Orient Beach

A Novel

Bill Woods

Ideas into Books: Westview®
Kingston Springs, Tennessee

Ideas into Books®
W E S T V I E W
P.O. Box 605
Kingston Springs, TN 37082
www.publishedbywestview.com

ISBN 978-1-62880-165-1

First edition, October 2018.

Cover photo by Bill Woods.

Edited by Benjamin Effinger.

Printed in the United States of America on acid free paper.

Orient Beach

Table of Contents

Tampa
Kissimmee
St. Petersburg
Sarasota
UNITED STATES OF AMERICA
Vero Beach
Fort Pierce
Cape Coral
Ft. Myers
West Palm Beach
Naples
Freeport
Fort Lauderdale
Miami
Coral Gables
Gulf of Mexico
Key West
Nassau
THE BAHAMAS
Havana
Matanzas
Artemisa
Sagua la Grande
Pinar del Rio
Colon
Santa Clara
Cienfuegos
CUBA
Moron
Nueva Gerona
Sancti Spiritus
Camaguey
TURKS A ISLAN
Las Tunas
Nuevitas
Banes
Bayamo
Holguin
CAYMAN ISLANDS (UK)
Manzanillo
Santiago
de Cuba
Guantanamo
George Town
US NAVAL BASE
GUANTANAMO
BAY (CUBA)
Cap-Haitien
Gonaives
U.S. MINOR OUTLYING
ISLANDS (US)
HAITI
Port-Au-Prince
Montego Bay
JAMAICA
Les Cayes
Kingston
Brus Laguna
NDURAS
Puerto Lempira
Caribbear
Puerto Cabezas
ARAGUA
Bluefields
Riohacha
San Juan de Nicaragua
Santa Marta
Barranquilla
Quesada
Cienaga
Maracaibo
Puntarenas
Puerto Limon
Cartagena
Machique
San Jose
COSTA RICA
Sixaola
COLOMBIA
La
M
El Carmen de Bolivar
Colon
Tolu
San Carlos
del Zulia
ad Cortes
PANAMA
Sincelejo
Balboa
Panama City
Lorica
El Banco

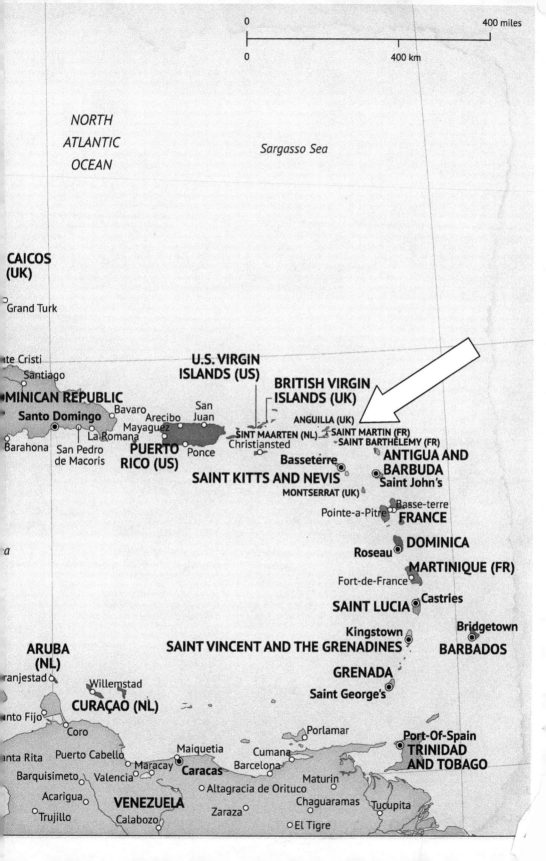

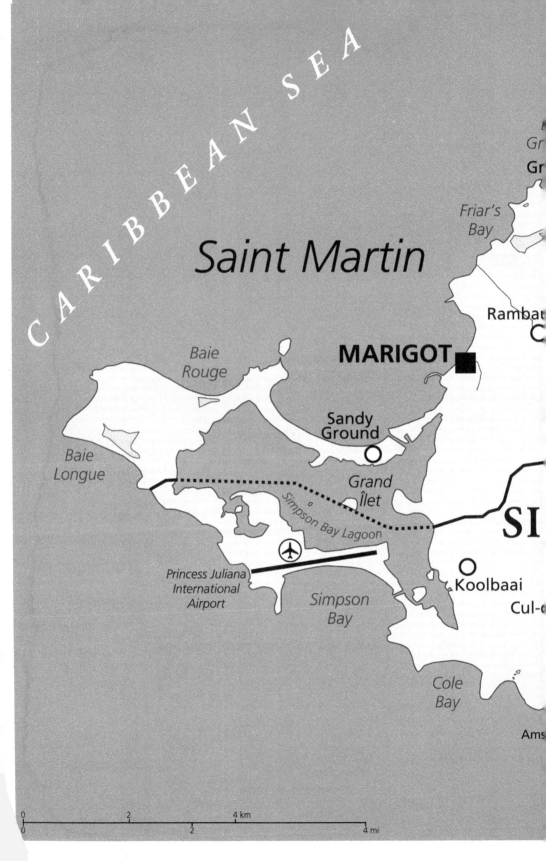

Prologue

Reason is God's shadow; God is the sun.
What power has the shadow before the sun?
—*Masnavi*, Book 4 Story 4

Legion is on the way to paradise when the glow of sunrise through his closed eyelids dims. He sits in lotus position, legs folded under him, the back of his hands resting on his knees, his middle fingers touching his thumbs. He had seen a statue of Buddha doing this and, of all the routes to paradise he has tried, this works the best. The only downside—it attracts a lot of weirdos.

"Have a seat, my friend. You're blocking my view," Legion says without opening his eyes.

The orange blares inside his head again and he begins to shrink to a single glowing point hovering over the beach. But paradise remains a floater at the edge of his vision that flicks away if looked at directly. When he opens his eyes, a golden carpet stretches across the water from the sunrise to where he sits; the ocean waves bow before him.

"Are you crazy?"

Legion blinks. He first thinks the question came from the sun and then he turns to a naked bald man, an inner tube of fat bulging at his waist, slumped on the sand beside him. Legion suspects the man is an apparition. Since he hovers at the blurred boundaries of reality most of the time, it does not frighten him.

"Maybe, I guess. They say if you think you're crazy, you're not. I think I'm sane, so maybe I am," Legion replies.

"I've been watching you come to the beach every morning and I wanted to ask before I have to go back. What are you doing?"

It seems obvious to Legion, but maybe not. "Worshiping the sun." Then he adds, "Like you, I suppose."

"That's what you believe? The sun is God?"

Legion turns to the dun disk cut in half by the horizon, newly molten, humble, approachable. In a few moments it will reign again, too spectacular to look at directly. He turns back to the man. The flesh looks solid but the vacant face makes him seem hollow. Legion is dubious.

"If I were religious, I could look up what I don't know in a book. It's not that simple. Considering the limitations of the human brain and language, a dog would have a better chance explaining atomic physics with barks. Maybe the mysteries of the universe aren't knowable."

The man's eyes jerk open wide when he realizes Legion is waiting for a response. He squints out at the horizon for a moment as if considering, but then his eyes deaden and turn to the sand.

Legion lifts both hands palms-up beside his head and shrugs. "Well, just stretch a myth between the things you do know. This works for most people. For me, I'm training myself to better tolerate the unknown, think less human—more like a dog."

They sit quietly together watching the ocean give birth to the sun. The lower edge of the blood-red orb stretches back to the grasp of the slate ocean before it tears loose and floats free and round like a soap bubble.

Legion closes his eyes again hoping the gurgling surf will flush the intruder out of his head.

"Dad," the man says.

Legion ignores him.

"Legion!" the man yells insistently close to his ear.

When Legion turns, he is startled to see the fat man has morphed into a younger version of himself.

"What are you doing?" his younger self yells.

Part 1

1580 - West Indies

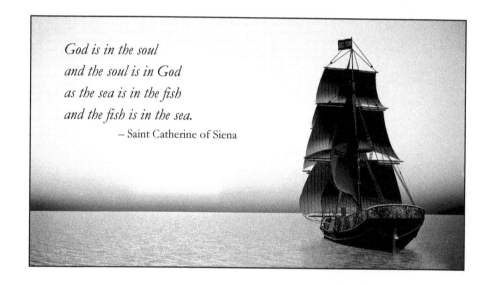

*God is in the soul
and the soul is in God
as the sea is in the fish
and the fish is in the sea.*
— Saint Catherine of Siena

Repent before it is too late.
– Spanish priest lighting the fire

If there are Spaniards in Heaven, I will go to Hell.
– Hatuey, Arawak chief as he burned at the stake

It became such a great pestilence, more than half the population died.
They died in heaps, like bedbugs.
– Toribio Motolinia, Spanish monk

Civilization was a plague set loose on paradise.
– Unknown

It can only be misery to live in folly, illusion, deception and ignorance,
but it isn't—it's human.
– Erasmus

Modesty is not natural to children.
Modesty only begins with the knowledge of evil.
– Rousseau

Speak of me as one that loved not wisely, but too well.
Who like the base Indian, threw a pearl away.
– Shakespeare

CHAPTER 1

The Shipwreck

The ship groans in pain. This does not wake Friar Simón; nor does the grinding hull as it pushes across rock. However, when a wave lifts the galleon and slams it solidly on the reef, he jolts awake.

All is dark. He rubs his crusty eyes, not sure they are open. In the haze of malaria, seasickness, and dysentery, nothing makes sense. He tries to reach into the blackness, touch something, anything for a clue, but canvas prevents him from extending his arms to the sides. *A funeral shroud?*

Nausea retches his burning stomach into his mouth. The convulsion leaves him sweating, shivering, exhausted. Out of the swirling fog in his head comes a disappointing conclusion. He is still in his tortured body—*not dead yet.*

His hammock still suspends him between the bulkheads of the tiny forecastle like it has since the ship left New Spain a fortnight ago. Desperate shouts from beyond the walls are muffled by the droning wind through the superstructure. *What's happening?* One of the sailors will tell him. His yells are too feeble to be heard. As he twists to dump himself onto the deck, he hesitates. Even if he had the strength to stand, the violent lunges of the ship would only slam him from wall to wall.

Lightning flashes through a porthole. The forecastle walls slant obliquely. As the ship quakes, he bounces above the deck trying to force the cogs of his brain to move. No, the hammock has kept him facing up, so the ship is listing radically to port. The sea must be over the sides. The ship is sinking.

The keel explodes like a cannon, followed by the musket fire of other timbers snapping. No longer buoyed by water, the ship shudders under the impact of giant waves. The side-to-side lurching of the ship teetering on its keel is replaced by a wallow as the ship slumps onto the reef. Wooden joints whine as they pull apart. Amid the crescendo outside, he listens for human sounds, frantic shouts, or slaps of shoe leather past the door of the forecastle. The crew has abandoned ship. He is alone.

Friar Simón, a loyal Franciscan Monk, closes his eyes to pray, not in desperation, but sublime contentment. In the pitch dark, his hand traces the silver chain around his neck to the gold cross. He lifts it from his chest and kisses it. Redemption is only moments away.

Simón wakes to the faces of frightful demons glaring down at him. *This is a mistake.* "Nooo," he howls. The devils jerk back and run out the forecastle door. Straggly heads peek around the doorway then dart out of sight as they mumble to each other.

He tries to raise himself to a sitting position on the hammock, but cannot muster the strength. With the effort, his bowel discharges foul mucus into his robe. Muscles still ache with fever. This should not be his reward.

A boy is pushed through the glare of the doorway. He tries to squirm between the men, but they shove him back in. Giving up on escape, the boy sticks out his chest with bravado. Black bangs above his eyes tremble.

There are no instruments of torture in his hands. He is naked, so nothing is hidden. The older demons blocking the doorway also wear nothing except hideous black scars on their chests and cheeks.

Simón extends the palm of his hand. "Depart from me, Satan," he says with menace.

The boy cowers back to a forecastle wall, eyes darting as he looks for a place to hide, as if it is he who is confronting the Devil.

Again, Simón tries to sit up. Again his bowel erupts, but with only a thunderous fart this time. The startled boy holds out his hands as if to fend off an attack. When Simón slumps back into the hammock, the boy snickers and then laughs out loud. It's an innocent, uninhibited laugh. In the doorway, the other Indians begin to snicker also. In spite of his trepidation and all his maladies, Simón chuckles, relieved they are only savages, not demons. Maybe they will dispatch him quickly without torture.

The Indians unhook his hammock from the bulkhead and haul him outside like a dangerous animal they've captured in a net. Lazy white clouds have replaced the stormy sky. The water is knee-deep on the warped and splintered deck. The ship's rigging and aft superstructures are gone. Dugout canoes are tied with vine ropes to the stub of a broken mast. Simón looks about for other captives. The crew must have swum ashore.

Still wrapped in the hammock, Simón is lowered into a canoe and trailed behind the others as they paddle to the beach a half-mile away. Women and children on the beach, nude like bronze Roman statues, slink back when his canoe is pulled ashore, examine him like a tuna the men have caught, giggle to each other in hungry anticipation.

A grizzled old man, yellow-streaked hair about his bony shoulders, parts the tribe. His stern face does not show the nervous curiosity of the others. After bending over the canoe for a closer look, he jerks back erect and pinches his nose. The boy who Simón had met in the forecastle stands beside the canoe with a wide grin also pinching his nose. Looking at the boy, the old man gives orders with grunts and hand signals. The boy cringes. The grunts and hand signals are repeated with more insistence. The boy pushes the canoe off the beach and tips Simón into knee-deep water. Simón thrashes to sit up, sputtering with only his head above water.

More orders are given. Three females tentatively wade in to surround him. He struggles when they stand him up and pull at his robe. And then, exhausted and weak, he lets them undress him. The boy uses a stick to drag the soiled robe down the beach. When the boy stops, the old one motions with his hands to drag it farther away.

While two females support him under his arms, a young girl, a year or two older than the boy, pours a sweet smelling potion from a conch shell over his head. As it streams down his body she lathers him thoroughly. After using the conch shell to rinse him with seawater, the females return to shore and leave him meekly covering himself with his hands against their scrutiny.

The old one wades out to inspect him more closely, pinching skin, probing with a finger. Behind the old one, the savages quietly mumble to each other, maybe discussing how he should be cooked, or how he will taste.

The sun dims. The savages on the shore blur. Simón wobbles and falls face forward into the water.

A cherub cradles Simón's head in her lap. Her delicate hand brushes his bald pate as she sings soothing psalms to him in contralto. He struggles to open his eyes, to see her lovely wings. His eyelids are too heavy. "Bless you," he thinks he says, but it's only a groan. Nothingness overtakes him again.

The voice returns, faint at first as if the cherub descends from a great height to hover just above his head. The comforting words are indistinct, but the singsong rhythm is familiar. An altar boy, one of his converts in New Spain, sang lullabies like this to his pet monkey. When Simón's eyes open, the Indian boy's face, only inches away, blooms into a wide smile.

"Who...?" Simón's mouth is gummy from dehydration, "Where...?"

The boy dumps Simón's head from his lap and runs away squealing.

Above, sunlight seeps through a thatch roof. Simón struggles to sit up and then falls back. There is only enough energy to twist his head. He lies on a woven grass mat under a lean-to of sticks and palm leaves. In the blinding glare of the low entrance, the boy is a dancing stick figure waving the rest of the tribe closer with one hand and pointing at him with the other. Behind the boy, the other savages creep closer, bending at the waist to peer in.

The boy grabs the hand of the old one and pulls him under the low roof. They kneel to either side of Simón's head. The old one studies him like an artifact. The boy mimics the old one's dire expression.

"Are you...leader?" Simón asks the old one. Simón's mouth is too dry to form words. "Are..." He stops trying; they would not understand Spanish anyway.

The old one pushes down Simón's chin, and with a gnarled finger of the other hand, pries Simón's mouth open wide. The boy crowds from behind to look in also. The old one snarls and elbows the boy back. Rough fingers pinch Simón's nose. He tries to shove the hand away to no avail. Short gasps rattle in his chest. The old one sits back on his heels, his brows furrowed in deep consideration. The boy is a half-size replica.

A malaria seizure stiffens Simón's body, turning his blood to ice. The uncontrollable shivering renews. He closes his eyes. *God,* he prays silently, *let the disease kill me this time. Or let these heathens murder me quickly. In your infinite mercy, give me peace...* Simón intends to continue his prayer until God grants deliverance, but his head lolls unconscious instead.

He passes into Hell. Demons pry his clenched teeth apart and pour scalding lead down his throat. His arms flail feebly to fight them off. *It should not end this way.* Again and again, they roust him from sleep to administer more torture.

Eternity. Forsaken. In delirium, Friar Simón howls curses at God.

7

CHAPTER 2

Bomba

riar Simón sleeps with two women. He does not realize this until his own moaning wakens him. He shoos them away. When shivering wakes him again, they are scrunched against his sides keeping him warm.

The girl attends him like a nurse. Each morning she brings a fresh coconut with a hole pierced through one eye. They still have not brought back his robe. He has tried several times to explain his need of it, but the girl does not understand. When she bathes him with a sponge, he tries to hide himself with his hands.

Episodes of diarrhea become less frequent. When it does occur, the girl calls in the old one and, while she props him up, he forces a bitter tea down his throat. At first, he thought this punishment for soiling the mat, but it might be medicine.

The girl brings him oysters in a wicker basket and drives a sharp stick into the edge of the shells with a rock. She tried slipping one off a half shell into his mouth. When he choked and almost passed out before coughing it up, it scared them both. Now, she minces an oyster in her mouth and dribbles it from her lips into his. The hair tenting over his face smells of mint; the hands that hold his face smell like coconut.

In the evening he is fed a bitter-tasting gruel made from long roots. The women start preparing this in the morning on a flat rock just outside the shelter by stripping off the outer casing of the roots with a shell and mincing the pulp inside into a paste on a rock. The result is scraped into abalone shells and left to steep in spring water for the rest of the day. In the evening, the water is poured off. If he acts pitiful and helpless, the girl will spoon this into his mouth with a scallop shell. When he points to a root and asks with his face for her to name it, she calls it bomba and points to his privates. Either the name of the root is because it resembles a penis, or the other way around.

As his sagging skin fills out, he worries if he is being fattened for slaughter. Every day the old one examines him with probing fingers, seemingly satisfied. Even if they are cannibals, there's a chance he could be spared, kept as a novelty, a pet.

The men sleep in a separate shelter a stone's throw down the sand berm. At night he hears an occasional laugh, and he wonders if the men are talking about him, *the pervert in the women's shelter with the children*. Even the boy must be over the age to sleep with the women. He is sure the men consider it as an indignity to sleep with the women, but sleeping in a pile of men is unthinkable.

He had lost track of time and begins scarring a support post of the lean-to with an oyster shell each morning. On the day he makes the tenth mark, he sits up. When he crawls from under the shelter and staggers to his feet, the girl yells for the other savages to watch. She walks around him with obvious pride.

The shelter is on a palm-shaded berm overlooking a placid bay. Blinding-white sand circles the azure water to hazy mountains on both sides of the opening to the bay a mile away. The tiny forecastle of his sunken ship sits like a privy atop the whitecaps of waves flowing over the reef. Beyond the gap is the darker blue deep ocean. Behind the sand berm, verdant mountain slopes ring a mirror-surfaced salt flat as large as the bay.

The boy comes running and leads him by the hand to the edge of the surf. When Simón collapses onto his bottom, the boy sits in front of him beaming his perpetual smile. Dangling around his neck from a leather thong is a silver bosun's whistle, probably taken from the dead owner's neck. Simón picks the whistle off his chest and demonstrates blowing it. A mistake. As the boy blows as hard as he can, the birds all around the bay jump into the air in terror. The women hold their ears and scream. The old one comes running. He blows it himself once and then hangs it around his own neck for safekeeping. As the old one walks away, the boy dances around him protesting, but he does not get it back. The old one cuffs him on the back of the head before he stops.

The boy, still pouting, kicks the sand as he returns to sit in front of Simón. Simón tries to overcome his mope by teaching him Spanish words. He scoops up sand with one hand and points with the other.

"Sand."

The boy's face clouds with confusion.

Simón points at his chest. "Simón."

The boy points to his own chest. "Seaman?"

Simón tries again. "See-moan"

The boy points to himself again. "Seaman." A grin spreads across his face when he understands. He rushes off to the other savages, jabbing his chest with his thumb and shrieking, "Seaman...Seaman." He darts from one to the next, pointing to himself, and saying his new name. If they say it back wrong, he makes them repeat it. Simón cannot think of a way to undo the error.

Frowning, the girl sits crossed-legged in front of him and points between her adolescent breasts. She wants a name too. Simón shields his eyes with his hands, then fearing the girl might take offense, forces himself to lower his hands to his knees. Her eyes follow his gaze. Between her thighs are delicate...

"Petals," he says.

She points between her budding nipples repeating her new name several times as her smile broadens. She points between his legs. "Bomba." Simón feels his face flush.

The boy joins them. She points, "Bomba."

The boy looks at Simón and points also, "Bomba."

This is the first word Simón learns in their language, the word the savages use thereafter when referring to him. He thinks it means erection.

The old one approaches and demands a name. He is named OldOne. The rest of the tribe line up for naming. Apparently, nobody had a name before. The four other men he names after the Gospels. The three women are given names that will be easy for him to remember: Cackle, Grande, and Sparkle (for her eyes). The two male toddlers are named Little and Big. The baby girl brought by Cackle he christens by dribbling water over her head to be Blabber. When the others see this ritual, they line up again for the same treatment. This is more souls than Simón saved during his entire six years in New Spain. "Father Bomba," he says aloud. It has a missionary ring to it.

That night he lies between Grande and Sparkle and thinks about his shipmates. There are no other captives, so could they be hiding in the hills, afraid of being eaten? When OldOne arrives the next morning, Bomba points toward the ship and uses mime to indicate men. OldOne grunts that he understands.

OldOne yells for Seaman, using his new name, and the three of them walk toward one end of the beach. Bomba's legs are rubbery and he holds to OldOne's shoulder. Seaman, bored by their slow pace, runs ahead chasing sandpipers. At the end of the beach the mountain is sloughed off, leaving a cliff on the mainland and an islet of boulders just offshore. Looking back across the lagoon, the savages are ants crawling on the white rim of a blue dinner plate.

Six sailors lie on the sand below the cliff. The rest of the crew must have washed out to sea. Sand crabs and scavenger birds have been at work. Some sailors he recognizes by their clothing. The odor is potent. OldOne and Seaman stand upwind as he kneels to murmur a prayer over each body.

His shipmates must have a Christian burial. With his hands, he scrapes a trench in the sand beside one of the bodies. OldOne walks up to watch. When Bomba tries to drag a putrid body toward the hole, OldOne, his face contorted with revulsion, grabs his arm and pulls him away. As OldOne shoves him back the way they had come, Bomba jerks away and falls on his knees for a final prayer. At least his friends had not been eaten—not by humans anyway. He makes the sign of the cross in the air before turning toward camp.

Seaman scampers ahead again, stopping to examine the flotsam from the ship. He points at the sand and yells back for them to hurry. They follow turtle tracks from the water to the undergrowth at the back of the beach. Under a palmetto, they find an unperturbed tortoise munching leafy plants. The tortoise, fresh meat for the ship's return voyage to Spain, had somehow escaped the hull of the wreck and made it to shore.

Bomba collapses by its side, laying his head against the hard shell. Another survivor. Marooned now like him. The blood in his veins crystallizes into jagged glass and he shudders as a seizure begins. More torture. Tears leak onto the shell. He and the tortoise should be dead, past pain, like their comrades.

The tone of OldOne's gibberish sounds like questions. Exhausted, too feeble even to look up, Bomba closes his eyes. The voice fades, chirps of a sparrow amid the roar of a waterfall inside his head.

When he wakes, the anxious face of Petals is inches away looking down, the familiar thatch roof of the women's shelter above her. He props on an elbow. She offers him half of a coconut shell filled with spring water.

"Thank you."

"Thank you," she echoes. Her smile warms him. He wants to pull her closer, to feel her warmth against his skin.

"How long...?" A gust of wind swirls hair over her puzzled face. There is no way for her to understand. He crawls from under the lean-to.

The sky is dark, the color of wet slate. The bay is a darker gray streaked white with the leading edges of giant waves. Dingy froth churned up by the waves exploding on the beach scutters across the sand. OldOne stands on the shore, waves running onto his legs, a gale wind streaming his straggly hair behind as he stares up at the sky. Seaman is at his side, also trying to read the billowing black clouds. The rest of the tribe squat on their heels, hands shielding their faces against the blowing sand, watching OldOne, waiting for his decision.

OldOne waves at the angry sky as he wheels to face the tribe. The tribe rises and he bellows orders like a ship's captain. The women herd the children toward an opening through grape trees. Petals scoots out of the shelter to join them. OldOne points toward Bomba. More orders. The men jog toward the shelter.

The men take turns carrying him on their back. A sand path meanders through thick brush beside the salt flat and then up a mountain slope. A lightning bolt cracks the sky and a hard rain begins. His bearer slips and dumps him face-first into mud. Wind-driven rain stings his back like bees; blowing sand pelts his eyes. Giant trees bend down to swat him with their limbs. Matthew and John drape his arms around their necks and pull him along, his feet dragging behind through the mud.

The tribe disappears single-file into a black hole behind a boulder. They prop him against the cave wall and crowd the entrance watching the sky darken to night. Lightning flashes flicker across their terrorized faces. The whistles and moans of the wind blowing across the cave entrance drown out their mumbling. His ears pop when wind gusts suck air from the cave.

Out of the dark, a woman's small hand brushes over his body, identifies his hairy chest, and then searches out his hand. She leads him into the midst of the tribe. They are squirmed together like spooked sheep into a single quivering pile. One-by-one the bodies go limp with sleep. Petals' silky head rests on his thigh. His head is cradled between Grande's familiar breasts. He stares out the cave mouth listening to the groans Jonah must have heard from the whale's belly.

CHAPTER 3

Treasure

A waterfall of rain cascades over the front of the cave for three days. In the gray light, the family mills about like phantoms, eating coconuts and dried berries from a stash. A freshwater spring trickling from the rear of the cave collects first in a cistern dug into the floor lined with stones, and then spills over into a trench running out the front of the cave. Cups fashioned from shells sit on niches in the cave walls. Downstream, at the cave entrance, is where they relieve themselves. This evacuation during a storm is a well-prepared routine.

On the fourth day, the roar of wind across the cave mouth subsides. The sky becomes lighter. A steady drizzle drips from Seaman as he crawls to the top of the boulder in front of the cave and calls back what he sees to OldOne. They wait another day. When Bomba wakes the following morning, OldOne is silhouetted in the entrance. The rain has stopped. OldOne turns and sweeps his arms toward the outside, waving everybody out. Four days of inactivity have renewed Bomba's strength and he walks down from the mountain without help. By the time they reach the salt flat, shafts of sun streak through the clouds.

The lean-tos have blown away without even a limb suggesting where they had been. From the top of the berm, Bomba looks out over the bay. The placid water fades chameleon-like from green to blue then back to green as mottled clouds drift over. Where isolated sunbeams touch the bay, turquoise Incan medallions seem to float on the water.

A few of the palms, undermined by encroaching waves, have fallen; broken fronds dangle from the rest. Otherwise, the beach is pristine. The sand that had been churned dingy-gray by the feet of the tribe is now smooth, gleaming white.

A rainbow arcs overhead. The message of hope sent to Noah. The past has been cleansed away, time reset. With the end comes a beginning. He had thought New Spain would be a Genesis, a fresh world untainted by old world sins, a new race of people eager to carry God's banner forward. It should have been. But the seeds of evil came also, in the holds of their ships like stowaway rats, in the hearts of conquerors. God's missionaries, their latent malevolence magnified by greed and unleashed without mercy. Murder, rape, enslavement of the blameless in their own land at the hands of soldiers who bore crosses on their tunics. Eden desecrated in the name of God. He too reeks of that debauchery.

Below him, the tribe walks to the water's edge. Seaman, arms flailing, shrieking delight after his confinement, charges into the undulating waves until he is swept off his feet. He yells back and Petals gracefully dives into a swell to join him. The others wade in knee-deep and wash the grime of the cave off their bodies.

Will he be their prophet or the catalyst of their demise? Did he bring corruption, like his soiled robe, ashore with him? Can he save them? With the innocence of children, maybe they are already protected by God's grace. Or was it he who has been sent to them to be saved?

He looks down at his nakedness. What had been unthinkable a month ago, the intimacy of wind and sun on his skin, already feels ordinary. The island is changing him, causing him to molt into some-thing bizarre, unpredictable. Soon, only the golden cross hanging on his chest will remain of Friar Simón. He falls to his knees. Clasped hands rise to his chin. "Lord, thy will be done…" A shaft of light warms the bald pate of his bowed head. Bomba, a different man, arises. He starts down the slope to the beach to be baptized anew.

One end of the rainbow falls on the narrow mouth of the bay. White-tipped Atlantic waves dissipate across a shallow shoal. In the storm that night, the ship's captain would not have seen the reef. The narrow inlet with calm waters beyond must have seemed the answer to his prayer, a miracle. Instead, hope born of desperation lured him to his demise.

The forecastle, the only structure above water after the shipwreck, had been knocked down by the second storm. Nothing is left to alert a passing ship of a wreck.

Marooned. This bay will be the extent of his world for the rest of his life.

After floating on his back admiring the wispy mares' tails that have replaced the overcast, Bomba stands on the sandy bottom, only his head above water, his body gently buffeted to-and-fro, watching the tribe work, enthralled by their ingenuity. The men drag fallen palm trees to the top of the berm where the women strip off the leafy fronds. The trunks are lashed with long tentacles of greenbrier to standing coconut trees to create frames for new lean-tos. The women lace the fronds into thatch roofs. They've said nothing since they started. The responsibility for each job is understood, their tasks coordinated without directions. The shelters are complete before the sun reaches noon. The women begin to weave palmetto leaves into floor mats while OldOne leads the men over the berm, probably to search for crabs in the salt pond.

The men are lean, muscles rippling beneath bronze skin with every movement, their faces conveying a dignified confidence. The only feature that distinguishes them from the Indians of New Spain is their feet, which have four toes, or rather webbing between their second and third toes. He can tell by the family's furtive glances at his feet they think he is the one with an embarrassing deformity. After being naked for a month, the only part of his body he is still self-conscious about are his toes, which he squirms under the sand when someone stands in front of him.

Bomba turns and looks across the gentle water to the mountains encircling the bay, their tops pastel blue behind a shroud of mist, slopes dappled bright green where the sun shines through, their reflections wrinkled below on the flat water.

At the distant reef is where the remains of the ship will be. He imagines how it must look underwater: squashed, ripped apart, ballast and cargo strewn among the rocks. Any wood above the hull—deck planks, masts—would have been wrenched away and washed ashore or far out to sea. As he wades out of the water, he spots dark lines far down the beach, inky streaks across bleached parchment that had not been there before the last storm, maybe the ship's masts. Seaman is suddenly walking beside him. He must have been watching from the shelter, waiting for an excuse to leave the women, eager to explore also.

"Bomba," Seaman says with his usual smile.

"Seaman," Bomba says back.

The boy laughs and runs ahead, spurts of sand kicking up behind his feet. Seaman likes his name.

Two masts lie where he had found his shipmates. The bodies of the sailors are gone, maybe thrown by waves of the second storm into the shrub behind the beach. He does not want to look. He paces beside the masts, both twenty feet long to the splintered ends where they broke from the ship. A spar is attached to one with sail and hemp rope wound around it. He and Seaman exchange a smile, both imagining what fun they can have with this. Another loose segment of rope is tangled in a grape tree at the back edge of the beach. Seaman climbs, drags it down, pulls it out straight on the beach to admire, dances around it with pride.

Bomba points, "Rope."

The boy says it back several times. Bomba nods that he is saying it correctly.

Seaman picks up one end and holds it in front of his face. "Rope," he says to it as if it is alive.

Bomba puts the end of the rope over his shoulder and turns toward camp, straining as he pulls. Behind, where the rope loops down, Seaman does the same.

Seaman remembers the exact spot where they had found the tortoise. It is still there, blithely browsing on the local fauna, none the worse for the storm. The top of the shell is the height of Seaman's waist. The boy walks around it, eyes narrow with caution, well back from the menacing beak. Bomba learned from the sailors that these giant tortoises are unique to the Pacific islands so this is the first one Seaman has ever seen.

"Weiwei?" the boy asks.

"Tortoise."

"Oris." Seaman struggles repeatedly to form the T with his tongue. He cannot do it.

"Weiwei." Bomba pats the top of the tortoise's shell. "Weiwei."

"Weiwei," Seaman confirms, smiling with relief that he does not have to learn the hard word.

Weiwei must be their word for sea turtle. This is the second word they share.

When they return, the floor mat of the women's shelter is finished and the women are weaving the mat for the men's lean-to. Petals runs out to greet them, to see what they are dragging.

They drop the rope and Seaman points at it. "Rope." They continue back and forth until she can pronounce the word. He points up the beach where they came from and amid his jabber, he uses Weiwei's name. His arms circle wide to show the circumference of his shell and he hears the name Petals had given him. Bomba must mean big, which is a relief. It will be less embarrassing to be named Big rather than Erection. Petals dashes back under the lean-to to tell the other women, teach them the new word. Seaman, he is sure, will tutor the men the same way when they return. They will be good teachers.

Bomba laughs out loud at Petals' chiding of the women who do not say the word correctly. The women stop their chatter and look at him, surprise on their faces. His hands cover his genitals, but there is no erection. Seaman walks close and points at his head. Bomba feels the crinkle of his sunburned cheeks. He is smiling. They've never seen him smile before or heard him laugh. He points to his face. "Happy." They all return his smile. He laughs aloud again and points in his mouth. "Laugh." The women turn to Petals to continue their lessons, pointing at each others' faces, laughing, practicing the words as he walks down to the water's edge to wash the sand from his shoulder. It will not be long before they can converse.

Something else has changed. He feels strong. Even after such a long walk, he is not tired. The diseases have left him. He screams ecstasy to the ocean. Seaman comes running, his face bewildered, following Bomba's gaze to see what he is looking at.

By twilight, the mat for the men's shelter is only half-complete, so the men join the women under their shelter and, like in the cave, begin arranging themselves for the night. Cackle pulls Bomba into their midst. Everyone's skin is slick with the minty ointment they've rubbed on each other. He had let the women smear it on him as well. It seems to prevent sunburn and ward off mosquitoes.

There is not any discrete pairing of men and women, no indication of which ones are siblings. They shuffle together indiscriminately until all have a leg or stomach on which to rest their heads. Blabber crawls from one of the women to the other, suckling with each, until she finds Cackle, the only one lactating. They are a family; that is as far as he can understand their relationships.

Through the open side of the lean-to that faces the beach, he watches the sprinkle of stars and a sliver of moon reflecting on the slack water. The small talk, like the hum of a beehive at first, subsides until there is only the gurgle of lazy waves lapping onto the beach.

As his mind becomes numb with slumber, there is a groan, then a sigh. He startles alert, unable to determine the origin. He is moving, gently swaying as part of the mound of humanity. A gasp. Copulation…somewhere in the pile sex is being performed. A hand seeks him out. Even in the dark, he can't hide his arousal. He brushes the hand away. His body throbs with anticipation, intently alert for more sounds, the swaying to resume. He can't get back to sleep.

At sunrise, they begin to untangle, stretch, and walk out on the beach. He searches the faces of the women for any sign of the owner of the hand. The women wander down to the water to wash without looking back.

After a swim and new application of ointment, he sits with OldOne and the men in the shade of the lean-to trying to communicate. Even with Seaman, who considers himself an interpreter now, OldOne doesn't understand his plan. Finally, Bomba gives up, coils the rope they found yesterday over his shoulder, and waves his arm for the men to follow him up the beach.

Bomba tries to lift the end of the smallest mast. He can't do it, but when the others see what he is doing, they eagerly join in, emulating his movements as they swing the masts parallel six feet apart. He begins to unravel the sail and ropes from the spar. When OldOne understands the task, he starts issuing orders. Seaman repeats everything he says, pointing and urging the men if they don't obey quickly.

When Bomba ties off a rope to the end of a mast and begins lashing on the deck planks that had also washed up, the men stand back to marvel. They've only used braided vines before and don't understand proper knots. The surety of the knots will be vital, so

Bomba stops to teach them the clove hitch and half hitch. He teaches OldOne first. Of course, Seaman watching over OldOne's shoulder learns the knots first and excitedly begins teaching the other men. Only Luke cannot master it. He looks away in shame while the others grin. OldOne assigns him to gather planks while the rest do the lashing.

Bomba demonstrates how to loop the rope around a board and the mast and then brace their legs on the mast to pull the rope tight. OldOne directs the tasks; Seaman assigns himself to verify the quality. An hour before sundown, the raft is complete. Everyone slumps onto their rumps on the sand, quietly admiring their work, smiling.

Using the rope he had brought from camp, Bomba fashions a harness to a hatch cover, also washed ashore, to make a sled. As they pull it toward camp, Seaman thinks he deserves to ride. OldOne shoos him off. When OldOne walks to the lead and Seaman thinks he is not being watched, he climbs back aboard. OldOne picks up a stick from the beach and slaps it across his palm. He doesn't break stride or turn around, but Seaman slips off the back of the sled and resumes walking.

They stop to load Weiwei. Seaman pats it on the back to show his bravery. OldOne circles around, away from the ominous beak, not knowing what to expect from such an exotic animal. It takes all of them to push Weiwei on the sled and then all of them to pull him on the sand. Whenever Weiwei extends his legs to crawl off, Seaman taps his shell with a stick and Weiwei retracts his legs.

The sun is on the horizon when they reach camp. They push Weiwei into a palmetto thicket. He seems to enjoy anyplace after being trapped in the hold of a ship for months. Tomorrow they will find him a freshwater stream with plenty of vegetation around it. If he is prone to wander, they'll have to build a fence.

The women bring food and the men eat sitting cross-legged on their new mat in front of their lean-to. As dusk turns to night,

OldOne, barely visible in the moonlight, points to the sky as he talks. Bomba tries to understand; he seems to be telling stories about the constellations. When the men begin to doze, they move the mat under their shelter and position themselves for sleep.

Bomba remains sitting in front of the shelter conflicted about where to sleep. Which would be the greater sin: sleeping with the men or the women? Sleep alone? He had never slept with anyone until coming here, but now the thought of sleeping alone horrifies him. He rationalizes that sleeping with the women, his original sin, was not a choice he had made voluntarily, so wasn't a sin after all. Continuing to sleep with them was still covered by this dispensation.

When he crawls under the women's shelter, they act as if they had been waiting for him and make room in the middle of their huddle. They resituate themselves to use him for a pillow. Blabber curls up on his chest. As she sleeps, warm pee dribbles down his sides. He listens to the mumbles followed by giggles from the men's shelter, sneers about him, he knows, but he doesn't care. This is where God wants him to be.

Late into the night, he lies awake, planning what he should do if one of the men were to crawl into the women's shelter. Should he leave? Protest? To his relief, there is no copulation that night.

At sunrise, the men trek back to the raft, eager to get started. Today they will test if their creation is seaworthy. As they walk, they work on their vocabulary. When Bomba puts his hand on something, he says the name in Spanish. They say their word for the object back to him. If the Spanish word contains T's or has many syllables, he agrees to use their word. They accept his words for "sail" because they have no equivalent word; "raft" is changed to "barge."

Bomba wishes he had thought to build the barge closer to the water. He uses the spar as a lever with a boulder as a fulcrum to lift one side. The men stand amazed when one side of the barge lifts out of the sand. With hand signals, he pantomimes for them to push when he lifts. That side moves toward the water a foot. Repeating this side-to-side, the barge is moved crab-like into the water until it floats. Twenty feet of sail rope left over after the lashing hangs off one end. He finds an oblong stone on the beach and ties it to the end as an anchor. They tether the barge in waist-deep water before wading ashore and collapsing in the sand to admire their craft twitching in the waves. Seaman stays aboard, running around the perimeter, jumping on each corner, before squealing back his approval. Bomba shares his proud smile. He can fashion a mast and sail later, but for now, it will do. Maybe he can sail back to civilization one day.

Bomba's face becomes somber as he tries to think of a way to communicate the next step of his plan. He searches through the flotsam for a plank that could be used as a paddle and then points to other planks for the men to follow suit. None of them move. He climbs aboard and demonstrates paddling. The Indians seem too primitive to understand even the most obvious.

OldOne watches, paces on the sand with a solemn frown. When OldOne sits cross-legged, the other men huddle around him, pointing to the barge and mumbling to each other. Seaman understands Bomba's plan and splashes the water with a plank, slowly propelling the barge around the anchor rope to show how it can be done.

OldOne waves his hand toward camp and the men jog up the beach. He lies back in the sand and closes his eyes, ignoring Seaman's pleas. Bomba sits on the side of the barge, feet dangling in the water, waiting to see how this plays out. Seaman squats like a vulture on a corner of the barge, pouting.

The men return pulling their two canoes through knee-deep water. Bomba had forgotten about the canoes that had been sunk in the salt pond before the storm to keep them from blowing away.

OldOne jumps to his feet and issues his orders. The plaited vine lead ropes are tied to the barge. Seaman pulls the anchor and stands ready for OldOne's next command. The men, two on each side, push the barge out to chest-deep water and then hoist themselves onto the deck. Gingerly they transfer from the barge to the canoes. As OldOne yells further instructions from shore, Seaman unties the anchor rope from the rock and ties up to the stern of the nearest canoe. The second canoe hooks up stern-to-bow in front of that canoe. They dig in with their paddles and the barge is underway. Bomba sits amidships, his mouth slack, astounded.

OldOne stands on the beach, arms waving, yelling instructions until his voice is drowned out by the waves crashing onto the reef ahead. Seaman jumps to the front edge of the barge, arm outstretched like a masthead, relaying Bomba's points to where the shipwreck will be.

Tangles of rope streaming toward shore mark the spot. Through the clear water, the hull of the ship, splayed open across the reef, comes into view. The wooden deck and superstructures have broken away. Bomba points at the anchor rock and Seaman pulls in the closest canoe, unties it, and reties the rock. He looks to Bomba for approval before lowering it. Bomba nods and watches the anchor play out. Six feet deep.

Bomba whistles. When all eyes are on him, he extends his arms wide toward the canoes. "Crew," then points to Seaman, "Seaman." The boy understands his meaning and beams with pride as he starts directing the men. Maybe twelve years old and already captain of a ship. The canoes are tethered aft and the men slither onto the barge.

Bomba jumps in feetfirst, cutting his feet on oyster shells, a lesson he will remember. He swims underwater, back and forth across the wreckage, looking for something worthy of retrieving. The gold bars he and Orlando, his father, had cast in New Spain had been stored in the hold for ballast along with the bricks of their kiln. He knows where to look and finds them easily. When he surfaces, he hands up a Mexica gold bowl to Seaman. It flashes in the sun as he holds it high for OldOne to see.

This becomes their routine for a week. They leave the barge at anchor over the wreck and pile their plunder on the deck. Seaman learns to dive down with a rope and slip a noose around the gold bars. John pulls them up and Mark stacks them like cordwood. Matthew and Luke transport them to shore a few at a time with the canoes. At the end of the day, they use the hatch-cover sled to pull the gold back to camp.

Luke is fascinated by the gold chains and loops them around his neck until he can hardly walk. He is so eager to show off to the women, he paddles a canoe to camp ahead of the sled piled with gold coins and emerald encrusted jewelry—originally intended for the royal family in Spain. The women wait eagerly by the shore and cheer when they see him coming. They fondle the ornaments and put the gold bowls on their heads like crowns.

Bomba saved a tortoiseshell comb for Petals. He had to demonstrate its use. Sparkle heaps the doubloons on the remnant of a sail and plops on top with a beaming smile. The women seem to understand the intrinsic value of gold, whereas the men are only interested in the utility of metal. Petals scolds Seaman when he throws a doubloon at a seagull. She makes him find it and bring it back. The women won't allow him near their treasures after that.

The last things they salvage are the kiln and the iron tools. Seaman grumbles when directed to dive for the useless kiln bricks, but Bomba insists. The kiln is the only link left to his father and his prior life as Simón.

Simón had taken the vows of the church, at least partly, to escape the choking fumes and dawn-to-dusk labor of his father's foundry. When his father had been given a commission from the King to melt the Indian gold of New Spain into more easily transportable gold ingots, he proposed to Simón they combine efforts one last time. In exchange for helping his father build a foundry in New Spain, his father would help him build a church.

Simón prayerfully wrestled with this idea and concluded this to be his calling, an opportunity presented by God to save the indigenous souls of the new world. He envisioned being appointed the first Cardinal of New Spain, canonized after his death.

His father had meticulously designed this kiln, had the bricks cast to his specifications in Seville, and had them plus his tools loaded aboard their ship to New Spain. Building their new foundry in Veracruz took three months and then they started processing a warehouse of confiscated pagan gods, breastplates, and armbands.

After two years, he and his father were ready to start on the second part of their agreement, but during that time silver had been discovered in the mountains. The Viceroy of New Spain knew the security of his job depended on the pleasure of King Philip and the King's pleasure depended on gold and silver. The Viceroy demanded Simón's father and he build a smelter to process the silver ore. The natives, Simón's future parishioners, were driven into the mountains to mine it.

Six long years after his arrival, Simón was finally free to start his ministry. However, after watching firsthand the atrocities of Spain and the Church, he had lost heart. The souls of the natives were not left to the persuasion of monks. Soldiers who carried sabers instead of Bibles converted whole villages in a single day and then subjugated them into slavery. Some of these Indians were worked to death in his father's smelter without ever hearing the word of God.

God's revenge arrived on a ship from Spain. Black Death swept through Veracruz killing half the population. Both he and his father were ravaged. He survived; his father didn't. When he regained enough strength, Simón disassembled his father's kiln and carted it, and the last load of gold ingots, to the port. He planned to personally present the gold to King Philip and suggest a cathedral be built.

He had bargained five gold doubloons he had minted himself for passage aboard a galleon that had just returned from the Pacific. The kiln bricks and gold ingots were loaded in the hull and an equal weight of ballast rocks thrown overboard. After provisioning to supplement the live tortoises left over from their Pacific voyage, the ship embarked for Spain on the first Sunday in July of the Year of our Lord 1580.

His illness began the next day. At first, he thought it seasickness. His body needed time to adjust. Instead, he became progressively worse. Even on calm days, he couldn't keep the gruel from the ship's mess in his body. By the time the storm hit, he had already given up on surviving the trip.

CHAPTER 4

Fire

OldOne is sitting in the shade of a palm when the white-skinned heathen comes walking up the beach with what looks like an arm-length log on his shoulder. More trash he and Seaman have scrounged from the sunken nest. No matter what stupid thing the new creature decides to drag back to camp, the boy is right with him eager to help.

Bomba places the object down gently, reverently, with a prideful grin, in front of OldOne for him to marvel. It is just wooden boards held together with black bands. The heathen introduces it as Powder like it has a spirit, a god maybe. When OldOne kicks it over in disgust, Bomba cringes and scolds OldOne like a child for his lack of respect.

Bomba carries Powder to the backside of the berm that faces the salt pond and then stands on the top of the berm waving his arms and squawking like a raven. Seaman says he is warning the tribe to stay away lest they evoke the wrath of Powder.

In many ways Bomba appears human, but obviously an inferior species. Although a head taller than the men of the family, he is weak and sickly. His toes do not have webbing between them to help him swim through Night like humans after he dies. He must be like the fish and birds that have no spirit after death.

When the men brought the creature ashore two moons ago, he was covered in anal secretions. Although he was not quite dead, OldOne had ordered his carcass be dragged to where the others of his kind had washed ashore, downwind so they wouldn't have to endure the odor as the crabs and birds disposed of his flesh.

But the women swarmed around the creature, doting on him like a pet iguana. Even after the women cleaned him up, he begged to be wrapped again in the filthy covering he had been found in. He has no sense of decency. If the women hadn't adopted him and nursed him to health, there wouldn't be this turmoil in the family. He should have beaten the naive women away from the creature with a stick.

The women call him Bomba because of his large cassava that springs into readiness whenever they're around. Now that he is well, he may be inclined to breed. He'll have to be watched. It is hard to believe any of his women would degrade themselves, but they are women and must be continually bred to be content. In his youth, OldOne remembers he could keep a whole tribe of women satisfied; however, of late, his cassava is unreliable. He has counseled the other men to reinvigorate their efforts to this duty, but only three of them can be counted on. The one Bomba named Luke, although constantly hanging around the women, refuses to breed them. He tries to breed the men instead although he is wrongly equipped.

Bomba named the boy Seaman. The boy won't even answer to Boy anymore. He was already headstrong, but after following this animal around every day, he has gotten worse. The woman Bomba named Grande should be whipped for birthing such an insolent whelp.

In the afternoon, Seaman led Bomba into the hills around the bay and they came back with a basket brimming with rocks, each one a different color. Now that Sun has fallen into Ocean, Bomba strikes each rock with a black stick he brought from his wrecked canoe. One creates little lightning bolts when hit, which makes Bomba excited and OldOne anxious.

OldOne follows Bomba behind the berm and watches him pull a stick out of the belly of Powder and pour black sand into a scallop shell. When he returns, he directs tiny lightning bolts into the scallop shell. OldOne yells for Seaman to stand back, that Lightning is dangerous but, of course, he has to put his nose into everything.

Lightning mates with Thunder. Bomba and Seaman lie on their backs with black vapors rising from their hair. When the women come running, OldOne sends them to fetch seawater in the gold bowls in case Fire attacks the shelters. Seaman jumps up and runs at full speed halfway to the cliff at the end of the beach before he stops and looks back. Bomba sits up and grins.

OldOne banishes Powder from the camp. Bomba nods his head (which OldOne has learned means "okay"), hefts Powder on his shoulder, and takes the trail to the cave. After regaining his courage, Seaman follows.

Bomba only returns to the beach to check on Weiwei. There are no other turtles like him on the island, but he doesn't know this, so he wanders into the woods searching for females. Bomba tied Weiwei's foot to a tree. He stays in his shell most of the time, depressed OldOne thinks, because he is kept from his purpose.

Weiwei shouldn't be punished this way. He should be killed and eaten, which is the purpose of male turtles, but Bomba won't allow it. The female turtles are responsible for bringing eggs to the beach, gifts to the family from Ocean. Half of the eggs are left to hatch and when the young turtles dig out of their holes; the purpose of the family is to escort them to the safety of Ocean before predator birds can get them. Every animal has a job to perform in order to keep Ocean happy. Bomba thinks he is superior and tries to impose his will on Ocean's animals like they are his possessions.

Seaman visits Bomba every morning, sometimes spending whole days at the cave neglecting his chores. Petals carries food to Bomba and stays overnight. She says Bomba is still sick and needs care. Suspecting this is a falsehood, OldOne follows her back to the cave.

He finds Bomba and Seaman feeding twigs to Fire, the offspring of Lightning and Thunder. Fire, he knows, has a voracious appetite and can grow so quickly it can devour entire mountains. Petals and Seaman sit next to Fire, both too stupid to be afraid.

OldOne kicks dirt on Fire and it flickers out. While he is chastising the children for playing with Fire, Bomba calmly builds another pile of twigs, pours on black sand, and begins mating Lightning and Thunder. With a poof, Fire returns.

With insolent grins, the children add more branches to Fire and let it burn to red coals. Petals scoots rocks around it and sets a black pot they had retrieved from the floating nest on top. When the water inside bubbles, she drops in oysters.

"Cooking," she says.

"Bomba has tamed Fire," Seaman explains smugly.

Sun has retired and Fire flickers a spell on their faces. OldOne stumbles down the mountain, wandering off the path into trees, greenbrier tearing his legs, trying to comprehend what he has witnessed.

Bomba insults Earth by making it produce Lightning, spawn Fire. Lets Fire run free. He must be a disciple of Maybouya, the evil one. The children have become corrupt.

"What is the world coming to?"

OldOne mixes the potion—guava berries, mushrooms, and snails—in a conch shell. He spits in it and lets it ferment in the shade for four trips of Sun, until the bubbling stops. When Moon is at her highest, he sits cross-legged on the beach facing North, the only star that does not move. He pours the concoction down his throat quickly, without stopping to breathe. The potion is poison. If his mouth alerts his stomach, the potion will be ejected. He waits grim-faced for the journey to begin to the edge of death.

Even with the help of the potion, he doesn't dare talk to North directly. He searches among the stars, his ancestors swirling around North, and finds the Wanderers, the sons of North. If he states his appeal clearly, maybe they will convince North to intercede.

Numbness creeps from his toes toward his head. He wavers then falls back on the sand. Only his eyes remain alive, looking up at the Wanderers, waiting for one of them to notice him. And then his spirit floats away from the husk of his body into Night.

OldOne visits Red first, the Wanderer who is the most sympathetic when the family is in trouble. As he approaches, Red glows crimson, as big as Sun. Red tells him his family is doomed and that it is his fault. He has sinned by allowing Maybouya to take root in Earth.

OldOne can't deny his guilt. He had felt North urging him to let Bomba die but had succumbed to the whining of the women and his own curiosity. After Bomba began his miracles, OldOne suspected he might be a Wanderer visiting Earth and was afraid to challenge him.

"Will I not be allowed to correct this?" OldOne asks. "Please ask your father to take pity and forgive me. I'm only a man."

"It's too late. Maybouya is too powerful for you to battle. Your people are infected already and cannot be salvaged. I'll advise North to allow Wind, the daughter of Maybouya, to wipe away the corruption, so Ocean can heal Earth. It's the only way."

OldOne tries to talk with the other Wanderers, "I'll go and kill him now," but they ignore him.

Petals stands in the cave mouth trying to understand what Bomba is doing. She would like to help, but his actions are mysterious, and she can only watch in rapture.

A boulder is rolled to the back of the cave as an altar and Powder set atop it. Then a salt cake, brought from the salt pond and dried before Fire, is ground in a gold bowl with a rock until it is as fine as sand. The salt is sprinkled on the walls and floor of the cave as he chants. He takes the metal vine from his neck and drapes it over an overhanging root above the cave so that the gleaming ornament suspends over the entrance.

Bomba takes her hand and they kneel together in front of the cave as he speaks—not to her, but apparently to Powder in the back of the cave. This part makes her skin crawl.

With these ceremonies complete, Bomba smiles and leads her to the fire pit. "Cook," he says. Petals fetches water from the cave as he builds a temple of sticks and summons Fire from a rock. When Fire burns to embers, she puts the bowl of water on to boil and adds oysters. They sit together on a flat rock, his arm around her because it is a small rock, and wait for the oysters to signal they are cooked by easing open their shells.

After the oysters cool, she begins to eat them off the half-shell, but he only watches, which makes her nervous that she did not cook properly. He falls off the rock clutching his stomach like he is sick. She can tell he is faking by his mischievous smile and kicks him playfully on the leg. He groans and thrashes on the ground like when he first arrived until she agrees to feed him. As she dribbles oysters into his mouth, her own stomach begins to ache like she had swallowed an oyster still inside the shell.

Is this the man-spell the women talk about? Is this how it attacks a woman? She looks down at the opening to her stomach and then at him. Even though the first signal of womanhood has come and gone, she is still too small.

Bomba feeds Fire. The light bouncing off the tall boulder behind Fire illuminates the cave. He leads her inside and they lie on the mat she had made to cover Earth. The cave is cold and they clasp to each other to ward off the chill. The oyster in her stomach, his man-spell, grows hot. She shivers although her skin feels hot against his. He pulls her closer.

She tries to remember how women entice men. She should have paid attention how the women cast their spell. She takes his hand and puts it on the moisture of her stomach to show him his spell is working. Even as his manhood readies, he pulls her to her feet and shoves her outside the cave. His face turns upward as he pleads to Night, then rushes back into the cave leaving her shaking with fear.

What had she done? What should she do now?

And then he charges out with angry face and drags her roughly into weeds to squirt his spirit. When he shudders and falls onto his back, he stares into Night, his mouth twisted in disgust. Slowly he gets up and walks beyond the sight of Fire and comes back peeling leaves from a limb. From over his shoulder, he thrashes his back. She breaks off a limb and tries to do the same to herself, but he stops her, directing her to whip him instead.

It is her fault. She is not fit to breed. The next morning she goes back to the camp in shame. When she asks the other women, they are puzzled also. Luke thinks Bomba prefers men. Each of the other men breeds her and say she is as good as the other women. Mark breeds her twice just to boost her confidence.

OldOne, fasting by himself at the shoreline, ignores her. When she approaches him for advice, he says she has shamed the tribe by breeding with Maybouya and banishes her back to the cave. "You're damned!" he yells as she backs away. "We're all damned."

CHAPTER 5

The Goldsmiths

The sand is bloody. The rats have eaten away enough of Weiwei's foot that he has slipped the rope that tethered him to his tree. Petals follows a shallow trough made by his shell sliding through the sand to the salt flat. In the middle of the pond, where the water is knee-deep, she sees the dome of his shell. He had crawled that far to find water deep enough to drown.

She sets the reed basket of oysters at her feet, lowers Cain from her hip onto a tuft of saw grass, and sits on the sand beside him. Her gaze is transfixed on the reflection of Sky on the flat water, looking for a ripple indicating Weiwei still struggles. His suffering is over, and she is glad, yet the harbinger of death causes a shiver.

Cain hugs her pregnant belly, frightened by her foreboding face. She pulls him onto her lap and squeezes him to her chest for reassurance. With her lips, she sucks the pus from the bites on his arms and legs. Bomba calls them Rats as if he has known them before. But until the end of the rainy season, when Sun tracked at its lowest in Sky, the family had never seen one before. Now they hide everywhere, coming out at night to scavenge among the oyster shells, digging up eggs left by the turtles, biting the children in their sleep. Only occasionally does she glimpse one, but she feels their eyes always on her, watching her now from under the palmetto fronds. OldOne says they came in the nest with Bomba. Bomba's demons he calls them.

Seaman sits beside her. As he walked to the cave, he must have seen what she had seen and followed her footprints from the trail. He lays his ax on the sand and takes Cain from her arms. The toddler snuggles under his chin. As Seaman looks out at Weiwei, he fondles Cain's feet, absentmindedly rolling each toe between his fingers. Like Bomba, Cain has five separate toes on each foot without the usual web of flesh between the second and third toes. When Seaman was learning to breed and being scoffed at by the other women for his awkwardness, Petals waited for him beside the trail from the beach to the cave to teach him what he should do. Maybe the new baby's feet will be normal.

"Will you go ahead; tell him before I get there?" she asks.

He doesn't look at her. Finally, he nods, the way Bomba does to mean *yes*, picks up the ax, and walks back to the trail.

Smoke and the smell of smoldering wood drifts down the crease between the mountains. Since Bomba keeps a fire going all the time, she has become accustomed to the haze of smoke and the stinging of her eyes. The clearing in the glade in front of the cave grows wider. Only tree stumps remain from the rainforest that once shaded the cave mouth in perpetual twilight.

Bomba douses water from the black pot onto flames that had erupted at one corner of the charcoal pit. Steam billows up and he steps back. His smock, an apron made from his boat's sail, is tattered with burn holes and streaked black from charcoal. Seaman shovels sod with a wood spade over the hotspots to keep them from flaming up again.

"Weiwei still," Seaman says.

Bomba stops and looks at him with a puzzled face.

"Spirit gone. Turned to smoke; blown away like spirit of trees."

Bomba drops the pot and pushes past Seaman at a jog toward the trail before stopping stiffly in front of Petals.

"Dead?"

He sees in her face that it is true.

For a long time, he looks at the ground without moving and then walks slowly back toward the cave. She, with Cain clutching her hand, follows. Bomba walks under the thatch roof they had constructed from above the cave entrance to the boulder six paces in front. The pile of charcoal stacked underneath is head high. Bomba walks out with his ax. Seaman follows him to the edge of the clearing where they are splitting a log in preparation for the next burn of charcoal. Bomba hands Seaman one of the wedges they had forged from gold ingots. Seaman holds the sharp edge in a crack while Bomba taps it in with the butt of his ax. When the crack opens, Seaman puts in the next wedge at the end of the split and they repeat the process until the man-length log falls open.

Seaman takes over with his ax splitting the half-logs into hand-width slivers. His ax, including the handle, is solid gold. Bomba had made it by cooking gold and pouring it into an impression made in the sand by his own ax. Since Bomba presented it to him, Seaman always has it with him, always shiny like Sun from polishing with sand and sharp from rubbing on a granite rock. His arms have grown large swinging it.

"We will cast Weiwei," Bomba says.

Seaman looks to Kiln, the shrine Bomba erected beside the cave where Fire makes gold like water. Doubt clouds Seaman's face. Weiwei is big, much bigger than his ax. Bomba sits on one of the logs surrounding the pit where Petals cooks. Seaman adds kindling before sitting beside him.

When she brings the pot filled with water out of the cave, both men are slumped with their elbows on their knees watching Fire come back to life. Their eyes are directed at the flames but she thinks their minds are seeing Weiwei in gold.

"We can do it," Bomba says still looking into Fire, talking more to himself than Seaman. "We have enough charcoal and gold to cast both. Same plan as before, only more. Weiwei first, before he begins to putrefy. By placing him upside down in the form box and packing the greensand around the top half of his shell, we can lift him straight up and leave a clean impression of the designs on his back. After we roll his casting out of the form box to cool, we can prepare the same greensand into a mold of the mermaid. The kiln will only have to be fired once that way."

After the water boils, she tips the oysters onto a flat rock to cool. With the tips of her fingers, she flings four back in the pot for herself and Cain. The clang of the oyster shells hitting the pot startles the men from their trance.

Just inside the cave opening, at the table Bomba made from a split log, she cuts the oysters with a gold knife into bite-size chunks for Cain. Outside, beside Fire, the men talk energetically as they open oysters. The words are a mixture of tribal words and new words Bomba has added. She can only follow parts of what is said because there are also hand signals used for some words, but Seaman grunts that he understands. Their voices become louder and faster with enthusiasm and then abruptly stop. She walks to the mouth of the cave. Seaman disappears at a jog down the trail to the beach. Bomba is scraping sand from the pit below Kiln, where gold flows when Fire is added to Kiln.

Her hand rests on Cain's head as they watch from the cave entrance. Bomba replaces the flat rocks in the bottom of the pit and then refills the hole half-full of sand—greensand he calls it although it is not green. She had helped him carry the fine powdery sand, found on the leeward side of sand dunes, back to the cave. He grinds a stick of charcoal between two stones until it too is like powder and sprinkles it from a gold bowl over the sand. To this, he adds wet clay from the banks of the stream.

When Bomba begins to knead the mud into the sand with his feet, Cain lunges toward the pit. She grasps for an arm but he is too quick. "Cain," she yells and gives chase. At the edge of the pit, he runs into Bomba's hands. Petals stops, closes her eyes, awaits the scolding words.

Cain jabbers a gleeful babble. Cain holds to Bomba's hands as they dance in a circle tramping the sand. She doesn't understand either of them, why they do things, how stomping mud can bring their smiles.

Petals follows them to the stream to rinse the clam sludge from the pot. Bomba washes the mud from Cain's legs. Cain gasps and holds his breath when Petals pours a bowl of the cold stream water over his head. Bomba mimics him, staring into Cain's eyes, cheeks swollen with air until their laughs burst out. Cain sits between them on a log, their feet in the stream.

"Weiwei...gold?" Petals' face conveys the *why*.

Bomba's face turns to the woods, then squints up at Sky. Cain follows his gaze looking for a bird. The spirits of the trees, their shadows, stretch across the splintered stumps and brown branches cluttering the clearing to hear his answer.

"Because I can do it. I know that I can, but I must prove it."

She doesn't understand the words and the *why* remains on her face.

He looks again across the clearing.

"Weiwei..." he points to Kiln and then uses the family's hand signal for *a great distance*. "Weiwei will live forever."

Bomba leans across Cain and startles her with a kiss on her mouth and then pushes her away. He points to Cain, then to her and then toward the path. She nods. What will come next, the firing of Kiln and melting of gold will be dangerous. She and Cain will have to live at the beach until it is over. Bomba's spirit teased her when they kissed and she leans toward him for another. He jumps to his feet, strides to Kiln, and begins adjusting bricks.

Petals' hands turn into fists, wishing he were close enough to hit. Why does he even touch her if he doesn't want her? Why does she stay with such a loon? Nothing he does makes sense; his spirit is happy one moment then infected by Maybouya the next. She kicks a spray of water from the stream and then lies down on her back in the water to cool off. Cain thinks it is a game and jumps on her stomach.

The voices of the men come from the trail, urging each other on. Seaman emerges with Matthew and John following with a pole on their shoulders. Weiwei dangles upside down from ropes tied to his feet, his head lolling at the end of his stretched neck. Bomba waves the men to the pit.

The men banter excitedly with Seaman as they pack sand around Weiwei's shell. They are so absorbed in creating their next miracle, nobody notices her take the path to the beach. Cain whines and struggles to loose himself from her grip and return to play with the men—to abandon her also.

As Petals walks away, Bomba stares at her shape, the squirming bronze buttocks just below the swaying tips of black hair. His sinful nature begs to call her back, leave the boy with the men, and lead her into the cave. He had once thought a cloistered life would rid him of carnal thoughts, but as she disappears into the foliage, he knows he too must battle the weaknesses of flesh. Already he has broken his vow of chastity. God's grace had accepted his pledge to sin no more. If only she would stop tempting him. Only work, continuous hard work, could keep sin at bay, redeem his transgression.

Bomba turns toward the pit, the tortoise on its back, Seaman directing the men how to pack the sand around the shell. He starts that way then stops. It would be a mistake to undermine Seaman's supervision. Seaman knows what to do as well as he does.

Once the kiln is fired, it will take three grueling days non-stop to melt the gold for the two castings. They will have to divide into two shifts with Seaman in charge of one. Bomba walks to the creek, lies down on his back in the creek with his ears underwater so he can't hear their voices, won't be tempted to intervene. He is proud of Seaman, the leader he has become, how much they have accomplished together in just two years.

At first, Bomba had only used the kiln to heat doubloons to a molten state to forge wire for fishhooks. With unraveled hemp rope from the ship, he had braided thinner cord and taught Seaman how to fish. Seaman, in turn, taught the amazed men who now troll every day from their canoes around the reef, sometimes catching fish with just a bare shiny hook. The women wanted more bowls, so they hammered ingots into golden platters for each of them. Each improvement he and Seaman made to the lives of his family gave them pride.

Bomba's first casting was gold poured into a simple impression made by a stick in the sand. He reheated the blank to a glowing orange, and as Seaman held it with tongs, hammered out the shape of a knife against the ship's anchor. Each man in the tribe wanted a knife of his own, so Seaman used this knife as a pattern and poured six more. Then they cast his ax using the one found at the wreck as a pattern. Not every effort was perfect, but to the Indians, every crude casting was a marvel. With each project, Seaman gained confidence.

Bomba had less luck teaching the Bible. He had arbitrarily picked a day as Sunday, and every seven days thereafter, he invited the family to the cave, which doubled as his sanctuary. Petals boiled fish and crabs and the family sat obligated to listen. His Bible stories inevitably contained camels, donkeys, or sheep. These supernatural creatures, sometimes drawn in the sand with a stick, made more of an impression than the point of the story. How could he teach them about Jesus' birth if they didn't even believe in donkeys? But there were parts they listened to intently. The star over Bethlehem they quickly identified as North, their version of the Supreme Being. The story of Jonah and the whale made sense to them.

He learned to adapt the Bible stories to their understanding of the world. Angels became mermaids, whom they knew were real, and God he called North. If they fornicated openly, he pointed to the sky and chastised them that North was watching. This had little effect during the daytime because they knew Night, where North dwells, was hidden by Sky. He also couldn't convince them North would disapprove anyway.

On a day he thought could be Ash Wednesday, Bomba taught the tribe about crucifixion. He had lashed together the trunks of two saplings into a cross and propped it against the cave entrance before they arrived. When he leaned back against the cross with outstretched arms, they watched curiously. He was prepared with a branch forked like a hand and a spike he had hammered out of scrap gold. As he splayed himself on the cross, he substituted the branch for his hand and tacked it in place. From their gasps, he knew they understood.

OldOne pushed Bomba aside. North would never allow such cruelty. When Bomba tried to go a step further and show them how to cross themselves, the Indians mimicked him, laughing at each other as they did. OldOne tipped the cross to the ground and ordered the family back to the beach. Bomba had never seen him so mad. Making such a sign was a salute to Maybouya, he warned. It would bring storms.

Some nights Bomba joined the family gathered around OldOne who pointed out stars and told stories about their ancestors who swim in Night. When they died, OldOne reminded them, they too would swim in Night. The family already had an equivalent to every Christian concept, so Bomba merged his message to OldOne's. The church of Spain would excommunicate, maybe burn him at the stake, if it became known. Each night he prayed to be absolved of this heresy. He faced the North Star when he prayed.

During the last storm, the ship's wooden figurehead broke loose from the bow of the wreckage and washed ashore. OldOne claimed the life-size mermaid as a gift from North sent by his archangel Ocean. "Mermaids are omens of prosperity," he said. He kept it propped against one of the palms that held up the men's shelter.

To Bomba, it had become holy also, a statue of the Virgin, but he kept this to himself. Mornings when he came to the beach to bathe, he knelt before it and with bowed head quietly mouthed Hail Marys. One day he opened his eyes and Seaman was kneeling beside him. The next morning, OldOne joined them. It became a morning ritual for the whole tribe. "Hail Mermaid full of Grace, North is with thee. Blessed be the fruit of Ocean's womb..." was the chant he taught them.

Bomba lingered after prayers to study the statue. The sea had scoured the paint off the figurehead. As the wood dried in the sun, a crack opened between her breasts and widened until it reached her navel. Every day her features became less distinct. In a few months, the figurehead would just be another piece of driftwood.

Her arms were stretched against her side, back slightly arched, chin tilted up, hair flowing onto her shoulders as if she were surfacing after a kick of her tail. Where the back of the figurehead attached under the ship's forepeak was flat. If he molded her facedown, the poured surface could represent her back. The split and the other dings could be cemented with mud long enough to make an impression in the mold. Draft angles and fillets needed to cleanly lift the pattern from packed sand could be added with mud also and then chiseled away from the finished casting after the pour.

He became convinced the mermaid could be cast, down to her hips at least. He discussed it with Seaman, now his apprentice, who in turn explained the plan to OldOne. OldOne at first declared this graven image would give offense to Ocean. But later, after waking from a trance, OldOne ordered the mermaid be made into gold. His only stipulation was that a pole be cast onto the bottom of the statue so he could mount the mermaid in the sand facing Ocean to show appreciation for the gift. The project became everyone's obsession.

CHAPTER 6

Black Death

The wave gently lifts the canoe and, after it passes under, the barge trailing behind. OldOne and Abel lie beside each other on the barge, their heads rocking in unison, first toward shore as the barge rides up an incoming wave and then seaward after the barge teeters over the crest. Like Bomba, the one-year-old and his grandfather seem to be studying the shape of the waves beyond the reef to judge if the water is deep enough for burial.

Bomba pulls the tether rope until he is alongside the barge and rolls out of the canoe onto the rough planks. He staggers to his feet on the shifting deck and looks to the shore. Seaman stands alone on the beach. How can he watch? How could he not? It is too far to see his face clearly, but Bomba imagines the torment of losing his father and son in a single day.

Bomba looks down at the bodies. Lumps under OldOne's skin distort his neck and torso. Open boils that had oozed corruption have dried. He kneels down and checks the knots at the gold ingot and then at OldOne's ankles. His feet are purple, like Bomba's father's had been at the end. Black Death. Bomba knows the symptoms well enough.

The Indian slaves in his father's foundry became sick first, stumbled out the door and never returned. When his father woke one morning with a rash, they both knew what would follow. His father begged him to leave, hide at one of the silver mines until it was over. Instead, he washed his father's sores with aloe and prayed. Earnestly he prayed. With tears dripping from his cheeks, while his father moaned in agony, he prayed.

When he too became sick, he pleaded from the doorway to passersby for help. They ran away. A town official pushed a small leather pouch of gunpowder under the door. "Put a pinch in your mouth," he yelled in, then nailed their foundry doors shut from the outside. When he had awakened from delirium two days later, flies swarmed over his father's festered body. He had been too weak to even cover him.

When OldOne is rolled into the water, he sinks to the end of the rope, then floats to the surface on his back. His half-lidded eyes watch Bomba tip the gold brick overboard. OldOne follows the ingot feetfirst, his arms trailing behind, face tilted up as he goes out of sight. There should have been words. There are no words.

He sits in front of Abel so that Seaman cannot see him tie his blacksmith hammer onto the baby's gray stomach. Before he releases the baby into the water, Bomba closes his eyes to avoid the image of the baby sinking. He rocks back, arms stretched wide on the deck, his mind blank to all but the orange through his eyelids and the gently undulating raft. Again he tries to pray, "Hail Mary, full of grace..." The usually soothing chant is wisped from parched lips and lost to the gurgling ocean.

From atop the bolder in front of the cave, Petals looks across the treetops to the bay. Even standing on tiptoes, she cannot see the beach as she had hoped and is about to climb back down when a dark speck just beyond the reef catches her eye. At first she dismisses it as driftwood and then there is a flash of sunlight from a paddle. A canoe and behind it a tiny square—the barge. Her legs tremble and she slumps onto the bolder to keep from falling. Her baby is being buried...and OldOne, maybe others of the family also. Her wails echo from the surrounding mountains.

It is too far away to see who is in the canoe, but it must be Bomba, the only man not yet incapacitated. The memory of Bomba wrenching Abel from her arms turns her face into a snarl. "Maybouya," she mumbles. She stands, stretching her arms with clenched fists, the sign for *evil*, toward the specs on the water. "You have destroyed us, Bomba." She wipes tears from bleary eyes and extends her fists again toward the bay and screams, "May-bou-yaaa!"

In the night, the swish of wind through the trees subsides and faint moans can be heard from the beach below. Pain or mourning? Beside her, Bomba's breathing is steady, listening also—or maybe asleep. When she quietly gets to her feet, a hand firmly grasps her ankle. She tugs briefly then lies back beside him. He holds her hand on his stomach, not out of affection or reassurance, she knows, but as an alarm if she tries to escape to the beach again.

At dawn, Bomba rouses Cain and leads him whimpering to the stream for a morning bath. Petals rises and follows, knowing that if she doesn't bathe and recoat her skin and hair with bitters, he will force her also.

She and Cain stand in the stream without talking or even looking at Bomba, ready for his torture. Bomba lathers them with the soap he concocted from coconut oil and ashes from the fire pit. When they are thoroughly scrubbed, she uses the black pot to rinse both her and Cain with the cold spring water. They stand shivering as Bomba slathers on the ointment the family uses to repel insects. When Bomba stands back satisfied, Petals refills the pot half-full for cooking and leads Cain to Fire.

Bomba grabs her arm roughly and pulls her face in front of his. He points to the trail and shakes his head. She stares back defiantly. He takes both arms and shakes her until she nods.

Bomba adds wood to Fire before walking to the trail. He ducks behind trees to hide, to see if she will stay at the cave like he had ordered. Hate, an emotion she had never felt before, supplants grief. She screams her fury, awful words in her language. Is this what it feels like when one's spirit becomes lost?

Cain, his wet hair in peaks, his skin shiny from the bitters, wraps his arms around himself as he dries in front of Fire. She twirls him in front of her looking with dread for the pink rash that had erupted on Abel's skin.

Abel's swollen body flashes in her mind, the shrieks of pain that faded to whimpers at the end. She clenches her eyes and unsteadily sinks onto a log in front of Fire. Her eyes open when Cain climbs in her lap. Tears drip from his cheeks also. She hugs him to her breast. He has been weaned for three rainy seasons, but she lets him suckle. It relieves them both.

After Abel quit breathing, while she still screamed, Bomba elbowed through the women and wrenched Abel from her arms. He held the baby's chest to his ear and then placed him beside OldOne who already dead. When she tried to go to Abel, Bomba lifted her off her feet, cradled her in his arms. She had seen then, in his eyes, that Bomba's spirit was gone. He had carried her into the surf and demanded she stay put until he came back leading Cain with one hand and the shell containing ointment in the other. He had washed them thoroughly in the surf, shooing back Grande who tried to console her.

He had dragged her and Cain by the arms toward the cave, but she kept pulling away, trying to return. With her draped over his shoulder beating his back with her fists and Cain under his arm, he doggedly continued to the cave. Her anguish meant nothing to him. OldOne had told her about men whose spirits become lost, how their bodies continue to move although they are dead inside.

When he stood her in front of the cave, she broke his grip and started back toward the trail. He caught her arm, slung her around, and slapped her across the face. Stunned, her hands rose to the sting on her cheek. He had never hit her before. His arm arched back again, his face twisted, cruel. Cain screamed as he clutched her leg. Afraid he would hit Cain also, she led Cain into the cave.

Petals' curses hurt. Bomba squats behind a tree stump at the edge of the trail so Petals won't see his heaving sobs. It is happening again, the plague, and there is nothing he can do for those already infected. If only Petals and Cain can be spared. He hasn't learned enough of their language to explain to Petals what is happening, what will happen. There is no point anyway. Who wants to hear their family will die in horrible agony?

When Petals brought food to the cave that morning, Abel wailed incessantly and Bomba took him from her hip, tried to comfort him while she talked.

"Matthew," she pointed to the sky. "Seaman," she made a paddling motion and then said the tribe's word for Ocean. Matthew had died. Seaman was burying his body in the traditional way.

Petals sat on a log and wept into her hands while water came to a boil in the black pot. Frightened by his mother sobbing, Cain crawled into her lap. Abel whimpered in Bomba's arms and finally relaxed into sleep. It was then, as he laid Abel on a grass mat, he had seen the red spots on the baby's chest. "Nooo…" he had moaned. The baby startled and then went limp again. Petals stared at him, wanting an explanation. There was no way to tell her. He didn't want to tell her.

After the oysters opened, Petals scooped out the shells onto a gold platter for them to eat. Petals watched curiously as Bomba minced the oysters with his knife, refilled the pot with fresh water, and put the meat back in to boil. While the pot simmered on the coals, he went into the cave and came back with a palm full of gunpowder to sprinkle into the thick broth.

With the bail of the pot in one hand and leading Cain with the other, he walked to the beach. Petals followed with Abel asleep on her shoulder. As he feared, the rest of the tribe was sick as well. All he could do was comfort them—or try anyway. Since he had previously survived the plague, he would be spared, but every member of the tribe would inevitably be stricken. Less than half the population of Veracruz had lived through that terrible summer. Survivors, like himself, were left pockmarked and weakened.

The family sat in stupors on woven mats in the shade of the shelters. Seaman, Luke, and Grande, who only had the splotchy rash on their chests so far, tended the others who already had the whelps under their skin they would have seen on Matthew. All were quiet, their heads resting on their knees, solemnly awaited their fate. OldOne seemed the weakest. Open sores on his throat drained onto his chest. He sniffed the broth then pushed the gold spoon away when he smelled gunpowder. "Powder piss," he sneered. Bomba spooned the mush into the others' mouths and they swallowed reluctantly. Abel was still too young for solid food. When Bomba smeared broth on Petals' nipples, he refused to nurse. He dribbled some from his finger into Abel's mouth, but he spit it out.

Bomba begged OldOne to pray. OldOne scoffed that North could not hear them until dark. Besides, he had met with a Wanderer in a trance the previous night; the family was doomed. Bomba argued, but OldOne turned away. Who was he to dispute a Wanderer?

Bomba crossed himself and knelt before Madonna, the golden mermaid stuck in the sand in between the shelters. As he prayed

Hail Marys out loud, Luke darted from under the lean-to at a run and dove into the surf. The family watched him swim past the reef and head for the vague outline of an island miles away. It was almost certain death, but no one called after him.

CHAPTER 7

The End of the Beginning

Petals sits on the edge of the pit where gold is poured watching Cain play at her feet in the sand. Bomba has spent every waking moment of the past three trips of Sun at the beach, but makes her stay at the cave with Cain. At noon, Bomba will walk up the trail with crabs from the traps for her to cook into broth to carry back to her family before dark.

Through the trees at the head of the trail, there is movement. She looks to Sun. Bomba is returning early. Part of her longs to see him emerge into the clearing, is grateful he is caring for her sick family. Another part loathes the sight of him. He won't answer when she begs to know what is happening, if her family is getting better. This, of course, means they are not.

She jumps up and runs to Fire. The water is not yet boiling. She is raking coals against the pot when she hears her name.

Seaman staggers across the clearing and falls to his knees in front of her. His face is swollen, his body a mass of festered boils. "Bomba say Petals, Cain dead. I no believe."

"We no sick. What of family?"

"Spirits go." He points to Sky.

"All dead?"

Seaman's head tilts forward, shoulders heaving.

Petals lifts his chin. "All?"

Seaman's eyes are shut, unwilling to meet her eyes, mouth open in a silent cry.

Petals feels faint. As her vision fades and she wilts to her knees, she reaches for Seaman to keep from collapsing. Although his chest against her face is hot, he shivers. She hugs him tighter. Their tears pool together between her breasts.

"Seaman spirit go also," he says.

"No!" she pushes him to arm's length to look into his eyes, to see inside to his spirit. Seaman must see the presage of death in her face and looks down. "No," she repeats with determination.

She pulls him to his feet, leads him to the stream. While he sits on the log, she lathers him, washes corruption from open sores. Although the day is already hot and she is sweating, Seaman continues to shake. After watching her smear aloe on Seaman's sores, Cain runs into the cave. He backs out tugging Seaman's ax through the sand. He must think Seaman will begin chopping wood as he does most mornings.

A hand grabs Petals' shoulder, pushing her aside. Bomba pulls Seaman to his feet, points to the trail. Seaman falls forward on his hands, looks up at Bomba's anger. Bomba lifts him to his feet and turns him toward the beach. Seaman stumbles forward as Bomba prods him on.

Halfway across the clearing Bomba staggers against Seaman's back and collapses to his knees. Seaman turns and stares across Bomba at the ax in Petals' hands. She follows his gaze to the ax, only then comprehending what she has done. As she tries to lift the ax again, Seaman takes it from her.

Bomba tries to regain his feet, moans, falls forward on his face. Blood seeps from a gash in the center of his back onto the dirt. The golden ax, arched back above Seaman's head, trembles.

"Do now. Send to Maybouya." Petals is surprised, alarmed by her own words, at how badly she wants to see Bomba's head split open.

Cain grabs Seaman's leg. "No!" he pleads.

Petals floats facedown in chest-deep water at the edge of the oyster bed. The langouste senses a predator, scutters between two rocks and crouches with claws outstretched. Petals gulps air and dives, driving the sharpened bamboo shaft between the claws. She stands, still pinning the langouste to the sand, waiting for the thrashing to end. The nauseatingly sweet smell of putrid flesh envelops her. She has not been brave enough to go to the lean-tos, but her mind sees the rotting bodies anyway, ravaged by rats, the swarm of flies. She holds her breath again, hoping the wind will shift. It doesn't and she retches into the water.

Seaman has made Fire roar. There is little smoke; Fire must be consuming the last of the charcoal. She dumps the langouste and the few clams from her woven basket into the steaming pot as Seaman stirs with a sliver of wood. The sores on his chest and neck are scaly scabs now, no longer surrounded by red. Every day he seems stronger.

Cain sits on the log staring blankly into Fire, seeming not to have noticed her return. She sits beside him. Still he will not look at her. When she follows Cain's gaze into the flames, she sees his spirit burning.

"Seaman."

He glances up from the pot. She points to Cain and makes the sign for *far away*. Seaman looks at Cain, still in a daze, then back to her, nods that he understands, says nothing. He tips the pot onto a flat rock by the fire; steam billows up. With his gold knife, he pries the meat from the shells onto a gold platter and throws the shells into Fire. Petals forces herself to eat. She turns Cain's head to look at her and pushes bits of the langouste tail past his lips. He mimics her chewing.

After they've eaten all their appetites will allow, Seaman takes the platter to Bomba, still leaning in a sitting position against the cave wall at the entrance. He hasn't moved or spoken since Seaman propped him there three Suns ago. When Seaman tries to push meat between Bomba's lips, he turns his head. Seaman leaves the bowl and walks to Kiln, the work area where he helped Bomba make many things. Seaman stands rigid, looking above the treetops to Ocean and the purple island sitting on the horizon. He is motionless so long, Cain thinks something is wrong and squirms to his feet. Petals grabs Cain's arm and pulls him back down on the log. Their future is being decided and she doesn't want Seaman interrupted.

Seaman turns to Kiln, picks up a chisel from among Bomba's tools, and pries at the square rocks until Kiln crumbles in on itself. "Kiln no magic," he says walking over to her. He lifts the black pot by the bail. "Pot evil." He gathers up the gold tools Bomba had made her for cooking. "Gold evil. Fire evil. All Bomba bring; all we make—evil. OldOne warn us." He returns to Kiln and gathers all of Bomba's tools into the pot, searches in front of the cave for other implements. Petals looks into the cave. Bomba is watching.

Bomba leans against the cave wall in an awkward slump that should hurt—but it doesn't. Below his shoulders no longer belongs to him. His arms burn as if wrapped in jellyfish, but he can still curl his fingers.

Bomba looks over at the pot of tools against the wall to his right, then to his left, at the stack of gold platters, their gleam, their slick surfaces begging to be touched. Seaman is looking at them also, feeling the same craftsman's pride, the lure of wealth the yellow metal invokes. Seaman glances at him, the trance broken, his face stern as he strides back to the fire pit, returning with his gold ax and standing at Bomba's feet.

Bomba closes his eyes, welcoming a final blow. His eyes flick open when he hears banging in the dark backside of the cave. The powder keg is off its shelf, powder spilling from a broken stave onto the cave floor. Seaman kneels beside it scooping the black crystals into a golden bowl. Walking on his knees, he carefully pours a ribbon of powder on the cave floor. When he reaches Bomba's feet, Seaman rises and they stare at each other. No words are said, nor does either of their facial expressions change, but a pact is made. Bomba nods.

Seaman's hands cover his eyes and a shudder quakes his body. When his hands return to his sides, charcoal residue streaks his somber face, a face of mourning, resolve. He nods emphatically, pivots out to the fire pit, and comes back with an arm-length stick burning at one end. Orange flames cast Seaman's wavering shadow on the cave walls. He leans the burning stick against a rock beside Bomba's hand. Bomba's hand inches to the cold end of the branch, grasps, lifts the stick to vertical to show Seaman he can. Seaman looks into his eyes again. *"Kolomo betta,"* he says, words Bomba had never heard before. A blessing or a curse? Bomba closes his eyes. Does it matter?

Outside—more words. Petals' frantic questions, Seaman's louder demands, Cain's frightened whine. And then the quietness of the cave rings in Bomba's ears. The stick wavers at the end of his half-numb arm, a tongue of blue stretching up from the end with yellow fading to orange at the edges, black soot spiraling into the darkness. Looking into the flame, the image of Petals forms in his mind, scowling down at him, wishing him dead. If he were to let the fire fall forward now, onto the powder, before his murderers get away…

He turns his head to the darkness at the end of the cave. Has he also become a killer? The face of Petals returns, but much younger, beaming adoration as he slips a tortoiseshell comb into her hair. Her smile makes him smile.

The face of Seaman replaces hers, not the morose man that just left, but the boy in the ship's cabin, shaking with fright while faking bravado, bursting into laughter at his fart.

Where had their joy gone? Was it he who had stolen their lives? Bomba remembers the paradise the island had been when he first arrived, the tribe's bliss and harmony. In appreciation, he had applied his ingenuity to make the Indians' lives even better, civilize them, save their souls. A mission from God...or a self-serving delusion? He was no better than the conquistadores who had raped Mexico. The results were the same. God had redeemed him from death into Heaven. If only he had realized, appreciated his good fortune, left perfect alone.

Cain waddles out of the darkness, like watching himself as a baby emerge, large ears and pointed nose already, tinge of amber in his hair—undeniably his. "Cain," he calls invitingly to the specter. If only Cain would run giggling, snuggle his warm body next to his. Cain alone could make his heart flutter, the only one he truly loved. But he was also an ever-present reminder of sin. He could enjoy their play only briefly before guilt, shame for ill-gotten pleasure, pushed the boy away. Cain sucks the tips of his fingers, glancing up from the floor furtively as he backs into the shadows.

To have it end this way, a plague. The laments of the family seem to seep from the cave walls, like a liturgy, one crying out, the others answering in unison. Like Job, watching his family die, he too had been forced to watch, watch and listen, as if it were his penitence.

A trial devised by the Devil, sanctioned by God to prove his faith. "Damn your tests," he says through clenched teeth into the darkness. "Damn you both."

The edge of sunlight marks time as it creeps into the dusky cave. Bomba picks out one of Seaman's footprints on the sandy floor close to the shadow. *When the sun reaches that spot*, he thinks. Then he looks at the guttering flame—*or maybe sooner.*

Even as Seaman adamantly points to the beach, Petals continues to argue. He shoves her toward the trail and scoops Cain into his arms to lead the way. They are at the edge of the salt pond when the mountain explodes. Seaman pulls her behind a tree until the rain of rocks onto the forest around them is over.

The canoe and barge are nosed into the beach at the end of the trail. Petals glances farther up the beach, to the shelters where the family would be. A sand dune in the foreground keeps her from seeing the bodies. She is relieved.

She steps into the canoe first and Seaman lifts Cain to her. Cain is limp and she lays him in the center. Seaman hands her a paddle, points to the front of the canoe. He climbs into the back, pushes away from shore with his paddle.

They head to a narrow channel through the reef, struggle through incoming waves into open water. Seaman points the canoe toward a ghostly island in the distance. In the trough of giant rollers, she cannot see the island ahead, only Ocean threatening to swallow them. Then the canoe is lifted and she feels hope.

It will be a long voyage; already she is exhausted. She turns from her knees to sit looking rearward. Seaman, muscles rippling as he digs into the water, looks beyond her to the next wave he will have to negotiate. His face is the boy, before he was named Seaman, but he is a man. Why hadn't she noticed? Behind him is a yellow gash in the mountain where the cave had been. Rubble of boulders and uprooted trees had slid all the way to the salt pond. White smoke billows up from darting yellow fingers. Fire has escaped, OldOne's greatest fear. It will spread for days, burning the whole island unless there is a storm. Maybe the rats brought by Bomba will be purged and the island can renew.

Against the thin white band of beach, the lean-tos are tiny black squares, between them the glint of the golden mermaid. Below the thatch Petals' family lies unburied. If she survives this voyage, she will pray to North to forgive this offense and allow them to swim in Night forever.

Cain sits up, looks toward the new island with marvel, a faint smile. Seaman glances at Cain, then at her, points to her paddle. *Far away*, he signals emphatically with one arm.

She turns back to her knees and begins to paddle with vigor. North will spare the three of them. Like coconuts washed onto a desolate beach, they will take root, become seeds of a family, and defend their new home against evil. She will not look back again.

Part 2

(417 years later)

August 2002 - Orient Beach, Saint Martin FWI

Sex and religion are closer to each other
than either might prefer.
— Saint Thomas More

I feel most deeply that the whole subject is too profound for the human intellect...let each man hope and believe what he can.

– Charles Darwin

Battle not with monsters, lest ye become a monster,
and if you gaze into the abyss, the abyss gazes also into you.

– Friedrich Nietzsche

Maybe this world is another planet's Hell.

– Aldous Huxley

It is easier to build strong children than to repair broken men.

– Fredrick Douglass

God alone creates perfect. Every bird is perfect.
Every tree is perfect—only different.

– Navaho tradition

Suicide – beating the grim reaper on his home court.

– Unknown

CHAPTER 8

Reunion

$\mathcal{P}$aul gasps after struggling to the top of the sand dune that separates the resort parking lot from the beach. His leather-soled loafers have given him little traction in the sand and his legs throb. He extends his arms outward like a scarecrow to let the breeze off the ocean flap his clammy dress shirt.

From the back pocket of his suit pants, he pulls out a brochure picked up at the airport. The picture of Orient Beach must have been taken from this very spot. A quarter mile out from the beach, white breakers flash on a coral reef. A few miles farther, a scrubby island, the outline of a whale breaching out of the turquoise water. The near end of the beach, to his right, abuts a rock jetty. To his left, a mile away, the tip of the crescent sweep of sugary sand ends at a tumble of boulders below a cliff.

At this early hour, the beach is deserted except for a couple walking hand in hand and an old man sitting cross-legged facing the ocean. The couple wears sunglasses and the woman has a rope of beads above her hips, nothing else. The solitary man is also nude, no sunglasses, not even flip-flops. Paul doesn't see what he came for at first and is turning to leave this disgusting place when the lone man lifts his hands, palms up, to the sides of his head in the familiar *voilà* gesture he remembers.

Paul's lips curl into a smug grin. There is no hurry now that he has found him. As he considers what comes next, his smile fades into a resolute stare. It crosses his mind to leave now, down the backside of the dune, catch a cab back to the airport. It had been stupid to come anyway.

As he slogs down the dune, Paul compares the man ahead to the father he remembers from a year ago. Mahogany skin stretches tightly over bone and muscle. At least twenty pounds of pudginess is gone. The hair, remembered as a distinguished black, flecked gray at the temples, is now sun-faded, streaked ocher. The long ropy strands tumbling to his shoulders make him seem feral, dangerous.

"Dad?" His voice is too tentative to be heard above the crashing surf. He repeats it with more assertiveness, but the man facing away remains in a trance. He leans in closer, "Legion!"

The face that turns to him is his father, but not the face he was expecting. The pale blue eyes that once blended with his sallow skin are now opals set in bronze. There is a serene smile Paul has never seen before. Paul turns his head away, looking down the beach trying to recall the prohibition: *the son damned for seeing his father naked; or the father damned for exposing himself?*

He turns back with a stern face, "What are you doing?" Paul's tone is more an accusation than a question, the way it might be said to a misbehaving child.

Legion's luminous smile drains away. "What do you want, Paul?"

"I need to talk to you, Dad, somewhere else so you can hear without me having to shout."

"I'm not quite through here, Paul. Can't it wait a little while? Go up to that restaurant at the end of the beach. Lily Ana will be the only one there right now. Ask her for a gin and tonic; tell her to put it on Legion's tab."

"Dad, it's not even eight in the morning."

"Paul, I don't know what you've got to say, but I'll need to be more mellow to deal with you." Legion turns back and closes his eyes to the glaring sun.

Paul waits but the conversation has ended, at least for now. He turns to the café front peeking out behind fan-shaped fronds of palmetto. The sand in his loafers galls his heels as he walks stiffly, flat-footed.

Although the café has waist-high half-walls to allow unrestricted views of the ocean, the inside appears dark after being on the beach. He pauses at the door to let his eyes adjust. The couple he had seen walking earlier sits at a table by the entrance on towels spread over the wicker chairs to protect their naked bottoms. They are holding hands across the table cooing like doves and don't notice him walk in. In the back, a woman sits behind the bar, her face framed by the shelves of liquor bottles behind her.

"Gin and tonic, please."

"For *Monsieur* Legion?" The inflections are songlike, the way English is spoken with a French accent. "And for you?"

"Do you have orange juice?"

"Of course, *Monsieur*," she sings.

Paul watches her put two full jiggers of gin in Legion's drink. Her complexion is Mediterranean dark, not just from the sun. The auburn braids at her shoulders are sun-kissed at the tips. She wears jean shorts, ragged at the hem and a nylon blouse that fits loosely over her thin frame. Paul had thought a bartender at a nudist resort would be nude.

"Does Legion drink like this every day?" he asks.

She stops pouring the orange juice and looks at him. This is a confidentiality not given out by a bartender in any country, but her expression says more. She had watched him on the beach with his dad; knows he is from Legion's past. The question is personal to her also.

"*Pardon?*" she says in French, feigning not to understand.

Legion, silent on bare feet, is suddenly beside him. Lily Ana hands him a towel from behind the bar, which he folds in half and spreads on the stool next to Paul. Lily Ana sets the drinks on paper napkins in front of them.

"Lily Ana, this is Paul, my only son, from the States. Paul…Lily Ana. In addition to being my personal bartender, she's the sexiest woman in Saint Martin. Can you set us up at a table? Paul here wants to talk."

After they settle at a table, Paul kicks off his loafers and quietly sips the orange juice thinking of different ways to say it. "Mother is dead." Paul looks for a reaction but there isn't one. "A car accident two weeks ago—killed instantly."

Legion turns to watch the surf climbing up the beach. "I'm sorry to hear that, Paul."

"You coldhearted son-of-a-bitch!" Paul's rabid intensity hangs in the air. Behind Legion, Paul sees Lily Ana crane forward over the bar with a scowl. Paul struggles to contain his voice but the fury is still there. "She was your wife, for Christ's sake."

The French couple sitting at the next table quietly leaves, returning to the beach. A pigeon, that had been waiting patiently in a palm tree at the café's corner flutters to their vacated table, its head bobbing as it pecks at the remainder of their croissants.

"Paul, she left me, remember? She filed for divorce as soon as she found out I was sick. I never wanted to hear from her or her lawyer again, and thus I'm here. How you ever found me, I can't imagine. I'm sorry for you, Paul. I know you loved her. She's been dead to me for a year."

"She didn't divorce you, Dad. You've been married all this time, until she died." The timing of the breakup Paul knew was true, but it wasn't like that, not the way it sounded when his dad said it. The rage pinches his face. "She said she still loved you."

"And I loved her—once." Legion finally engages Paul's eyes. "I thought that was all it took. But being in love takes two people and your mother was never in love with me, or any other man. She never understood love, like a blind man trying to understand purple. To her it was just a superlative, the next degree above like."

Lily Ana is beside them, touching Legion's elbow. Legion looks up and smiles to assure her. "Another, beautiful, but only one shot this time should finish me up."

After Lily Ana leaves, Legion adds, "If your mother didn't divorce me after I left, it wasn't for love. Maybe she couldn't love, but her hate was forever. Her lawyer must have convinced her it would be more economical to wait for me to die and get it all rather than settle for half."

"You don't look like you're dying, Dad." Legion is gazing out toward the breakers at the reef, his lean muscles rippling as he twists for the view. "You've never looked so healthy."

Legion turns back to face him. "Yep, ain't that a hoot. I came down here to die in peace and now I can't seem to get it done. I'm thinking that my biopsy got mixed up with some other guy that died six months ago. It's either that, or all this clean living, or maybe just a miracle."

"I don't think you rate a miracle."

"It's the clean living then. I walk every morning at daybreak and every night at sunset to the far end of the beach, two miles round trip. It's a tradition for the die-hard nudists who live here. They believe the sun cures everything. And I swim whenever I get hot and Lily Ana feeds me fish, and salad, and fruit right here."

When Paul looks skeptical, Legion adds, "Yeah, I'm dying. Everybody's dying. It may take me another month, or maybe twenty years. The timing's not so important. But when I die it will be right here. I've got nothing to go back for, no unfinished business. Nobody except my lawyer needs to know. Nobody back there will care, including you, Paul."

A gull streaks in out of the sun and banks into the wind, hovering motionless in front of their table. Folding its wings, it dives to a coconut husk on the sand, which it tests with its beak. Convinced it is not a baguette thrown out from the café, it catches the wind and sails down the beach.

"You see that girl over there?" Legion scoots his chair to face Lily Ana, pointing so Paul will have to look also. Lily Ana, who hasn't taken her eyes off them, fidgets knowing that he is talking about her. She waves her hands *no*, not to tell whatever he is telling, but Legion continues. "She's from Italy. She got to Saint Martin as part of the crew on a yacht out of Barcelona. There was a dispute with the captain over sex. He sent her ashore at Marigot in a rubber dinghy to restock the wine, and while she was ashore, the boat pulled anchor. She watched from the jetty as her home motored through the port mouth into open water. She was left with her bathing suit, a sarong, a case of French wine, and the dinghy—no passport, no ID. She sold the wine and the dinghy the next morning and was here looking for a job in the afternoon. We arrived on the same day."

They watch the beach out front begin to fill. From the path beside the café, clients wave and greet Legion in French or English. Three little girls, all under age twelve, trot playfully ahead of their parents. Their evenly tanned bodies are perfect, like innocent nymphs on a Grecian urn. "Any civilized country would put their parents in jail," Paul sneers.

A petite young woman, Kewpie doll face framed by a bob cut of dazzling white hair, walks in from the path. Legion rises and stoops forward across her pregnant belly to receive kisses to each side of his neck. Her belly button protrudes and blue veins streak her taut sides. Her gorged breasts point down, the chocolate nipples ready to burst. Legion takes her hand and turns her for an introduction, but Paul is walking away to find a bathroom.

Paul expects Legion to be fuming when he returns. Instead, he chuckles.

"Correcting your rude behavior is not my responsibility anymore, Paul. You are free to be an asshole if you wish. Here, you can be anything you want." Legion throws his head back finishing his drink. "And yeah, I'm still an asshole too, but a different asshole than you remember, one you don't know at all. My life has turned basic. My wants and needs are simple."

Paul starts to respond but is cut off.

"And it's my life, mine alone. Your opinion of my lifestyle means nothing, so don't bother. And my life is right here and right now—no past, no future." He looks past Paul to the bar. "I love Lily Ana, Paul. And even more important, she loves me. Look at this thing I am. Who could love a half-crazy, naked old man? She makes me happy and I try my best to make her happy. We don't anticipate the future and the past happened to different people in another life. For me, Paul, this is all there is, all I want."

"Look, I'm happy you're happy," Paul doesn't feel happy. "But there are things to settle."

"Not for me, Paul. You know my lawyer. He's got the power to do anything that needs doing. I don't even want to know how it works out, and he knows that."

Paul thinks of a rebuttal but then lets it go. It is always pointless to argue with the old man.

CHAPTER 9

Paul

Paul squints against the glaring white sand behind Legion. Legion shouts over Paul's shoulder, "Lily, it's time for breakfast."

From behind the counter, Lily Ana brings a baguette and swimming trunks.

"You drink in the nude, but wear clothes to eat? Nobody will believe this, Dad."

Legion pushes back from their table and slips into the trunks. "You coming?"

Not knowing what his dad is talking about, Paul shakes his head, feeling it safer to decline.

Legion walks out to the surf, just twenty yards in front of the café. A yellow dog that had been waiting by the doorway twirls and whines, apparently begging for the bread. When Legion wades in, the dog prances and barks at the waterline. Legion stops when the water is at his waist. Breaking the baguette so half is in each hand, he holds them at arm's length and sticks the broken ends below the water.

Paul flashes a sarcastic smile at Lily Ana, standing beside him, but she is watching Legion so intently she doesn't notice. This strange ritual must have meaning to her also.

At first, there is the slightest disturbance around the ends of the bread, like drops of rain hitting the water. A growing shadow coalesces around Legion and the water begins to churn violently. The tips of spiny fins zip by from all directions. Hand-sized fish, yellow with vertical brown stripes, flip into the air out of the roiling mass.

The dog rushes out when a wave recedes, growling ferocious threats at the thrashing water, only to be chased back by the next wave. The three girls who had passed the café earlier wade in as close as they dare, shrinking back giggling when fish jump their way. In under a minute, only the end nubs of the baguette remain.

Several gulls, also materializing from nowhere, hover above. Legion holds the nubs above his head for them to see then tosses them into the air. The gulls swoop all at once. Two gulls catch the bread while still on the ascent and then race away with the rest of the birds in pursuit trying to steal the prizes.

And then there is only Legion watching the gulls fly out of sight. The ominous shadow that surrounded him in the water has dissolved. There is no evidence left that any of it actually happened. Paul gives Lily Ana a questioning look, but again she doesn't notice. She is with Legion in the water, feeding the animals vicariously. The edges of her mouth widen into a smile when Legion waves.

The pregnant woman had watched from the shade of a palm. After the girls came back to their sand castle and the dog loped off down the beach, she wades out to Legion. They talk a moment before Legion swoops her into a hug, clasping her head to his chest. He lifts her so that she floats on her back, supported by his arms. Her distended belly and breasts rock with the waves.

Paul looks up to Lily Ana who is still standing by his chair. "Is the slut's baby his?"

Lily Ana glares then turns back to the bar only to whip around after a few steps. "Zuzu is my friend. She is Legion's friend. We are all friends here." She is not shouting but the music in her voice earlier is now shrill. She walks up close, lowering her face to look directly into his eyes, "Until the *chiot* arrived." And then she is gone back to the bar.

Paul reaches to his jaw; he feels the sting of a slap, although she had not touched him.

"Your girlfriend called me a 'shit,'" he tells Legion when he walks up, still dripping.

Legion glances to Lily Ana, busy behind the bar. He chuckles. "It seems you have not made a favorable impression on *Mademoiselle*. But I don't think she said 'shit'; she would never use that word. She might have said *chiot*, which is French for puppy. What happened between you two?"

"I asked about the pregnant woman. I asked if it's your baby."

"Lily Ana is not the jealous type, but not very tolerant of rudeness." Legion settles himself in the opposite chair. "I wish you could be more subtle."

Legion gets Lily Ana's attention with a wave and then continues. "No, although I love her, the baby is not mine. I don't know the father, a paramour from France who brought her here six months ago. He paid for a year's lease on a cabin, in cash up front, and then rushed back for urgent business. He hasn't been here since. Her tab is paid from a business address in Paris. She should be all right until the baby, but—" Lily Ana places a bowl filled with papaya and pineapple chunks between them, Legion smiles up at her. "We worry for her."

Legion rises, kisses Lily Ana on both cheeks as if greeting her for the first time, then embraces her firmly. Lily Ana melds to Legion perfectly, hands lightly to his back, head nestled under his chin, her eyes closed. Neither of them seems to care they are making Paul uncomfortable. He had never seen Legion hold his mother this way. Had he ever seen his parents kiss? How much of their civility toward each other had been a pretense for his benefit? Paul shuts his eyes, his face twitching as he fights away smoldering anger.

After Lily Ana leaves, Paul and Legion fork the fruit from the bowl directly to their mouths, stopping only to tear mouthfuls of baguette with their teeth or sip wine punch.

"Do you ever get bitten?" Paul asks, motioning with his head to the beach where Legion had fed the fish.

"Hurts some and makes little pink marks, but never breaks the skin. But that's the reason for the trunks." Legion chuckles. "And there's a nasty barracuda, about four feet long, that rockets into the ball of fish sometimes—never know what he might want for breakfast."

Paul winces at the thought of razor sharp teeth passing inches away. "Damn."

"If you're going to be around tomorrow, you can give it a try." They both smile knowing that's not going to happen.

"I'm in a motel on the Dutch side, by the airport. I don't know how long I'll stay. But before I leave, I think I'll drive around, see what's here."

"There are high-rise hotels on the strip between the airport and the cruise ship harbor, hundreds of duty-free shops and endless traffic jams. And then in the countryside, mansions for the rich foreigners, and concrete huts for the locals—nothing in between. There are some nice overlooks, however, and plenty of nice beaches. Cupecoy, near where you're staying, is superbly beautiful, where most of the gays go."

"And what's that supposed to mean?"

"Nothing, other than Cupecoy is beautiful."

"So you still think I'm gay. I'll bet I've had more women than you. I'll hook up tonight if I get back to Philipsburg in time. You disgust me, Dad."

"Let me show you Galion Bay; it's right behind us. We'll get some conch fritters."

"I'm not gay, Dad."

"Paul, I've given up lying since I've been here. It's not some moral thing; it just seems pointless."

"Damn your sorry soul. I hate you. I want you to know that."

"I know you do, Paul—and you should. I was not a good father and I was mean to your mother. But I'd still like to spend some time with my son, if you're willing."

Paul wants to storm away, but he has nowhere to go. And he doesn't think it would have the same effect on Legion as it had in the past.

"I've got a fishing trip planned for tomorrow. Do you want to come?"

"I hate fishing. I'm not going to lie anymore either. Fishing's stupid."

"I'm OK with that. But I'll have to go. If I cancel, the charter captain will lose a day's pay. I'll be leaving at daybreak and won't be home until dark."

"I'll be gone when you get back."

"Why not hang out here tomorrow and I'll show you around the island the next day?"

Legion pushes back and walks to the bar with Paul slowly following. "Paul's going to be staying with us for a few days," Legion says to Lily Ana. "I'll lay out some steaks to thaw and we'll grill out before our walk this evening."

Lily Ana asks something sternly in French. Legion starts his reply in French, but she lifts her palms for him to stop, that she has heard enough. She turns back to cutting limes, never looking at Paul.

CHAPTER 10

Zuzu

The Flores girls are rebuilding a sand castle damaged by the morning tide when they see Legion slosh into the water. After Legion breaks the bread, they join the yellow dog at the water's edge, eager for what comes next. Zuzu can't help but giggle when the girls scream and the dog barks at the jumping fish.

After the fish have had their breakfast, Zuzu wades out, relieved as the water begins to support her pregnant belly.

"So how is the boy this morning?" Legion asks. Lily Ana had declared, with no explanation, that the baby is a boy.

"Big. Too big, I think," she says with a heavy accent. She had learned English since Legion could not carry on a conversation in French. "And a football player—kicking my insides all over."

"How are you really? Lily says it could happen any day?"

"I hurt. I'm tired of hurting. Every day some place new hurts. I wish it would happen now. But he has not dropped yet, do you think…?"

"I don't know about those things, but you will be a mother soon. You will be a wonderful mother."

Zuzu smiles drearily, impatient to hold the baby in her arms rather than her belly. "I'm becoming afraid," she says.

She lets herself be swept into his embrace. She nuzzles the silvery fuzz of his chest, surrendering to the musk of him, thinking nothing, content in his swallowing grasp.

"Let me take you to Philipsburg, closer to the hospital. In case—"

She pushes her head away from his chest to look at his eyes. "No! It should happen here. You promised. I want only you and Lily Ana to help me."

"So you're not afraid our plan is a mistake?"

"No, it's only me and what comes at the end. Lily Ana says it is normal to be miserable and afraid at the end. She thinks everything is as it should be."

"What if there is no time? What if—"

"*Arrête!* Stop it; you're scaring me."

His eyes water. "I'm afraid also."

She clings tightly to him, wishing he would stop talking. She needs to allow herself the illusion he has not changed, that she can continue to rely on the strength that has kept her alive these last six months. He is like a rock breaking into sand, slipping through her fingers; the harder she tries to hold on, the more he crumbles. How could she live without him?

"And how are you today?" she asks.

"I'm better, I think."

She wants to ask more, make him tell her the truth, but she really doesn't need to. He is losing weight steadily, eating less and drinking more each day, a shadow of the prince who woke her with a kiss just a few months earlier.

After she had finally accepted it, that she had been abandoned, hidden away, she wanted to die, had tried to die. It had been Legion who had dragged her to shore and, like a god, blown life into her. He and Lily Ana had nursed her, one of them always by her side, even after her lungs had healed from the salt water, afraid to leave her alone. She had hated them at first for forcing her back into her disgusting life. They had endured her surly manners and refusal to talk. She hadn't felt her life could have value to anyone and didn't trust their kindnesses. But they had been persistent in saving her from death and then became equally determined to save her from life.

Her mother was a *vulgaire prostituée* on the streets of Paris, her father unknown, probably even to her mother. She had grown up alone, in one walkup apartment or another, locked up when her mother was away at night, then again as her mother slept during the day. As her mother lost her looks, they began to slowly starve. She started to bring men to their apartment, a different class of men that couldn't afford hotel rooms. One man had been more interested in her than her mother. There was a row, an exchange of yells and slaps, before her mother could get him to leave. After that, Zuzu hid in their only closet when she heard the key turn in the door. She had listened to the gasping of the men and the sighs of her mother (which she could tell were contrived) and their ridiculous banter.

During her recovery, she did not know English and Legion knew only a little French, so Lily Ana was the only one who could talk with her. When Lily Ana spoke to her of God's love, trying to create in her a reason to live, it was the word "love" that caused her to clasp her hands to her ears in revulsion. It was her mother's word, the word she used with men, the word used by the man that brought her here. It was a shameful word that meant lies and deception. She didn't want any man to love her, even God. And if He did anyway, He was a typical man, a mean man that could not be trusted.

"Everyone is loved by God," Lily Ana explained, "there is no choice. Whether to love in return is the only choice." Zuzu tried not to listen but began to trust that Lily Ana and Legion were attached to her in that way. They had chosen to save her without reason, without her consent; her only choice was whether to return their devotion in kind.

It was for them that she had conceded to live. It was for them she would have this baby. They too were incomplete, with holes in their lives that this baby could fill. They would do this together. They were bound together, as if sharing only one life, one life between them; with its only purpose being to nurture this new life she carried. She marveled that the remains of three broken people could combine to create something splendid. They were shards of sea glass washed together into a pattern on the sand. The next wave would rearrange them, maybe bring new glass, or wash some of them back into the sea.

"Everything is all right, Legion. I'm just being a ninny. The water has awakened him. Do you want to feel him kick?"

She floats onto her back with Legion supporting her lightly with his arms. Her stomach squirms and they both laugh. They practice the things that Lily Ana had taught them, correcting each other when something is forgotten.

"And now what do you say," she quizzes.

Legion remembers. "Breathe! Breathe deeply! Now push! *Mettre bas!* Push him out, my little angel!"

He would not be much use during the birth, she knew, but it would be worth the pain to hear him yelling these things.

"So, who was the young man with you before breakfast?"

Legion's smile turns to gloom. "He's my son."

"Your son? You weren't happy to see him?"

"I don't know. He just showed up—surprised me."

"I think I surprised him."

"He didn't know whether to shit or go blind when you walked up."

Her chuckle brings back his smile.

"I apologize for his manners. I could never teach him anything." Legion bends his face down close to her stomach. "With you, it will be different; do you hear me in there?"

CHAPTER 11

Webb

ounging at the beach bars had been relaxing when Legion first arrived at Orient Beach, but even paradise becomes monotonous after a year. This fishing trip was just what he needed. He had been looking forward to it for a week. It was just like Paul to drop in out of nowhere and expect everything to stop for him. Sure, he could have rescheduled and made it up to the captain, but——. The tip of a wave over the side of the Anguilla ferry slaps Legion's face like a wet hand; as if the ocean had been listening to his thoughts and couldn't take any more of his bullshit. Legion's face transforms from startle to a fuck-you grin and he shakes a fist at the ocean. "Stay out of my head," he sputters.

The truth the ocean knows is that Legion had been thankful for the excuse not to continue the spar with Paul today. The life he had run away from a year ago had found him and, being a coward, Legion is running again.

After clearing customs at Blowing Point, Legion steps out into the dusty commotion behind the ferry terminal. As Webb had said on the phone, there are a lot of white vehicles in the line of waiting cabs, but only one driven by a white guy. Webb recognizes Legion by his blue shirt and Panama hat and waves for him to hurry. He holds open the passenger door of the rusty Suzuki Samurai, impatient to get under way.

"The handle on the inside is broken, so if you need out, reach through the window and use the one on the outside," Webb says as he slams the door. The door window is missing so it won't be hard to reach through to the outside handle. Webb uses a bungee cord to secure the driver's door after he gets in.

The vehicles on Anguilla are all left-hand drive, like in the States, but because of the British heritage, it is customary to drive on the left side of the road. Since there is no centerline, Webb takes the center of the road until there is oncoming traffic. Legion feels a flush of panic when vehicles approach from the opposite direction.

After they negotiate a few roundabouts, they are in open country on the road that traverses the spine of the island. Webb's boat is moored at Island Harbor on the east end.

"Morning," Webb says reaching his hand across for a shake. "Half day of fishing, right? Big stuff if we can find it. That's what we talked about. I'll get you back for the two o'clock ferry."

Legion returns his wide smile, the business smile they both use. "No, that's not what we talked about. Half a day means four hours of fishing. Considering the travel, we'll barely get in three. And if there's fish to clean—" Legion cuts his sentence short when Webb slows onto the shoulder of the road.

"We won't be keeping any fish. There won't be time to clean fish." Webb looks up the road for a moment longer, then turns to Legion. "Do you know what day this is? The sailboat race starts at two. My boat is the rescue boat. I've got to be there. I'm supposed to pick up my cousins at Sandy Ground. As it is, it'll be after two before I'm there. The race will be started already."

Webb's forced smile softens to a plea for Legion to understand, but Legion's face hardens.

"Look, I'll do the trip for half price, or we can do a full day trip another day at the half day rate." When Legion still looks sternly at him, he adds, "Look man, they rescheduled yesterday's race to today due to weather. It couldn't be helped."

"If I insist, will you do the trip as we agreed for the full four hours?"

Webb closes his eyes and lowers his grimacing face to the steering wheel. "Yes."

"Then I've got a proposal. I want to see the race. I'd rather see the race than fish. We fish until the start time, and then you take me with you to the race."

Webb throws himself back in the seat, his arms locked stiff against the steering wheel as if bracing for a crash. His doleful face transforms as he works through the possibilities. Combined with his sandy hair and freckles, his jubilant smile makes Legion think of Christmas and Paul tearing open presents. Paul's freckles, like his smile, have faded over time, but Webb is a reminder that pure joy is possible.

They lock onto each other's eyes and laugh together; not knowing what it means, only that it means something. Two boys, sharing the rush of an adventure, replace the hard-nosed men. In that moment, they bond like brothers.

"Yeah, it will work! We'll catch fish, you will see. We will go out to the canyon and catch something big; then troll back to Sandy Ground in time for the races. We will get in the full four hours fishing that way. The races will be over by four and we can fish on the way back if you want."

"As long as you get me back in time for the last ferry, it's a deal."

"Sure. Last ferry is at six, no problem," Webb says as he pulls back on the road.

The highest point of the island is only two hundred feet above sea level, so there are no spectacular vistas, only thorny scrub, and concrete block shanties that crowd the road. As they descend into Island Harbor, Legion is glad to see the water again and feel the breeze.

A narrow beach surrounds the bay on three sides with a rocky island in the center of the fourth side. Gaps between the shore and the island provide access to deep water. Dilapidated buildings indicate the island is deserted, probably abandoned after a hurricane. The road ends at a concrete pier stretching fifty yards out into the harbor. Homemade fishing boats are moored in the turquoise shallows on both sides.

Webb pulls the Suzuki under a sea grape tree behind the beach. Unlike in Saint Martin, where the beaches have been cleared to accommodate more tourists, the sea grape trees here overhang the water.

"Let's get a beer first," Webb says as they walk toward a tin-roofed shed.

A charter captain that drinks in the morning? Legion thinks. *Or, are my jitters so obvious that he knows I need a drink?*

A stand-up bar extends across the entire front of the shack. There is only enough room between the bar and the plank shelf of liquor bottles behind for a bartender to stand. The awning over the bar hinges at the roof so it can be folded down to lock up the bar. The awning is propped up, but nobody is there.

Legion follows Webb around behind. Several elderly barefoot black men in faded T-shirts and tattered shorts sit on the trunk of a fallen palm tree. Their kinky black hair looks dusty and flat in the back from when they were sleeping. They watch a cast iron pot suspended on a tripod over an open fire. The steam smells of rotting fish.

Webb says something to the group in a language Legion does not recognize. He heard his name so he takes it for an introduction.

"Legion, these are my cousins." He points to each one and gives a name.

"What language is that?" Legion asks.

"English, of course."

"That's not English."

"Yes, yes. Listen." He says the introduction again slowly. Legion recognized some of the words but the meaning doesn't come through. The men laugh to each other.

Webb holds up his hands before Legion can ask another question. "Don't even try. Some words are combined into one word and the words are out of order. I can't explain it, but it is the island dialect of English. It goes back to the slave days when Negroes were brought in to work the cane fields. The masters spoke English so they picked it up best they could. They teach proper English in school now, but most islanders still speak the dialect among themselves."

Webb says something to one of the cousins who rushes to the bar.

"I'm not really a beer person," Legion says. "Does he have vodka?"

Webb smiles and trots around the corner of the bar with his cousin. Legion nods to the remaining cousins. They respond with a perfect "Good morning."

"Good fishing today," one says as he gets up to stir the cast iron pot. This seems to be all they have planned for the day.

Legion follows Webb and the cousin as they haul the cooler between them out to a boat tied to the pier. It is an old twenty-three footer that was once white but is now creamy with age. A canvas bikini top stretches back from the windshield to cover two side-by-side captain's chairs behind the console. A single fighting chair faces rearward looking over two outboards mounted to the transom. Stubby rods stick up out of holders along each side.

"You keep a clean boat," Legion says.

"It's my office, my livelihood. I take care of *The Little Lady* and she takes care of me."

Webb puts away the bumpers that kept the boat away from the pier while the cousin on the dock unties the lines front and back. They coordinate without the need to talk or even look at each other. Webb starts one motor and steers through the moored boats out of the harbor. He opens a hatch built into the port gunwale and selects several baits that he displays on the fighting chair.

"Which one will catch them today?"

"I thought you were the expert."

"There is no expert. There is only luck. Sometimes they go for the brightly colored ones and sometimes white. Sometimes they are deep, sometimes by the shore. So you pick; you look like a lucky fellow."

"I think white and silver ones down deep and the chartreuse at the top. And let's try deep water."

"You've fished before, I see. You are a serious fisherman." He pushes the throttle and does a final adjustment on their heading before clipping the baits to the rods. One at a time, he lets out four lines. Two are weighted to go deep and the baits on the other two skip through the waves at the surface. They are all out at different distances to prevent tangles in the turns. After a final adjustment of the reels' drags, he returns to the wheel to steer toward the canyon thirty minutes farther out. They squint out over the water looking for the birds that will signal a ball of mullet where the game fish will be.

Webb's sunglasses dangle from a cord around his neck while he slathers a translucent film of zinc oxide cream on his face, rubbing it in except for his lips, which remained a thick smear. With his long-billed cap, a curtain sewn to the back to protect his neck, and long-sleeved shirt, he is well protected from the sun. Legion imagines him walking down Second Avenue back home; even the street people would stop and stare.

"Where are you from, Webb?"

"Right here—born right here. Way back, my ancestors were Scottish. My great-great- whatever was brought over to run a gang of slaves, be an overseer on a sugar cane plantation, back in the seventeen hundreds. He did not like that line of work so he came down to this end of the island to be a fisherman. He learned to fish from a tribe of Arawak Indians living on that island you saw in the harbor. Legend is the Indians used gold fishhooks. My father said he had one when he was a boy and then somebody stole it.

"Don't know the name of the ancestor from Scotland, but he had a brood of kids with the Indian maidens. His kids inherited webbed toes from the Indians. The English called everybody on the island Webb. That is where my name comes from. My family has been fishing out of Island Harbor ever since. My father taught me and his father taught him."

"What happened to the Indians?"

"Indian was bred out of them after the English arrived."

"But what about your black cousins back at the dock?"

Webb laughs, first with his eyes that dance, and then he cackles with his mouth wide open. Legion finds himself laughing also but doesn't know why.

"Yes, yes. I see what's bugging you now. Almost everybody on this end of the island is related to me, cousins of some sort, both white and black. My people were not picky about who they mated, only who they married. As far as I know, there are no Negros in my bloodline."

They reach the canyon, six thousand feet on the depth finder, and troll for another hour with no hits.

"Fishy, fishy, fishy. Come little fishy." Webb sings like he is calling a hog. "Come on, help me talk to them."

"If we got a strike right now, I'd think about it. What I really think will help is a drink."

Out of the cooler, Webb hands Legion two green bottles of soda to open while he sloshes in the ice for the liter bottle of vodka.

"Vodka and Ting are made for each other. You'll see."

Webb drinks down his Ting and carefully adds a little vodka. Legion drinks half of his. It is grapefruity, but not sweet, very refreshing. He tops the bottle with the vodka.

One of the reels begins to click.

"I told you a drink would do it," Legion says as Webb springs to the rod.

The clicking stops and Webb freezes waiting to see if the fish is still there and then jumps back into action when the spool of the reel starts racing.

"Put on the belly strap and get in the fighting chair."

When Legion is ready, Webb hands him the rod.

"Now lean back and reel fast to set the hook and we'll see what happens."

The fish is small. The rigs can handle three-hundred-pound marlin, so they are not sensitive enough to enjoy a small fish. It is just a matter of winching in the five-pound mackerel and hoisting it into the boat. Webb lets it bounce around the bottom until it lies still long enough to clamp it against the deck with his foot.

"Calm down, little buddy," Webb says to the fish. "It will be over in a minute."

The fish makes a final shudder before Webb uses pliers to extract the hook.

"It's too late," Webb says, then looks at Legion, "I tell you this because you are a fisherman and already know; the sun is too high for marlin. We should have been at the canyon at daybreak for a real chance."

"Yes, you're right of course. But this is okay. We'll go for marlin next time."

"So how long are you staying at Saint Martin?"

"I live there now...at Orient Beach."

"But it will never work if you come over by ferry."

"We'll figure it out if you want to do it. I can stay on Anguilla the night before."

"Or I could motor over to Orient while it's still dark and pick you up. We could be here at the canyon at sunup."

Webb's eyes are dancing again. He clearly would rather fish than go on these excursions with the tourists. They discuss the arrangements for the next Sunday when Webb normally doesn't book charters. He will pick Legion up at the beach in front of La Belle Creole. Legion will pay for the gas and vodka. This then became their routine every Sunday. They would fish with the faith of all fishermen; one morning a school of marlin would await them and all would be made worthwhile in one glorious day.

CHAPTER 12

Lily Ana

A bronze-tinted china doll with coal-black hair and rose-smudged cheeks waves to Lily Ana from the path to the beach. Betty is back. Her terrycloth beach cover falls to the sand as she waves greetings to the other regulars. Half the crowded beach waves back.

Lily Ana slams an empty Jack Daniels bottle into the trash can behind the bar just to hear the beer bottles shatter. Immediately she is ashamed that Betty can agitate her so easily—without even trying.

Having a perfect body is not a fault, but the way she flaunts it—parking herself by the café door to be walked around by every customer. When she is sunbathing, beer sales double. Legion demurs that she chooses that location for convenience, but he always moves from the bar to a table overlooking the beach when she arrives.

For her, flirting is as ubiquitous as breathing. Her seductions are not obvious, maybe not even intended. She should not blame Betty—or even Legion for ogling. He would do more if given the chance. Any man Betty wanted could be had for the price of a lingering smile. Maybe it had already happened.

Betty's ingratiating politeness towards her, Lily Ana suspects, cloaks a condescending pity. She likes to think of herself as slender, but men would call her skinny. Her nipples are like dried stalks of cut flowers sticking out of her flat chest.

The blunt feeling of inadequacy knots her stomach. *Jealousy. Envy.* She sighs and turns toward the kitchen, out of sight of the beach, chastising herself for the sins in her heart. She will have to pray for forgiveness twenty times a day until Betty leaves.

Paul enters the café at four, still in his dress clothes from yesterday. His eyes are on the floor as he maneuvers through the tables to the bar. Another man, from a year ago, flashes into Lily Ana's mind.

"Where is the town?" Paul asks. "I need to buy a few things."

"What do you need? Maybe they sell it at the resort store."

He looks up with a smirk. "Bathing suit for one."

"I'll be going to Grand Case when my shift is over." Already she regrets mentioning it. "A cab will be waiting at the gate to the compound in an hour. You can ride in with me."

"You don't mind? Look, you don't have to pretend…" He looks down at the bar. "Thanks for letting me stay the night."

"It's Legion's cabin."

"It's an imposition on you, not him. I'll be leaving in the morning if I can get a flight."

She tries to reconcile the snarky kid from yesterday with the congenial gentleman of today. He is different when Legion is not around. *What's happened between these two?*

"I'll see you at the cabin at five."

"Thanks." He turns to the side door that leads to the cabins. Again, the flickering overlay of the man from a year ago. Had her first impression of Legion been any better?

Lily Ana swung her legs off the couch and immediately went back into survival mode, heart pounding. Cradling her face in her hands, she willed the fog of sleep away. Stagnant air reeked of mildew and stale beer. The coo of a pigeon and the rhythmic crash of surf drifted through an open window. She must be in one of the resort's beach cottages. The calamities of the previous day came flooding back. The man…

In the twilight, she could barely make out a round table with four chairs in the center of the single room cabin and a bed on the far side. A strange man lay on his back across the bed, his shoes still on, snoring. Did she even know his name? She shook her head and forced her gaze away. She could deal with him later. If she were going to survive this, she would have to get ahead of events rather than allow her mind to wander. What to do next?

There was breakfast. She didn't know the time, it was still early, but she needed to get to the café quickly. She rushed to the bathroom mirror, hoping she wouldn't look like she felt. Bedraggled and dirty, her stringy auburn hair matted against her scalp. The bathing suit and sarong she had slept in were her only clothes. She stared into the mirror. Frightened hazel eyes looked back. How could she have let this happen? But there was no time for self-loathing. She couldn't do anything about her clothes right now, but she could shower and braid the hair.

Eduardo was already at the café when she walked in barefoot from the sand path onto the cold concrete floor. He waved for her to hurry. Eduardo, dumpy with thinning hair, was the cook who had hired her only the day before. He spoke Spanish and a little French but mostly directed her by pointing. How had they ever gotten through the interview? She didn't even know her salary.

He pointed to the oranges, which she thought he wanted squeezed, but then to a knife for her to peel and cut them into chunks. After the other fruits were cut into bite-sized cubes, it was all stirred together with grapes and fresh strawberries in a punchbowl. Lemon juice poured over the top kept the bananas from darkening. He showed her how to brew the strong coffee the customers preferred. At the bar, Lily Ana poured steaming cups for Eduardo and herself. The coffee lay molten in her empty stomach. Eduardo filled two salad bowls with the fruit and pushed one to her. *"Usted come,"* he said jabbing at her bowl with a fork.

A truck arrived with bread, which she stacked in the pantry. The smell of fresh bread mingled with the aromas of fruit and coffee, overpowered the dank smell of the seaweed washed onto the shore out front. Sunrise around the edges of the shutters streaked across the tables like prison bars. Her head tilted to one side of the glare then to the other as she laid out place settings.

After setting the last table, her eyes roamed the interior looking for anything out of place and finally settled on Eduardo who had been watching and waiting. He signaled thumbs up, the tables were set to his satisfaction. With a flick of his hand, he waved for her to follow him to the shutters.

The waist-high walls of the café were capped with a flat board. Varnished wood shutters, hinged at the ceiling, hung down to the walls. Slowly, methodically, he showed her how to raise the shutters using the cords routed through pulleys at the ceiling, looking at her after each step until she nodded. After Eduardo demonstrated the first one, she raised the rest herself. Some of the chairs had to be scooted out of the way to lift the shutters. Tomorrow she would remember to move these first.

Eduardo leaned against the kitchen doorway. She detected a slight smile (or was it just the absence of a frown?) before he disappeared inside. She could do these things herself, before Eduardo arrived in the mornings, to show she could be trusted to open. She took a deep breath and surveyed the room one last time before throwing open the double doors facing the beach.

The resort clientele began to arrive. Most were American couples, but also some French families with children. All seemed to know each other, at least well enough to exchange greetings. They drank coffee standing at the bar and some ate croissants. They were quickly out the front doors, chatting as they walked towards the far end of the beach. This morning walk must be a sunrise ritual.

As they trickled back an hour later, they dished themselves bowls of fruit and placed orders for eggs that Lily Ana awkwardly relayed to Eduardo by pointing and hand signals—a whipping motion for scrambled, hands pressed together for fried hard.

She greeted and introduced herself to each new customer, did her best to carry on a light conversation in whatever language they spoke. Her native language was Italian, but because she had worked ten years at the international resorts at Monaco, she could speak French and English almost as well. After eating, the sunrise crowd ambled to the beach or back to their cabins.

When the café finally emptied, Lily Ana flopped into one of the chairs and looked out the front doorway at the white beach, turquoise water, and the islands in the distance. For the first time that morning, her tense muscles began to uncoil. A drop of sweat ran to the tip of her nose and she swabbed it away with the bar towel draped over her shoulder. The morning breeze from the ocean picked up to offset the rising heat and humidity. If her destiny was to be marooned on an island, it couldn't get much better than this.

Eduardo came to the doorway of the kitchen, wiping his hands on his apron until he was sure she was paying attention. She imagined there was approval on his face, but maybe not. He flicked a switchbox on the doorframe. Above, ceiling fans began to twirl. Okay, she indicated with a head nod, she would do it tomorrow.

When he went back in the kitchen, her shoulders slumped; and then she jerked herself erect again. She was exhausted but also encouraged. She could do this. If she could keep this job, her fall could be arrested; a new life forged from calamity. The betrayal was at the edge of her mind, but she willed the memory away. There would be time later to ruminate the past, but for now, she had to stay in the present, plan ahead. The terror of a new place, strange people, would be surmounted by the routine of work. One day she would breathe again, a full breath, uninhibited by the anxiety that gripped her stomach now.

Around ten, the man from the cabin wandered in with tentative steps like each footfall was painful. He wore the slacks and dress shirt from yesterday, now wrinkled from being slept in. He sat at a center table and lowered his forehead to the tabletop as if his neck could no longer support the heaviness. Lily Ana brought him coffee and the wastebasket in case he was going to be sick. When he noticed her legs approach from the corner of his eye, all he could manage to say was "water."

He gargled a mouthful of the water she brought and spit in the wastebasket before draining the rest of the glass. He looked clownish. His pink nose and cheeks, the sun's doing the previous day, contrasted with the greenish-clay circles that the sunglasses had covered. With a dire frown, he squinted out to the ocean, through the kitchen door at Eduardo, before finally turning to her.

"Where am I?" he asked.

"La Belle Creole."

"I can see I'm at a café." Impatient, he glared at her. "I mean what country am I in?"

"French Antilles—Saint Martin."

He looked away at nothing as if trying to recall. He stood up abruptly and rammed his hands into the pockets of his slacks. He produced a wadded-up boarding pass, which he spread on the table.

"SXM? Where the hell is that?"

She didn't answer. He didn't make any more sense now than the night before when he was fall-down drunk. A smile crept onto his face like he had discerned her disgust. She forced a smile. A cheerful greeting to even the most obnoxious customers would bring the best tips. She vowed to be more disciplined.

"Thanks for the coffee." He sat back down and took a sip. "I'll be better when I get this down. And thanks for last night, taking care of me and all. I do remember that."

He had drunk gin last night past closing time, until his head flopped on the bar. He was still there when she finished securing the liquor and cash register. She would have abandoned him, locked the doors and left, if she had had any place else to go herself. But her plan, the only thing she could come up with, was to sleep at the café, maybe some place in the pantry.

She had watched his slow, inevitable slide off the barstool. If left alone, he would be crumpled on the floor in the morning, probably bleeding. Eduardo would not be happy. But dealing with drunks was not a bartender's job, at least not in Europe, where there was always a bouncer. Here she was on her own and would have to learn new rules as she went.

He had left the key to his cabin on the counter to show where to charge the drinks. She slipped herself underneath one arm and he shuffled, with her encouragement, back to his cabin. She let them in, flipped the light switch by the door, and pushed him onto the bed. He went instantly asleep. She collapsed exhausted on the sofa. A moment of rest was all she intended but didn't remember anything until this morning.

"Thank you for taking care of me last night," she said with a devious smile.

His gaze again went to some indeterminate place. "What happened last night?"

She turned out her lower lip feigning anguish. "You don't remember? You don't remember promising to marry me?"

"I think I'd remember that. But to be honest, everything this side of Miami is a little hazy. I asked this friend of mine, this travel agent, to get me out of town. Told him I didn't care where, as long as there were a beach and naked women."

"Well, he must have done a Google search. If you put in 'beach' and 'naked,' I'm sure this place would come up first."

He broke into a laugh and slapped the table. "That's exactly what that son-of-a-bitch would do. That's it exactly!"

Eduardo stuck his head out the kitchen door to check if the man was disturbing other customers. There were no other customers.

"Do you want something to eat?"

He grabbed at his stomach, but his face retained a grin. "Lord, no. I don't think I could hold anything down."

He seemed to be sobering up.

"Mystery solved. I know how I got here. But I still don't know exactly where I am. What's this place like?"

"I can't tell you. I've only been here a day myself. And all I've seen is this café."

"Then let's investigate. Can you get away?"

Eduardo still lingered at the kitchen doorway. She pointed back and forth between Legion and herself and then made her fingers walk through the air. Eduardo waved her on with the back of his hands, then extended ten fingers, ten minutes. She flashed the ten fingers back, then closed her fists and flashed ten fingers again. His face soured but he brushed with the back of his hands again.

"Twenty minutes—I've got to be back in twenty minutes."

"Is that how you two talk?"

"I don't speak Spanish and he can't speak any of the languages I speak."

The man pulled off his shoes, socks, parked them under the table, and rolled up his pant legs to the knees. Lily Ana draped her sarong over the back of a chair. When they walked out into the blaring sun, he held his hand at a salute to shade his eyes.

"Are you going to be here long?" she asked.

He didn't respond immediately, as if this was the first time he had thought about it. "I think so. This place has a good feel to it. And besides, I've got no place else to go."

"It's expensive here. Can you afford to stay?"

"Actually, money is the only problem I don't have. I might stay here forever, now that I think about it."

They walked casually, like any other couple on the beach, except for their clothes. She was more self-conscious in her one-piece bathing suit than the others seemed without anything. She knew the nudity would not startle her in a few weeks. Not that she would ever go nude, but she could get used to the mores of the customers in time.

"I just sold a factory to a conglomerate. I have an obscene amount of money right now. So, I can afford anything. The questions are: What do I want, and is it for sale?"

She wasn't sure she liked this pompous braggart who had turned his face to her, expecting her to be impressed. She walked on, matching her strides with his, without returning his gaze.

"How about you? You just got here too?"

"Yes, yesterday—came in by boat. I needed a job and some-body told me about this place. Eduardo didn't ask a lot of questions."

"Oooh. Sounds intriguing."

"Not really, but it's a long story, longer than we have time. We'd better start back. The short answer is, I don't have a passport. If the word gets to the authorities, I'll have to leave."

"I hope you're not telling everybody this. First disgruntled customer and you'll be out of here. Why do you think you can trust me?"

"I don't know. Maybe I shouldn't. I guess I'll have to be careful about making you mad."

"Not to worry. You're the only friend in the world I have right now."

"Well, Mister… I don't know your name."

"Legion."

"Well, Mister Legion—"

"No, just Legion. I'm not as old as I look."

"Well, Legion, I'll let you decide if I'm a friend or not. I've got a favor to ask." She walked on stiffly, gathering courage. "Did you know I slept in your cabin last night—on the couch? I was gone before you woke this morning. You see…I don't have a place to stay and no money. I'll be living on tips until my first payday, whenever that is. I'm asking if I can sleep on your couch until I can find something else, until I get paid."

They both walked looking straight ahead saying nothing.

"You don't know me and I can imagine what's going through your head," she said. "That's why I wanted you to know about the passport. If anything goes wrong, if something gets stolen, if I do anything you don't like, you can call in the *gendarmes* and I'll be deported. I'll pay you, anything reasonable, but it will have to wait until I'm paid, or until I can get enough in tips."

"I don't need your money."

"I know, but I will have to pay or I can't do it. And I'll pay in money. You'd have to agree to that part. I'm not offering you anything else."

"I don't want your pay, money or otherwise. If you need a place to sleep, you've got it. I don't have anything to steal anyway. I pay for everything by credit card. The bill goes to my lawyer and he pays from my account. I guess we can work out about the panties on the towel rack later."

"Thank you." She felt lighter, like her feet could barely reach the sand. She had a place to sleep, with no strings attached if her intuition about this man was correct. "Thank you," she repeated with prayer hands below a beaming smile.

"Well…you should hold that for a while. I'm not exactly domesticated."

"I'll do the cleaning. You'll see. I'll do everything."

When they walked back into the café, Eduardo was behind the bar serving drinks to a French couple. He looked relieved to see her return.

"Go to the store, where you checked in," she advised, "Get yourself some suntan lotion. You'll be sick if you stay out in the sun today."

When she took over at the bar, Legion followed Eduardo back to the kitchen. She could hear them well enough, but couldn't understand the Spanish they spoke.

Legion left and then came back to the bar about two. His styled haircut, still damp from a shower, gave him the look of the executive he claimed to be. The morning stubble was gone. He wore new clothes, tasteful khaki shorts—with belt, Hawaiian shirt—tucked in, and leather deck shoes—with socks. Lily Ana hid her face with her hands when a giggle overcame her. This is as casual as he knows how to be. He is handsome, but he will stick out like a clipped poodle in a nudist resort.

He walked stiffly straight to her, his jaw clenched, glancing at her furtively. Her heart dropped. He had reconsidered their arrangement and come to tell her.

"Fix me a gimlet, make it a double," he said.

She didn't know how to make one, so he talked her through it. When she pushed the drink in front of him, he cradled the glass with both hands without returning her smile. He rocked his head back and downed it with one gulp. He grabbed the bar with arms stiff, his head tilted down, waiting for the alcohol to kick in. "You did good. Another just like it."

"Shouldn't you slow down? It's barely past noon," she said.

His eyes rose to hers for the first time, full of fury and loathing. "Give me another," he demanded with a stern voice.

She mixed the drink and set it before him. He stared into the glass a moment then threw it down like the first. The muscles in his cheeks, which had been rippling under his skin, began to relax. He pulled himself onto the stool in front of her.

"You know that little secret, the one you told me earlier? Well, this is my secret. I'm an alcoholic. I'm not one of those 'drink-to-have-a-good-time' drinkers. I'm a full-blown drunk. I'm going to stay drunk until I die. Do you hear what I'm saying? And I won't have..." he moved his face in closer and spoke quietly but emphatically, "I won't have a woman around hounding me about it. I'm through with that. Do you understand?"

He shuffled over to a table bumping chairs as he went. When he was seated, he raised his hand for another drink. She mixed the third drink and brought it to the table, scooted it in front of him. His gaze stayed on the beach.

"It's a deal," she said as politely as she could muster. "I'll never mention it again."

When she came back to the bar, Eduardo caught her attention and with a movement of his head beckoned her into the kitchen. Through the doorway, he pointed at Legion, then to her, and then clenched his hands together.

She shook her head. No, they were not a couple.

Again, he pointed at Legion then made an "X" out of his pointer fingers while shaking his head. He then pointed to her and followed that up with a pushing motion with both hands. He was admonishing her to stay away from this no-good drunk.

Her eyes rolled as she sighed in exasperation. She was not that stupid plus he should stay out of her business.

Eduardo shrugged before walking back to his stove. She watched him scraping the griddle with a spatula and marveled that they could have such an intimate conversation without saying a word.

Her shift was over at three. Legion was slouched back in the chair still watching the beach activity and didn't notice her leave. When she entered the cabin, she found a paper sack on the bed. On the bag Legion had printed in block letters that he had negotiated a one-hundred- dollar advance with Eduardo. A pair of blue jean shorts, two blouses, two panties and twenty dollars in change were inside. She stripped off the bathing suit and rushed to the shower. After drying, she luxuriated in the silky feel of the new underwear. And surprisingly, he had guessed right on the size.

The woman looking back at her in the mirror didn't seem to be her at all. This face, although not young, looked younger. But something else was different. She combed her wet hair into a helmet and pinched color into her cheeks before again comparing what she saw to the desperate woman of only that morning.

CHAPTER 13

The Ocean

From the fighting chair, Legion watches the eastern horizon where white cumulous clouds build into indigo cathedrals. One cloud turns into a thunderhead. The squall underneath blows in front of Scrub Island, erasing the black ridge as it sweeps across, then the rainbow at the trailing edge repaints it. The wind is pushing the weather farther east so there is no danger.

Nausea catches him by surprise and gold flakes sprinkle before his eyes. He stumbles to the boat rail as the world dims. The breeze past the boat's windscreen cools his clammy face. It is not seasickness, but something new. Maybe it will pass, or maybe this is just the first time for a new symptom and it will continue until the end. Nothing he can do about it either way.

"Are you hungry yet?" Webb yells over his shoulder from the helm chair.

The thought of food doesn't help Legion's nausea. He moves to the seat beside Webb so they can talk over the noise of the motor. "I could eat, but I didn't bring anything."

From the jumble of fishing tackle on top of the cockpit hood, Webb digs out a cellphone sealed in a zip-lock sandwich bag. Legion listens to one side of a conversation in the dialect. There seems to be intense negotiation and then finally Webb's grin widens.

"We will stop by Prickly Pear Cay. My cousin works there. She will bring us chicken legs." Webb points to a white spot on the horizon in front of them that is only distinguishable from the frothy tips of the waves because it doesn't dissolve away.

To the port side of the boat, the volcanic mountains of Saint Martin rise from behind low-lying Anguilla. The two islands look like one, although they're twenty miles apart. This may have been the view Christopher Columbus saw and why he claimed only one island for Spain as he sailed by in 1493. Legion imagines himself a sailor aboard that caravel, with square sails flapping above, trying to make sense of it all. Sailing toward the edge of the world that could come at any moment.

On his right stretches the infinity of blue sky over bluer water. In that direction, to the north, they could motor for weeks and never see anything except the ocean until they reached Iceland.

As the water becomes shallow close to the cay, Webb reels in the deep rigs. He steers around dark boulders under the turquoise water. In the clear water, the rocks look like they are just under the surface but the depth finder says they are twenty feet deep. As they pass a coral outcrop, the reel of one of the rigs begins to sing. Legion mounts the fighting chair and sets the hook; there is an instant battle. Because of the shallow water, the fish cannot go deep, as is its instinct, but races from side to side with amazing speed.

"Keep it away from the reef; it will break off," Webb advises. "We need this one."

Legion considers what he said, but doesn't see he has any control over the darting fish. When he pulls back, the fish jumps, exploding spray into a halo of rainbow colors.

"A barracuda!" Webb yells. The fish runs at the boat and the line goes slack. "Reel fast! Keep it tight or he will throw the hook!" Webb grimaces with each jerk of the line as if he is the fish struggling to free himself.

When the fish has given up, Webb hooks the gaff into its gill and yanks the ten-pound barracuda aboard. They watch it flop, shimmering iridescent as blood flecks the gunwales. When it lies still a moment, Webb pins it to the deck with his shoe.

"Die quietly without such a fuss. Leave me some fingers," Webb tells the fish as he extracts the hook from the spiked jaws.

The frantic struggle suddenly stops, the gills left open wide in the last attempt at breath. The glassy sheen of a doll eye facing up turns to putty. Legion is glad of the quick death; relieved the fish's terror is over. Couldn't they play the game, enjoy their contest, without this finality?

This feeling of remorse shames Legion. Hunting and killing is a measure of a man's worth in every culture. When he looks at Webb's satisfied smile, he envies his ease. He kills every day as his life's work, but also for pleasure.

The barracuda too had been a killer. If cut open, they would find victims that had succumbed to his superior speed and agility before he himself became the victim. It seemed a contradiction that a merciful God purposely created such savagery. But when looked at with the cold logic of an engineer, he had to appreciate the brilliance of a self-perfecting process. The best hunters survived to reproduce. The most elusive and swift survived also. Even an omnipotent God had design constraints if He wanted to perpetuate life without constant intervention.

Webb reels in the other shallow rig and secures all the hooks to the rods before standing them in the rod holders. He motors in slowly until the boat grounds on the beach, then throws an anchor off the stern and pulls the boat out deeper so the hull won't bump the bottom when dropped by a receding wave.

Two charter catamarans are also anchored just off the beach. Their clients lounge under red and blue umbrellas just out of reach of the surf. In the shade of the tree line behind the sunbathers, gray smoke wafts above the grills. A hefty black woman emerges from palmettos and heads their way. Her head is wrapped in a vibrant scarf and her body draped in a billowy dress equally splashy. Legion wonders how much of her outfit is to fulfill the tourists' expectation of an island woman. She wades out and tosses two aluminum foil packages onto the bow. Webb is ready and hurls the barracuda and the mackerel they caught earlier into the surf at her feet. They don't try to talk over the gurgling breakers. She grabs the fish just above the fan of their tails, one in each hand, and pulls them out of the surf with their heads dragging in the sand.

"Will she cook those for the tourists?"

"No, no. For them, she cooks salmon from Alaska and sea bass from Chile. She will take these fish home to feed her family. The local people like the taste of fish. The tourists want fish that look like fish but have no taste."

They tear at the chicken legs with their teeth, wiping grease on their shirtsleeves. With drumstick in hand, Webb climbs onto the bow, using his free hand to shield his eyes as he studies the sky and sea.

"It will be too rough to troll in open water," he pronounces.

By the time Webb removes the baits and puts the rods in the galley under the forward deck, the wind has picked up even more. He retrieves the anchor and idles back through the boulders and past the reef.

The waves slap the side of the boat drenching them with spray. Their course to Sandy Ground will be across the flow of the whitecaps so they will have to be careful not to get caught under the collapsing crest of a giant wave.

Webb steers in the troughs between the waves as long as possible, the sea towering above them on both sides. When a wave begins to lift them, he steers up the roller at an angle with only sky in front of the bow. At the crest of a wave, the boat rockets into space, leaving them weightless as it hammers over. This clear delineation of the edge of death is thrilling. The orgasm of sensation leaves Legion limply satiated and yet yearning for more.

Webb slaps at the wheel readying the boat for the next wave, his lips pressed into the grim smile of battle, eager to test his skill against a worthy challenge. He will likely lose a bet to this monster one day. This ocean, which he worships, can also demand him as a sacrifice.

The sunlight dims again, and with it comes the nausea. Legion scoots back in the passenger's chair hoping for it to pass. The spray from the waves slapping the upwind side of the boat keeps him conscious. The grimace that draws his lips tight across his teeth morphs into a sneer. This malignancy gnawing at his brain feels fear also. It is redoubling its effort to complete its work before the sea terminates them both. This ferocious sea, with its promise of supremacy, calms him.

CHAPTER 14

Lightning

W hen they enter Long Bay, the cliff on the windward side moderates the unremitting swells of the open ocean. On the far side of the natural harbor is the expansive beach called Sandy Ground.

Webb jumps out of the captain's chair and stretches his arms toward the beach. "The big day is here. Every weekend in July we have the preliminary heats at the different harbors around the island—all-night parties after. The finale is always here, the first Saturday in August. This is the Super Bowl of Anguilla. The fishing was not so good today, but you are a lucky man to see this."

"There should be plenty of wind for the race," Legion says.

Webb appears startled when he turns, his usual smile gone. He passionately squawks something unintelligible, then catches himself, and resets to his stilted version of the Queen's English.

"Too much wind!" he restates. "Last year we had this much wind and we lost three boats."

"They're not good sailors then. They should be able to control a sailboat in this kind of wind."

"No, no. They are good sailors. Some are my cousins. They have been sailing all their lives."

"So, why did they lose their boats?"

"The winner will be the one who takes the most chances, the one who pushes to the limit and gets away with it. If the sails are trimmed to get the most out of the wind, an unexpected gust will send the boat over. It can't be helped."

"It could if they allowed for the gusts."

"Yes, but if they are cautious, they will lose. My father owned one of the boats that my cousin raced. When it went down in a race, my father did not hold it against him. However, if he had come in last, he and my father would never have spoken again. There would have been too much shame."

"You people take racing seriously."

"Yes, yes. It is our tradition. For some islands it is soccer; for others, it is baseball. For Anguilla, it is sailboat racing. Today everyone on the island will either be watching from the cliff or, if they have to work, listening on radio."

Webb steers to the right of the sailboats to pick up his cousins. The competitors are equally spaced with their noses tethered twenty feet offshore. Their naked masts erratically stir the air as the boats toss in the waves curling ashore.

Two white women in floral print bikinis wait in the surf, the older one stocky and the younger a willowy teen. Webb throws an anchor off the bow and allows the wind to swing the stern toward the beach. He hangs a ladder off the transom and steadies the older woman as she struggles to climb aboard.

"This is my Aunt Agnes," he introduces, "and this is Cheri, her granddaughter visiting from Guadeloupe. She wants to see the race too." Webb throws a towel atop a cooler for Cheri and helps Agnes into the fighting chair. "Aunt Agnes is my spotter. We will pick up the crew if a boat founders."

In the island dialect, Agnes and Webb discuss the boats, gesturing to the ones they know.

Webb sees Legion struggling to understand their conversation. "We think *Lightning*, the black one with the gold lightning bolt on the side, will be the winner. It has a good record this season. But we will be rooting for *Scooby*, the yellow one beside us; the skipper is our cousin."

Legion tries to pick out the skipper from the swarm of black bodies in and around the yellow boat; there are at least thirty. In the midst of this commotion, a girl lies quietly against the interior of the hull nursing her baby, its tiny legs dangling beneath her pullover shirt.

Children play in the surf between the boats and the beach. Crowded along the water's edge, scantily-clad brown bodies gyrate to reggae blaring from a stage at the far end of the beach, perhaps a mile away.

Agnes answers his astonishment. "The young ones have been partying since yesterday—never went home last night."

There is no organization, no sense that a race is about to begin. Legion had expected a more competitive atmosphere: men looking at watches, orders being shouted.

"When does it start?" Legion asks Webb.

"When it is time. A horn will go off when it is time."

Webb and Agnes continue discussing the boats.

"But when will it go off?"

"When it is time."

Cheri giggles. Both men look as she smirks at them like old fools. Webb had not realized Legion thought there was a specific start time until she laughed.

"It could be any time now. The judge will wait until he thinks the wind is right for a clean getaway." Webb smiles at Cheri. "We are on island time in Anguilla, aren't we, *Mon Chéri?*"

Webb and Agnes continue their discussion and Cheri pretends to listen. Legion doesn't think she understands the dialect either since Guadeloupe is a French island. Cheri is at that metamorphosis between cute girl and beautiful woman. Her budding breasts don't fill the halter-top and her hips are just beginning to spread. She reminds Legion of the high school girlfriend Paul never had and the beautiful grandbabies he would never see.

Cheri turns slowly and deliberately to face him when she notices herself being appraised. Her face is a scowl intended to make a dirty old man turn away. He engages her eyes with an assuring smile. *You will molt into a gorgeous butterfly,* he wants to say. She reads this somehow and shyly smiles back.

Finally, the air horn blares and there is instant mayhem. Many on *Scooby* leap into the water, while others heft themselves from the water and slither over the gunwales into the boat. The bow anchors keeping the boat trussed in place are well up the beach; Legion expects crew members to be rushing to retrieve them. Instead, the ropes are loosened from the boat and thrown overboard. Sturdy men wading chest deep push the bow around to face open water as the sails are being raised on board. The woman who had been nursing hands the baby across the gunwale to one of the men in the water just as the wind catches in the mainsail. The heavy boom swooshes just above her head. The sails of the other boats up the beach are filling also.

"This is the most dangerous part," Webb advises.

Without speed the rudders are ineffective, so the boats lurch menacingly at each other. Agnes points out boats darting on collision courses. At the last possible moment, *Lightning* swerves and barely misses a competitor. The rules observed by gentlemen in their regattas elsewhere are meaningless here. Bravado mixed with seamanship. A battle is underway and the only rule is to win.

Where seconds before Legion watched individual people and components of the boats, now he sees the boats as a whole. He can no longer comprehend the separate bones and sinew of the charging animals. Where the yellow boat had been referred to as "it" while it slumbered tied to the shore, Agnes and Webb now refer to the boat by its given name or respectful innuendo. "Tighten the jib, *Scooby*!" they coax. "Stay the course, babe! Keep your nerve; make *Lightning* turn!"

When the first boats reach the mouth of the harbor, Webb pulls his anchors and begins securing them in a locker under the foredeck.

Agnes reports to Webb from her perch on the fighting chair. "*Scooby*'s headed back. Bent the boom in a collision with *Lightning*. Nobody appears hurt."

"*Scooby* can still sail with the bent boom, but stands no chance of winning," she explains to Legion. "Better to quit now than risk being last."

Agnes and Cheri wave to *Scooby* as it tacks to shore. Nobody waves back. The jib is pulled in and the main lowered to half-mast. As it approaches the beach, it turns into the wind. The sail flutters. Life smothers out of it.

They follow the race in case other boats get in trouble, but the enthusiasm is gone. The sailboats run before the wind on parallel courses. The dangerous games of chicken are over. The main sheets are deployed to one side of the boats and the jibs to the other to keep the sails from robbing wind from each other—a flock of herons, their wings outstretched, gliding in formation above the water. Colorful spinnakers balloon in front of some, although this is risky with gusty winds. *Lightning*, the leader, moves in closer to shore for smoother water and deploys a white spinnaker emblazoned with a gold lightning bolt.

Legion now has time to admire how the boats are made. There is no superstructure at all, only the open hull. The mast is mounted in a block amidships; taut cables stabilize the mast to the sides. The rudder hinged behind the stern attaches to a long tiller handle held by the skipper. The boats are about the same size as the luxury yachts moored in the harbor but without the fluff and gadgetry of the elite crafts. As they follow *Lightning* close abeam, Legion counts a crew of twelve. Only two are actively sailing the boat.

He leans to Webb so he can be heard over the roar of wind and motor. "Why such a large crew?"

Webb looks away as if thinking how best to explain. "This class of boats evolved here on Anguilla to carry freight. They had to have shallow keels for these waters, but the cargo provided enough ballast to keep them upright. If the cargo was light, the skippers had to throw in rocks for extra ballast."

Cheri shifts around on the cooler so she could lean in and listen. Legion thinks she had been wondering about the boats herself but didn't want to appear stupid about what every child from Anguilla grows up knowing.

"When the tourist trade picked up in Saint Thomas and other islands, the boats started taking people along to work. There were no jobs on Anguilla at the time. They discovered if they took enough people at one time, they didn't need cargo or extra ballast. The people could shift around in the boat to apply the weight where needed to make them faster. That's how the races got started. The skippers would convoy together for mutual safety anyway, so they started racing back and forth between the islands. The fastest boat had bragging rights until the next tourist season."

The planned racecourse was to the end of Anguilla and then up the other side between Anguilla and Saint Martin. But before the start, the Race Committee had called off the leg of the race on the far side of the island due to the high winds. This is where the three boats were lost last season. The contestants round a buoy at the tip of the island and head back to Sandy Ground against the wind. As they tack across their intended direction of travel, it is hard to judge who is in the lead.

"This is where the race will be won or lost," Agnes yells over her shoulder to Legion.

Webb takes a direct course through the sailboats crisscrossing in front and behind him, always careful to stay far enough away from their courses not to hinder their maneuvers. Agnes and Webb point whenever a boat reverses tack, sneering if it is done poorly. They follow abeam but downwind of *Lightning* when her starboard tack brings her close to them. The wind tilts the boat toward them so Legion can observe everything going on inside.

The leeward gunwale is just inches above the water. On this side, one man crouches in a pool of water feverishly bailing with a plastic bucket as tips of the waves splashed in. On the far side, the windward side, the rest of the crew is crowded as far up the side as they can get. About half of them have their feet hooked under a rail across the ribs allowing them to sit on the gunwale and lean their torsos out over the water. The rest huddle at their feet. All, except for the bailer, are rigidly still so the skipper can balance their weight against the force of the sails with the rudder.

Lightning hits a wave broadside causing her to shudder and leap. One of the outstretched bodies loses its perch, and with arms flailing, falls out of sight behind the boat. The leeward gunwale dips, allowing water to gush in. The skipper releases the main sheet just before the boat swamps. The bow swerves to face the wind and *Lightning* rights herself. The skipper continues the bow around with the rudder and yells, "Hard alee." The bodies flow like mercury from one side of the boat to the other. When the wind fills the mainsail again, the boat lurches away in the opposite direction of only seconds before. But the unplanned maneuver has cost *Lightning* the lead. No one in the boat even looks behind to see if they can spot the man who went overboard.

Webb maneuvers his stern to the man treading water and lowers the ladder. When he tumbles in over the stern, Cheri offers the towel she has been sitting on. He pulls the towel over his head and crouches in the corner of the transom. Humiliation drips off him like the seawater.

"Damn!" he spits from under the towel. His body heaves as he yells it again even louder. Legion can't tell if he is talking in dialect. 'Damn' is probably 'damn' in their dialect as well.

CHAPTER 15

The Fathers

O n the return trip to Island Harbor, they motor close to shore to avoid the larger waves that charge past the sheer rock wall that is the north edge of Anguilla. The cliff hangs above them, occasionally blocking the sun. Webb darts from one boat rail to the other checking clearance between the hull and the rock slides that littered the shore. He seems to know the location of each submerged hazard before it comes into view.

The boat bangs into the waves and the headwind blows the spray from over the bow chilling them. There is plenty of time to get to the ferry for his return trip to Saint Martin, so Webb meanders at half throttle on one of the two outboard engines. No one is waiting for either of them. No hugs of relief that they are safely home; no eager faces to listen attentively to their boasting. With a boney, liver-splotched hand, Legion grasps the top of the windscreen, feeling old and faded, an empty husk to be whisked away by a gust of wind.

Legion eases out of his seat beside Webb and opens the cooler. He levers the tops off two bottles of Ting with the opener on the cooler side and pours half the contents overboard before mixing in the vodka.

"Do you have kids?" Legion asks as he nudges Webb with a bottle.

Webb jerks around, a mischievous smile emerging under the smear of zinc oxide salve on his lips and cheeks. Legion thinks he is not the first client to ask this question when fishing got slow. Webb hesitates as if deciding which story to tell.

"Yes, I have a son. He lives in England. His mother was a nurse here on the island. She enticed me to her condo one day and forced me. She was a big woman; got on top and forced me." There is an injured frown when he turns his face away and then he jerks back with a devious grin to see if Legion believed it. They rock in their seats overcome with infectious laughter.

"The part about her forcing me is not true, but the son and her being a nurse is true. She called me after going back to England and told me she was pregnant. Said she was not in love and would not consider moving back. But she wanted the baby and wanted to know if it was all right. There would be no obligations, no further contact. She didn't want anything but to have the baby. She would have an abortion if I said no."

For a moment, Webb freezes in thought, his eyes narrow as if trying to see something in the distance behind Legion's shoulder. "He must be sixteen now. He knows he's my son. She told him everything. He came to stay with me one summer when he was seven. I introduced him to his cousins and we fished every day. But the next summer she said he didn't want to come back. I haven't heard from either of them since."

An unusually large wave lifts the boat and heaves it towards the rocky shore. Webb battles the steering wheel as the boat darts and bucks defiantly in the surge. After the wave passes under, it explodes like thunder against the rocks just a few feet away sending spray back at them.

Webb continues as if nothing has happened. "It is better the way it worked out. I do not have a fatherly instinct. And I could never make him love the island. He was embarrassed by me, I think."

Webb steers behind a coral outcrop and pulls the motor to idle in front of a small pristine beach butted against the rock wall. "You can only get to this beach by water or by climbing down the face of the cliff." He motions to a steep trail cutting diagonally down the slope. A rope hangs beside the trail to assist climbers.

"This is where he was conceived, I think."

The shudder of the boat ceases when Webb cuts the motor. They drift at ease on the flat water darkened by the shadow of the cliff. After churning in the open sea all day, the stillness feels peculiar, unnatural.

"What about you? Do you have kids?" Webb asks.

"I have one son also. He's grown now, or at least he thinks he is. We're not close. I guess when his mother left me, he and I were divorced also. I was not a good father."

"The father thing is a mystery to me," Webb says.

Legion continues, "I wanted to be a father. I was the softball coach, the scout leader…tried to do the right things. But the bottom line is, we never liked each other. If he didn't look like me, I'd swear he belonged to somebody else. Everything I did or thought was irksome to him. As he got older, he mimicked his mother's attitude toward me. I wasn't a good husband either."

"But you are a good fisherman and you are learning to appreciate the races. You do not seem like such a bad guy to me."

"These things aren't important."

"Of course they are important. Who says they are not important? They are important to me. They are important to you. Let the sons live their own lives. They will do so anyway."

"Let's talk about fishing or the races…anything else. I'm sorry I brought it up."

"So we will not talk about it. The sun will come up tomorrow if we do or if we don't. At the end of the day, we either caught fish or we did not. You can regret not catching fish if you want. This old ocean does not care one way or the other."

Webb starts the motor and maneuvers to the opening of the cove.

Legion tries to blank his mind to all but the pastel granite, limestone, and coral rocks littered beside the beach.

"Why did she call?" Webb yells over the noise of the motor reverberating off the cliff face.

"What?"

"She could have had the baby and I would never have known about it. So why did she call?"

"Do you wish you didn't know?"

Webb turns to him, his lips twisted in a grimace, his eyes dark for the first time. "Why did I have to decide if he lived?"

Webb guns the boat back into the ocean at full throttle, deliberately crashing through waves as if to punish them. Legion holds to his seat, catching his breath between the poundings. "Stop it. You'll break her spine."

And then it is over. Webb eases the throttle. The sudden squall has been ridden out. He stares ahead, jaw clenched, quiet.

They continue at a leisurely pace up the coast of Anguilla while they drink. Webb points and names every landmark and relates stories of the presidents and Arab princes who had stayed in the palatial villas atop the cliffs. As he brags on his island, his wispy smile is of a man who continues to be mesmerized every day by the woman he loves.

Neither of them checks the time until the mouth of Island Harbor comes into view. It is already too late to reach the ferry port before the last trip of the day. If Legion had been sober, he would have been mad. But this is the Islands, where time does not hold the same significance for measuring the day as it does elsewhere. Webb bypasses the harbor entrance and continues to the passage between Scrub Island and the eastern tip of Anguilla.

"We will make Orient Bay before dark," he says.

On the way, they hatch a plot to save the world by blowing up the United Nations building. They will fill the boat with explosives and extra gas and explode the boat in the harbor in front of the skyscraper. They are working through the details when the vodka runs out. They conclude neither of them cares enough for the fate of the world to justify such a long trip.

"Somebody would probably start a war with Anguilla," Webb ponders, "drop a bomb or something. It might be fun, but I do not want my island blown away."

When they coast onto the sand of Orient Beach, Legion can't manage to crawl over the gunwales. Webb throws out an anchor to keep the boat from washing aground and they sleep on the deck.

CHAPTER 16

Island Dog

A t first light the next morning, Webb rolls Legion into the water and drags his sputtering limp body to shore. While they doze stretched on the sand, Legion glimpses (or dreams) Lily Ana, hands on her hips, watching from the front door of the café. Her image fades back into sleep and then she suddenly reappears standing over him pouring a bucket of ice water in his face.

His squawking wakes Webb, who turns to his side laughing convulsively.

"Ting cocktails made us wise," Legion sputters to Webb while using his finger to squeegee water from his eyes, "but now, we're dumb as usual."

Lily Ana doesn't laugh. "I prefer you dumb."

After staggering to his feet, he is adrift inside a thick fog. Lily Ana has disappeared.

"Are you coming?"

He tries to follow her voice but stumbles into the water. An unseen wave growls and froth runs up to his knees. The receding water erodes the sand beneath his feet. With the slant of the beach and no horizon, his arms flail to retain balance. "Lily?" The next wave crashes, coaxing him farther into the ocean.

Lily Ana grabs his hand. "Come on, before you drown." She orients him toward the far end of the beach and pulls him along.

Legion looks back. Webb and the boat are already lost in the fog. "Next Sunday. Pick me up here. We'll settle up then."

There is no reply.

"I don't know where your son is. He was asleep on the couch when I came in last night, but was gone when I woke this morning. His clothes are still strung around the cabin, so I guess he's still here somewhere."

The sand mutes Betty's approach from behind and she passes Legion with her quick purposeful strides before he can get a good look at her profile.

"Beautiful morning," Betty says glancing back with her confident smile.

"Getting prettier by the minute. Welcome back," Legion says as she fades into the mist ahead of them. Legion's pace quickens as he tries to keep her in view.

Lily Ana jerks back on his hand like he's a dog tugging at a leash. "Stop it!" she hisses under her breath.

"Look at how it moves in every direction all at once. Watching that girl's ass is like watching a dogfight; a guy shouldn't look but he has to."

"She's a Jezebel, Legion. Yesterday she had Bella massaging her feet—right there on the beach for everybody to watch. There's no end to the humiliation she'll put that poor woman through just to show off."

Legion smiles at how easily Lily Ana fits people into neat categories.

Bella, a hefty deaf-mute black woman, strolls Orient Beach barefoot in her flowery print muumuu selling straw hats and shell necklaces to the tourists. She holds up fingers to indicate the number of euros or dollars when someone points at the merchandise draped about her body. She raised her grandson André, the beachboy, doing this.

Every trip Betty buys crap she'll never use. Her cabin must be full of the stuff. It seems she has found a better way to give Bella money without the proud Negress thinking it charity.

Lily Ana walks stiffly ahead, still fuming about Betty. Legion follows a few steps behind not wanting to get too close until her fury subsides. She might turn her sharp tongue on him next.

Out in the bay, he hears the throb of Webb's boat motor at idle. He squints into the swirling fog. It would be chancy navigating through the reef with visibility so low. Webb could do it and not get a scratch on the hull.

In the bay, shadowy silhouettes of chartered catamarans at anchor lazily twitch with the wave action. These glorified houseboats of the jet set hardly resemble real sailboats. It is obvious they have no soul. There is nothing intrinsically sexy about a fiberglass box. Sailing a catamaran would be like sex with a whore; you could appreciate their efficiency, but could never fall in love with one.

Paul jogs along the waterline where the waves rush up and melt into the sand. His footprints and those of a dog stretch behind intermittently, the surf having washed away long sections of their trail.

The dog lopes effortlessly beside him, tongue lolling to the side, head turned to Paul enjoying their camaraderie. Its short hair is burnt orange except for a peppering of black mixed into the muzzle, eyebrows, and the tip of the tail. The ears are turned down at the ends, giving its face a dull, houndish look. Paul, dressed in his new jogging outfit and matching sneakers, finds it annoying to be seen with such a mongrel.

Ahead, mixed in with other flotsam, Paul spots a stick. When he stops to pick it up, the dog gives a gleeful yelp as it dances, anticipating the throw.

"Get out of here…shoo!" Paul's face distorts into a scowl as he slashes menacingly at the dog.

The dog's tail stiffens; the hairs above its shoulders bristle. When Paul tries to run again, the dog rushes at him, nipping at his legs. Paul backs into the water to get away. The dog continues to bark threats as it paces back and forth at the water's edge.

Paul looks up and down the beach for help. In the haze that hangs above the thrashing breakers, a splotch of color bounces. It floats closer and a nude angel steps out of the fog.

"Stop! Careful of the dog. It'll bite you."

"He's not after me."

"It wasn't after me either—at first, but now it wants to kill me."

She stops in front of Paul, beside the dog that sits innocently on its rump looking up at her. She smiles patently a moment before wading in with her hand extended. "Better give me that." She throws the stick and the dog bounds away. "He'll let you out if you stay with me, if he thinks you're my friend." They wade to shore before it returns. "Hold my hand." The dog drops the stick at her feet. Paul stiffens as the dog circles sniffing at his heels. "Relax," she says as she leads Paul up the beach.

"It's your dog?"

"No, he's an Island Dog."

"So, why does it mind you?"

"He doesn't mind anybody." The dog prances ahead of them, its tail swishing back and forth. "We walk together in the mornings."

They stroll toward the granite cliff seen above the haze at the end of the beach. Paul sneaks a peek as his eyes follow the dog frisking around her. She turns her face away from the wind shaking her head, allowing the wind to fluff her short black hair around her puckish face. Turning back, she sweeps the hair aside with her hands into a part above her left eye. Her short stature makes her figure all the more voluptuous. When he thinks she is looking ahead at the cliff, a surreptitious glimpse turns into a stare. He can't make himself turn away.

Her cheeks lift into a coy smile before a quick sideways glance lets him know she is aware. "Don't do anything quickly because of the dog."

"You're warning me not to try anything? You'll sic it on me?"

"Not at all. That's not what I meant." She laughs, the cluck of a dove. "It's just that Beau might try to protect me."

"I thought it wasn't yours."

"He doesn't belong to anybody. We're just friends that walk together."

"What kind did you say it is?

"An Island Dog."

"Is that a breed, like a Poodle?"

"I guess that's right. But you won't find it in any dog book. People have been bringing dogs to the islands for centuries, different breeds, from all over. They've run loose, and so all the different breeds are mixed together. That's what an Island Dog is, all breeds mixed together."

"If you average all dogs together, this is what you get?"

"That's it. They don't need humans to take care of them. They eat food scraps thrown out by the restaurants, and with the warm climate, there's no need for shelter. But they still like the company of people."

"It looks like a mutt."

"I think he's handsome." She chuckles at his frown of disbelief. "It's sort of selective breeding in reverse. Island Dogs are what dogs were before people started tinkering. They're like the original dog, I guess. And they're smarter than most purebreds."

They walk easily now, still holding hands. They reach the tumble of blue boulders spilled into the water beneath the cliff and start back. The dog is still out ahead. Other walkers emerge from the haze in front of them.

"So, you live here?" he asks.

"No, no. I'm from Chicago. But I come down at least twice a year, with my boyfriend."

"*Bonjour*, Betty," Lily Ana hails as she walks out of the fog. Legion is trailing behind. The dog races up to Lily Ana, sniffs her legs, then on to greet Legion.

"*Bonjour*, Lily Ana."

"I see you've met Paul."

"So, this is Paul. I didn't know his name."

"It looks like you've known each other for years," Lily Ana says with a disparaging grin.

Startled, Paul drops Betty's hand.

"I had to rescue him from Beau."

"From Beau?" Lily Ana looks back at the dog getting his ears scratched.

"It attacked, tried to bite me," Paul explains.

"Who knows what goes through Beau's mind? The guards will pick him up if he bites somebody," Lily Ana warns Betty.

"They should do it now, before it bites. It should be put down," Paul says emphatically.

All three look at Paul for a moment before the two couples continue their walks in opposite directions. Beau follows beside Legion.

"Like Legion," Betty says. "Beau is handsome like Legion."

"You think Dad's handsome?"

"Of course. The way older men can be handsome, but not pretty."

"Women are strange."

She giggles but does not respond.

"So, you're Betty?"

"Yep, Betty Boop."

Paul stops and looks at her unabashedly for the first time. She also stops and does a Betty Boop pose, standing on one leg with the opposite knee turned in, her eyelids fluttering seductively. If he could imagine a slinky black dress, the cartoon character would be complete.

"Amazing," Paul says as he takes her hand and they continue to walk. "Is your name really Betty Boop?"

"My name's really Betty, but I add the Boop when I come down here."

They follow an erratic line of sea grass that has accumulated where the surf plays out. The sun has burnt away the haze. Flames spiking above clouds that fringe the horizon give her body a pinkish glow.

"So where's your boyfriend? Doesn't he like to walk?"

"Sometimes."

"Sometimes he likes to walk, but he can't keep up with you?"

"No, some of my boyfriends like to walk and some don't." She looks sideways to get Paul's reaction. "And none of them can keep up with me."

Ahead, a beachboy arranges lounge chairs into pairs facing the water and screws umbrellas into the sand between them. He wears surfer pants and a yellow T-shirt with the name of the resort across the front and back. The yellow contrasts with his amber skin. His black kinky hair seems incompatible with his narrow delicate nose.

"I suppose he's handsome too?"

"André? André lives here. He's worked at the resort ever since I've been coming. And no, he's not handsome yet, but he's pretty."

Betty giggles at Paul's puzzled expression.

"He's black," Paul says.

She waves and André waves back.

"You think he's black?"

"Well, he's not white."

"He'd be offended by either term, I think." She squeezes Paul's hand and smiles up at him. "I'd introduce you, but I don't think you two would like each other. He's an Island Man."

When Lily Ana looks back, the ghostly form of Legion is barely discernible. She stops and waits. "Legion, can you not keep up?"

He continues to amble along the beach at the same pace without answering. As he comes closer, she sees his gaze is toward the ocean, lost in some daydream, and hadn't heard her. Legion is startled when he bumps into her.

She takes his hand before continuing. "Where were you just now?"

"Fishing. I was out there with Webb."

Lily Ana doesn't believe him, but won't press him further. He had tried to explain when they first met the blasphemous things that go through his head. She had tried to save his soul, but he only seemed bemused. He won't discuss it with her anymore because she can't help getting upset. The Devil plagues his mind and tortures his body—or maybe God is testing him like Job.

She turns her head away so he can't see her bleary eyes. "I love you, Legion—Lord only knows why." She is confident God has put them together for a purpose. Legion had been sent by God to rescue her and now it is her turn to save Legion for God.

The café is just ahead where their days will begin, she tending bar and Legion the only steady customer.

"What do you think of Paul?" Legion asks.

"He is not you."

"That's good."

"Not in my opinion. He's such a boor. As bad as you are sometimes, you could never be so snobbish. Was he always that way?"

"Maybe not always, not as a little kid. I think the thing with his mother and me damaged him some. There's some history I haven't told you."

Lily Ana gives him a questioning glance, wanting more, but his eyes stare down at the swirl of the water.

"So his bad manners are your fault? I don't buy that," she says.

"Is he so bad? I mean, I don't really like him myself, but he's the only family I have. I'll put him up somewhere else if he bothers you."

"No, it's not that I hate him or anything. I feel sorry for him actually. I'll try to make him feel welcome for your sake. You'd do the same for me, I know. But what are you going to do?"

"Nothing. What should I do? If he's getting on your nerves, I'll run him off."

"He's your son. Surely, you two can patch things up. He seems to need his father right now."

Sandpipers skittered on the beach a few yards ahead of them, sprinting on little stilted legs before again dipping their heads to browse on sand fleas washed up by the surf. Legion feints a rush at them, interrupting their well-ordered routine by making them fly. He's feeling mean.

"He was an accident this woman and I had twenty years ago. I've paid the price and he's on his own. The only thing he needs is for me to feel guilty."

Lily Ana strides ahead on the way to the café and then turns and walks backward. "Think about it, Legion. He needs you whether he wants you or not—and maybe you need him."

CHAPTER 17

Betty Boop

She lies stretched on her back in all her glory wearing only a wide-brimmed straw hat tilted forward over her face and dark sunglasses.

"Betty, is that you?"

"You didn't recognize me?"

Of course he did. Paul had memorized every pore in her skin on the beach this morning. "Well, pretty women are all alike, you know."

"Really, I thought I was special," she says as her legs spread slightly. She takes off the sunglasses to reveal a mischievous smile.

Realizing his baggy trunks are beginning to tent, Paul lowers himself onto the sand beside her. She sits up too, throwing the straw hat in his lap.

"You've got a mean streak," he says.

"Maybe, but I know how to get a man to sit beside me on the beach."

Paul returns her naughty smile. "You don't have any modesty?" he asks, deliberately scanning her body, trying to make her blush.

She props back on her elbows stretching her legs in front, admiring herself down to her painted toenails. "What do I have to be modest about? Isn't this just the standard equipment?"

"Above standard, I would say." Paul gives a hard look at one of the tourists walking by. "It doesn't bother you to have these old geezers ogling you?"

"Heavens no. This is why they come. This is why I come."

"To see the men?"

"Of course not. Girls don't care about that. They want to be seen, to be appreciated. Old men can appreciate too, you know.

Whether they're young or old or fat or well endowed, doesn't matter. It's whether they think I'm attractive, whether I can see it in their eyes."

"You're a tease."

"Do you think so? The old men seem to understand, but you young guys read too much into it."

The beach is full. Half are lounging on rented beach chairs, paperbacks in hand, watching the other half stroll in the surf. All, except the day-trippers from the ships, are nude. The vacationers from the hotels at the other end of the beach strip also when they pass the sign permitting nudity. They've booked rooms farther up the beach as a cover for their real purpose, which is to walk naked on a public beach. But their tan lines and the bathing suits held in their hands make them easy to spot. When they walk by, face forward, their eyes behind mirrored sunglasses dance around. If it is a couple, they hold hands for reassurance, but never look at each other.

"Too bad the girls back in Nashville aren't like this," Paul says to himself, but out loud.

"They are."

"No, I mean like this, walking around in the all-together."

"Don't the young ones wear the shortest, most see-through things they can buy? It makes their day to feel men's eyes all over them. They'd walk around nude if they could get away with it. They might not admit it to you, or even their girlfriends, because it's not ladylike, but this is every girl's secret fantasy."

"That's not true."

"Okay, whatever you say. It amazes me the fables guys make up about girls. Girls know instinctively before age six how boys think, but boys never understand girls. Boys are always trying to think like men—and, of course, you can't tell men anything."

"Some men might think you're a whore." Paul grins to soften the word, but not the intent.

"Some men probably would, but I'm not. I'm still giving it away. Later, when the flower begins to wilt, I'll turn into a whore. All women are whores you know; just some wear wedding rings. I'll find a sugar daddy, probably in a few years. Then I'll never come back here—become a prude."

"You're something else; that's what you are."

"I'm Betty Boop. Here, I'm who I want to be. This is my escape from reality, or maybe to reality, not sure which. Whether you think I'm a lady or a whore makes no difference to me. I'm not in the mood to pander to your expectations."

Paul cocks his head and gives her a squint-eyed look. "How much of this rot you're spouting do you really believe?"

Betty gives him a playful shove. "I'm just like every other girl you've ever met, only without the pretense."

Paul imagines himself nude in a typical bar scene, picking up a girl who can plainly see what is on his mind. It would probably save on the useless small talk. Although it would be tough to stay in the closet if you got an erection whenever the busboy bent over a table.

"What are you smirking about?"

"I was just wondering how this nudist thing got started. But I guess nudists wonder how the clothes thing got—"

"Are you one of those deep-thinker types? I don't worry about it, at least not anymore; just trust my feelings and go with that."

"Where's your boyfriend?"

"At the airport, waiting for the next plane to Miami. He didn't feel as comfortable with this as he thought he would. I'm going to stay on for another week before flying back to Chicago."

"What do you do in Chicago?"

"You really wouldn't recognize me in Chicago. I'm a paralegal in a prestigious law firm. It's strictly business suits and pantyhose. Can you imagine me in a business suit?"

Paul narrows his eyes. "It's a little hard to get that picture right now."

"I'm a little miss-nobody at the office. I have to stay under the radar of the jealous wives. But it's just a job, right? You don't have to like it, just be good at it. And I'm good at it. I've saved butt so many times around that office, I pretty well write my own ticket."

"Is your boyfriend from work?"

She takes the hat off his lap and puts it back over her face as she lies back chuckling. "Heavens no. No flirting with lawyers or clients. Not that I haven't been propositioned a few times, but I've got more sense than that." She tilts up the hat brim with a finger. "Sexy does not equal bimbo, you know."

She squirms herself back into the depressions her body has made in the sand. "Freddy is a guy that picked me up at a bar. When I told him what I wanted, where I wanted him to take me, he lit up like a slot machine. But when we got here, he was a little possessive. Got the idea we were in love or something. I told him the score from the start, but he believed what he wanted to believe. I feel bad about it. You may think I'm a tease, but I'm not a bitch that likes to lead men on."

They sit on the beach crowded with sunbathing nudists with the voyeurs parading by at the waterline. The residents pay as little attention to tourists as they do the seagulls hovering overhead, a different species to which they've become accustomed and ignore. Paul feels the furtive, questioning glances from the nudists lounging close by at this outsider who has ventured too close. With the right provocation, they would collectively swarm to shoo him away.

"How about you, Paul? What brings you here?"

"You know Legion, my father? I came here to tell him Mother—his wife died."

"Wow, that's heavy. I didn't know he was married. How'd he take it?"

Paul flushes with the memory of his father's callous reaction. He looks out to the horizon thinking how the truth would sound.

Legion didn't care; neither of them cared. They wanted each other dead. Paul is the one who feels naked now, wanting to cover himself from Betty's eyes. "Look, my father's an asshole."

"Oops, I didn't mean to pry. I'm sorry about your mother."

Betty sits up again and studies his face sternly. "People here like Legion," she says flatly, without empathy, "and Lily Ana, too."

Paul takes it as a warning. Betty will be among the first in the nudist colony to rally behind one of her own.

"Is Dad her sugar daddy?"

"No, it's not like that with her. As far as I know, she's never taken a dime from Legion. He bought her a car about six months ago, and it sat in the parking lot until the battery ran down. She wouldn't even sit in it. She's one tough broad. Legion would like to be her sugar daddy, but she won't have it. It drives him nuts, but he respects her. And everybody admires her for putting up with Legion. He can be a pill sometimes."

"Like I said, all women are not like you."

"Yep, you've got me there. But I look at it as the difference between girls and women. The ultimate fantasy for a woman is to be respected, to be loved for who she is, rather than her body. I'm going to stay a girl as long as I can, but when I grow up, I want to be like Lily Ana. I want to be, but who knows what I'll turn into."

Paul again grazes down her body, the delicate perfection of a butterfly. He tries to imagine her without wings or the desire to fly. He knows he will never understand. The female thought process is as mystical as calculus.

With the same perplexity, he had tried to understand his mother, who had never been a girl in his eyes. In his preschool years, when they bathed together for convenience, she chided him for the effect his birth had on her body. With her fingers, she would stretch herself to show the potential effect of surgically lifting one thing or another. In later years, it was from him she sought reassurance that age had not eroded her beauty.

When Paul's eyes move from Betty's delicate manicured feet back up her body, he is seeing his mother—her body. Betty's knees lift to conceal her sex. When he reaches the mounds of her breasts, her arms cross, cupping them in her palms.

"Stop it!" she demands.

He looks questioningly at the startle in her eyes.

"You're making me feel...naked."

Her cheeks are pink with agitation, with violation, the blush he had tried to invoke before. He had changed her, without touching her or saying anything, with only the reflection of a repugnant woman on his face. She thinks the loathing is for her.

Paul smiles an apology.

Her forehead furrows in challenge. "What?!"

CHAPTER 18

Legion

$\mathcal{P}$aul dresses in the khaki shorts, polo shirt, and canvas deck shoes he had bought in town yesterday. Legion puts on the nicest clothes he owns, frayed jean shorts and a sky blue button-up shirt imprinted with sailboats. He even tucks in the shirttail. He is past being self-conscious no matter what he wears or doesn't wear but he is tired of the looks of disgust from Paul.

Legion slathers Paul with suntan lotion, "You're going to burn anyway, but this will make it less painful."

They take a path through a tunnel of lush tropical scrub behind the cabins. Every bush has pink or red flowers and thorns. They emerge onto a sand trail wide enough for them to walk side-by-side atop the exposed reef that separates Orient Bay from Galion Bay.

To their right, a lone stork steps lightly through the mirrored surface of a shallow salt flat. The stork folds one of its orange twig legs into the grey fluff of its stomach and freezes on one foot, its dagger-thin beak poised to strike at the scurry of a brine shrimp. On their left, the contrasting thunder of ocean waves blasting into the coral rock sprays shimmering diamonds into the air. A quarter mile farther up the trail, the turquoise water of Galion Bay peeks through the trunks of bushy-headed coconut palms.

"Is this going to be another walk-and-talk?" Paul asks, referring sarcastically to when he was growing up.

Legion halts suddenly, slapping at his pockets. "I've forgotten my wallet; wait here." He turns and with purposeful long strides walks back. After being swallowed by the undergrowth, he bends over and takes deep breaths until the suffocating panic begins to release him. Is it the hangover or the craving for more booze causing him to fade to a shadow? Or is it the onset of a blackout? Lately, Legion has been mysteriously awakening in places not knowing how he got there, either a symptom of what was killing him or the uninterrupted booze—hard to tell.

Legion creeps back to the opening to the trail and pulls apart branches of a scrubby tree to look secretly at Paul investigating fossils beside the path.

How could they be so different?

As a child, Legion had endeavored to become what his father expected. As a teen, he had never gone through, didn't fully understand, the rebellious attitude of his peers. If asked by a well-meaning adult what he wanted to be when he grew up, he would bow his head in perplexed embarrassment. The question had seemed absurd. His father, of course, would tell him at the appropriate time. He went to college because it was expected. He made good grades and kept his nose clean because it was expected. He became an engineer, not because he liked building things, which he did, but to fulfill his father's wishes. After his father's death, he ran the factory under the often-demonic fear of letting his father down.

Paul, on the other hand, had always been obstinate. Legion had taken him on many walk-and-talks over the years when things boiled over at home. Paul never resisted, but their walks ended with increased frustration for both of them rather than the chumminess Legion wanted.

Their talks followed a predictable scenario. Legion played the sage pointing out the errors of his son's thinking and behavior. When Paul offered a defense, Legion never attempted to understand. Right or wrong was never the point anyway. Wringing out a commitment to conform to what he wanted was all that mattered.

He'd been more a manager than a friend, directing him like a subordinate at work rather than his own flesh and blood. He'd never learned his son's feelings, nor had he let his son know his. Maybe he didn't care. At least, that is the way Paul would have interpreted it when he had become old enough to catch on to these manipulations.

Paul would have seen his lack of empathy with his mother as well. Arguments with his wife had been about domination rather than resolving disagreements. When either he or his wife tried to draw Paul in for support, he would slink away, refusing to participate. By his early teens, Paul had become distant, secretive about his life, not interested in theirs.

When Paul began high school, Legion gave up, ignoring him as best he could. He put in even more hours at work, letting his wife deal with the snarly kid. It was obvious his family was falling apart. He'd hated the feeling of defeat but had not put out the effort to fix anything.

Looking out at Paul through the tree, Legion's face contorts with the memory of that farce. At breakfast the day before, Legion had seen in Paul's eyes a true reflection of the husband and father he had been. It was the unexpected arrival of his former self rather than Paul's prickly attitude that was so alarming. The specter of himself as a father nudges at his elbow now causing his heart to race. This callous, superficial man that Paul has become is his creation, his inescapable legacy.

Paul looks good; he has to give him that. He still has the trim, lean frame with a little more muscle in his upper body probably from a gym. He seems taller, but that of course, that couldn't be since he was fully grown when Legion last saw him a year ago. Legion himself must have shrunk and Paul seems taller by comparison. Legion's own father had been six inches shorter than him when the hunchbacked and shriveled man died. Legion appraises himself, throwing his shoulders back, running his hands across the slight paunch at his waist. He is not vain, at least not anymore, but wonders how he appears to Paul.

Paul has his mother's smooth, babyish skin and his grandfather's pronounced chin that gives his face a look of self-assurance. His face is a facade concealing the insecure, no-so-bright kid Legion knows him to be. But in business, Legion imagines eyes would migrate to the promise of his strong features when leadership was needed. These affirmations from his associates might give him the confidence he would need. But having the look could only take him so far.

Legion thinks back to his own career, of his successes that he suspects were undeserved. He had inherited the factory from his father, the founder. With no more qualifications than the founder's strong chin, the employees had turned to him like sunflowers to the sun. Their livelihoods, their families' futures, depended on him. He had come to understand why his father worked himself to death, the pressure he must have felt.

The senior managers, having been with his father from the beginning and having built the company, had known Junior Legion (his father had been Mister Legion) since kindergarten. They liked him well enough but were also leery of a misstep from Junior. They just wanted to retire with their pensions intact.

He would have sold out then if there had been a buyer for a run-down factory making an obsolete product. Although the company still made a profit, market share was slipping. Without updated products, it was just a matter of time. The company had some cash left, enough for a redesign, but just enough. Nothing could go wrong or cash flow would run short. The vultures would swoop in if that happened.

So the restructuring was not the bold move he would be credited with later, more desperate than bold. After concluding he had no choice, he did his best for the sake of the employees and their families.

He had called in those senior managers and put it bluntly. If they wanted their pensions, they would have to agree to stay at least another year, until they'd trained their replacements, until they had redesigned the product. Otherwise, he would pay off the creditors now, there was enough cash for that, and close the doors. They'd either work together on this or they'd all, including himself, walk away empty-handed.

They had agreed. "After all," one old-timer said, "it might be fun, like in the beginning."

He hired new engineers, pronounced new grandiose goals that were declared profound by the young managers he brought in. How much of the turnaround was due to his tall frame and jutting jaw, this illusion of leadership and management skills? If at any point this illusion had been stripped away, the frightened shadow left behind would have fallen in a heap.

His wife, especially, recognized his pathetic lack of substance; in fact, she married him because of it. That his need for approval invited manipulation had been to his credit. Her mother had taught her how to lure the right kind of man, a man like her ball-less father. When he overheard his fiancée brag to her mother about him before the wedding, it sounded more like pride of ownership than love.

Not until he had been on the island a month, isolated away from all that had previously defined him, was he startled by the emergence of a different personality that felt more authentic. In comparison, his previous life glared all the more absurd and laughable. There were periods of relapse, but it became ever easier to give himself over to this new unfettered lightness; a balloon released to the wind, its destination carelessly uncertain.

But the excitement with the new Legion was tinged by an underlying fear that it was a delusion, that the new persona taking hold was insanity. How would he know? Without knowing the old Legion for comparison, how would anybody here know? Or, as he finally concluded, in the short time he had left, would it even matter?

Paul is examining a fossilized trilobite and is startled when Legion yells, "Got it!" when he charges back out of the undergrowth. He falls in beside Legion and they resume their short walk.

"It's called Galion Bay because a Spanish ship tried to take refuge here during a hurricane back in the 1500s. Although the lagoon looked ideal from a distance, they discovered too late there is no entrance." Legion points to a froth of white on the far side of the bay. "The coral reef is less than six feet deep across the entire front. The ship broke up and everyone went overboard. The hurricane raked them across the coral like cheese on a grater. History has it that everyone died. But according to island legend, survivors are part of the ancestry of the locals. As with all shipwrecks, there are rumors of sunken treasure, but none has ever been found."

They walk through the sea grape trees onto a pristine beach bordering the lagoon on three sides. The reef out front completely dissipates the power of the ocean waves so there is only a slight ripple on the water. Black families are camped under the shade of sea grape trees, fathers cooking ribs over makeshift grills, mothers watching their toddlers play in the sand at the water's edge. Paul stops and stares at children, barely older than the toddlers, wading fifty feet from shore.

"This is called Baby Beach by the locals," Legion explains as they resume walking toward a shanty at the center of the beach. "There's probably two square miles in this lagoon. On the far side, there are areas that are six feet deep. But on this side, almost a square mile, the water is no deeper than your waist.

"A French concern bought this corner of the bay in the early '70s to build a resort." Legion points ahead to the massive concrete skeleton of a three-story hotel looming behind the shanty beach bar. "It was the most elite family resort in the Caribbean for maybe ten years. The French guests would hike over to Orient Beach to sunbathe on the deserted beach. That's how Orient Beach got its reputation for nudity. But then the hurricanes started coming—hit the island five times in seven years in the '90s. As soon as they got the hotel repaired after one, the next one would hit. In 1995, two hit a month apart, just before tourist season, and the owners finally gave up. This property has been tied up in the French courts ever since. Except for that concrete hulk and a few giant coconut palms they planted around the beach, everything reverted to nature.

"Anything of the slightest value was stolen by the locals. Pascal used scavenged wood to build his little café out front. Since there are no clear property owners, there is no worry about trespass. The locals get here by a sand road used during the resort's heyday, but there are no tour buses. The cruise ships don't promote this beach because there are no tourist traps to give them kickbacks."

Legion leads Paul under a thick canopy of flowering vines into the cool dark of Pascal's café. The structure would be considered a shed in Paul's native Tennessee. Salvaged light poles support a simple truss roof covered by shingled planks over the rear to protect Pascal's kitchen from rain. The front half of the roof is a thick mass of flowering vines entangled about exposed two-by-four rafters. The building's ends, facing up and down the beach, are the entrances. The bar that separates the kitchen from the dining area is made from repurposed marble kitchen counters. Four local men sit on stools with their backs to the bar watching windsurfers over the plywood half-wall.

Paul and Legion settle at one of the picnic tables randomly arranged on the sand floor. Legion waves two fingers in the air and a stocky man with stubble beard wearing a wife-beater T-shirt brings two bottled beers. "You want food?" he asks.

"What you cooking?" Legion returns.

"Conk fritters, like always."

"Sounds good for me," Legion says, smiling at Paul's yuck expression. "Bring my son here a burger and fries…and two more Caribe's when you bring the meals."

The stocky man looks back and forth between them with raised bushy eyebrows. "You have a son?" Without waiting for an answer, he turns back to the kitchen.

A little yellow bird with slate-colored wings helicopters from the vines above and dances around on the table pecking at crumbs. It reminds Paul of the candy chicks his mother bought him at Easter. Paul nudges a French fry left on the table toward the bird. It suspects a trap and jumps back into the vines. The bramble of vines above is full of these yellow birds getting lost among the flowers that are also yellow.

"Canaries?" Paul asks.

"No, they're called sugarbirds. They come here to eat too."

"They act like they own the place. Do you remember that pair of raccoons that raided our packs when we camped on the Fiery Gizzard Trail? Those guys let us know pretty quick who owned that campsite." Paul chuckles.

"I don't remember you thinking it was so funny at the time."

"They hissed like wildcats when we tried to run them off; scared the piss out of me."

"Paul, don't try to make it into something it wasn't. I know you hated the camping and fishing trips. I liked those things and thought you'd learn to like them too, but I know you never did. Thanks for going with me and not making a big fuss about it. I shouldn't have forced it on you. I feel bad about that."

"Yeah, I didn't like it at the time, but looking back there are some great memories. I wish I could have been a chip off the old block. We're just different."

"Where are you with that, Paul? I wish we could just talk, put it on the table. Trust me, I'm not trying to change anything. I've learned my lesson. I just want to help."

Paul looks hard at Legion knowing where this is headed, then out at the placid water, the children splashing and giggling. "What do you know about it? I don't need your help."

"I've known you were gay since before you even knew what it meant, when you were ten or so. Don't know how I knew; can't put my finger on any one thing. At that age, you didn't know about sex one way or the other. I thought I could correct it as you grew older. So there were the Boy Scouts you hated and the sports I nagged you into. But it was there already, from birth, I guess. I still don't understand, but I accept it now. I'm not glad you're gay because I think it makes your life hard, but it doesn't make me think less of you or anything like that."

"We're just different Dad, in all kinds of ways. If you're going to keep up the gay talk, I'll have to leave."

"Paul, you're the one that hasn't accepted it."

"Fuck you, Dad!"

Legion gives him a long stare before shifting the conversation. "So how's work? What's happening at the old factory these days?"

"It's good, I suppose. I don't work there anymore."

Legion's expression of surprise Paul knows is not authentic, just more of the duplicity he had grown to loathe. He had found out about Legion's agreement with the new owners to keep him at his job for at least a year. When that year was up, they had reorganized him out.

"Moving on? Great idea, actually. What are you into now?"

"Do you care?"

Legion turns his gaze toward the beach, a spectacular view, but Paul doesn't think he is seeing any of it.

"Life's short, Paul. Try not to waste it."

CHAPTER 19

The Animals

*P*aul turns to the shouting from behind the café's counter. A skinny man in surfer shorts and tie-dyed T-shirt bellows in French at Pascal's back as he cooks at the grill. Pascal patiently scoops the calamari onto a plate with a spatula and sets the plate aside. He reaches to a plank shelf above the grill and exchanges the spatula for a butcher knife before turning.

The skinny man, his dreadlocks flying, jumps out of Pascal's reach and scrambles around the end of the counter with Pascal in ponderous pursuit. The man still blusters defiantly as Pascal backs him out of the café onto a trail leading away from the beach. The man shuffles backward until his foot hangs on a root. As he twists to catch himself with his hands, Pascal leaps forward slashing with the knife. The young man recovers in a desperate dash through the grape trees.

Pascal wipes rivulets of sweat from his forehead with his apron as he lumbers back to his grill. He reaches into a cooler of ice and using an opener on the side pops the caps of two beers before bringing out their meals on a tray.

"Trouble with the help?" Legion asks.

The curls of hair leaking from the neck and armholes of Pascal's grease-splattered shirt mat against his body. "He is the cousin of my wife. I had to give him a chance even though I'd heard he was a thief."

After Pascal leaves, Paul asks, "Would he have used the knife if he had caught him?"

"Maybe not. But the guy wasn't hanging around to see."

"Will the police come to investigate?"

"Oh no. *Gendarmes* don't come down here. Besides, nothing happened. I didn't see anything and you didn't either. Even if he'd killed the guy, nobody would have seen it. You understand?"

After the meal, they watch the mothers in their cut-off jeans and halter tops playing in the water out front with their naked babies. Legion switches to drinking dark rum straight and Paul tries to keep up although he mixes his with Coke. The shadows of the palm trees elongate out into the placid lagoon marking the passage of time.

By late afternoon, Paul has a serious buzz and thinks Legion does too. Paul just wants to let the day wind down without any further fuss. He tries to remember jokes, one of the few passions he and Legion share. They had always swapped the funny stories they heard at work or school as a way to spend time together without things getting contentious. After a year apart, they both should have plenty stored up.

"This man woke up in a hospital after a car accident. He shouted 'Doctor, doctor, I can't feel my legs!' The doctor replied, 'Of course; I've cut off your arms.'"

Legion picks up on Paul's cue and has his first joke ready.

"Did you hear about the priest who went bird hunting with a member of his parish? When they flushed a covey of birds, the parishioner took a shot and missed. 'Damn!' he yelled. The priest crossed himself and forgave his salty language. When the next bird flew up, the man missed again. 'Hellfire!' he said before he caught himself. The priest wagged his finger. 'You must control your language, my son, or God will punish you. After the third miss, the priest heard the man mutter 'For Christ's sake!' under his breath. 'That's it,' the priest proclaimed. 'God will surely strike you down.' A dark cloud formed, thunder rumbled, and a bolt of lightning struck the priest. From the heavens, a deep voice boomed, 'Fuck me! Missed again.'"

The jokes would not have been so funny if they had been sober, but they laugh with open mouths, slapping the table with each punch line. When the jokes run out, they gasp with laughter at the snorting sound Legion makes when he laughs. The more they laugh, the more he snorts. Soon they are rolling on the sand floor.

Paul lies on his back, the flowers of the vine roof twirling above him, not sure he can get up. Pascal kicks sand in his face when he walks up and stands beside his head. Paul feels himself being rolled onto his stomach and hoisted by the back of his shirt onto his hands and knees. He waits for the touch of the blade that will slit his throat. Instead, Pascal continues to lift him under his arms to his feet. Paul teeters as if trying to stand on a beach ball. Pascal pushes him backward onto the bench seat of a picnic table. They look at Legion asleep on the sand floor.

"I think he's done for the day," Pascal advises.

"Get up, Dad," Paul demands with a familiar voice, his father's voice. His father's embarrassing behavior is empowering. "Legion, get up!"

Legion doesn't move and Paul looks more closely at his slack face before turning to Pascal. "Hey, man, I didn't know this could happen. He drinks continuously; how can he pass out?"

"He can drink rum all day. He does it here all the time. But then he's passed out before, too. It's not the rum, I think."

"Is he sick?"

"You don't know?"

Disheveled hair drapes across Legion's gaunt face. He looks like a decrepit drunk Paul might find sleeping it off in a Nashville alleyway. How do you tell the difference between old, sick and drunk? "He says he's dying."

"He is very sick, I think."

"Help me get him up. I've got to get him home."

"No, let him come around on his own. Stay away from him for a while. He's dangerous right now."

"Dangerous?"

"Believe me, it is true."

"You are afraid of him?"

"He is somebody else right now. That is the man I fear."

Paul looks from Pascal's serious expression to Legion curled up on his side.

"He tried to kill me a few weeks back. He fell over like this and I thought he had drunk too much. I kicked him and pulled him to his feet; told him to get his queer ass back over to Orient with his queer buddies. He stabbed me in the throat with a fork. Usually, I can see a man calculating before he decides to fight, but I didn't even know he had stabbed me until the fork was dangling from my neck."

Paul looks again at Legion, lying lifeless at their feet. "That didn't happen. Why are you telling me this lie?"

"Careful what you say. I'll mash you like a bug."

They stare at each other. Paul still does not believe, but also does not want to pick a fight with this gorilla. Pascal pulls a sweat rag from his neck and points to four pink spots in a line.

"He meant to tear out my jugular. The fork hit muscle, but he came very close." Pascal gingerly kicks at Legion's foot to see if there's any reaction. "I carry a switchblade; it's as much a part of me as my own hand. I had it pointed at his throat before I thought, before I even pulled the fork from my neck. He pushed his neck into the blade. And when I didn't plunge the knife, he grabbed my hand to do it himself. He said I couldn't kill him because he was already dead and I was stupid to threaten a dead man."

Pascal looks from Legion to Paul, "And he is right, I tried to kill him, but he hexed me and I couldn't. But he can kill me, I think."

"Why does he still come here? Why do you let him?"

"He came the next day after he stabbed me as if nothing happened. He asked why I had the bandage on my neck. He doesn't remember any of it."

The picnic table bounces when Pascal sits beside Paul. Legion's arms and knees remain pulled to his chest like a sleeping baby.

"I've never spoken to him about it. Nobody that was here will bring it up—I won't allow it. As far as he knows, it never happened. He won't remember this either, I think."

Legion's legs suddenly thrust out stiff, his toes pointed, causing Pascal to jump to his feet, switchblade already open. Every muscle in Legion's body is taut, his body twitching as muscles spasm. Gradually the seizure relaxes and his legs and arms retract back to the fetal position.

"Legion?" Paul reaches forward to take an arm. At his touch, Legion jumps to his hands and knees like a startled cat. His head slumps, his eyelids closed as if what awakened his body has not yet reached his brain. Slowly the eyelids creep up like window shades into a menacing grin that causes Paul to freeze. Something primitive glowers back, a predator nonchalantly holding its helpless prey under its paws. Paul is transfixed as long as those eyes engage his, but he can't make himself look away.

Pascal jerks Paul out of Legion's reach. "Leave him alone. It is not over."

The eyes continue to hold Paul even after the eyelids slowly close. He knows if he moves, the eyelid will fly up again and teeth will rip at his throat. As Legion's face goes limp, Paul senses a demon slinking away, leaving only the hull of Legion's body to crumple on the sand floor.

Paul is totally sober now—beyond sober. With his body throbbing with adrenaline, intense sensations flood over him. The light breeze sweeping in from the beach feels as tangible as a feather being dragged across his face. Sights and sounds, unnoticed before, are suddenly stark. His eyes dart to the flutter of a bird, a child's laugh; everything demanding his attention at once. Paul risks a look at Pascal, wanting to ask something, to have it explained.

Legion's body shudders as if being struck by some unseen club. Eyeballs wallow behind half-closed eyelids. He becomes a beheaded snake slithering in the sand. Struggling to his feet, he stumbles in a circle searching for a way out. He staggers onto the beach in the direction of the trail back to Orient Bay. The children stop their play and stare warily as he passes. Paul follows at a distance.

At the far end of the coral outcrop, with the pounding surf beside him sending shimmering sprays of gold and silver nuggets at the setting sun, Legion turns and waits. "Come on, Paul...keep up," he yells above the crescendo.

Legion stands with head slumped as Paul cautiously approaches. With a sudden lunge, Legion sweeps Paul's head into the crook of his arm and clamps his head against his chest. Paul's muscles coil for escape, yet he can't persuade his body to resist.

"I'm a drunk," Legion says. "I'm sorry, but your father's a drunk."

Legion releases him and takes the lead off the trail onto the narrow path through the undergrowth. Branches fly back into Paul's face and fangs of thorny vines attack his legs. It is twilight when they arrive back at the cabin. When they emerge from the thicket beside the cabin, Lily Ana, backlit by the overhead light inside, is scowling through the open window above the kitchen sink.

"I'm drunk," Legion announces as he throws back the screen door. "And my head hurts and I want sex. Paul could you leave us for a little while?"

"Paul, stay where you are. This sot couldn't do anything with me anyway."

Legion stops abruptly and stands board-stiff, returning her glare. "Paul, it is better to dwell in a wilderness than with a contentious woman." The screen door spring screeches again as Legion storms back outside.

"Angry woman!" she yells after him. "You know the verse as well as I do."

When there is no reply, Lily Ana goes to the door searching the shadows thrown through the doorway. "Legion?" she calls softly.

"He got sick," Paul tells her.

"So he threw up? Went a little too far this time."

He wants to correct her, tell her what really happened, but there doesn't seem to be any words that fit.

Legion's head is a balloon floating in a black void. His hands reach to his neck for assurance his body is still attached. Warm water rushes onto his legs and he feels the familiar crunch of wet sand underfoot. Ahead, starlight reflecting on the foam at the leading edges of the surf looks like ghostly snakes squirming and hissing. In the distance the outline of black mountains with the Milky Way above seems vaguely familiar, a distant memory. He continues to shuffle forward, looking about for something he recognizes, trying to remember how he got here.

Mixed in the dank air he detects a musk scent and remembers a bear that had approached his car while the family drove through the Smoky Mountains. Then too, the smell of the animal had alerted him before it reared onto the open window of his car door.

Legion's head twists from side to side, squinting into the black. The animal's eyes would be adapted for hunting in the dark. It is looking at him now, following him. He is overcome with the impulse to run, but in what direction? The thrash of every wave sounds like the charge of an animal. His heart races with panic; his leg muscles twitch with the overload of adrenaline.

It attacks from behind with claw-studded paws, pushing him down onto his stomach. When Legion flips to his back, it straddles him, the faint reflection of starlight in its eyes. A liquid tongue explores his face, feeling in the dark where to sink its fangs. Legion squinches his face against the drool from its mouth, the putrid smell of its breath.

And then it leaps away. The smell is still strong and Legion imagines it sitting patiently beside him on its haunches, in no hurry to finish off its prey. Legion's annoyance at the animal's self-assurance starts to overcome his terror. He tries to get up, go on the attack, but his muscles are immobilized like in a dream. He can't even yell his contempt at the animal.

It nuzzles him, prodding about his body with its nose. Then there is the ripping sensation of his stomach being torn open. A head bores into him eating his entrails. Fear is gone now that his death is inevitable and his temper rages at the animal eating his still pulsing organs. His hands grab the head gorging inside him and wrest the bloody jaws apart.

Blackness turns into ethereal white. Legion lies on his back afraid to move. The pulse throbbing in his ears makes him think he is still alive. The white billows out with each breath and he realizes a sheet is covering his face. Again, he wonders if he is alive.

The smell of the animal is gone, but the memory of it is still vivid. He cautiously pulls the sheet down. His hands and arms are streaked brown with encrusted blood. Throwing the sheet aside, he checks his stomach. It is sore, like it always is, but there is no sign of a wound.

Lily Ana, asleep beside him in their bed, begins to stir. There's a gurgling snore from Paul scrunched on the couch against the far wall. Legion eases out of bed and stumbles to the bathroom to look in the mirror.

"Legion! Legion, what's happened?" Lily Ana's voice startles him and he swings the bathroom door shut.

He doesn't know how to answer. He turns on the shower, but it is too late to pretend not to have heard. "What?" he yells back.

"What's on the sheet? Is this blood? Are you hurt?"

"It's nothing. Don't worry. I got a little cut on the walk yesterday. It started bleeding in the night."

Legion opens the medicine cabinet behind the mirror and takes out his safety razor. He unscrews the handle and dumps the blade onto his hand. He slashes the blue veins on the heel of his left palm. In the shower, a rivulet of fresh red flows with the brown he washes from his arms.

CHAPTER 20

André

Betty stands in the doorway of La Belle Creole watching the nudists parade at the waterline, some toward the far end of the beach and others returning. Their giant shadows, thrown by the rising sun, undulate on the bay; the overlapping shadows of couples have two heads and many legs. Betty knows most of these sunbathers, but from where she stands, they're just tan blurs against a turquoise backdrop. Betty is nearsighted. But Betty Boop doesn't wear glasses and contacts at the beach are a bad idea.

With no one to hold her hand, she feels like an interloper. As she approaches the returning couples, she exchanges greetings but does not stop to chat like she would if there was someone with her.

Away from the shore in the powdery white sand, she spots the familiar swatches of yellow over green, the uniform of the resort's beachboys. That would be André opening the rental umbrellas and unstacking the beach chairs, always his first tasks of the day. He stops for a moment when she waves but doesn't wave back— maybe he didn't see her after all. Her meandering gait turns into purposeful strides towards him. A smile grows on her face as she thinks about André and their unlikely friendship. They are like brother and sister—or like two sisters would be more correct. André is grimacing with effort as he screws an umbrella shaft into the sand when she prances in front of him.

André greets her with a forced smile. "Hello, beautiful. I like your outfit this morning."

She twirls around as if spinning the hem of a new sundress instead of nothing at all. "You like the color? I couldn't think which lipstick would match."

They both like dresses. Sometimes they would take André's old Saab into Marigot to shop together, and later, to his little house in Grand Case, to try on the outfits they had picked out, play dress-up, and giggle the afternoon away.

"What do you think of my new guy?" Betty asks.

"Which one? The one you came down here with, or the guy you were with yesterday morning?"

"Paul, the guy you saw yesterday. Quite a hunk, huh?"

"He's a looker all right. I think I'm in love too. But you've got no chance with him."

"You're jealous! What if I told you I have a date with him tonight?"

"I'm still saying I'd have a better chance."

Betty's smugness turns to open-mouthed astonishment. "Oh, no... you're wrong. He's my Prince Charming. He's not like that. I'll have him in my bed before the sun sets. I'll tell you all about it in the morning."

"Oh, you might have sex, but don't get any ideas about Princess Charming falling in love with you."

"You don't know. How would you know?"

"I can't tell you how I know, but I do. It takes one to know one."

Anger flicks across Betty's eyes before the composed smile returns. She and André have the same taste in dresses, but she had never thought about them having the same taste in men. He was wrong about Paul and would learn it the hard way if he tried to flirt.

"Have you seen Beau? I've got nobody to walk with me this morning."

Startle replaces André's smug smile. His gaze, instantly bleary, falls to her feet. His shoulders slowly slump forward as if he is being deflated.

"Whatever is wrong, André?" She pulls him close, pressing his face to her chest, patting the back of his head like she would console a child.

"Beau is dead," he sobs.

She pushes him away, holding him at arm's length, searching the eyes looking up from his bowed head. "No! What do you mean? He's not dead."

"I found him this morning floating in the surf. I dragged him back behind the dune before anybody could see. I'll have to bury him when I'm through here," he says sniffling.

Betty drops her arms, turning to the dune behind the beach, her lips pressed into an angry line.

"You don't want to see him. He's all messed up."

"What do you mean? What happened?"

"I don't know what happened. His snout is all mangled. His mouth is wrenched open, his lower jaw just dangling." André shudders.

Betty continues looking at the top of the dune, imagining what lies behind. "Nobody could do that to Beau. He would eat anybody alive who attacked him."

"I think somebody drowned him first and then did that to him. If somebody got him in the water—"

"But who would do that?" André's bottom lip puffs out as their eyes question each other. Beau swam beside his human buddies every day. The day-trippers pointed it out to each other with astonishment. But for the residents, it was just a normal event.

The face-off between Beau and Paul the previous morning flashes into Betty's memory and her hands rise to her mouth. "Do you think it was Paul? He was mean to Beau yesterday. Beau may have chased him into the water again and Paul got the best of him."

"Could be. But Beau wouldn't have gotten in the water with Paul; it would have had to be someone Beau trusted. And besides, Paul would not be the type to do the other part—mutilating him afterward."

The return of her anger with André intensifies her scowl. "How would you know what Paul would do? You two have never even met." She wants to slap him—to slap somebody.

CHAPTER 21

The Demon

Legion doesn't join the morning walk. He doesn't feed the fish. Where did the blood come from? Was it all a dream? The questions plague him, but the answers scare him more.

Lily Ana comes to the cabin after the breakfast rush. She pulls his arm across the kitchen table and removes the bandage, working without speaking, methodical, efficient. The cut gaps open, but the bleeding has stopped.

"You need stitches," she says.

He looks away. Her head moves closer to chastise him, but then she sits back with a sigh to continue her work: folding the old dressing into a wad, washing with peroxide, applying ointment, wrapping again.

"How did it happen?" she asks again. "Do you not remember?" His eyes close. "You should have a tetanus shot. At least, you should do that. I'll call a cab."

"No," he says.

She stands, looking down at him, rigid, hands on her hips. "Sometimes..." the anger in her voice is barely controlled. "Do it for me. See a doctor. Before it gets worse." She waits for an answer and then turns and pushes through the screen door. The spring screeches as it pulls out, then screeches again as it contracts. The door slams.

After lunch, he goes to the bar for a drink. It is not the liquor that causes these blackouts. Perhaps the alcohol even helps. He asks Lily Ana for a double. She scowls; nothing left to say. He pours his drink in a paper cup and walks onto the beach to avoid her glare.

The sun is bright, too bright. Multicolored sparks twinkle at the edge of his vision. Laughter comes from a group of bodies passing by. Someone greets him and he mumbles something back.

He wades out chest deep where the waves begin to curl into breakers. The water buffets him forward then back as he searches the beach. Voyeurs bussed over from the cruise ships walk at the water's edge gawking at the spraddle-legged nudists as they nap.

Again the questions pester him. He searches his sketchy memory. The smell of the animal that stalked him is familiar. If the blood was not his, it must be from the animal.

He swims down to Pedro's where Beau usually lunches on discarded rib bones. For an hour he watches the beach and then comes ashore and walks back toward the café. The Flores girls are tossing a Frisbee between them. Beau would never miss that.

The reflection of the sun off the sand makes his head hurt. Legion ducks under one of the resort's beach umbrellas and slumps onto a lounge.

"It needs to happen now—before it gets worse," he mumbles. He slumps onto his back and throws an arm across his eyes. "Before the demon hurts somebody."

"Mr. Legion."

His eyes pop open to the yellow canopy of the umbrella. He remembers where he is.

"Mr. Legion. Are you okay?"

He sits up. His eyes will focus now. André walks around from behind the lounge so Legion can see him.

"André. What time is it?"

"Almost six. Time for me to be putting things up."

"André...? André, have I been here all day?" Legion shakes his head. "I can't remember..."

"Everything is fine, Mr. Legion. You took the spot I set up for Wilma. I couldn't wake you, so I set her up in a better location. She's okay with it."

"Damn my sorry soul. I'll apologize to her tomorrow. Thanks for covering for me."

CHAPTER 22

The Couples

Reflections from the neon lights of the cafés surrounding the wharf wrinkle in the water in front of their table. The waiter removes the leftovers of their smoked salmon and salads. They sip the last glasses of the Merlot. Betty had advised against Merlot with salmon, but Paul had gone with it anyway.

At a table to Paul's right, a blonde woman with penciled dark eyebrows and a swarthy man with slicked-back black hair lean into each other, their eyes engaged like there is nobody else in the universe. Paul tries not to look at them directly, but he can hear the seductive smiles in the lilt of their voices.

To his left, a mulatto woman sits with a squat Latino man whose sunbaked skin is darker than hers. They both lean back in their chairs listening to each other attentively and don't appear romantically involved. The man is animated trying to make some point while the woman's voice sounds skeptical. On the back of the man's snagged and stained T-shirt is the picture of a sea turtle. Above the turtle is printed STAFF; below the turtle, *La Grenadines,* apparently the name of a yacht. The woman is wearing a newer version of the same shirt.

Both couples speak in French. Not that Paul can understand anything, but the melodious voices are soothing to him. When he closes his eyes, he imagines an opera, half spoken and half sung.

"What are you thinking?" Betty asks.

"I'm thinking how lucky you are to have met me."

"I'm thinking you're not going to be so lucky if you keep ignoring me."

"Only kidding. I'm the lucky one."

"Then why do I feel like trash when you look at me?"

Paul reaches for her hand, but she pulls it back.

He straightens in his chair. "Do you want to leave then?"

"No," she says, although her face is still sullen, downcast. "I just want to be courted." She motions with her eyes to the next table. The swarthy man had intertwined his arms with the blonde over the top of the table, their faces only inches apart. They sound like a prelude played with flute and oboe.

Paul forces a smile. "You won't let me touch you. We can do that if you want."

"No, we can't."

He reaches for her hand again and again she pulls back.

"You don't love me," Betty says with a pout.

"We just met. I don't know you."

"We can't do that because we're not in love."

"We just met! Can't you give it some time?" Paul snatches the napkin off his lap and throws it on his plate while looking about the café, everywhere but at Betty.

"You could never love me; I can tell already. And I don't love you."

"What do you want, for Christ's sake?" He shifts his chair to face the harbor so he won't have to face Betty and can't see the couple. The boats in the harbor jerk at their moorings like edgy circus animals amid the fantasia of color reflected in the water by the lights.

"I'm ready to go," she says dabbing at her eyes with a napkin.

"Me too." Paul waves for the check.

"Don't be mad. I'm sorry. I'm in a funk, I guess."

"You weren't in a funk before dinner."

"No, it was them."

When Paul looks over; the couple is all but having sex on the table.

"Then let's get out of here. I'll take you back to the resort," he says pushing his chair back.

"Please don't be mad." Betty is trying to smile now. "Will you stay with me tonight?"

"For Christ's sake!"

"In the dark, we can pretend to be in love."

CHAPTER 23

Friends

Betty is awake, lying on her back. *It's the difference between tofu and prime rib; they'll both keep you from starving, but...* When she turns her head, Paul is also looking at the slow twirl of the ceiling fan, probably thinking something similar.

When the cabin door creaks, they both turn their heads to see the outline of André backlit in the doorway squinting into the darkened room.

"You OK? I didn't see you on your morning walk and got worried," he calls in.

"Come kiss me good morning, André." Betty sits up and beckons with both hands. André tiptoes on bare feet, his eyes cautious. "Paul, this is my friend André; you saw him on the beach the day we met."

Paul turns back to the ceiling fan. "The pretty one—I remember. Another of your boyfriends?"

"Don't be mad. It's not like that—"

"She's like my sister," André says leaning down to kiss Betty on both cheeks while still looking at Paul. "I love her, but we're not lovers, if you know what I mean."

Betty smiles that André is so bold to a stranger, so open about being gay. She reaches behind his head and pulls him down for a kiss on the lips.

The bed bounces as Paul flips to his side to face them. Betty continues to hold André's lips to hers, her eyes shut, shoulders tense, waiting for Paul to yell, or maybe slap her. She wants André to see Paul's jealousy. When nothing happens, she releases André and opens her eyes. The boys' faces are only inches apart. But there is not the glare of hatred she had planned for.

Without even looking to her for permission, André strips down his bathing trunks and slips under the sheet facing her. His face nestles between her chin and breast, arm stretched down her body, his hand at the fluff below her stomach. The boys' eyes are still locked, neither even glancing at her. Paul positions his body toward hers exactly the same as André, as if answering his challenge. When their hands meet on her stomach, they tussle like small animals. The struggle ends with their hands lightly clasped.

It is unbearable. In a rage, their arms are thrown aside as she scoots off the end of the bed taking the sheet with her. A withering glower answers their startle. Wrapping the sheet around herself, she stomps to the bathroom and slams the door.

A flush of pink underlies the tan face in the vanity mirror. *Humiliating!* She should go back out there and slap them both. The flat of her hand bangs the door instead. Grabbing a sundress from a hook on the back of the door, she storms into the bedroom.

She stands at the foot of the bed, looking back and forth between them. They sit on the sides of the bed with their feet on the floor, their heads anxiously turned to her with contrite expressions like toddlers awaiting punishment.

She tries to renew her hard frown but instead finds herself fighting to keep the corners of her mouth from curling into a grin. These boys who will never be men are also slaves to sex, however misguided. It is not like they have chosen each other over her; this just isn't about her anymore.

The initial indignity subsides, replaced by jealousy that love has chosen them and not her. What these two felt when they looked into each other's eyes was unmistakable, that moment of rapture when all else vanishes, when passion overwhelms and demands to be satisfied. She has known that white-hot euphoria only rarely, but the memory lingers in her body like an addiction.

Her expression softens. "I'm going for a walk," she says.

"I'm sorry, please don't be mad," André entreats.

"It's just me...disappointed, I guess."

"Don't leave." André reaches for her hand. "You're my best friend."

Paul's face is slack, eyes full of question, apparently not knowing how he should feel or what to say.

"I'm the odd man out here; you two want to be alone," she says.

"Please stay." André pulls her onto the bed so she is kneeling between them.

"Neither of you wants me, I know. How can this work?"

André's pleading face turns into a mischievous grin. He had already been thinking about that.

"Then can everybody agree to at least play fair?" André nods his head vigorously and she and André look to Paul. He stares back, startled eyes shifting between them before his head also nods. She shoves them roughly onto their backs and dives between them. She twists onto her back, squirming her hips for them to give her more room.

She knows she is not the source of their craving, but also that her body and experience is ideally suited to quench their lust. What goes through their heads when they look at each other, or at her, is mysterious; however, their bodies are those of men and surprisingly simple to operate.

Their separate fires become one consuming blaze, leaving their sweltering bodies tangled like corpses tossed in a heap by some horrendous violence.

CHAPTER 24

Nature

$\mathcal{B}$etty's eyes fly open in a start, not instantly knowing where she is or whose arms entwine her. They lie to either side facing her, their arms draped across her to touch each other, eyes closed in exhausted slumber. Her body aches after the contortions and strain, but her lips stretch into a contented smile. She has never felt so thoroughly ravished.

Suddenly she bolts upright, her face full of fright again. In the heat of the moment, she had forgotten about protection. At that instant she knows she is pregnant. It isn't a passing thought that it is possible, but a certainty.

She looks back at them, still in sex-induced comas, innocently unaware of the portent of what they've done. She wouldn't even know which of them was the father. Of course, neither of them would want a baby, nor be of any value in raising one. There would have to be an abortion when she got back home. Neither of them needs to ever know.

She lowers herself back between them and stares into the stifling silence. Until now, pregnancy had been abstract, something stupid girls had to contend with. She had often doubted her body was even capable. She looks down at her breasts that would swell, then to her flat stomach. The nucleus of a human being grows already, nurtured independent of her control like a parasite.

There is a baby. The thought brings apprehension, but also a twinge of excitement. The initial horror morphs into fascination with being part of a miracle. Her distraught face relaxes into a radiant smile. *Does conception alter a woman's brain as well as her body?*

She scoots to the end of the bed, picks up the sundress off the floor, and slips it over her head. The boys still sleep as she eases open the screen door. Her eyes squint against the glare of the sugar-white sand. There is barely room at the beach to walk between the resort's yellow umbrellas and lounge chairs. She throws the dress on an empty chair before wading in up to her breasts. The water is warm and soothing as she splashes off the lovemaking.

Looking back toward the beach she recognizes most of the crowd of sunbathers. They'll be eager for their usual gossip—not what she wants right now. The raft anchored in deeper water is empty, so she swims out.

She stretches on her back, eyes closed to the sun, letting the undulations of the waves under the floating platform rock her to sleep.

André's leg is crossed over his when he wakes and Paul lies still, staring at the ceiling, not sure what he should do. He throws André's leg aside and pushes him to the edge of the bed.

André startles to his feet, looks back at Paul; the beginning of a smile until he reads the anger in Paul's face.

"Look, kiddo…André, or whatever, I'm not used to sharing my whores. This room is rented for the day; you need to move on."

André jumps across the bed trying to punch but there is only a flailing slap. Paul catches his arm and holds him as he gets to his feet. "I should beat you to a pulp," he says before throwing André onto the bed.

André sobs facedown into the pillow.

"I'm not gay. Understand?"

André turns onto his back, his face a snarl. "I know what you are. You're mean. Leave her alone. You don't deserve to touch her—or me." André pulls on his swim trunks and T-shirt as he rushes to the door.

Paul follows, "Wait," not knowing what he will do if André stops. But André doesn't stop, pushes wide the screen door, and trots onto the beach. He goes down to the water's edge, looks back and forth, then runs up the beach. Paul expects it to be Betty he is running to, but instead, he runs into the arms of a fat black woman carrying straw bags over her shoulders. She wraps André in her massive arms. She lays her cheek atop his head; he sobs against her breast. No questions asked; no explanations given. Her eyes glisten, sad because he is sad, not needing to know why.

Paul imagines how André's tears might feel on her breast, the feel of his hair between her fingers. Isolation, emptiness returns like the creep of night. Tears blear his eyes also.

After napping away the middle of the day, Betty flips to her stomach and rests her chin on her folded arms. The gentle tilting of the floating platform makes the shore rather than the platform seem to rock. Her girlfriends stand in knee-deep water in floppy hats, paper cups in hand, tanning themselves in the reflection of the sun off the water as they talk. *Which of them has children?* But asking one of them what to expect during pregnancy was out of the question. They would want to know about the father and that discussion was off the table. Betty didn't want their smirks or sympathy.

A smile creeps onto her lips as she thinks about André, her usual confidant. It seems absurd that she can discuss with a gay man what must be hidden from her women friends. Who knows what he would do if he thought he was a father? He would have to be spared.

She was on her own to think through this, make sense of what happened, decide what to do next. Her mind rehashes the morning's events, not as a participant, but as a cold-eyed observer. Not only the boys but herself, as well, become specimens under a microscope to be probed. This discipline of thought, the ability to gain emotional distance, she had learned was essential to understanding complex behavior.

She sighs. The flip side of this detachment had proved disastrous for her personal life. Understanding has its price. Over the years, it had become ever harder to simply enjoy passions without stepping back for analysis. Orgasm, once a rocket into outer space, was usually faked these days. The bliss of falling in love seemed irretrievably beyond her grasp. It is the examined life that is not worth living. If she were granted a do-over, she would gladly become a dental hygienist, a stripper at a truck-stop lounge, anything but a psychologist. But there was no putting the genie back in the bottle.

Betty thinks back to the beginning, to the fascinated girl who interned during college as a clerk for the most prestigious law firm in Chicago. Their criminal law practice was a distillery for the irrational and bizarre. Insatiable curiosity about the firm's clients caused her to change her college major from pre-law to psychology.

Their law firm was top tier, with lawyers chosen from the highest percentile of the best law schools. But, as could be expected with these engorged egos and millionaire pedigrees, they had little understanding or empathy for the sleazy lives of their clients. Even before graduate school, she had her own office and the lawyers made appointments with her for help with their messy cases. A side benefit had been a full-boat grant to pursue her penchant for psychology to the doctoral level.

Her first sabbatical had been to Africa to study ethology. An enclave of scientists had set up shop in the habitat of the common chimpanzee on the west bank of the Congo River. They would cross the river in dugout canoes to study the bonobo, a separate species of chimps that had split from common chimps a million years ago. Humans branched from a common ancestor five million years prior to that.

While the common chimp is aggressive in protecting territory and possessive of the females, bonobo behavior is more like a hippie commune. Bonobo females are always available for a tumble with whomever, and the males don't act like the females are a finite resource to be hoarded. Although the bonobos seem the happier of the two, their free-spirit behavior apparently is not favored by evolution and they are on their way to extinction. The human complement of instincts contains a smattering of both chimp species, plus some unique to humans.

Of all the apes, only humans form long-term relationships with their mates. Many lower animals, however, do bond as couples and jointly raise offspring. Who knows what a swan couple feels when they pair? It appears to be the equivalent of humans *falling in love,* but attributing romantic love to animals is sappy anthropomorphism. For swans, the instinct to bond must be satisfied before the instinct for sex can be initiated. This rational ordering assures necessary protection for the offspring. The comparison to humans breaks down at this point.

Much of what she has learned about love—too much—has been firsthand at the expense of heartache. Some men arouse in her the raw urges of sex, while with others she feels a bond forming even without sex. At Orient, she is attracted to Paul's father, Legion. He is a useless old drunk, but there is something about him that touches her vitally. This is not unique to her; sexy young girls fall in love with ugly old men every day. It is frightening to realize she has no control over whom instinct chooses for her. Her eyes clench at the sudden image of waking up beside Legion every morning.

Paul, on the other hand, is handsome, young and virile—every girl's fantasy. But he is also shallow and callous. She had known quickly enough they would never bond. Girls pick up on these signals quickly and she bets Paul's love life is a series of first dates. A marriage made in Heaven would be if the instincts for sex and bonding align for a couple. It happens—but rarely, and never for her.

Instincts, as with physical traits, are hard-wired into the genetic code—most obvious and their usefulness apparent. Others are as mysterious as the human appendix and tailbone. Modesty does not exist in other animals nor is there any known cause for it to have evolved into humans. This mystery is why Betty first came to Orient Beach three years ago and why she keeps coming back—to gain insight into modesty by observing nudists. In her mind, the nudists' behaviors should be the norm unless modesty serves some as yet unidentified advantage to survival or sexual selection. Her latest speculation is that clothes are the equivalent of the trinkets collected by bowerbirds to impress their mates.

Homosexuality is also a paradox she studies at Orient Beach. In surveys, two percent identify themselves as homosexual, although less intrusive studies estimate the number at six percent. Up to a third report same-sex experiences or desires, and if categorized, would be bisexual. Paul probably.

But homosexuality is not just a human phenomenon. One summer at Orient, she observed seagulls and albatrosses bonding into same-sex pairs about a third of the time. In theory, it shouldn't happen at all. This tendency is a reproductive dead-end and should have erased itself from the genetic code millions of years ago. So is it just a failure of the mechanism of evolution? Or is homosexuality preserved in DNA because it serves some function critical to the larger society, like worker bees in a hive? Another mystery. Where is Darwin when you need him?

And now she has the opportunity to study the maternal instinct firsthand. Already she feels hormones reformatting her brain. Is it worth the twenty years of raising a kid to learn this? Would it even be an authentic experience to raise a child without a partner? Yes, single mothers are becoming the norm, but none of them will say it is preferred or that it feels natural. She has given up on falling in love, but maybe she can entice a man to fall in love with her—

marry her. The thought of living with a man she doesn't love causes a shudder. Plus there would be the guilt of lying.

It is Paul then. Homosexual, bisexual, who knows—not even him it seems. If she were going to condemn a man to a loveless relationship, he would be the most deserving and the least harmed. Besides, the baby is his anyway—at least it wouldn't be hard to convince him of that. He might step up, or maybe not. There is only one way to find out.

She jumps to her feet and dives in, emerging in a crawl stroke toward the shore. Her girlfriends watch as she pushes out of the surf onto the beach, her face an intense grimace. No one calls after her. She snatches the sundress as she jogs toward the cabins. Struggling it down over her wet body isn't worth the time. When she swings open the screen door of her cabin, there are only the sheets strung across the floor.

Paul is gone.

Chapter 25

The Heavens

Legion leads Lily Ana by her hand closer to the water's edge so the surf will run up their legs as they walk. Ahead, the blue roofs over tan walls of the Mount Vernon Hotel stretch atop the bluff overlooking the far end of the beach. The windows reflect the setting sun like an array of mirrors.

"How do you feel?" she asks.

"I'm good. Feel perfect. How about you?"

"I worry. You're losing weight."

"That's a good thing. Thanks."

"You know it's not a good thing."

"You're gaining weight and that's a good thing. Remember that scarecrow when you first arrived? I could count your ribs—"

"Stop it. I want to know how you are really."

A good woman who needs to hear his lie, even though she won't believe it. He tries to deflect Lily Ana's glower with a playful smile.

"I get scared, Legion. I can't stand the thought of going on without you. I have to think of later, when we'll be together again in Heaven."

The heaven game again. Frustration turns to anger. Why can't he just speak his mind without weighing each word to coddle her? "I won't be going. You'll have to start being a bad girl if you want to see me later."

"Stop it! If anybody deserves Heaven, it's you."

"I don't believe. You know that."

"It doesn't matter. God sees your heart. You'll be there, even if I don't make it. Promise you won't take up with some angel. I can't stand that thought either."

"Well now, you're ruining paradise for me. I'm secretly a Muslim and plan on killing some infidels in the name of Allah so I can have the seventy-two virgins. Unless you become a virgin again, you'll stand no chance."

Her hand becomes wooden in his grasp. She looks away. Legion would cut out his own tongue if he could have the words back. She doesn't deserve to be the victim of his snide sarcasm. He's never seen her cry and doesn't want to see it now.

"Look. When I'm gone you'll be filthy rich—and Zuzu too. There's a million in insurance. My lawyer has it all taken care of. You'll move to one of those cliff-side villas overlooking Bay Rouge and have the beachboys over every night. You'll forget about me soon enough."

She squeezes his hand so tight it hurts. It seems the harder he tries to steer around her melancholy, the more misery he inflicts. It's frustrating, yet also heartening, that he cannot simply purchase contentment for her. Money could not buy her at the start, nor will it soothe her at the end. If she were that superficial, she would never have allowed herself to fall in love with a dying man anyway. Compared to her, his past lovers had been empty shadows.

Some people are not brave enough to fall in love. When the party is over, someone must pay—an unavoidable yin-yang. It is unfair that Lily Ana alone must foot the bill for the love they share, while death will give him a free pass. He imagines how he would react if the tables were turned and he was forced to watch her slowly waste away. His eyes clench.

"Thank God..." he mumbles.

"What?"

"Lily, don't make me lie. Don't ask me to say what you want to hear. I just can't turn it on and off like that."

He wishes he could believe—for her sake. He had considered lying, but that would make him deserving of Hell even if there isn't one. He could try to explain his thinking again, but he won't.

Lily Ana's beliefs will not permit his life to come to a simple end. She must save his soul. But it is her salvation that concerns him. He wants peace for her, not in the afterlife, but now.

Neither gambles with upsetting the other by talking further. They walk silently with synced strides, hands clasped, arms swaying like a rope tethering them together.

Once, when they had first met, Legion had attacked her chaste piety as a strategy to shame her into his bed. The ploy had backfired. He soon began to admire her steadfast convictions in the face of his reason. He became envious of her religious certainties, so natural to her, which he could never have. In the beginning, he had ridiculed her convictions; now he would fight any man who did the same.

Legion understands the lure of Heaven. It is a comforting hope. But wanting to believe is not belief. He suspects many of the devout are not bestowed with the gift either, but fake convictions to others—themselves—even to God in prayer. However, for Lily Ana, the afterlife is as definite as the next wave.

How many versions of Heaven are there? Paradise morphs to suit each individual. His reward will be nothing. He is pretty sure he can count on that. When he can get his mind around the concept of nothing, it seems superior to what religion offers anyway. It calms him to think of it now; it is what gets him through the tough spots—that it will end. The torments of his body will cease. The recriminations that harp incessantly in his brain—injustices he has received or those he has inflicted on others—will dissipate like smoke in the wind. A smile overtakes him as he realizes this is just another variety of Heaven. She thinks he doesn't believe in salvation but he does.

"I'm not scared, Lily; you think I am, but I'm not. If I've got it wrong and I wind up in Hell, then so be it. If I wasn't created perfect and God wants to torture me for His mistake, then there is nothing I can do about it."

"Please quit." She squeezes his hand but won't look at him. "Why can't I talk to you without you getting this way?"

"I don't think I'd want to be around a god like that anyway. Even if there were a Heaven, I wouldn't want to go. When I read the Bible God doesn't come across as such a nice guy. I'd probably punch Him in the nose."

"Legion, listen to yourself—all this anger toward God. Do you know what that means?" Her face brightens. "You believe."

"Of course not. Don't be silly."

"You've been ranting about God ever since I've known you."

"So?"

"How can you be so mad at someone who doesn't exist?"

They stop and stare at each other a moment and then she smiles. She takes the lead now and pulls him along, her pace lively for the first time.

Warmth from inside tingles his skin. His eyes blear. He doesn't deserve her. His Heaven is right now, on this lovely beach, holding her hand. If only this moment could be extended to eternity. He wants to squeeze her, force his joy into her. But he doesn't; she wouldn't understand. He walks silently beside her, their fingers interlaced, together and yet each alone, unable to speak a common language.

When they turn at the boulders for their walk back toward the café, Legion notices the wind and the surf have slackened. The undulating sea beyond the breakers is purple, a mixed reflection of the orange sun and blue sky. The waves scouring the sand in front of them have left a froth of bubbles. Each bubble reflects a miniature world of him and Lily Ana with the Mount Vernon as a backdrop. A million tiny worlds.

The sun squats atop the dune behind the beach like an orange tabby cat. A stick figure, silhouetted against the sun, jumps up and down waving both arms in exaggerated arcs.

"Is that Paul?" he asks Lily Ana.

She follows his point and studies the figure with squinting eyes. "Yes, I think so. Something's wrong. It's Zuzu!"

They both start to run but Legion slows after a few strides, gasping, heart pounding. Whatever Paul is waving about wouldn't be helped by a heart attack.

CHAPTER 26

The Birth

Zuzu, that pregnant girl who hangs around the café freaking everybody out, taps on the doorframe and steps through the open doorway. The combination of white hair and dark tan makes her look like a photographic negative. She is barefoot, but at least wearing clothes—a pleated smock with the front bulged out below her breasts.

Slumped on the couch, beer in hand, Paul waits for her to say something. "There's nobody here," he says finally. "I mean, I'm here, but Legion and Lily Ana are walking."

She nods her head, but her face looks bewildered like she doesn't understand his English.

"On the beach…walking," he repeats, pointing out the door, then making two fingers of one hand walk across the palm of the other.

She glances over her shoulder, at the path that leads to the beach. Her hands grasp the sides of the bulge in her dress when she faces him again. "I wouldn't make it. Can I sit down and wait?"

Before he can answer, she takes unsteady steps to the couch. As she lowers herself gingerly to sit, her water breaks. It floods onto Paul's bare feet.

Zuzu walks with her arms around the necks of Legion and Paul down the path from the cabin to the ocean. Lily Ana jogs ahead to the café for things they might need. When they emerge onto the beach, Paul feels Zuzu's legs give way as she moans through clenched teeth into his ear. Her cry weakens Paul's legs also and he and Legion lower her to her hands and knees. When the contraction subsides, they struggle past the breakers into waist-deep water. Legion lifts her so she floats faceup at his waist, stabilized in the rolling waves by his arms at her back.

"Support her head," Legion says. Paul stands away, still unable to grasp what has happened, what is going to happen.

"Paul!" Legion shouts. "You've got to help. When she contracts again her head will go under water."

Paul sloshes to her head and clutches her face to his chest. She clenches the crook of her arm around his neck, bracing for the next contraction. Without warning, Zuzu wrenches Paul's head underwater. Zuzu, her breath held against the pain, is all right, but Paul hacks to expel salt water from his lungs. An elbow catches him in the eye before he can hold her arms again.

There is only a hint of twilight now plus the dim illumination of a security light from behind the dunes. Lily Ana is back with a towel around her neck, the glint of a knife held between her teeth like a pirate. When she wades between Zuzu's legs, her cotton blouse balloons in front of her. She thrusts the knife at Paul. "Hold this." When he is slow to react, she deftly twirls the knife in her hand and punches at his stomach with the handle until his hand rises to take it. She pulls her cotton blouse over her head and throws it toward the beach before taking back the knife.

"Strip her," she demands. When neither man moves, "Do it now, quickly before the next contraction."

Legion skins the dress over Zuzu's head and throws it toward the shore while Lily Ana pulls down Zuzu's panties. In the surf, the white garments squirm like the underbellies of dying fish.

"It is happening quickly," Lily Ana reports, "there's a crown already."

Zuzu alternately gasps for breath and then growls with intense effort until her strength is gone. She pries at Paul's grasp. "Let me go. I can't bear any more. Push me under."

In an instant, Lily Ana slaps her twice, once with either hand, until Zuzu focuses on her face. "If you die, the baby will die also. Do you understand?" She leans in close, so Zuzu can see her eyes in the dim light. "You must endure. There is nothing left but to endure. So shut up and get on with it."

With this, Zuzu strains intensely, her eyes bulging; until her body slumps limp. Paul looks at the face he holds against his chest, peaceful now after the agony—dead. He looks imploringly at Legion, then to Lily Ana still between Zuzu's legs, her face barely discernible, intently performing some task by feel.

"She has fainted. Legion, support her head. Paul, I need you here," Lily Ana orders.

Lily Ana thrusts something at Paul, nudging him twice with it before he takes hold. His first instinct is to drop the slimy blob. Realizing what it is, he fishes it up, grabbing what he thinks are tiny legs.

"Wash it thoroughly, especially the face. Be careful of the cord. Legion, we need to get her to the cabin quickly, in case she is bleeding badly." With Zuzu cradled in his arms, Legion slogs toward the shore.

Alone in the dark water, a creature he cannot even see in his hands, Paul is close to panic. "What do I do?" he shouts.

"Wash it gently, then bring it on," Lily Ana calls back while jogging behind Legion up the path.

"Wait! I can't do this—it will drown!"

"It can't drown. It's not breathing yet, not till you take it out of the water," she yells back. And then they are gone past a dune before he can make a further protest.

Trying his best to follow such brief instructions, Paul alternately holds to an arm or leg with one hand and swishes water against the tender skin with the other. A slick leg slips from his grip and the baby is lost in the darkness. He ducks into the water and brings it to the surface cradled in his arms.

The baby is limp, lifeless. He has killed it. Paul holds it against his chest and staggers to the shore. As he reaches the path there is a wiggle, a gurgling gasp close to his ear, and then a blaring cry. As he navigates the silvery path through the undergrowth Paul accompanies the baby's wails with his own, neither knowing they are yelling, ancient instincts compelling them to holler as loudly as they can.

CHAPTER 27

The Sons

Zuzu wakes to the screaming, not sure if it is coming from her, if the birth is over. She is inside now, lying on a bed under the glare of an overhead light. Legion and Lily Ana stand with their backs to her running water into the kitchen sink, their heads turned looking into the darkness beyond the open doorway. The incongruous bawling and whooping are coming from outside.

Paul's yells abruptly stop as he emerges from the black and stands stiffly just inside the door frame, squinting into the light looking perplexed. He turns to look behind him into the night as if he too wants to know where the yelling came from. Lily Ana reaches for the baby on his shoulder, struggling at first to pry it from his grasp.

"I need to wash the salt water from its eyes," she explains. The baby whimpers at being washed so roughly. After drying it and wrapping it in a towel, she moves toward Zuzu, but then turns to Paul, standing like a statue, arms still raised to his shoulder.

"You performed well…better than I expected," she says returning the baby to his arms. Turning to Zuzu, "It's the boy we were expecting, a perfect little boy."

Lily Ana lies facing the wall on the sofa with Legion scrunched in behind her, both in exhausted sleep. Paul is drained too after the adrenaline has subsided. He sits in a kitchen chair in the center of the one-room cabin. The single overhead light throws stark shadows across the floor. His ears ring from the quiet stillness.

Only the distant faint rumble of the surf affirms that time itself has not stopped. His body jerks back erect when he dozes. In his stupor, he stares at Zuzu and the baby lying peacefully asleep on the bed.

On their backs with a sheet covering them to their waists, they seem carved in relief into an alabaster slab. Zuzu's cheeks and lips are smudged the same shade of pink as the baby's body, painted with the same brush by the artist to indicate their chiseled bodies are alive. Her blonde, almost white, hair combed neatly into an androgynous dovetail this afternoon is sprayed in an aureole on the pillow.

In her sleep, Zuzu turns on her side to the baby who startles awake. Its arms reach to touch her, hands instinctively grasping, and then it is asleep again. Lost children, Paul thinks, both of them unclaimed children. Even as he tries to convince himself the emotion choking him is pity, he realizes his desire to cuddle Zuzu is not compassion for a desolate child. He detests the arousal he feels.

Paul gets up and flips off the light, intending to sleep on the floor. As he goes to the bed for a pillow, he hesitates and then lies beside Zuzu on his back looking up into the black. He reaches across her to feel the baby to confirm that in the dark it is still there, that it is real. She catches his arm and pulls him onto his side and spoons back against him. He freezes waiting for her to move again, to speak, but she is asleep. He lies with his arm across her, his hand on the baby's chest feeling it rise and fall. Neither she nor the baby move, nor does he until the dawn light begins to reveal the palms outside the window. Too tired now even to think he drifts into sleep, his face falling against her neck.

When Paul wakes, his mind tumbles trying to comprehend where he is and who is under his arm. His fingers are sticky from leaking breast milk. Jumping to his feet, he wipes his hand on the sheet. Zuzu lies undisturbed as if in a coma, lips slightly parted. He feels her forehead fearing a fever but finds her face cool yet moist from the day's rising heat. The baby facing her jerks fitfully with its eyes closed, clutching at her warmth.

Watching the baby until he begins to fuss, Paul positions the baby's face in front of a nipple and pushes his face against it. Remarkably, the baby recognizes what he has been seeking and, after determining the exact location with his nose and tongue, pulls it into his mouth. Paul turns to the wall, away from her should she wake, willing his erection to subside.

CHAPTER 28

The Women

The following morning Legion takes over for Lily Ana at the café allowing her to tend to Zuzu. Lily Ana imagines him delivering pastries and coffee while announcing the news to all who will listen. He will be drunk in a few hours. She will have to go back. Paul also had gone to the café for coffee but had rushed back with it still in his hand. She continues at the sink washing and sanitizing with a bleach mixture while Zuzu and the baby sleep.

"Is she OK, you think? Should we go to a hospital?" Paul asks Lily Ana while flopping into a kitchen chair.

"She is good. They are both good. Nothing to be concerned about."

"I thought last night that she had died, that they both were dead. How could anybody survive such barbarism?"

Lily Ana looks out the window in front of the sink and sighs. *Who is he to call them barbaric?*

"Men don't understand. They know things but they don't understand. Women give birth every day. Of the women giving birth right now, this very minute, how many do you think are in nice hospitals? How many have doctors to pump in drugs so they won't feel it? Since the beginning of time, women have gone through this. Women are made for this. You men think that women are made for your enjoyment, but everything about a woman's body is for making babies. It's only a trick on men that they find these baby machines irresistible. The better equipped a woman is for babies, the more a man is attracted."

She turns to Paul expecting him to engage with some rebuttal, but Paul is wilted in the chair looking at his feet.

"But not all survive." Lily Ana continues, "I don't know if either would have survived last night without your help." He still does not look up, so she walks in front of him and lifts his chin, surprised to see his eyes glistening. "Thank you," she says. "God sent you here for a purpose; we just didn't know what it was until last night." And when he still does not respond: "Now go get into bed. You look worn out."

Paul looks over at mother and child, still sleeping soundly underneath the swirl of the overhead fan. "What can you tell me about her?"

"Well, she arrived here from France six months ago, already pregnant—"

"No, no. Legion has already told me that. I want to know…" He stops mid-sentence, his mouth open. He either does not know what he wants to ask or can't bring himself to say it.

Paul looks out the window, "What will happen to them?"

"She is the daughter I never had; the daughter Legion never had. We love her, and now the boy, as our own."

"But you can't expect her to stay here, raise the baby here. We can't let that happen."

Lily Ana wonders where the *we* came from but lets it pass. "She will be fine here until something else happens. She will stay if she wants, or be taken away by some American tourist. You can't plan what she will do. But as long as Legion and I live, they will always have a home here."

Paul is quiet as Lily Ana continues with her chores. Suddenly, she wheels around to look at Paul unabashedly, pondering his eyes until he looks away. She thinks she sees the symptoms.

A person can fall in love, and yet be unaware. She had learned this the hard way. An Italian boy's enthralled eyes flash before her mind's eye, accompanied by the pang in her gut that always comes with the memory. It had been months after he had left her for a prearranged marriage that she realized the import of what they had lost.

She had not suspected Paul was even susceptible.

The screen door slams startling Zuzu from a dream of being pushed underwater by a monster. "Lily?" she calls out as she opens her eyes and sits up.

Paul turns over his chair getting up. He stands, mouth slack with indecision, alternately looking between her and the door.

"Paul, are you OK?" Zuzu asks.

"Yeah. Lily Ana just left. Do you want me to go after her? Is anything wrong?"

Zuzu tries to swing her legs off the bed. Pain shooting through her abdomen jolts her out of the fog of first waking. She throws back the sheet. "I have a baby!" she declares pulling it onto her lap.

The baby's face wrinkles into a snarl and little arms thrust out with clenched fists as if to punish whoever woke him. "I did it. I'm a mother." Zuzu says with growing amazement. She presses the baby's face to a breast when it begins to whimper.

Paul turns his face away.

"Would you bring me a glass of water? Bring a chair over. Let's see what we have here."

They both admire every move the baby makes until he falls back asleep against her chest. She checks the diaper, but there is nothing yet. Paul examines each finger and toe separately, obviously fascinated.

"Thanks for sleeping with me last night. I'm used to sleeping alone, but I needed someone to snuggle last night. It was all so scary."

Paul sits back, his face serious. "What will you do now? Will you contact the father?"

"No. He doesn't want anything to do with us. He's probably expecting to pay child support, but I'll never contact him. I don't want to ever see him again or for him to have any rights concerning the baby." She searches Paul's eyes, deciding how much to tell him.

"I don't know if Legion said anything, but he will be the father. We're legally married; did you know that? He wants me to register the baby as his natural born child. I don't want the baby to ever know about his real father."

Paul stares at her blankly. She can almost hear the thoughts grinding in his head.

"Would you leave me now? I need to take stock of myself and don't want you watching. Go to the café and tell Lily Ana that everything is all right, but I need to talk with her when she can get away."

Paul is opening the screen door when he stops and looks back. "I want to be the father."

"What?"

Paul rushes back, sits again, leans forward over the baby. "Dad is dying; he can't be the father."

"It's just to give him a name, so the baby won't be illegitimate."

Paul's gaze drops to the slumbering baby and then his eyes are pleading with her. "I want this to be my son. I want to marry you."

"Paul, what are you saying? You don't even know me." Her face turns from shock to sternness. "I know you're not attracted to me. Betty and I are friends. She tells me everything."

"That was a mistake. Yes, I do want you and the baby. You make me feel things I've never felt before."

"Even if that were true, it still wouldn't work. See, I don't want you." She was surprised to see Paul's eyes moisten. "No, I don't mean it like that exactly; it's just that I don't ever want to be touched by a man again. The thought of it disgusts me."

Paul's face softens, "I understand—"

"No. It's not what you're thinking. I don't like women over men. I just don't trust men—all men. I could never fall in love or get married—not really married. Do you understand?"

Paul runs to the door, throwing the screen door wide.

CHAPTER 29

The Second Coming

aul stumbles down a footpath, trying to get as far away as he can without swimming. The path leads him over the coral ridge that forms one side of tranquil Orient Bay to the tumultuous Atlantic side of the island. After the sand trail runs out, he carefully steps from one jagged rock to the next to get as close to the cliff edge as he dares.

Looking down, mountainous waves crash against the vertical wall with thunderous spray. Raw sensations blot out his befuddled thoughts. Sunburned cheeks crinkle as he roars defiantly back at the ocean, yells lost even to his own ears amidst the clamor.

After the initial collision of a roller with the wall, the wave gurgles through voids in the coral beneath his feet and erupts in spewing geysers behind him. The atomized water from the crashing waves in front and the geysers behind flash rainbows all around.

He traces one of these tunnels to a car-size chasm. An intruding wave fills the depression to the depth of a bathtub, and then immediately begins leaking back through the porous rock. A sand floor is exposed for a few seconds before the next wave. After watching a few waves churn in and out, he carefully climbs down the wall. Below the rim, the staccato crash of the waves becomes the muted rumble of distant thunder.

The gushing water threatens to knock him against the jagged sides so he sits on a smooth copper-colored boulder in the center of the sand bottom. Above, past the rim, is blue infinity. Being hidden away inside the earth where time and events pass unnoticed comforts him.

He slides down the boulder until his back is propped against it. The next incoming wave swirls around him until only his head is above water. When it recedes, he pulls off his T-shirt and wraps it around his sneakers to form a pillow. When the water gushes in again, his head anchors him as his arms flail and his weightless body floats free of the sand. When he closes his eyes, the universe becomes small, just large enough for him. Nothing exists beyond the brick-clay hue of his eyelids.

A voice is barely audible above the thumping heartbeat of waves and churning digestion of water slushing through the coral voids. "With you, it will be different."

When the flow reverses and the water rushes out, he screams at being flushed into an alien world.

Lily Ana relaxes on a stool behind the bar, recovering after the lunch crowd. Paul stumbles to the back door of the café wearing a wet bathing suit, sneakers, and pullover T-shirt. His legs are splotched with dried blood from scrapes and scratches. She had seen this before when naïve tourists tried to walk on the coral rock on the ocean side of the reef. He holds onto the door frame a moment as his eyes adjust from the sun, then reaches out for the bar for stability as he stumbles toward her. The anger on his face frightens her.

"Give me a Jack Daniels, straight."

There are a dozen questions she wants to ask but instead, she just stares in disdain.

"Using alcohol to treat a hard day is a slippery slope."

Paul's eyes narrow into a drop-dead glare. It is the look Legion would have given her if she had said that to him. Until now she hadn't seen any resemblance between father and son. When angry the flame in their eyes is the same. She starts pouring the drink before either of them can say anything they would regret and sets it on a coaster.

"Will you call me a cab, Lily Ana?"

"Going into town?"

He covers his face with his hands, rubbing the palms into his eyes, "I'm leaving. I've got to get away from this God-forsaken place before it drives me crazy."

The empathy she feels surprises her. She doesn't know what has brought this despair, but she knows the feeling well. "Don't go," she entreats.

Their eyes lock. Paul seems to be questioning if she is sincere. "I mean, don't go because of me. I know I've—"

"No, no. This is nothing to do with you. I've just got to go. I need to leave right now." His hands cover his face again, to hide teary eyes. "It's just me. I'm all fucked up." He wipes at his eyes with the back of his hands and looks at her. "Will you call a cab—please?"

Lily pivots to the phone on the wall behind the bar and calls the resort's reception desk. She speaks briefly in French before hanging up.

"It will be here in twenty minutes—out in front of the office. I don't know where your father is; you can probably find him on the beach."

"Good, I don't want to see him."

Instant anger surges through her. "You can't go without talking with him!" she shrieks. "He'll think—"

Paul pounds the bar with both fists, "I don't give a damn what he thinks!"

Paul's ears roar. Faces are leaning over him, mouths moving. He tries to recall why he's lying on the floor. This dumpy guy had grabbed him by the back of his shirt and shoved him toward the door. When he had turned to take a sock at him, everything went black.

That dude's face, hanging over him now, freezes when Paul smiles. Paul feels a sense of release akin to joy. He tries to tell the man that he wants more, but his mouth won't open. He takes a feeble slap hoping to provoke another punch. Lily Ana, her eyes dripping, grabs at the podgy guy's arm but it's too late.

And then the faces are gone leaving him to the most peaceful sleep in days.

Lily Ana wraps ice in a bar rag to put across Paul's forehead. His innocent smile belies the drool of blood from the corner of his mouth. When he doesn't respond to her imploring words, she bends to kiss him on the lips. His smile seems to grow, but his eyes still do not open.

She rushes through the front door to the beach thinking how she will explain this to Legion. After stopping and looking both ways, she jogs along the beach asking everybody she knows but nobody's seen him.

She should call an ambulance. When she runs back into the café, Paul is gone. Eduardo wipes sweat from his face with his apron before he shrugs and points towards the resort office where the cab would be waiting.

CHAPTER 30

The Prophets

T his is him," Legion hears someone whisper behind his back.

Legion looks up from his drink, not at the men who settle onto stools to his right but at Lily Ana. She is looking at him out of the corner of her eye as she wipes down the bar, a look of apprehension like she expects him to piss on the floor at any moment. He wonders why she is not coming over to get drink orders from the two men.

Legion recognizes the bald fat man from the beach the day Paul arrived. He is still naked with the same lost-kid naivety on his face. Legion grabs his arm.

"Hey man, ain't you got a towel? Don't you know it's rude, downright unsanitary, to put your bare ass on a seat."

The dumpy man jumps up looking around embarrassed. The only other customers, a graying couple sitting at a table by the entrance, hadn't noticed.

Legion waves to get Lily Ana's attention, but she is already staring at him. "Do you have an extra towel back there? We need a towel."

Lily Ana reaches under the bar and hands Legion one of the clean towels she keeps for just such occasions. Legion folds it in quarters and spreads it over the stool next to him.

Legion gestures with his hand for the man to sit, "If you're gonna hang around a nudist resort, you need to learn some etiquette."

"Are you all right, Legion?" Lily Ana asks.

"Sure, sure. I've got it taken care of. Thank you, Sweet. Can you bring us another round?"

The dumpy man tentatively resettles himself on the stool as if expecting another reproach.

"We've talked before, but I must have missed your name."

"I'm Enoch," he points over his shoulder with his thumb, "and this is ah…my friend, Elijah.

Elijah doesn't need a towel. He is draped in a thick beach cover, more like a bedspread, from the top of his head down to his hippie sandals. A luxurious beard fluffs out of the folds of cloth under his chin. Stern dark eyes under bushy eyebrows and a long, hooked nose give him a haughty look. Enoch also has a beard, a kinky coarse splotch on his chin of what looks like pubic hair.

When Legion first arrived at Orient Beach a few months back, he would have found these lonely old men who wandered into the bar annoying. But tonight he feels relieved to have their company.

"Elijah. Do people call you Eli?"

Enoch turns to Elijah. He seems to pass some signal with his eyes and Elijah nods.

"No. But you may call me Eli if you wish."

"All right, Eli. So what brings you and Enoch to Orient Beach? Here to sun your buns?"

Enoch giggles like a little girl. He twists around to Eli and repeats, "Sun your buns."

Eli's face remains severe, like chiseled stone. "You forget yourself, Enoch."

Enoch's grin is gone when he turns back. "No, Legion, we're here for a more serious purpose. I was telling Elijah about our talk earlier, about your interesting ideas, and he wanted to meet you."

Behind Enoch, Eli's head is nodding agreement. "We think you're the right man to help us understand."

"Sure. You've got the right guy. I know everything there is to know about this place. Ask away."

Lily Ana returns with his gimlet but still ignores the other men.

"Lily Ana, bring two more of these. Don't be rude to my guests."

"Stop it! Just stop right now before… Go on back to the cabin and try to sleep. I'll check on you when I get a break."

Legion feels embarrassed. Lily is usually congenial with his friends, friendly to new customers. She must think these two are troublemakers.

"Lily, just bring the drinks."

Lily Ana's eyes water. "Please, Legion, you know it scares me when you get this way. Can't you—"

Legion hunches his shoulder and looks to the stools beside him, "Can't I what?" His new friends are looking away uncomfortably. "What'd I do?"

Lily Ana wipes her eyes with the bar rag, turns to select the gin from the shelf behind, and begins mixing the drinks.

Every night Legion drinks alone at the bar, waiting for Lily Ana to close and lead him home to rub his neck until his migraine subsides enough for sleep. Each morning his eyes snap open the moment she stirs before waking. Then he has to wait, no matter how tired he gets, for her to coax him back to sleep again the next night. He can't sleep without her. When did that happen? Legion's head falls forward. "Fuck me!" he yells at the bar, his face clenched with pain. He had become the doting old man he had sworn never to be. He can't live without help anymore.

Enoch is on his feet again with a look of shock, gazing around like he had broken another rule of etiquette.

"Forgive my language. It wasn't meant for you. I'll answer your questions."

Eli had risen also and was adjusting his robe to appear more dignified. "We can't stay here, Enoch, it's not proper. Get on with this. We've got to get back."

Enoch resumes his seat next to Legion and Eli reluctantly sits behind him.

"Why are you naked? Why are all these people naked? Don't they feel…embarrassed?" Enoch asks.

Legion stares a moment in disbelief and then chuckles. "Enoch, in case you haven't noticed, you're naked too. Aren't you embarrassed? You're at a nudist resort, for God's sake, surely I don't have to explain that."

The two men simultaneously look to the ceiling as if expecting it to fall.

"Yes, Legion, I am embarrassed. But I can't do anything about being naked."

"Sure you can. Buy yourself some spiffy clothes; start hanging out at the casinos on the Dutch side of the island."

"No, you see, when I was taken I was copulating with one of my concubines. I had seven so I was out of my clothes a lot—"

Eli gives him a nudge from behind. When Enoch glances back, Eli is shaking his head.

"I can't explain exactly, but I'm stuck without any clothes. When Eli was taken, he was dressed in his rabbinic robe."

"Taken?"

Enoch freezes with his mouth open as if a thought has just left him.

Eli thrusts his face past Enoch's shoulder. "Look," he says with indignation, "you should feel ashamed. We want to know why not. Since the beginning of time, since the fig leaves, everybody has worn clothes. It was decreed as punishment. Don't you know that?"

Enoch scoots his stool back so Eli can talk directly to Legion without straining. Legion locks eyes with Eli. There's something peculiar about this obnoxious SOB, but Legion can't quite put his finger on it.

"Well, maybe I should feel that way but I don't."

Enoch finds his tongue again. "Legion, you're acting like Adam before the apple incident, before he knew Good and Evil, before God afflicted him and all his descendants with modesty."

Eli is unable to stay out of it. "So why are these people the exception? That's what we're trying to understand. Only gods are exempt from modesty. Don't you feel any shame about exposing your genitals?"

"Genitals? What's with you two—this obsession with genitals. I mean it's just sex equipment, right? Why should I worry about people seeing my balls any more than my elbow?"

"See? That's what I was telling you," Enoch says to Eli.

Legion is losing patience. "It's the sex thing, right? You think sex is immoral so I should hide my penis. Have I got that right?"

"Procreation is a blessed thing," Eli clarifies. "There was nothing in the penalty prohibiting that. Women are forever punished with the pain of childbirth, but nothing else."

"I mean, sex is no more immoral than eating, is it? And as far as the genitals thing, you don't see a dog running off to hide behind a tree every time his penis comes out."

"I tend to agree, but—" Enoch jumps when he gets jabbed again, "but you see, other animals didn't get the curse. They don't know about Good and Evil. Only men know that."

"So, let me see if I've got this: I'm supposed to be ashamed of being nude because of the curse put on Adam, and you're here to find out why the curse isn't working."

Enoch glances back to Eli who nods. "We might have said it differently, but that about sums it up."

"Well, I don't know if I'm buying into this curse business but I have to admit most people cover their sex organs."

"So Eli has this theory," Enoch says diplomatically, "that the Devil is involved, that he's taken away the knowledge of Good and Evil from some people. Is that it, do you think? Is this the Devil's doing?"

Eli has his nose in the air. "I'll bet you don't know Good from Evil! I'd bet you steal and kill people and who knows what else."

"Listen, bub, if you're working up to nudists being bad just because they aren't shy, then you can go to Hell."

Eli has driven himself into a frenzy. "You're going to get your buttocks blown away by a lightning bolt if you're not careful!"

Legion just smiles back which infuriates Eli even more. Being instantly vaporized in a flash actually sounds pretty good, considering the alternatives. Legion, his face suddenly serious, leans toward Eli. "Could you make that happen? I mean, you two seem to have some pull. I'll go stand on the beach and wait."

Eli slumps forward and begins bumping his forehead on the top of the bar.

Legion glances at Lily Ana wiping the cocktail glasses for the hundredth time, watching them surreptitiously. She probably wants him to throw these guys out.

"We don't really do that sort of thing. We could maybe, but we don't." Enoch pauses and watches Eli continue to bump his head. "But that's the other thing we wanted to ask about. You see, Elijah and I were both called directly and never got to go through it ourselves. We were wondering…what's dying like?"

Legion's whole body jumps. "Do you smell something?" Legion pushes his hairy chest into Enoch's face. "Do I smell funny?" Enoch jerks back, his eyes popping wide.

The face of Dodd, the beloved head engineer at the Legion factory, looms in his memory. When Dodd had been diagnosed with cancer, after all treatment was abandoned, it was Legion who became despondent, where Dodd became rejuvenated with excitement. "I'll finally get to know," Dodd exclaimed. Assuming Legion, like with the company's research projects, would want to share in his discoveries, he cornered Legion alone in his office one day. "Can you smell it?" Dodd wanted to know. He was giddy with anticipation. "I can smell it."

Legion couldn't smell it and wondered how a man who smoked two packs a day could smell anything. Legion had convinced him it was a trick the cancer played on his mind. But later, after cancer further consumed his friend, he could smell death, too.

"Dying! Sorry for laughing, but it's just hard for me to understand why you know-it-alls would ask some drunk sitting at a bar about that. Who've you two been talking to about me?"

Eli jumps to his feet. "He's right, Enoch. He wouldn't know stewed cabbage from camel dung. Let's get out of here."

Enoch continues to sit and stare at Legion, waiting for an answer.

"Yeah, I'm dying. Isn't everybody?" Legion's face crinkles with a chuckle and then goes blank. "You're telling me that both of you are dead?"

Enoch nods *yes* and Eli shakes his head *no*. "Well, technically, we're not dead because we never died. That's why we want to know what happens," Enoch says.

"You just rot, and that's it. Or maybe you get whisked away to paradise to have sex with virgins forever. A few of my kinky-headed friends back in Nashville profess this but seem a little reluctant to put it to the test. Are you two of those everybody-goes-into-cold-storage-until-judgment-day types?"

Enoch and Eli look at each other somberly but neither replies.

Legion smiles. "Most days I'm confident there's nothing at the end. Then other days, I know I'll burn in Hell."

"Legion!" Lily Ana is holding the sides of his head, her face inches from his, demanding to be recognized. Legion wobbles on the stool, unable to steady the weightless apparition his body has become.

"Lily...?"

"They're not real, Legion. Whatever you see is not there. Do you understand?" He goes limp in her hands and she lowers his head onto a towel folded on the bar. "I'm closing early. Don't move while I put everything up." She turns and starts returning liquor bottles to the shelves.

Legion's face is turned to his right, toward the empty barstools. It's true; they're not there. There's only the folded towel where Enoch had sat. In the center of the towel is a brown streak. Legion's arm struggles to bring it to his nose. "That's real," he whispers to himself. He turns to Lily Ana, her back to him closing out the cash register. He tries to call to her, but his mouth won't form words. *It's just as well,* he thinks, *she'll say this shit's all in my head.*

CHAPTER 31

The Battle

Legion reaches through the dark to the row of liter vodka bottles on the nightstand. His fingers count three before picking up the one closest to him and swirling it to judge his progress. The rest of this one and the other two will be enough; surely, it will be enough.

His teeth bare when the fire in his gut rekindles. The flame is thrown back into his throat. He bends to the trash can beside the bed, but then the spasm in his stomach releases and the vodka stays down.

He has drunk, as fast as his stomach would allow, for the last two hours to get this far. His body is so accustomed to alcohol that it takes copious amounts to get seriously drunk. There is no enjoyment in it anymore and he gulps it down like medicine.

The beast eats him voraciously now. He had known this time would come. It had always been his plan to cheat the beast in the end, to give advantage to alcohol, the other demon. But he needs to speed things up while he still has some control. He had resolved this plan yesterday when he was sober—relatively sober. If he reconsiders now, it will just be the booze softening his resolve. Now the plan is in motion, there's no need to think about it further.

Maybe halfway through the next bottle, his body will become numb. Breathing will be too shallow to sustain life, and he will drift into the unknown. But at this moment, the tipping point between life and death, he floats free of his body into the twilight realm where gods dwell. This kingdom, prohibited to the sane and sober, is where wisdom ceases to be an illusion. He's been to this precipice before, but never so close to the edge.

Out of the dark, the image of his mother lying in a coma on her deathbed materializes. She had not moved in days, and although he was standing at the foot of her bed looking at her face, he hadn't noticed when her breathing ended. When his father guided him to the study, he didn't know the import of his trembling hand. They sat across from each other, searching each other's eyes. His father's gaze rose to the paintings of praying hands on the wall behind Legion's head as he explained that Legion's mother had gone to a better place; that she was well now, and happy. When his father's face tilted back to him, his bleary eyes were imploring, wanting assurance that what he had said was believable, so that he too could believe and be consoled. There was grief in his eyes, but also uncertainty and fear.

His father said—but did not mean—that he was happy her suffering was over and she was in Heaven. He said—but did not mean—that he was eager to join her. If there had only been a shade of difference between his father's words and what was written on his face, Legion could have forced the two to be compatible. But this stark dichotomy had been Legion's first glimpse into the perplexing mire of an adult world.

Legion had crumbled forward, holding fast to his father's knees. He had steeled himself for his mother's death; but the rock of certainty that had been his father had slipped away also. His jerking sobs were not so much for a dead mother, or even his father, but for a child who had discovered himself an orphan.

As a teen Legion had declared himself a non-believer and openly derided his father's attempts to appear pious. His father would continue this charade for five years until it was his turn to die. What fortune he had not spent on earthly miracles offered by doctors, he had given away to evangelists to hedge his bets for the afterlife. At the funeral, sitting on a front pew looking at his father in an open casket, the scriptures proffered by well-meaning clergy to console seemed a flimsy fraud. This had been the day he had set his life's goal to achieve where his father had failed—to understand.

Although he majored in engineering to satisfy his father's wish, he had considered this no more than a trade school curriculum, a dead end as far as understanding anything important. Humanities became his driving focus. Even then, he knew that knowledge by itself was not wisdom, but thought it an essential ingredient. He explored philosophy and religions of all persuasions with the intensity other boys pursued girls and sports. But the more he learned, the more he realized he didn't know. Rather than the clarity hoped for, the chasm between what he learned and what he understood became ever wider. Uncertainty became a snowball rolling downhill.

Even the default of atheism he found hollow. A true non-believer would assume extinction at death and be relieved by the prospect. If he could only accept that. Atheism he determined was a belief also, as elusive as any theology.

On into his senior year, he had maintained the assumption that what he needed was more knowledge. Engineering taught him that all is understandable using the laws of physics. If something seems fantastic, it is because science does not yet understand how to apply the laws governing the phenomenon. Three hundred years after Newton, science still grapples to understand gravity, yet every serious scientist accepts there is a rational solution. Then his logic professor put his never-ending quest for knowledge in perspective with a thought experiment Legion had memorized:

"Imagine a clock—the old design with a mainspring and gears—that becomes suddenly self-aware and endowed with an engineer's faculties. The clock has nothing to do all day but sit on an end table and think.

"Would your existence not be proof of a clockmaker? You haven't seen him, but he must exist, or have existed at one time. You hear the ticking inside your bezel and feel the gears turning.

Some force is making you move. It also is invisible, but again, self-evident. You trace the source of this energy to a constantly unwinding mainspring. You conclude that when the energy is expended, you will become inert like the end table. Would this prospect not frighten you? Would you resolve to keep perfect time in the hope the clockmaker will returns and reward you with a second winding?

"Does anyone see fault with the clock's logic?"

Some students' hands shot up and meekly came down again before the professor could call on them.

"So everything needed by the clock to draw its conclusions are present. No additional knowledge will alter the basic logic. But what about the unwinding mainspring? Does the clock have any choice but to assuage its fear with the hope the clockmaker will return and be pleased?"

The memory of his father's confused face seems a consolation now. These battles with uncertainty must have raged inside him as well. His father's face morphs into Paul's face. Had Legion ever treated his father with such blatant disrespect? Had his father considered him a fool also? A just God would claim all three of them as innocents, as utterly confused by life and devoid of blame as newborns.

Legion's lips quiver. "I'm sorry, Father," he says into the dark. His slurs do not sound like words. Legion clenches his eyes shut trying to blank out his shame.

Now, at the end, if he could just ruminate on the good memories. Lily Ana's smile emerges then turns into a stern frown. He had picked a fight with her earlier and sent her away to stay with Zuzu for the night. Right now, she was probably complaining to Zuzu about his meanness. His eyes water with humiliation. Why did they have to remember him this way?

Legion's numb hand wanders like the head of a cobra searching for the nightstand. He finds the bottle lying on its side where it had fallen into the crook of his arm, most of its contents mixed with his sweat on the bed. It takes a full minute to guide the neck of the bottle to his mouth. When the rim clatters against his teeth, he fills his cheeks before squeezing it down. The last of the vodka dribbles down his chin, past his neck into the pillow. The bottle falls to the floor as his body wretches in rebellion. Lips stretch over clenched teeth until the ground glass in his stomach becomes bearable.

He lies naked on top of the sheets, his body slick with sweat. Does he want to be found this way? He should have thought about this indignity before he got too drunk to dress. But why bother? This is how Lily Ana knows him, his normal self. They would only have to gather the sheet around his body for it to be ready for disposal.

She would likely have him dressed and displayed at her church before burial. This horrid thought sends his mind to panic before reason calms him again. He, of course, would not be there. His body would be a thing, a possession of others. Lily Ana would need the trappings of a Christian burial. They had discussed it and he had agreed. What did it matter?

When his hands brush over his chest and stomach, he can't tell where his fingers end and his torso begins. Is this how men should die, alone, staring into the dark, waiting?

Legion imagines Adam lying on a grass mat under the stars, his hand touching Eve for reassurance as she sleeps beside him. Adam is thinking about his son who had mysteriously ceased to move, the corruption that had distorted his body causing him to stink. Would this happen to him as well? Was this a further punishment resulting from the apple? When Eve's naked body snuggled to him for warmth, he would have felt betrayal as well as arousal.

Legion holds in his mind the saddened face of Adam lighted by a moonbeam through the trees of the garden. Adam's pronounced chin resembles his father's—and also Paul's. The stringy unkempt hair is his. This fantasy fades as he drifts into unconsciousness.

His head lolls back and forth with each impact. There is the sound of the slaps, but there is no feeling. His eyelids part only slightly to Lily Ana's face hovering over him pounding on both cheeks. Vomit oozes from his mouth and she rolls him onto his side.

"Should I call a doctor?" A voice out of view shrieks above the squall of a baby.

"No. If he survives what I'm about to do to him, he'll live. Grab a leg."

Legion's bottom bumps to the floor. As he is dragged, his arms trail limply. He is propped in the shower with his head held erect by a corner.

"Turn it on," a stern voice commands.

The cold torches his skin like fire and he groans. Struggling onto all fours to escape, he vomits into the shower drain.

"He'll live...at least until he tries this again, and then I'll kill him. Why don't you leave while I clean him up?"

"No. You're so mad; you might hurt him. You take the baby and go outside—have a cry and calm down."

Legion hears the voices, but the meanings of the words do not register. His head slumps to the shower floor. The screen door slams. The cold water stings his back as he waits for the next torture.

"You made me live. Do you remember?" Zuzu grabs his ears and lifts his head so he has to look at her. "Now, I'll see to it that you live—whether you want to or not. Do you understand?" She turns the water to warm and begins to scrub his face with a soapy rag.

CHAPTER 32

The Passage

*T*t is Sunday and Legion is waiting when Webb noses his boat onto the beach. Legion throws a paper sack into the boat and struggles to hike himself over the gunwale. After several attempts, Webb motions for Legion to turn around so he can lift him under his arms to a sitting position on the bow. Webb feels bone under the sagging skin where there had been muscle only weeks before.

He boosts Legion into the fighting chair. "It should be calm. Where should we go?"

"Let's go to the canyon, the deepest part. I know that's where you keep the marlin you save for the tourists."

The boat reaches plane as Webb follows the buoys out of Orient Bay. Going with the flow of the waves the bow climbs the rollers and then glides down the backsides. After rounding the eastern point of Anguilla, Webb stops the engines and starts rigging the rods for trolling.

"Let's not fish today," Legion says as he looks out to the horizon. "Go on out to the canyon."

Webb's stomach clenches. He searches Legion's face, which seems peaceful, almost joyful. "It is not time yet," he says.

"Yes, it's time."

Webb restarts the engines and heads to the mile-deep gorge where they had fished many times. His hands tremble at the boat controls.

When the boat stops again, Legion slides from the chair and squats beside a tackle locker until he finds what he needs. He slips five one-pound bullet weights into each of his front pants pockets.

Without looking at Webb or saying anything, he works methodically as if he had rehearsed every movement. From the bag he had thrown aboard, he pulls out duct tape and wraps silver bands from below his pockets, over his belt line, and several inches onto his shirt. After a final check of his preparations, he stands looking over the stern and takes a slow deep breath as if savoring the scent of the ocean.

When Legion turns to face him, Webb slides from the helm chair intent on rushing at Legion and wrestling him to the deck. But his hands seem to remember a promise made and clamp tightly to the steering wheel. The internal battle burns in his taut muscles, throbs at his temples.

"Thank you, my friend," Legion says backing up to the side rail, "I will never forget this… I guess I'll forget it all in a moment. So much for farewell speeches."

As Webb lunges, Legion flips backward over the rail like a scuba diver entering the water. Webb bends over the gunwale watching a quavering ghost sink out of sight.

He plunges feetfirst looking up at Webb's face distorted by the water. The stab of pain in his sinuses, imploding under the growing pressure, eases when his eardrums rupture. Soon there is only the wavering sun above and the silent water, ever colder as he sinks.

This will end in terror, he knows. When the instinct for survival finally prevails, his hands will claw at the weights pulling him down until a desperate gasp of seawater fills his lungs. In his mind, he has endured this final horror already and accepted the price, knowing that it will be brief.

His lungs burn as panic creeps closer. A final look up at the shadow of a tiny boat against the wrinkling light. Hypoxia fills his starved brain with flickering images of a baby—Zuzu's baby? Paul? Or is it him?

And then a different vision intrudes. A strange man stands on a boulder atop Petit Cay, a small offshore islet at the edge of Galion Bay, one of Legion's favorite meditation spots. The man is looking back at him. Although he doesn't wave, Legion feels the man is waiting for him. He looks like Elmer Fudd wearing a bulky diaper. Legion loses his last breath to the irresistible urge to laugh.

The boat drifts with the prevailing wind ever closer to Scrub Island, a serrated edge of continental plate thrust from the ocean at the eastern edge of the canyon. The sun behind the island casts emerald green shadows onto the turquoise ocean. A row of gulls silhouette at the pinnacle of the cliff, their bodies turned into the wind, equally spaced like beads on a necklace. Below the gulls, terns circle in front of their nests in the dark craters that pock the face of the craggy outcrop. An ephemeral silver band, where the waves bash with a rumble into the vertical wall, separates rock from ocean.

This choreography is there to be seen and heard and felt, but Webb is numb to it all. He stands cantilevered over stiff arms propped on the gunwale squinting into the glare of the water, frozen by that image of Legion looking back at him as he faded out of sight. The body that was his friend still sinks below into ever-darkening water. It will likely hang on the jagged wall of the canyon before reaching the bottom. His flesh will be eaten by a myriad of fish, relatives of the same fish they had lured to their death. After a few weeks, his bones will be freed to reach the bottom. Eventually, the bones also will be consumed by mollusks or dissolve until there is nothing except the elements life had collected to construct him.

A traditional funeral would have defiled his friend, his body segregated in a vault like shameful corruption unfit to be returned to Mother Earth. When the fishing was slow, he and Legion contemplated such aberrations of the civilized world to which neither felt connected.

In the ocean his elements will mix with the elements of other men lost at sea in these waters over the centuries and with ancient sea creatures extinct before the advent of humanity. He will become the Caribbean Sea itself, to wash against its beaches, to become new life constantly being reborn. It eases Webb knowing his friend will always be near; there to greet him each morning when he opens the shutters of his beach cottage.

CHAPTER 33

Siddhartha

S iddhartha stands atop a blue-green boulder at the pinnacle of the tiny offshore islet looking down at the frail man walking across the water from the mainland. He has encountered other men who walk on water so he does not think this unusual.

When the man is halfway to the islet, Siddhartha sees he is not walking on water after all, but sloshing the hundred yards on a knee-deep ridge of sand formed by the waves converging behind the islet. A secret underwater path only a native to the area would know.

It is too far away to see his face clearly, but his slow methodical gait reminds him of another man he had met during one of these meditations. Siddhartha smiles at the memory of the disheveled little man who had passed from illusion to reality right before his eyes.

His illusion had been forced to drink poison because it had explained reality to the young men of his city. He had discovered that sane men are so frightened of reality that they will torture or kill the bodies of those who become enlightened.

Their stories had not been that much different. Siddhartha laments that his efforts at teaching have also been futile. If only he could explain it more clearly. Reality is like torchlight, invisible as it travels through the air in every direction. The light creates illusions. However, the light itself, which cannot be seen, is all that is real.

When the illusion of a man's body is finally shed, only invisible light remains. Enlightenment is when these invisible lights intersect creating a shared reality. Since enlightenment has no substance, the rules governing illusions do not apply. Notions of geography lack meaning and time does not progress in a single direction.

Siddhartha has learned these encounters during meditation are the only source of wisdom. But try explaining this to the bonehead novices that follow him around like lost orphans. They are drawn to him out of their own emptiness, the haunting suspicion that life is not what it seems. The eager acolytes try hard, even after he tells them it requires the opposite of effort. One must cease to struggle; give oneself over to the nothingness of pure light.

Most never lose their blank stares, become lazy tag-alongs on someone else's professed wisdom. Some become so frustrated they scoff at him as a deceiver. Siddhartha doesn't blame them. His best effort at explaining reality sounds ridiculous—a contradiction. When younger he also would have been skeptical of someone leading him around in a circle this way.

Maybe enlightenment cannot be taught. Maybe it can only be found, if found at all, at the end of a private journey. His most promising disciples have left him to continue their search on their own with only their own light for guidance. Their lives are arduous, as his has been, with no certainty of success. The most tenacious will reach reality, as he thinks many have. He will never know unless they meet again through enlightenment.

As the gaunt figure wades ashore, Siddhartha climbs down the backside of the cliff to sit on a sliver of beach to wait. The green hills on the mainland across the bay seem familiar. Shielding the sun's glare with one hand, he studies a white ribbon of beach. It's too far away to see people, but there are blue roofs over terra-cotta squares of what must be buildings. If this is the same beach, there had been only thatch huts when he last visited.

The tattooed man he had met there had put himself into a trance and crossed over into reality. The berries he had eaten were poisonous and his illusion lay outstretched on the beach at the point of death. Other illusions, all naked and streaked with tattoos also, walked around him without concern. The children would squat briefly to watch his labored breathing and then run off to play.

The man's reality explained that he was their shaman. It was his job to go into these trances so he could protect his tribe from illusions. His people knew he was not in the body on the beach, so they didn't bother him. The shaman had asked if Siddhartha was a Wanderer. He said he was.

From behind, Siddhartha hears the heavy breathing of the man climbing down the boulders.

"I thought I told you never to come here again," the man says.

Siddhartha remains cross-legged facing the ocean, showing no effect of the man's rudeness. Siddhartha is always astounded that he can understand what is said. Reality must have a universal language.

The man steps in front of him. "Look, I don't want to sound mean or anything, but…" The man stops mid-sentence, his mouth hanging open.

The man wears funny clothes Siddhartha has never seen before. He is too tall to be from the tribe of the shaman and there are no tattoos. He also doesn't know whether the man is from the past or the future, using the terms of illusion. Not that it matters.

"Hey, man, I thought you were someone else."

"I'm nothing," Siddhartha explains.

The man looks up and down the short beach that is confined at both ends by heaps of rock. He seems to be debating if he should leave. Finally, he walks into the surf allowing the waves to rush up his legs and dips the water onto his face with his hands. When he turns, his eyes squint as if disappointed. Siddhartha watches placidly as the man settles next to him on the sand.

"Who are you?"

"They call my illusion Siddhartha."

"You're not real, are you?"

"Yes, I am—and you are too." And then after a moment, "I guess neither of us is, except to each other."

The man is quiet for a long time, looking out to the ocean waves rolling in, occasionally glancing suspiciously at Siddhartha.

"My body is out there—at the bottom of the ocean. I didn't expect anything after that. So what happens now?"

"I don't know; I haven't gotten that far."

"Well, where should I go?"

"If I were you, I'd stay here as long as I could. I mean, this is a beautiful spot."

The man stares and Siddhartha can tell he wants more.

"You can't go back to the old illusion; all that's behind you. After our enlightenment, you will remain a light beam without any form or substance until there is another enlightenment. Or maybe you will be reborn into another illusion and start the journey anew. Would you like to be born again?"

The man stares harshly into Siddhartha's eyes. "Do you know how silly that sounds? You're not sane."

Siddhartha's eyes open wide. This man seems to understand. "Are you sane?"

The man laughs out loud. "I guess not if I'm seeing you."

He does understand. "I'm happy for you."

They sit for a while longer, quietly looking out to sea, until Siddhartha squirms with agitation. "Look, it's been fun enlightening you, but I've got to go back." After saying this, however, he continues to sit with his legs crossed. "My illusion is dying," Siddhartha manages a parting smile, "like yours has."

Reality fades away. Siddhartha is suddenly slapping at the slick fur of rats as they skitter across his lap. His bottom feels sticky from the pool of blood he sits in. Although the pain is intense, a smile remains for the man on the secluded beach. He wishes their lights could have mingled together longer. Maybe they will illuminate each other again another time.

CHAPTER 34

The Flight

Changing planes in Miami, Paul spots Betty standing in line ahead of him waiting to board. When he steps on the plane, Betty is already seated on the aisle in first-class thumbing through a magazine. Boarding stalls as passengers stuff carry-ons into the overheads and he is forced to stand beside her, his hand almost touching her shoulder. A paunchy man with a goatee sits next to her looking out the window. Finally, the press of passengers pushes him past.

In line for customs in the Juliana Terminal, he catches her sideways glance. She seems at ease hanging onto the paunchy man's arm explaining what he'll need when he reaches the customs booth. Her strapless black dress parts over one thigh when she walks. She's already made her transformation into Betty Boop. He imagines her on the beach, her short quick stride, body squirming with each step. Paul thinks this guy won't keep up either.

Paul positions himself at the luggage carousel so he won't see her.

"I'm sorry." She says lightly from behind him.

When he turns, she places her hands on his shoulders and kisses him on both cheeks in the French custom. Behind her, waiting by the carousel, her companion strokes his goatee and watches suspiciously.

"A friend from Orient emailed me about Legion. I'm so sorry," she says.

"I expected it, I guess, but not so soon."

A smile remains in her eyes although the corners of her mouth turn down. There's a pinkish blush under her usual tan. "I'm sorry about the other things too."

"Forget it. Sometimes things don't work out." He immediately wishes he had not said it that way. He wants to hug her, but the paunchy man is eyeing them as he waits for their luggage. "Where did you find this guy?"

"Prentice Women's Hospital. He's a doctor."

"Have you been sick?"

Betty chuckles and beams a Betty Boop smile. "Not really. Just one of those woman problems you men don't want to know about."

"You could do better."

"How can you say that when you've never met him?"

"Do you love him?"

Betty looks down at the floor a moment and when she looks up there is a glisten to her eyes. The sad face is back, the face of mourning. "Paul, I need—"

The luggage conveyor starts. "Betty," the paunchy guy calls to her.

She turns as if to walk away and then pivots back extending her hands to his chest. She leans in to kiss him on both cheeks again. "I'll see you at the service tomorrow."

"So you're coming? I'm glad. Will you sit with me?"

"No, that would be too awkward." Without turning her head, she motions with her eyes to the paunchy man. "Besides, you should sit with Lily Ana and Zuzu." Her face becomes stern. "Promise me you'll be nice, as nice as you can be, for their sake. If you can't be nice, you shouldn't even go."

"He was my father."

"Yes, but they loved him. For once, think about somebody besides yourself."

"You make me feel like an asshole."

"You don't have to be." She steps back and assumes her demure Betty Boop pose with eyelids batting. "In Saint Martin you can be anybody you want to be."

CHAPTER 35

Memorial

Webb thinks Cathedral Grand Case will be all that is left after the eventual Category 5 hurricane wipes away the surrounding cinderblock shanties. The church is massive, not in capacity, which is small, but in robustness. Tall windows recess into the three-foot thick stucco-over-concrete walls. Thick oak shutters pivoted on bulky wrought-iron hinges are as strong as the walls. The stained glass in the arches atop the windows depicting scenes from the Gospels, sprays a kaleidoscope of color across the interior.

Today, a typical perfect day, the shutters are swung open. A lavender-tinged sea breeze ruffles Webb's hair as he admires the vaulted ceiling. Chiseled teak beams remind him of the hulls of the caravels that lumbered through the Anguilla strait just five hundred yards and five centuries away. It is as if one of those ships had turned upside down on top of him.

The priest is repeating in French the same liturgy he has just spoken in English, so all present can follow the service. Webb closes his eyes and his mind drifts to what Legion called the Ting Agreement—why he is here.

They drifted in the open sea, the motors off since they had quit fishing. Webb worked at retrieving the baits before the lines became tangled while Legion probed in the cooler for two more bottles of Ting. Webb forced himself to concentrate, not wanting to lose a rig overboard due to his drunken condition.

Legion drank half his Ting and refilled the bottle with vodka, then handed the other Ting and liter vodka bottle to Webb. That day, Legion's eyes seemed even deeper in their sockets. Sallow skin stretched taut above the hollows of his cheeks. He looked seasick, but Webb knew it was more than that.

They slouched on opposite sides of the boat on coolers, backs to the gunwales, arms spread along the railings, absently watching Scrub Island off the stern. The rolling waves silently lifted the boat as they charged toward the ocean's relentless battle against the black guano-stained cliffs.

"How is it today?" After a year, Webb no longer spoke delicately of Legion's condition. Legion needed to confide truthfully to someone, but had to spare Lily Ana.

"It is killing me quickly now, I think. There was blood on the sheets this morning. Lily Ana had to bleach everything." Legion stepped to Webb's side of the boat looking down into the inky blue. "If I fell overboard, I wouldn't want you to fish me out." And then looking at Webb, "Can you promise me that?"

Webb met his eyes, his mind hazy, not sure he understood. "I couldn't do it," he said finally.

"Soon it will be beyond anything Lily Ana can deal with. The pain will be more than I can stand. I'll have to go back to the States to some hospice to be doped out of consciousness until I finish rotting."

Webb bent forward, his elbows propped on his knees, the heels of his hands pressing against his eyes. The waves slapped at the boat rhythmically as he tried to think through the vodka haze. "Don't ask me, Legion. Please…please don't ask."

Legion gave him no room. "I'm asking."

Paul swings open the varnished double doors, walks through the vestibule, and stops. Before his eyes adjust, the church is a dark cave. The only person he can see is a slight man highlighted by a window sitting on the back pew. Sun-streaked hair, swooped back to a ponytail, dangles over the collar of a faded orange angler shirt. The shirtsleeves rolled to his elbows make him look as misplaced as a jelly glass in a fine restaurant. His eyes, black buttons sewn to a crinkled leather face, gaze edgily at the windows like a caged animal planning an escape. Then, as if overcome with grief, the man's face turns to the ceiling, his eyes closed in prayer.

Sunlight from the opening door alerts the mourners of a new arrival and their faces turn to Paul. He searches out Betty and her new boyfriend sitting in the middle of a pew halfway down on his left. Her face contains a question, as if she is trying to recall a name to put with a face she recognizes. When she shifts to look back, the boyfriend turns also. Unlike at the airport the previous day, he seems self-assured, his smile sincere, understanding, sympathetic. Paul takes a deep breath and nods to Betty. With her admonition of yesterday fresh in his mind, he resolves to play the role of a grieving son. He wants Betty to see he can do it.

Grief-smitten smiles from familiar faces are returned as he walks. He had never bothered to learn their names. The three girls he recalls from his first day at Orient Beach are tiered down in age on one side of their parents. Their sun-kissed ponytails are tied with black ribbons. Paul feels conspicuous in dress shirt and tie while everyone else is dressed casually. But for the nudists, these colorful shirts and sundresses used for shopping trips to town are likely the only clothes they have. They make the church seem festive.

Lily Ana sits on the front pew by the aisle with Zuzu beside her, their shoulders leaned together, left hands clasped, heads bowed to the baby peeking from beneath a blanket in Zuzu's lap. Paul walks in front of them and they look up in surprise. Zuzu's white hair, backlit by a sunbeam from a stained-glass window, is a pink halo around her face.

Paul glances up at the congregation. The anxious faces anticipate a callous act that will confirm their expectation of him. Betty's glare is demanding, threatening. Only the baby, looking up innocently from Zuzu's lap, offers him a second chance. His arms reach to Zuzu before he thinks. The priest stops mid-sentence. All is still and quiet except for the blood swooshing in Paul's ears. Zuzu lifts the bundle to him and scoots down the pew so he can sit beside Lily Ana.

He feels the sideways glances from the women at the confusion they must see on his face. Suspicious emotions, never allowed before, manipulate him like a puppet. Holding the baby in his lap with his right hand, his left arm circles Lily Ana's shoulders and pulls her head to his. Her eyelashes swish against his cheek. He finds himself brushing her forehead with a kiss, not knowing it was coming. Zuzu leans her head against his other shoulder and snuggles closer. The warmth of the women's hips and the baby in his lap saturates him.

Lily Ana squeezes his hand and he turns to her. Her face is stern with dry-eyed challenge. The person reflected by her eyes cannot be trusted. Her face becomes blurry and he blinks to clear his eyes.

He tries to jam his mind into gear, to rationalize away these bizarre sensations. His teary eyes are not for his father, who he hadn't loved, but for the pain of these women who had loved him. Looking to the pulpit, Paul is astonished by the priest's knowing smile. The priest sees what he could not. He loves these women also.

"Bless this family in their time of grief." The priest says and repeats this in French.

Lily Ana heaves forward, her face in her hands, her back jerking spasmodically. Paul covets her grief. He wants to collapse on top of her; to press his body to hers so what she feels can migrate into him. He wants to be immersed in grief, empower it, claim it as his own.

When the service ends, the congregation crowds the aisle, some headed to the back of the church, others walking toward Lily Ana to offer condolences. Webb would like to hug her also but is frozen with indecision. She might not want to see him. What would he say?

As Lily Ana bends to accept hugs from three girls, she spots Webb and jerks erect; eyes lock on him with an icy stare. In the courtyard, before Webb can get away, a hand grasps his shoulder and spins him around.

"I know what happened." Lily Ana's voice is scathing.

The chatter between the parishioners abruptly ends. He tries not to look embarrassed as she fumes in front of him. He fights the urge to embrace her, knowing consolation is not what she wants from him. "Nobody knows what happened but me."

"Then tell me."

"Accidents happen at sea, Lily Ana. I'm so sorry. I'd do anything—"

"Anything but tell the truth." Her scorn becomes livid. Legion was a strong swimmer. Even in his weakened condition, he swam every day. The authorities bought it as an accidental drowning, but she never would.

"Don't make me tell it again, Lily Ana. I can't tell more than I've already said."

Indeed, this had been the final clause of the Ting agreement. Lily Ana must never know. She would not be able to reconcile suicide with her Catholic faith. Both he and Legion would be murderers in her eyes.

Lily Ana slaps him hard across the face. Webb stands unflinching, ready to take more. Satisfied he can't be shamed further, she spins and rushes back toward the church. She stops abruptly in front of Zuzu coming out of the vestibule. The stranger who sat with her in church holds her baby on his shoulder.

As Webb walks to the street, the crowd is hushed, looking elsewhere, pretending not to have seen.

"Webb!" Lily Ana cries at his back. When he turns, she pins his arms to his sides with her hug, and then pushes him to arm's length. "Thank you for being his friend. You would do anything for him, I know. You were his best friend."

"You were his best friend, Lily Ana."

CHAPTER 36

Revelations

From the church steps, Betty watches in awe as Paul holds the sleeping baby against his shoulder while Lily Ana and Zuzu accept hugs in the churchyard. This image, Paul's relaxed smile as he snugs his cheek against the baby's bare back, is disorienting, incongruent with the snarky malcontent she knows.

After the parishioners melted into the parade of tourists on the street, Lily talks to Paul, a back-and-forth Betty cannot hear, ending with Paul's head nod. Zuzu takes the baby and kisses Paul's cheek before she and Lily Ana walk toward the highway for a cab. Lily must need to get back to La Belle Creole to prepare dinner for the guests.

As Betty watches Paul walk away, an arm encircles her waist from behind.

"You should tell him before we leave," Betty's new man says.

Betty leans back and smiles up at him. "Of course."

They follow Paul across the street into La California. Paul stops at the bar and places an order before walking to a table on the balcony overhanging Grand Case beach. He is vacantly looking at the sailboats anchored in the harbor when they walk up.

"May we join you?" Betty asks.

Startled, Paul jerks around and then stands with a grin. "Sure."

The man pulls out the chair opposite Paul for Betty and gets a chair from an adjacent table for himself.

"I didn't get a chance for introductions yesterday. Paul, meet my fiancé, Doctor Larry Fritz."

With a beaming smile, Larry extends his hand across the table. "Sorry about your dad. Betty has been telling me what a great guy he was."

Paul gives Betty a quizzical glance. "Fiancé?"

Larry continues, "We've decided to get married as soon as the baby is born."

"No—" Paul says in disbelief before Betty nods.

"She's pregnant. Did she not tell you?"

"I must have missed it."

"About three months now. She's beginning to show a little." Larry reaches to pat Betty's stomach and she catches his hand and pulls it to her lips, smiling lovingly into his eyes, extending the tender moment while Paul absorbs the news and decides how to react.

"Congratulations."

"Oh, it's not mine. Betty told me about her and your dad. She tells me everything. It's so sad, him getting sick before they could get married." Larry covers Betty's hand with his on the tabletop. "But if it hadn't happened this way, Betty and I would never have met. I'm her obstetrician. It's a girl, by the way. We named her Nicole last night. The birth certificate will say Sterling Legion is the father, but I will adopt Nicole after Betty and I are married and give her my name. Nicole Fritz. I got clipped after my first marriage, so Nicole will be our only child."

"How convenient."

"So you will have a half-sister. And I'm like your step-dad, or something—once removed maybe. Anyway, we're all family. I was telling Betty she should talk to you—let you know about having a sister and all—before we fly back."

Paul is glaring at Betty when the waitress sets a Bloody Mary in front of him. *"Pour vos invites?"* the waitress asks. Paul does not seem to hear and she walks away.

"Larry, that really looks good. Would you get me one? Without the vodka, of course, and two stalks of celery."

Larry gets up. "I'll have one myself," he says headed for the bar.

Paul looks out to the harbor. "You're having Legion's kid…or so the story goes."

"It's his, all right. Legion would stop by my cabin after his evening walk every day. We weren't in love. More of a mercy-fuck than anything. I knew he was dying. You showed up a few days after I discovered I was pregnant. I seduced you because I thought you would be a better father than Legion."

"And…"

"One date changed my mind. Better a dead father than you."

"I'm glad I didn't make the grade."

"You hate me, don't you? You think I'm a bitch."

"You'd have to gain esteem to rise to the level of bitch."

"I'm not innocent little Betty Boop anymore, am I? Even make-believe characters have to grow up."

"You once told me you would become a whore when you grew up and find yourself a sugar daddy. My impression is you and this fool deserve each other."

Paul gets up, finishes the last of his drink scowling into her eyes, face twitching with anger, and then walks toward the stairs leading down to the beach. Betty stands at the rail watching him pull off his socks and roll up his trouser legs.

"I know what I am, Paul. When your fantasy grows up, wonder what you'll be?"

"Where did he go?"

Betty turns to Larry standing behind her with a blood-red drink in each hand.

"You've been crying. What did he say?"

"No, no. It's just me. Hormones acting up, I guess." She takes the drinks and sets them on the table before nuzzling against him. "I love you—have I told you that today?" She glances out at Paul walking in the surf. "It's been a long day, Larry. Would you take me home?"

Paul walks a half-mile to the deserted end of the beach behind the town cemetery. Here the waves, tame against the gently sloping beach, become outraged monsters sending up glimmering spray like shattered glass when they batter the boulders. The white hull of a fiberglass sailboat, a fatality of some past storm, lies on its side half buried in the sand, sinking to its final interment beside the human cemetery.

Overhanging trees shade the nook where sand abuts the rocks. Driftwood logs surround a stone fire pit. This would be where the local teens hang out on weekends to do what teens do. A furrowed path leads inland into the mouth of a sinister dark tunnel of overarching sea grape trees.

Paul looks back at the divots of his footprints half washed away, then farther down the sweeping white crescent to the town wavering abstractly in the haze. Among the buildings backed up to the beach, he picks out the balcony of La California.

A mercy-fuck…better a dead father…what will you be?

Paul collapses on a log, hurriedly putting on his socks and shoes before running to the path. Tangled emotions, too raw to touch, stalk after him, screaming to be deciphered. One quiet evening after too much to drink, he will force this day to make sense, but now he needs to walk fast, outdistance it all—walk to exhaustion.

The path emerges at the highway between the cemetery and a schoolyard. A woman with cropped sandy hair walks beside the road. From her hand trails a blue nylon leash attached to an indeterminate-breed dog walking stiff-legged behind. The woman and the dog are the same relative age and Paul imagines them becoming acquainted on the beach and adopting each other as companions. Her pace is purposeful but slow to accommodate the stuttering strides of the old dog. She seems to have a destination in mind, which Paul does not, so he follows.

Past the school, they veer onto a side street that had once been paved with asphalt but is now mostly gullies. Paul pretends to study the blooms of a flame tree as the woman and dog negotiate around a cattle gate blocking the road. Beyond, the remnant of road continues up a steep hillside. Trying not to be perceived as stalking, he waits by the gate until they are past the crest of the hill.

On the summit, the road turns into a roundabout. A rotting wood sign in the center reads HAPPY BAY in peeling paint. Driveways spoke away to abandoned chalets overlooking the ocean above the tree canopy. Paul follows the only road going downhill, where the woman and dog must have gone. The road turns into a myriad of footpaths through head-high elephant grass. They all lead somewhere he has never been, so he picks one at random and walks into the yard of another dilapidated chalet. A man only a little younger than Paul, shirtless, ribs reading through his taut skin, leans against an open doorway. Faint white smoke drifts out the door past him. The young man turns and says something inside and apprehensive faces appear at the shattered windows.

The boy calls out in French. *"Parle Francais?"*

Paul can only shrug. "English. I only speak English."

The faces seem relieved and move away from the windows.

A jerk of the boy's head flips long black hair out of his face revealing a grin. He waves Paul inside.

"We...thought...*gendarmerie,*" he says in stuttering English. He points and rattles off the names of two other boys and three girls. They sit cross-legged in a circle on a stained cotton mattress, eyes droopy, passing around the stub of a roach held with an alligator clip. The longhaired boy elbows the others aside to make a place for Paul to sit.

Paul does not remember the rest of that day and can only sketchily recall the next three months. From one of the commune, he learns that Happy Bay was a time-share jointly owned by hundreds of Americans. When some insurance company declared the hurricane damage beyond repair, the losses were written off on income taxes and the resort forgotten. Anything worth toting away was looted. Even the copper pipes and wiring were stripped from the walls. Ownership was questionable, so nobody cared. The remaining carcasses of Happy Bay were being reclaimed by jungle vines creeping in open windows and bashed roofs.

The days run together into one long day that begins with lying in the shade of a sprawling tree on the tiny beach below the chalets and ends with a communal soaping in a freshwater lagoon. The nights are also indistinguishable, the daylight fading to the orange glow of a roach being passed around. The girls are not pretty but in the dark, nobody cares. One of the girls, *Cuisses de Tonnerre* (loosely translated as Thunder Thighs) receives money from rich parents who think she is away at nursing school. None of the others have an income, so she buys the drugs. Paul prefers her for sex. She is never concerned with his orgasm, only her own, and is never clingy afterward.

Mornings, when he wakes first amid the tumble of flesh on two dank mattresses pushed together on the floor, he wonders with half-sober lucidity why he is here.

CHAPTER 37

Mars

S anta's sleigh is a farm wagon with rubber tires pulled by two mules with cardboard antlers strapped between their ears. Santa, in the traditional red coat and stocking hat trimmed with fake fur, sits in back tossing out candy from a washtub. His white wig and whiskers emphasize Santa's black face. Below the coat, hidden from the crowd by sideboards, he wears Bermuda shorts and flip-flops.

The Happy Bay commune, all wearing green tights and elf hats, dance and toot in the kazoo band that follows. The percussion section behind them, snare drums and tambourines, set the tempo. Paul and his friends had restoked with *Marie-Jeanne* on the walk to Grand Case and are zealously twirling and high-stepping to "Jingle Bells". Tourists cheer them on from the street sides and cameras flash.

Paul is grooving to "Silent Night", impelled to tears by how beautifully they play when a hand grabs his arm from behind and pulls him out of formation. His first thought is he must have done something lewd and is being ejected from the parade, but a squat black woman jerks him around to face her. She wears three hats stacked atop each other, a dozen bead necklaces, and sparkly bangles crammed to the elbows of her arms. In his foggy mind, she seems familiar, but he pulls away and rushes back to his spot in the parade. The fat woman follows, bumping his fellow band members out of the way, scowling as if he is a misbehaving child she is about to whip. The music from the rest of the kazoo section trails off. Even Santa stops his Ho-Ho-Ho's to watch. The whole festive mood is broken.

This time it is Paul who drags her to the curb.

"What do you want?"

She points to him, then herself, and then up the street in the direction of the parade.

"What?"

She swishes her hand in front of her mouth and reaches for his arm.

Paul jerks away. "Get away from me."

Her face forms into sadness as they stare at each other; tears well in her eyes.

"Fuck you, lady." Paul turns and then stops short when it hits him where he has seen this face before—Orient Beach, holding the head of a boy against her bosom, crying into his hair.

"André?" he yells at her back, but she keeps waddling away. He runs and taps her shoulder. "Is André here?" he says when she turns.

A smile grows on her face as she vigorously nods.

Paul follows her up a side road, ever farther away from streetlights, until her white kaftan becomes a specter floating through the dark. When he falls behind, she stops and takes his hand, pulling him past the jagged white teeth of a picket fence onto a stone path. The outline of a house materializes against the starry sky. Paul assumes it is abandoned because no light comes from the open front doorway. She pulls him by the hand through the doorway toward an orange glow from an open archway into a kitchen.

Two men sit at a table with a kerosene lamp between them playing cards. Paul can only see the back of the skinny man closest to him. The man on the far side looks up, his grin growing into an open-mouthed but silent laugh as he slaps the table and points. Paul imagines how ridiculous he must look in the elf costume and takes off his beany hat. The other man turns. His face, backlit by the lantern, is gaunt and shadowy.

"Hello, Paul."

"André? Is that you?"

Paul squints in the dim light, trying to make out André's expression, afraid he is still mad. Their last time together, the angry words fast-forward through his mind. He imagines the scene is playing for André as well, a different camera view of the same ugliness. André finally smiles and Paul is relieved.

"Excuse my uncle, but you do look funny."

The uncle's shoulders still heave with his soundless laugh, his eyes darting about in an unnatural way. The black woman walks in front of him wagging her fingers like a metronome. The uncle's face tilts down, remorseful eyes looking up at her like a child asking forgiveness.

André waves his arm to get the woman's attention. "Gra-mere, perhaps Jonah would like to hear a story," André says very distinctly.

The woman studies the three men individually, her face sheening with perspiration in the lamplight, and then nods. She takes the lamp base in one hand and with the other leads Jonah out a back door onto a deck. They disappear up a stairway against the outside wall to the roof. He and André are left standing in the dark, still staring at, but not seeing each other. Paul wants to reach for him, squeeze him, kiss him. These urges do not seem unnatural or shameful anymore.

"Do you not have lights?" Paul asks.

"No. I guess I'm used to sitting in the dark. Maybe I can find a candle."

Paul hears André fumbling in a drawer.

"Neither of them talk, by the way, but I guess you've figured that out. My grandmother can't hear either. The best I can understand, Jonah was shocked as a baby—just crawling around on the floor and chewed on an extension cord. Almost killed him.

He never fully recovered. Gra-mere threw the breaker on the power that day, thirty years ago, and hasn't cut it back on since."

In the dark, the strike of the match is like an explosion. The candle is on a tin base and André lowers a glass globe over it.

"Let's go up top. You'll want to see this."

Gra-mere and Jonah sit in ladder-back chairs facing each other. The lamp, wick turned low, sits at their feet. Paul and André ease quietly into a glider.

André whispers, "This is where we spend most of our evenings. Much cooler."

Gra-mere alternately points to the sky and moves her hands jerkily in front of her.

"She is telling him the Christmas story," André murmurs. "Don't say anything, just watch. She is pointing out Mars. Her sign for Mars and Jesus is the same. I've watched this so many times I think I understand the story. Mars comes to earth once a year wearing a red coat and brings presents and candy to eat. Then he jumps back in the sky, to Heaven, until the next year. She is telling Jonah that when he dies—I think he understands death from fishing, what happens when a fish quits squirming—when he dies he will be able to jump up into the stars with Mars and have sweet things to eat every day. This is Jonah's favorite story. He gets excited when she gets to the jumping into the sky part. She says they will both be whole again up there, like everybody else."

Paul watches enthralled, trying to understand the signs, and then he reaches for André's hand. "I'm sorry—can you forgive me?"

"Paul…" André continues watching Gra-mere's story. "Paul, you need to know… I'm dying of AIDS."

CHAPTER 38

White Lies

The bonfire, stoked by the wind, crackles and orange embers whisk out of the globe of light into the night sky. The clan sits cross-legged upwind of the smoke, the sheen off their black skin reflecting the flames like darting yellow tongues. Their bushy heads are turned to the fussing baby in her lap, the nipple of a wrinkled breast in its mouth sucking out her life.

"Betty?"

The baby spits out the gnarled nipple, kicks its legs, pees on her stomach, and howls. The naked men cover their ears with their palms. The women, some with babies at their tits also, glare with disdain.

"Betty? Is that you?"

The baby—something must be done. Betty looks into the menacing unknown beyond the firelight, and then at the flames stinging her face. She struggles to get to her feet, but her body is paralyzed.

"Betty, wake up!"

Terror throbs in her throat. The baby is screaming; she is screaming…

The sun sets, signaling an end to Zuzu's last shift of the day. She walks toward their cabin with Bud on her hip—tired, glad Lily Ana will be closing up. The path passes in front of Betty's cabin and, to Zuzu's surprise, the door is open. It has been locked up for nine months. A baby's wail comes from inside. She cautiously approaches the screen door.

"Betty?"

Through the screen, Zuzu can see someone stretched on the bed.

"Betty, is that you?"

A moan mixed with a baby's cries sends a shiver through Zuzu. Throwing the screen door back, she rushes in. Betty roils on the sheet, her sweaty face contorted.

"Betty, wake up!"

Betty's eyelids flutter and then open wide, eyes darting, cringing as if being attacked.

"Are you all right?"

She squints at Zuzu as if a stranger, and then sits up with her arms outstretched, pulling Zuzu into a hug. "It was a dream, wasn't it? A horrible dream."

The squalls of the baby intensify. Zuzu lays Bud on the bed and walks to the bassinet across the room. The baby is on its back kicking, a half-full baby bottle beside it. Reflexively, Zuzu sticks her finger in the paper diaper—wet. The bottle is cold. She pulls a fresh diaper from a bag beside the bassinet, carries the baby against her chest back to the bed, and starts changing the diaper. Betty watches, not offering to take over.

"This is the first time I've had her without a nurse. I don't know what to do," Betty explains.

"Do you have baby wipes?"

Betty jumps to her feet, but only looks around in confusion. Zuzu goes to the bathroom and comes back with a wet washrag. It is a girl with curly black hair and long eyelashes like Betty.

"She's beautiful. Three months old, I'm guessing. Where is the father? Is it the man you were with at Legion's memorial?"

"No, no," Betty smiles, but a sad smile. "We broke up before we got back to the States."

"You're here by yourself?"

"I should have brought a nurse, but Nicole's regular nurse is married and couldn't get away."

The bawling subsides to a whimper. Bud seems to sympathize and whimpers also.

Zuzu stacks pillows against the headboard to prop herself up. "Hand her to me," she says as she pulls up her halter top.

"No, your baby needs—"

"Don't worry. Bud is mostly on baby food and I could feed an army. Now hand Bud to me." The babies face each other blinking as they nurse. "Nicole, meet Bud."

Nicole seems starved and slobbers milk into a pool collecting in the hollow of Zuzu's stomach. "Greedy little thing," Zuzu says with a chuckle. "Betty, would you get me a towel? Aren't they the most precious—"

"Yuck! How can you stand that?"

When Zuzu looks up, Betty's face is scrunched in revulsion.

"If I need to explain, then you'll never understand. I thought one baby at my breast was the ultimate, but two…"

Betty retrieves a towel from the bathroom and sops up the milk from Zuzu's stomach, being careful not to get any on her fingers, and then tucks the towel under Nicole's chin.

"So who is the father?"

Betty slumps onto the end of the bed and studies her hands, picking at the cuticle of a thumb as if deciding on a manicure. "Promise you won't be mad?"

"Why should I be mad?"

"It's Legion's." Betty does not look up from her hands. "Are you mad?"

"No, I'm not mad because it isn't true."

Betty's head jerks to face Zuzu, "Yes, it is. He's on the birth certificate. I had the baby's DNA tested. If I can find some of Legion's hair, I can prove it."

Zuzu looks out the door, calculating. Betty's baby is three months old. It was conceived a year ago. Bud has just turned one. Betty was here at Orient when Bud was born. Betty was dating Paul…

"Paul? Nicole is Paul's? You told me about your little fling with Paul right before Bud was born. Remember?"

"No, it was Legion…" Betty entreats. Then, seeing Zuzu's scolding glare, Betty hides her face with her hands. Her shoulders lurch with sobs. Zuzu had never seen Betty cry, had not thought it possible.

"Paul's DNA would match Legion's also. Very clever. So Paul doesn't know?"

"Of course not. Paul's gay. It's not like we could get married and live happily ever after. Zuzu, please don't tell him."

"I haven't seen Paul since Legion's memorial. He probably won't ever come back to the island. I'm thinking of Lily Ana—if you keep spreading it around about Legion being the father."

"Paul believes it, but if someone told Lily Ana, she wouldn't. She would just hate me even more."

"You're right about her hating you, but she would believe Legion is the father. Every time you came down, she suspected Legion was sneaking off to be with you. I could never talk her out of the notion. It drove her nuts."

Zuzu looks down at the babies napping in the crooks of her arms—Nicole, just half the size of Bud, her lips still puckered to the shape of the nipple.

"Why did you come back? Why not stay in the States and skip the drama?"

"Northwestern has offered me a research project studying the aborigines in New Guinea for six months. That's what I want to do."

"You would take the baby there?"

"I thought about it. I guess I had this vision of living with a tribe, raising the baby the way they raise theirs."

"You can't do that."

"No, I can't. It's not the hardships of living in the bush. I'm just not the mother type. You can see how inept I am. I've tried, believe me, I've tried. I thought the mothering instincts would kick in and there would be this bonding like with you and Bud. It didn't happen—and it won't happen." Betty looks at Nicole; her hand reaches and then draws back. "When I look at Nicole I see a ball and chain. The older she gets, the more I resent her. We would make each other miserable. Bottom line, I've got to accept how things are—who I am, and who I'm not. I'm not mother material, or wife material, for that matter. It's not in me to provide the family life Nicole needs. She'll wind up being raised by a nanny."

"Why are you telling me this?"

"I thought about putting her up for adoption and then I thought of you. I came back to offer you a proposition for keeping Nicole for the next six months. What I'm feeling may be just one of those postpartum things, you know, and I'll want her back."

Zuzu glares her contempt. Betty walks to the screen door and looks out before continuing.

"Think what you will; I want to do right by her. You can have my cabin. It would be tight living with Lily Ana and two babies in one small cabin. I'll sign it over to you. And I'll have my paycheck direct-deposited into your account. In the bush, I won't need money anyway. It's twice as much as you make at La Belle Creole so you can hire a replacement. You'll be her temporary guardian. I could arrange that with a notary in Marigot tomorrow." Betty turns with her eyes closed and takes a deep breath, "Zuzu, please save me."

Zuzu stares at Betty and then glances down at Nicole before struggling out from between the babies. Both startle and then drift asleep again. She pulls down her halter top, puts pillows on both sides of Nicole, and situates Bud on her hip.

"Betty, you are the most selfish, most manipulative…" Zuzu throws the screen door wide and stalks away. "I wouldn't extend a hand if you were drowning in shit."

Even as she walks away, Zuzu feels Nicole calling her back. That young, she will need feeding again in an hour. Betty will be clueless when she starts to fuss. At her cabin, she lays Bud on the bed and fluffs pillows to put beside him. Clicking off the lights, she walks out in the moonlight and climbs to the top of the dune overlooking the beach to watch the glistening waves roll in.

It had been a night like this when she first arrived. A honeymoon he had called it. A honeymoon while they waited for his divorce. After being abandoned, it had been a night like this when Legion had dragged her ashore and revived her. When Bud was born, there had been a full moon like this one.

Bud will be the only baby she will ever birth. Soon he will be weaned. He only nurses now because she encourages it. Motherhood will continue, yet she feels something slipping away. Her breasts drying up will mark an end. *A girl*, she thinks, remembering the long dark curls against her shoulder, Nicole's lips so much gentler than Bud's, her eager tongue locking them together.

An hour later Zuzu finds herself in front of Betty's screen door looking into the lit room as Betty packs a suitcase. Tomorrow they will be gone on the 2 PM flight to Miami. The cabin will be put up for sale and she will never see either of them again.

"I'll do it," Zuzu calls in.

Betty squints at the door. She knows Zuzu's voice but cannot see her in the dark. She faces the door and talks to the phantom. "Thank you. Why did you reconsider?"

"Don't get the idea I'm doing you a favor. Let's just say you left an egg in my nest and go from there. If you are going away for six months, I'll need her birth certificate, that DNA test, and the other stuff you talked about."

"I'll have it all to you within a week. You won't have to do anything but sign a few forms."

"By the way, Legion is her father again. Lily Ana will only accept your kid if she thinks Legion is the father. I'd rather have my tongue cut out than lie to Lily Ana, but it's the only way."

"I understand."

"I'll be back to feed Nicole in an hour. I'd like you gone. Just continue your packing and leave her in the bassinet. I'll be moving in tonight."

"Can't I stay? Can't we be friends?"

CHAPTER 39

Jonah and the Whale

A ndré's eyelids blink at the darkness, unsure if he is awakening from sleep or death. He struggles out of the chaise lounge and holds to the balcony rail for equilibrium as he floats amid the Milky Way. Between Ursa Major and its quivering reflection on the placid bay, a strand of minuscule Christmas lights twinkle, the shoreline of Anguilla twenty miles away. The beacon at the airport swishes bright and then fades as it rotates.

The sky begins to gray and separate from the blacker ocean. The shadow of Anguilla sits atop this split with a puff of purple clouds above it. When the emerging sun peeks over the ocean's rim, the fringes of the clouds glow salmon and Anguilla turns the green of the namesake lizard. André's world is created this way from a void every sunrise and then dissolves in reverse order at sunset. It is always the same, yet always different.

Below in Grand Case Harbor, something is changed—out of place. Their red jon boat, usually tied to a mooring directly in front of their cottage, is missing. He spots it in the middle of the harbor twisting and bucking as the ebb tide pulls it away from shore. Its ropes must have worked free during the night. If it reaches the reef a hundred meters farther out while the tide is still low, it will be splintered and sink.

Underneath the balcony, André hears his uncle Jonah loading fishing gear into his wheelbarrow. If he were to yell down, Jonah would immediately dive in and swim after the boat. Even if he were able to catch up, he wouldn't know what to do next. He could put the painter in his mouth and swim it back to shore. But he wouldn't think of that. He would heave himself over the stern and, without a paddle, just sit there wondering what to do until the boat crashed onto the reef. The boat isn't worth that risk.

His uncle uses the tethered boat as a weather vane to predict the fishing, so he will see the boat is missing in a few minutes. By then the boat will be too far out for Jonah to reach by swimming. André waits.

"Whoop!" his uncle yells up to him.

André struggles to stand and then holds to the banister looking in the direction his uncle is pointing. André covers his face as if hiding his sorrow. When Jonah moves his arms as if swimming, André crosses his arms and shakes his head. They both quietly watch the lost boat a moment before Jonah begins to fish from shore a few feet in front of the balcony.

Jonah sails a slice of day-old loaf bread just beyond where the surf begins to curl and froth against the beach. He collapses into a squat with his buttocks resting against his heels, his lower arms propped between his knees and jaw. For him, this transition into a crouch is as practiced as a gull folding its wings after landing. His canvas trousers, a lighter shade of the same color as his bare sunbaked chest, are as natural to him as feathers. He waits patiently, as motionless as the blue boulders protruding from the sand beside him. There's no breeze yet. Except for the gentle lap of the waves, the beach is deserted and quiet. Jonah's tongue darts in and out of his toothless mouth to taste the air like an iguana.

The bread begins to twitch as if coming alive. Little by little, the slice dwindles to crumbs as the water around it swirls. He breaks apart another slice into stamp-size pieces and throws these to the same spot. Immediately the water churns. The water is clear, but Andre cannot see anything moving except the bread.

His uncle stands and gathers his nylon throw-net onto his arm, carefully adjusting the tiny edge weights to dangle uniformly. With arms and legs perfectly coordinated, he pirouettes like a ballet dancer ending in an arabesque. The net spirals open before hitting the water in a perfect circle. With short jerks, he cinches the net closed before pulling it onto the beach. Dozens of finger-size flashes of silver flop in the web.

He sorts the fish of the right species and size into a gallon pickle jar of water. The rest are flicked aside to the waiting gulls. The net is cleaned of shells and sea grass in the surf before being rolled neatly and placed in his wheelbarrow. He picks up a liter plastic soft drink bottle with thin wire wrapped around it. As he walks back to the water he tests the sharpness of the hook on the end with his thumb. The wire is carefully uncoiled to full-length parallel to the beach, and then he walks back with the hook end so that wire lies doubled and untwisted. A baitfish is impaled just below a lead weight. He twirls the end like a shepherd's sling. The wire whines as it cuts through the air. When he releases it, the line arcs out beyond the breakers. He tightens the line so he can feel a bite and again waits in his crouched position.

The sand bottom seems to undulate as the swell of waves pass over. Tentacles of sea grass stretch first toward shore and then, as a wave ebbs, out to the ocean. They seem unsure to which world they belong. One of these patches of sea grass keeps André's attention and he doesn't immediately know why. But then it definitely moves, slowly like the shadow of a cloud passing over. When it lies still again, the shark cannot be distinguished among the dark rocks and seaweed.

The first morning breeze cools André's sweaty forehead. His legs feel rubbery and he lies back on the wicker chaise lounge and pulls a patchwork quilt up to his neck. A shiver stiffens his body.

The front door slams and he hears the creak of the floorboards as Paul walks up behind him.

"Are you having a fever?"

André doesn't answer or look at him. Paul reaches to André's forehead but André shrinks back from his hand.

"Stop that. I can't catch anything from just touching you."

Paul goes to the rail and watches Jonah crouched below with the wire taut between his fingers.

"Tell me," André says.

"No. The fever will pass in a moment and it will be too late. I'll fix coffee."

"Tell me." André does not look at Paul directly, but he knows Paul is looking out at Anguilla and thinking where to start the story André always asks for when he gets a fever.

"Snow is like—"

"No. Start with the river. Start with the fishing."

"I'll make coffee first. I could use a cup myself. Give me a minute."

The coffee pot and cups clink from behind. The breeze is pushing the boat faster now toward the thrashing water at the reef. Below, the shadow in the water moves again, closer to shore, just in front of Jonah. The glare keeps Jonah from seeing it.

Paul returns with two pottery cups. André cradles his coffee in trembling hands. Paul goes back for another blanket to cover André until the uncontrollable shivering is over, and a kitchen chair to sit beside him.

"The Hiawassee River is like liquid ice in the winter. It runs too fast to freeze, but the rocks along the shoreline shimmer with a glaze. Behind the rocks are steep cliffs with tall white pines and cedars on top. The cedars are like black boats with their bows pointed into the sky."

"Tell about the other trees…the ones with no leaves."

"And there are oaks and maples that lose all their leaves in the winter and look like skeletons. But they are still alive—down below ground in their roots—and in the spring they put on leaves and become beautiful again."

"Deciduous. They're called deciduous."

"That's right. And I thought you didn't really listen."

"It's a miracle, don't you think? We don't have that kind of tree here."

Paul looks out to Anguilla again. "Yes, I guess it is. I've never thought about it, but I guess if I'd never seen it before, it would be a miracle."

"Tell about the water…how the water feels."

"The only reason to get in the water is to fish for trout. Dad took me once when it was snowing and made me wade out so he could teach me to cast. Even in the insulated waders, my feet began to throb and then went numb. It's stupid to go through all that for tiny fish."

"I wish I could do it. I've never been cold before. When I get the chills, I think I know what it would feel like. Is it like that do you think?"

"Yes, it makes you shake and your teeth chatter. I had chills when I was about ten—when I had pneumonia. It feels just the same."

"Tell about the snow now."

"You've already heard everything about snow. Don't make me tell it again."

They are quiet, watching the old man below crouching like a bird.

"Did you see that?" Paul jumps to the rail and points down at the water.

"Yes, I saw it earlier. It's a baby whale shark. Keep your voice down and stop pointing or you'll kill it."

Paul turns with a puzzled face.

"If Uncle Jonah sees you pointing, he'll stand up and see it too. He'll wade out, sit on its back, and kill it with his knife. It will just lie there and let him do it. Whale sharks are too big and dumb to be afraid of anything."

"He wouldn't do that."

"Call to him then. It will be quite a show. But in the end, the fish will die."

"Would he eat it?"

"That's not why he would kill it. I don't think he would know why either, but he would have to do it."

Paul watches Jonah fish just yards from the shark. When Jonah looks up at the balcony, Paul turns his head away and sits back down.

"Whoop!" Jonah yells.

Paul jumps back to the rail in panic.

Jonah is pulling the wire hand-over-hand as it jerks. "Whoop!" he yells again as he glances at the balcony to see if they are watching. A glistening tube the size of Jonah's arm is pulled onto the sand. Its body doubles back on itself as it flops. Jonah kicks sand on it to make it easier to grip before picking it up and breaking its spine across his knee. He holds the limp fish above his head for them to admire before washing it in the surf and dumping it in his wheelbarrow.

"*Bien cuisiner*," André yells down to him through the balusters of the handrail.

Jonah's toothless mouth gapes wide as he laughs. His arms wave about and his hands bounce off each other.

"It's a needlefish and he wants to cook it right now for breakfast."

"He said all that?"

André smiles for the first time. "Yes, and more. The fish fought bravely and the wire cut his hands." André chuckles. "You've never seen him talk before, have you? Only *ma gra-mère* and I can understand him. Bella is a deaf mute and Uncle Jonah is simple-minded, so I guess they kept to themselves when he was growing up. Uncle Jonah never learned to talk like other kids. Those two worked out their own sign language. When I was twelve—when my mother found out I was different—she dropped me off for *Gra-mere* to raise. Over time, I've learned how to read their signs."

Jonah dumps the rest of the baitfish on the sand. They sparkle as they flip around. Gulls circle above, waiting for him to load his tackle in the wheelbarrow and start for the cottage before swarming in. Jonah disappears under the deck and they listen to the butcher knife hacking against a plank as he cleans the fish.

"Does he know how to cook?"

"Of course. He will cut it into steaks, rub on his special seasoning and pan-fry it. You're in for a treat."

"Is your chill over? Can I get you anything?"

André turns his head on the pillow and frowns up at Paul. "You shouldn't stay. I'm not so helpless that Jonah and *Gra-mère* can't care for me. I don't want you here at the end."

"You're getting better, don't you think? We'll go to the States together…to the mountains. We'll go this winter when the snow—"

"Stop it!" André throws back the covers and reaches for the balcony rail to pull himself to his feet. The sudden exertion makes him swimmy-headed, so he holds to the rail to keep from swaying. "I'm not a child. You should leave."

Paul stands at the rail beside him, his face toward Anguilla. "I won't go."

"There is nothing you can do here. Your visa is expired. *Gendarmes* will come looking for you. You have to go."

"I won't go."

"Why do you have to be so…*obstiné?* Don't you understand I don't want you here anymore? You're hurting me. When I see your pity, the pain is double. If this were turned around, would you want me to watch? I wouldn't do it, you know. If I had any place to go, I'd leave you and never look back."

André looks at Paul and then follows Paul's gaze to a dark splotch under the turquoise water below. If it is the shark, it is lying still on the bottom. "It's gone," André says. "I saw it swimming out."

"You'd stay."

"No, I wouldn't. How do you know what I would do?"

"You're right, I don't know—and you don't know either, so stop all this bluster."

"Take a hint, will you, and stay away from me."

"André, I've never told you the end of that story about trout fishing in the mountains. I hated the fishing, but I'd actually been looking forward to spending time with Dad. I thought out in the wilderness things might be different and we could talk. But after lunch, he started nursing a hip flask. It was usual for him to be drunk before sunset. I knew the routine. He would act chummy for a while; by dark his eyes would be glazed.

"The overcast began to hide the treetops and it started to snow. We pitched our camp under a cliff overhang and built a big fire out front. Dad rolled out our sleeping bags in the tent and I crawled in to stay warm while our cans of beans heated on rocks beside the fire. 'Your mother's leaving,' he said. 'We can't stay together any longer.'

"I'd been expecting that; it was a relief to finally hear him say it. He said he didn't want either of us to have to go through a move, change schools and stuff.

"Dad stuck a plastic spoon into each can and used his fishing vest as a mitten to put the cans on a log in front of the tent. He said, 'I'll be the one leaving.'

"After the fire died, he put the rocks from the fire pit between our sleeping bags and we lay on our stomachs watching the glowing coals turn to ash.

"'You're gonna leave me too?' I asked him. He didn't answer. He just turned away onto his side and went to sleep.

"I lay awake on my stomach the rest of the night listening to the gurgle of the river. At first light, when I could barely make out the tree trunks against the snow, Dad started muttering. I couldn't see his face in the dark tent and he never moved. I thought he was talking in his sleep. 'You've got to go,' he whispered. I thought I had imagined it, but then he mumbled 'Just gotta man-up and get the hell out.' I rolled toward him and picked up one of those rocks between our sleeping bags. I wanted to bash his head in. If he couldn't turn me into another him, he was going to desert me like I was nothing. 'I'll never be like you,' I yelled at him.

"Dad got up without a word and started gathering wood for a fire. It had quit snowing in the night and where we'd tramped around the fire in muddy boots the evening before was clean and white again. While I watched from the tent, he scooped snow into a pot and put it beside the fire and spooned in coffee. 'You can be better than me, Paul. Try to do better,' he said.

"André, when I needed Dad the most, he turned tail and ran. I hated him for it. But when Dad was dying, I was the one who ran out on him. We were different in so many ways, but in this, we were the same. That's what you expect from me, isn't it—just catch a plane and bail out?"

Paul was waiting for a response, but André couldn't make himself look up.

"I need to do the hard things, André, don't you see? I have to prove I'm not like that—not just to you, but to me."

A red dot bobbing at the horizon catches André's eye. "Whoop!" he yells down. When Jonah walks out from below the deck, André points. Jonah shields his eyes and looks also.

When Jonah turns, his arms wave above his head and his legs dance wildly. "Whoop!" he yells up to them. His tongue darts around in his laughing mouth. Somehow the red boat had made it through the reef. Soon it would be out of sight and gone forever. It might drift into the open ocean or wind up against Anguilla's rocky shore. But for now it is safe and Jonah is happy.

CHAPTER 40

An Unlikely Family

 he procession is already halfway between Bella's house and the cemetery when Zuzu catches up. Bella, flanked by two women in black dresses and hats, follows behind the simple pinewood coffin. When the four pallbearers enter through the cemetery gate, two men's heads pop up from the grave they are digging. The men throw out their shovels, crawl out, and slap sand from their pant legs. The casket is set on two ropes stretched four feet apart at the end of the grave. There is no ceremony, no moment of reflection, only the fluid motions of the pallbearers lifting the casket with the ropes over the grave and lowering it.

After the ropes are pulled through and the gravediggers prepare to begin again, one of the pallbearers, the only white man, walks to Bella. As they hug and cry quietly on each other's shoulders, the rest of the entourage, whispering in pairs, meander back toward the gate. Only one of the pallbearers remains by the grave. He is oddly dressed in a long-sleeve white shirt buttoned to the top tucked into tan canvas pants cut off at the knees. At first, he smiles brightly down at the coffin and then dances frantically in circles waving his arms when the gravediggers begin shoveling in the sand.

Bella and the white man rush to him and the three motion signs to each other. The white man looks to the sky and pleads, "No, no," in frustration before returning to signing with the black man. Zuzu had not recognized Paul until he stuck his prominent chin in the air and his long hair fell away from his face.

Bella and Paul each take an arm of the black man. He stumbles between them, still looking over his shoulder as they walk away from the grave. When they emerge from the brick gateway at the cemetery entrance, Zuzu reaches out to touch Bella's arm.

"I'm...so...sorry," she says distinctly so Bella can read her lips. Bella nods and puts her hands, one atop the other, over her heart to show her appreciation. She looks back and forth between her and Paul who is staring wide-eyed. Bella smiles and pulls the black man by the hand toward her house.

"Paul, I almost didn't recognize you. You're skinny as a rail. I bet you haven't cut your hair since the last time I saw you."

Paul looks away with his pointer finger under his chin as if thinking. "You're right, I haven't," he says. "You're looking good as ever."

"I hope Bella will forgive me for being late. I went to the church first and nobody was there."

"Yeah...well. The old priest said he couldn't do last rites in the church because André was openly gay—some papal cannon or something. That tore Bella up, so I talked him into doing the ceremony at Bella's house." He looks at Bella and the black man walking away. "I need to help Bella with Jonah. He's...confused. He's got the mind of a three-year-old and was expecting to see André jump out of the coffin and fly up to Heaven. Bella and I will have to find some way to explain all this." Paul extends his arms toward her and when Zuzu, unsure what the gesture means, puts her hands in his, he pulls her into a back-patting embrace, his cheek laid atop her head, arms trembling. "Sorry. I wasn't expecting that either. Guess I needed a hug." He takes her hand and turns toward Bella's house. "Walk with me."

"I'm sorry about André. I didn't know you two were close. So you have been living with Bella?"

"For the last few months. They took me in after... I was sort of messed up for a while."

"Have you been on the island this whole time and didn't come to see Lily Ana?"

"I couldn't face her, not after Dad…" Paul looks ahead, his face hard, and lets out a tense breath. "The son-of-bitch wasn't faithful to Lily Ana either. After the memorial, Betty told me about her and Dad. I know this is bursting your bubble about Legion, and I'm sorry, but I just couldn't go back to Orient and pretend—"

"Paul…" For a quick moment Zuzu considers the lie, the lie everyone believes, and how it must remain the truth. "Paul, I know about Betty and Legion. And Lily Ana knows too." They stop and stare at each other. "Paul, there's so much I need to tell you. You need to see Bud—just beginning to walk. And there is someone else I need to introduce you to."

(Three years later – April 2006)
It is Sunday. Lily Ana and Zuzu are restocking liquor to the bar. They turn to giggles coming from the path to the cabins. Looking over the half-wall, Paul walks stiff-legged, rocking back and forth like Frankenstein. When he walks through the doorway, he has one giggling child clinging to each leg.

"Save me," he cries to Zuzu and Lily Ana in fake desperation. "I've been attacked by two ferocious crabs."

Zuzu has to tickle Nicki into helplessness before she will let Paul loose. After handing her to Lily Ana, Bud insists on the same treatment before he can be pried away.

"Aaah. Free at last. Either of you girls need a break?"

"It looks like you're the one who needs a break," Zuzu says taking back Nicki and leading Bud by the hand out to the beach.

Paul steps behind the bar and finishes unloading the case of vodka Zuzu had been working on. Lily Ana leans in the kitchen doorway, struck by how the three of them mesh together like oiled gears. Any one of them can run the restaurant plus tend bar, or cook, or bus tables if need be. And they love keeping the kids equally. They are family, the family she had never had growing up—or later as a young woman.

Paul looks so much like Legion. He had been muscular when she first met him four years ago, but now he is string-bean lean like Legion and he has let his hair grow into a ponytail like his. She misses Legion, the warmth of him at night—even his crazy antics.

She looks out past the half-wall at the beach allowing herself an idle moment to enjoy the sea breeze. Among the strolling nude bodies it is easy to spot Bella in her flowery muumuu.

"Paul. Go greet Bella. Here..." Lily Ana picks an apple from a basket on the bar. "Take her something to eat. I'll finish up here."

Paul searches the beach, beams a smile when he spots her, and trots out the doorway. They pucker kisses at each other's cheeks before signing to each other. Bella had been wearing that same dress three years ago when she brought Paul here. They had stood at that very spot, her signing to Paul and Paul shaking his head. Bella had turned him toward the La Belle Creole and given him a shove.

Lily Ana had not known what to expect from Paul that day— or from herself either. At Legion's memorial, he had acted so mature, sincere. Zuzu had hoped they could mend fences and become friends again. They had left with his promise to come by Orient before returning to the States. But like after Bud was born, he just left without even a good-bye. Zuzu had run into him later; he had never left the island but had never visited them.

Their meeting that morning had been awkward, both wary that the other harbored a grudge. Then he started coming with Bella on the bus every day she worked Orient Beach, loitering at the bar with either her or Zuzu. He immediately became attached to the kids, playing with them like they were his own. If he missed a day, Nicki and Bud would pout. And then he began sleeping in Betty's cabin with Zuzu and the kids, babysitting at night while Zuzu worked.

Zuzu had explained before she asked that there was nothing romantic going on. "Paul is gay. He'll never talk to you about it, but you need to know. And I'm not interested in a relationship with anybody. So we'll live like a family, for the sake of the kids— but it will also keep men from hitting on either of us."

So Paul became Uncle Paul, an adoptive father. Guests often complimented her, for her lovely daughter, Zuzu's devoted husband, and her beautiful grandchildren. At first, she had felt embarrassed when guests made these assumptions, as if not setting them straight was a sinful lie, but now she just glows with pride. They had evolved into the family people saw, a happy loving family.

CHAPTER 41

Sugarbird in a Flame Tree

O he male hops sideways, fans his tail, puffs out his handsome yellow breast, and chirps an invitation. Facing him a meter away, the female matches his dance exactly, quick flamenco stutter steps with rigid pauses so he can admire her statuesque pose. When the male responds with a new step, she plays hard to get and flies up to a flame tree limb.

Webb sits at the kitchen table watching the sugarbird couple through the open doorway performing their mating dance—the first sign of the coming dry season. Next, the bare flame tree overhanging the patio will burst into fire-red blooms, and then it will be time to fish seriously. The billfish will be herding the ballyhoo out of the Puerto Rico Trench into the canyon where he can reach them out of Island Harbor in *The Little Lady*.

When the female drops back down in front of the male, she flutters her feathers. He can't resist. She crouches onto her stomach to steady herself. Mating takes only a second and then he flaps up into the tree. She flutters again calling him back. He's hooked.

The male's carefree bachelor days are over. She'll want a nest in the flowering flame tree. Webb will get to watch their progress over the next week. Only the best materials will do. If the male tries to pass off a stick as good enough, she will jerk it from his beak and drop it to the ground, squeaking her irritation like a rusty hinge.

He will feed her for two weeks while she broods the clutch and then regurgitate most of what he eats into the gaping mouths of the hatchlings for another three weeks after that. With the breeding cycle ended, they will all fly off, leaving the poop-stained nest as the male's only reward.

Webb's eyes glance at the broom behind the door. He should shoo the male away, break the trance being cast by the female. Of course, this wouldn't save him. There's only one thing going through his pea-sized brain right now, and it won't be denied. A couple of weeks after this first family leaves, he'll be back prancing around the patio, none the wiser, calling out to every female that flies by, ready for his next servitude. If he performs well this first time, the same female will be back.

The email had been from EPWorthy with a British domain suffix. A full-day charter. It was the slow season and he needed the money. His reply confirmed the date, just a week away. He had told EPWorthy fishing was picking up, lied about all the fish he had caught just yesterday. He asked who recommended him. There was no answer, but a few days later a deposit arrived in his PayPal account.

In front of the pier, a woman wearing a loose fitting blue jumpsuit and canvas deck shoes stepped out of a cab. A pink sun hat, brim held to the sides of her head with a ribbon tied under her chin, shaded her face. Rose-tinted sunglasses turned to the beach bar where Webb sat with his cousins. After she waved and he waved back, she walked straight to *The Little Lady* tied at the pier, lowered herself in, sat in the fighting chair and waited.

Something, the gait of her walk maybe, seemed familiar; the nurse flashed in his memory and then he dismissed it as impossible. His cousins, horny bachelors, grinned at Webb. He took a last sip of coffee and grinned back.

She kept her head tilted down as he climbed aboard and greeted her. "Good morning." He was about to go through his usual disclaimers; *if you'd gotten here earlier…a front's moving in—*

"Hello, Webb."

He froze, one leg on the pier and one leg in the boat, the cast line he had been uncoiling from a cleat limp in his hands.

"How have you been?"

His head jerked around, mouth open and mind blank.

"Long time, no see." She took off the sunglasses and smiled, the cheery smile he remembered when he thought of her.

Webb finished pushing off from the pier, then sat on a cooler staring at her while the boat drifted. So many questions, each crowding to come out first. "Twenty years…" he stuttered.

"Aren't you glad to see me?"

"Yes, yes." He jumped up to hug her.

She stood, turned her back, propped her arms on the chrome rail atop the gunwale, looking out at the island at the harbor entrance. "Are we going to drift in the harbor all day?"

"But—"

"I want you to take me to Petit Cove."

"But—"

"I've hired this boat for the day—and the captain as well. I want to go to Petit Cove. If you want to hug me, it should be there."

Webb stored the bumpers and prepared the boat for the run. As he maneuvered through the rocks between the reef and shore, she stripped down to a bikini, throwing her fishing clothes through the doorway to the cabin under the foredeck. When he gunned through the outlet at Shoal Bay, she stood beside him, holding onto the top of the windscreen, letting the air stream her long auburn hair behind. She was still beautiful.

Webb idled behind the boulders into the little cove and pointed the bow at the tiny beach still half shaded by the overhanging cliff.

"Hop to the beach when I nose in."

"No, let's anchor out. We can swim ashore later. I've got something to discuss with you first."

Webb threw a bow anchor onto the beach, then idled back and dropped an aft anchor so they would be suspended in the flat water in the middle of the cove. After he cut the motor, he searched her eyes trying to guess what this was about. His eyes fell to her ample cleavage, the nipples reading through the thin white halter. When he felt his shorts begin to bulge, he turned to adjust the aft anchor.

"I see you missed me too."

The nurse pulled off her bikini, slowly, hanging each part separately on the two throttle control levers. Walking around to face the fighting chair, she grasped the arms and leaned forward, bracing her legs wide. "I have something to talk to you about, but I need your attention."

"You've got my attention."

"No, not until after. You will be able to listen after."

Webb remained frozen, trying not to stare, staring anyway. "I won't do it this way."

She turned her head to grin over her shoulder. "Yes, you will. Unless you've changed, there is nothing that can stop you."

Dropping his shorts eased the throb. The breeze made him uneasy. "You think you can make me do anything, don't you?"

"Please, just stop thinking about it. I want to feel you. I want this badly too."

And he did—stop thinking. The beach, the ocean, everything except her became a blur in the background. The sun blotted out. A tsunami jolted him to his knees. Little bursts of fireworks flashed in the corners of his vision as he slumped to the deck panting to make up for not breathing.

The water splashed when she dove in. He crawled to the side of the boat, pulled himself to his feet in time to see her lie back on the sand. He slouched into the captain's chair watching her stretched out, eyes closed, contentment hinted at the corners of her lips. He waited for her to look his way, call to him, but she seemed to be napping.

Webb dogpaddled ashore holding towels above his head. Even when he stood over her shaking his wet hair like a dog, she still didn't open her eyes. Unfolding one of the towels, he lay down beside her, covered his eyes with an arm.

"Andrew's dead," she said.

Andrew? It took a moment before the face of a snarly seven-year-old flashed into his mind. Their son. He had visited Webb once during a school holiday—fifteen years ago.

"I'm sorry. I didn't really know him."

"He died just last month. Do you want to hear about it?"

He didn't. "Of course."

She turned her head to look at his face. She walked to the water to rinse off the sand, dried herself with the other towel, and folded it to sit on. "I need to tell you anyway." She sat cross-legged at his side looking down at the sand in front of her legs. Her smile was gone.

"The boy you remember from the visit didn't change much as he got older. He was never happy, never content. Something about him, chemicals in the brain maybe, was imbalanced, made him depressed. At least, that's what I tell myself as an excuse for my failure as a mother.

"When Andrew was a toddler, I knew everything about raising kids. I read all the books, knew all the answers. He would go to the best schools, have all the opportunities England could offer. I daydreamed how successful he would become, a doctor maybe, how much he would adore me..."

Her face contorted as if being tortured, as if she might scream. She put her hands over her face, took a deep breath, and began again.

"Anyway, the older he got, the dumber I seemed to get. He rebelled at whatever I tried to get him to do. Every day was a fight. Everything I tried seemed to drive him further away. I was working long hours at the hospital, mostly at night. I should have seen it coming, but I didn't.

"He fell in with the punk scene at school. Things got worse from there. I found out about the drugs when he was expelled from high school, but it had been going on for years, I guess. We did the rehab thing…several times. Counseling. Antidepressants. Nothing helped. He overdosed in a flophouse. I didn't know until a constable came to my apartment looking for someone to bury him."

"Damn."

Her eyes flashed wide and her head jerked to face him as if she had forgotten he was there. The agony in her eyes sent a tremble through him.

"I'm sorry, Webb." She reached over to touch his arm. "You didn't need to know, except…" her eyes closed again. "There's a baby—with a girl at the flophouse, another heroin addict. She brought it to me after he died—before she went to prison for shoplifting. They'd both been caught several times. Anything for a fix—you know how that story goes. After the baby, they got into prostitution as well. Andrew was pimping her, she told me."

Webb got up, walked to the water's edge, looked out at *The Little Lady*, imagined them idling out of the cove before the nurse could say more.

"William. That's the baby's name. I had the DNA tested; he's Andrew's."

He could feel her eyes on his back, waiting for him to respond, ask a question, something. He couldn't face her.

"Do you understand? William is your grandson."

"I've got a couple of thousand US dollars I've been saving up for a motor overhaul. High season's coming and I could send maybe a hundred—"

"Webb, come here and talk with me." When he turned, she was waving for him to sit beside her. "Yeah, I've come back to ask for something, but it's not money. I make more in a month than you'll make all year."

He felt naked for the first time. Inadequate.

"I'm moving back to Anguilla. I'll be teaching nursing at Saint James. It's been in the back of my mind ever since I left. I should have come back to have Andrew here. Things might have been different."

"You'll bring the boy here?"

"He's here now. I left him with your mother before I came this morning. I told her about Andrew, and William, and everything else." She paused and a faint smile crept onto her face. "I told her what I want from you."

"I've got *The Little Lady*, a tin roof shack. Not much has changed. What did you tell mother?"

"I wanted to see if you could still make my toes curl. That was the most important thing. Second, I wanted to see if I could still make you snort like a pig."

"You didn't tell her that."

"No, I didn't."

"I don't snort like a pig."

"Third, if one and two were a go, I want you to take me back."

"Just like that? Me and you?"

"And William."

"What makes you think I'd be such a good grandfather or husband?

"Husband? I'm not proposing marriage if that's what you're thinking. I want you as a lover again. Your mother told me you never married, but you've had a string of live-in girlfriends. That's all I'm asking."

"You didn't think I was such a good prospect twenty years ago, and I'm still the same guy."

"You were a good man, Webb, but I was a scared little girl. We wouldn't have lasted a year. It's me that's changed. That's why it will work this time.

"I'm too set in my ways."

"If this arrangement turns out badly—for either of us, William and I will move to The Quarters, closer to my work, and you can have your life back, no strings attached."

Webb looked out at *The Little Lady*, bow nodding in the gentle waves. "Let me think about it."

She walked to the end of the beach, leaned back against a granite boulder, looked out the cove entrance at the ocean. He followed.

"Back in England, on rainy weekends, I'd daydream about this beach, the sun, rumble of the waves against these rocks, the breeze on my skin while we… I'd try to block it out of my mind, but my body remembered. A woman's body remembers her first lover like he's chiseled into her skin." The dreaminess on her face faded and she looked up at the cliff. "The fantasy got me through some bleak days."

She finger-combed her drying hair behind her ears, stepped forward and kissed him lightly on the lips. "Today is real, Webb, don't you see? This can be our second chance. Maybe I don't deserve it, but I'm asking anyway. Give me a second chance."

His body reacted to her closeness. He couldn't remember what she said.

"You think with your dick, so I'm appealing to your dick. I'll fuck you to exhaustion. Your cousins will have to carry you to the boat in a wheelchair when you have a charter. You won't have the energy to chase other women."

The mating dance. Webb watches.

He picks out an over-ripe banana from the fruit basket on his kitchen table and lays it on the sill of the open window. When she's through with him, he'll need to eat, build up his strength.

Through the window, Webb sees movement at the flame tree. A little rump sticks out from behind one side of the trunk and half a head peeps around the other. A hand reaches to the rear pocket of the rump. Webb charges out just as William is taking aim with his slingshot at the distracted sugarbird pair.

"Hold up there, Will."

"Pops, you scared 'em off. I could have got one for sure."

"Maybe or maybe the window glass. We done talked about you shooting that thing around the house. Besides, them birds are my pets. Don't you see me feeding them?"

"Sorry, Pops, I forgot."

"Maybe leaving that thing on the kitchen table for a few days will help you remember."

Will shuffles forward, his head bent down, his arm outstretched with the slingshot. Even when Webb holds his palms forward that he isn't going to take the slingshot after all, Will still looks glum.

"Why not..." Webb was about to suggest Will go down to the water, shoot at the gulls, then thought about all the boats, the busted windscreens. If only there were other kids to play with. In his mind, he searched the neighborhood, mostly retired older couples who kept to themselves. The only people out in the heat of the day would be his cousins, gruff old bachelors hanging around the dock. His grandma had already warned William to stay away from the dock. He thought back to Andrew's visit, and then further back to when he was growing up. The neighborhood had been boring even then.

"Hey, I've got an idea. Let's take *The Little Lady* over to Orient to see Bud and Nicki."

Will's face lights up.

"We'll have to fuel-up first, but if we start right now we can be there by lunch and be back by dark."

They grin at each other.

"I've got a pair of skis here somewhere. Bet I could teach you kids how to ski. You go check in the tool shed, see if they're there.

I'll call to let them know we're coming. I'll leave Nursey a note. No need her worrying if she gets home and we're not here."

Webb dials his cell phone, strums his fingers on the kitchen table as he waits for Lily Ana or whoever's tending bar at La Belle Creole to pick up. This will be fun, watching these kids play. So much he can teach them—driving the boat, fishing. He thinks back to when his father taught him, how he couldn't sleep at night for thinking about what they would do the next day. It was all mundane work now, stuff he did without thinking, just a job. Teaching the boys will be like doing it again for the first time.

His heart jumps a cog when he thinks of Legion. He had talked about teaching Bud to fish one day, even though Legion knew he wouldn't be around that long. It was never mentioned, but Legion seemed to know Webb would fill in, that it would go on without him.

It was silly for a dying man to marry a young girl and adopt her bastard kid. Zuzu was just a kid herself. One day while they were fishing and drunk, Webb had told him so.

"Webb," Legion said, "I think I learned this from Zuzu—or because of Zuzu anyway. A man can be dead and still walking around. Or he can live on after his body quits. It's not a God thing or a pass-on-your-genes thing either. Don't you see? The continuum is all that matters."

Continuum. Webb had thought about that word a lot. One day he planned to look it up, but it would likely be explained with other words he didn't understand. Just one of Legion's drunk philosophy words.

Outside on the patio, the sugarbirds are at it again. They hadn't even taken a break for the banana on the windowsill. The male hops jauntily from limb to limb in the flame tree, singing his heart out as if losing his freedom is something to celebrate.

CHAPTER 42

Damnation

As Lily Ana walks down darkening *Boulevard de Grand Case*, the gilded cross at the pinnacle of the cathedral flashes in the setting sun like a beacon. Across the street is the parsonage of Father Cornelius. Bernadette, his housekeeper, opens the door and looks through the screen. After exchanging polite greetings, Lily Ana pulls her fanny-pack to the front and unzips it.

"This is for Father Cornelius for…" Bernadette cracks the screen door open and Lily Ana hands an envelope through. "Tell him it is from Lily Ana; he'll know what it's for."

"Lily Ana? Is that you?" Father Cornelius's voice from inside. "Come in, come in. Greet a lonely old man."

Bernadette grins and steps aside. The priest struggles out of a recliner and props forward on a cane as Lily Ana curtsies. Jesus looks over his shoulder from a portrait on the wall, His face welcoming.

"Father, I have brought—"

"I know what you brought. It isn't necessary."

"It is necessary for me, Father."

"Bernadette, go in the kitchen and close your eyes." His arms extend towards Lily Ana. "If I hug this woman, you should not be a witness."

Lily approaches and places her hands in his. His hands jerk with palsy. His collar, stiff with Bernadette's starch, is rough against her skin when she kisses his cheeks.

"Tell me of Zuzu and the grandbabies. Such a beautiful family you have. And with you as their godmother, I know the children will be raised properly."

Father Cornelius's warmth floods over her and then the shame returns and her eyes blear.

"Sit and tell me why you have come."

"To bring your money for the baptisms, a contribution—"

"You could have mailed that to me. There is something else."

His eyes are kind but penetrating and insistent. She looks to the floor.

"Bernadette," he talks loud at the open kitchen doorway, "Please bring us glasses of peach brandy."

"We don't have peach brandy," Bernadette calls back.

"Please, before the store closes. Get money from my wallet."

The back door closes behind Bernadette.

"Sit." He crouches back toward the recliner and then falls in the seat. He pushes forward, hands propped on his cane to listen. "A confessional is such a bother, don't you think, for a crippled old man anyway. Would you rather move your chair to face the wall?"

Lily Ana pulls a straight-backed chair in front of him, but cannot lift her eyes to meet his. "Father, forgive me, for I have sinned."

"What sin could you possibly commit?"

Lily is quiet. He is patient.

"So many. Every day I sin."

"Can you name them? It will be hard to forgive them if I don't know what they are."

"I have confessed to you already, Father. I am a bartender at a nudist colony. I know this is a sin and yet I continue. I slept with a man who was not my husband, who was married to my daughter. This too I knew was a sin, and yet I would do it again."

She glances up, wanting to be chastised, but he is quiet. His irises are brown, lighter than his wrinkled black face; the whites are clear marble—young compassionate eyes.

"I confess but I am not repentant. My heart is full of sin. No need to tell me to go and sin no more, because I will, Father. I am doomed to Hell."

"Faith is the only requirement for Heaven, Lily Ana, and I know you have faith. Everyone sins—that's the nature of man. We are redeemed by God's grace."

Lily Ana's head slumps forward and she hides her face in her hands. Tears fall onto the waxed linoleum in front of his house shoes. "Crying again. I'm sorry, Father. Why can't I visit you without crying?" She wipes at her eyes with her sleeves. "What would Bernadette think if she came back right now?"

"Bernadette is at the café drinking coffee, waiting for you to leave. I hate peach brandy. It's just my way of telling her to take a break." He smiles. "My lie is a sin. I'll bet I'll sin again."

Lily Ana returns his smile and then feels the moment of respite flicker away.

"God's grace will save us," he says.

"No. I'm not repentant. I should go to Hell. I want to go to Hell."

Their subtle smiles, the priest and Jesus behind him, hide the contempt of spurned men. Their eyes bore into her. Her eyes clench shut and shame runs down her cheeks. The words, shooed from her thoughts for so long, have been said aloud, to a priest. With her teeter between Heaven and Hell now decided, she feels relieved.

"I don't want us to be separated…not forever."

"From Legion?"

"When it's my time, I want to follow him. He'll need me."

"Did you know his heart? Everyman must find his own path. He may be in Purgatory. We should pray for his soul."

"No, Father. Much of what he said I didn't understand, but he was not a Christian. Hell for us both is the only way."

"Lily Ana, think about what you are saying. You are a Christian and if you believe, you cannot go to Hell. Can you stop believing now? And what about your daughter and your grandchildren? Would Hell not separate you from them?"

"Yes, but…" Lily Ana interrupts then freezes with her mouth still open.

When she and Zuzu had met with Father Cornelius to arrange Bud and Nicki's baptisms, Zuzu had shown Father Cornelius her marriage license and Bud's birth certificate to confirm his parentage. Nicki's birth certificate listed Legion and Betty as her parents. Betty's power of attorney gave Zuzu authority to have her baptized.

God knows the truth, she decides, *I'm going to Hell anyway, so there is no further harm in telling his disciple.*

"Zuzu is not my daughter. Legion is not Bud's father."

Father Cornelius sits back in the recliner, puzzle on his face. Jesus in the picture behind continues a knowing smile.

"Zuzu was already pregnant when God brought her to Legion and me. The marriage was to make the birth seem legitimate. And Nicki is Legion's illegitimate child by another woman. She is all I have left of Legion and I'd do anything for her. You wouldn't have baptized the children if you knew; you wouldn't have made me their godmother. I'm not repentant of these lies either."

Father Cornelius stares at his hands buttressed atop his cane.

"Father, please tell me Zuzu and the children are saved—that they are safe. If they should die, surely God would take them in."

"Lily Ana, Bud and Nicki are innocent of their parents' sins. Now that they are baptized, rest assured they are within God's fold. Zuzu and Legion were married in a civil ceremony so it was a lie to the government, not to God. However, tricking me and the Church into baptizing the children was a grievous sin. We should pray to God for forgiveness."

"Don't ask me to lie to God again, Father. I'd rather go to Hell."

Part 3

(Fifteen years later)

September 2023 – Balneaire Resort, Saint Martin FWI

At the end of all our exploring,
we arrive where we started
and know the place for the first time.

– T.S. Elliot

The mind is its own place,
and in itself can make a heaven of hell,
a hell of heaven.

– Milton

A swirling opaque fog
at once isolating and co-joining us all.

– Unknown.

One never goes so far as when one doesn't know where one is going.

– Goethe

Legends contain truths distilled from the collective mind.

– Unknown

Women are never so strong as after their defeat.

– Alexandre Dumas

CHAPTER 43

The Wave

The resort's guests have evacuated, but six of the staff have chosen to ride out the storm in the resort's grocery store. The concrete building, a hundred yards inland from La Belle Creole, is sturdier than their rickety homes. They sit on the checkout counter and frozen food cabinets.

With no windows and the sliding glass entrance covered by a steel storm door, it is utterly dark inside when the power goes out. Paul reaches to Lily Ana on his right, pats her leg for reassurance, then turns to Zuzu on his left. Zuzu jumps when he lays his hand on her leg. She grabs his arm and pulls him closer. He can feel her trembling, her silent sobs.

Lily strikes a Bic lighter, as blinding as a camera's flash. From her raincoat pocket, she pulls out a handful of the squat little mood candles used on the tables at the restaurant. Everyone applauds.

The wind outside moans ever louder until it is like being in the stomach of a roaring monster. Metal roofs from surrounding cabins clang against the walls. Zuzu jumps with each crash, burying her face in Paul's shoulder. Candlelight flickers on the circle of faces, lips stretched tight and eyes tilted to the roof. Will it hold?

Lily Ana calmly thumbs her rosary. "Thank God the kids are not here."

"Pray for us, Lily," someone yells above the clamor.

"I'm not a priest. Pray for yourselves. Ask for absolution, in case it is our time."

Zuzu mumbles against Paul's chest, as if sending her prayers through him. Her tense muscles begin to soften. The storm subsides slowly at first and then all is quiet except for the ringing in the ears that comes after sustained noise.

"Open the door," someone says.

"No," a frightened voice answers.

"It's over. Let's see what's left."

Paul slides the glass door open, unlatches the storm door, opens it a crack. He thinks of Noah sending out the dove, wishes he had a dove to shove out the door. When he looks out, nothing is where it should be, as if the little store had been blown to a different island. Slate clouds billow above but the rain has ended, the wind only a gentle breeze. He steps out and the others tentatively follow, gasping at what they see.

Lily charges out and takes a quick look. "Zuzu, go to the cabins. See what's left. Meet me at the restaurant. Paul, see if the car will run. You need to check on Bella if you can get there. It might have been worse for them."

Paul starts toward the parking lot.

"Paul."

He turns, ready for her next instruction, surprised to see her confused, indecisive, as if she has something to say but cannot remember the words in English.

"Be careful, Paul."

He turns again toward the car.

"God loves you," she calls after him.

Paul stops and looks out through the spiderweb of fractured windshield at the pavement dipping beneath the floodwaters. Just another mile to Bella's house. So far, he has not confronted any debris he couldn't coax the Land Rover over or around, but ahead is the low-lying stretch beside the salt pond behind Grand Case. Once he starts down this there will be no room to turn around between the storefronts on one side of the road and the drainage ditch on the other.

An image flashes in Paul's mind of Bella on the roof of her bungalow, Jonah clinging to her, hiding his eyes against her chest from what he does not understand. Below, giant waves crash through the rear door into their living quarters.

He had tried to make her leave with him yesterday, ride out the storm at Orient, but Jonah was afraid of cars. When she finally gave up on coaxing Jonah into the Land Rover, she ushered him back to the house and turned on the stoop, waving with the backs of her hands for Paul to leave.

"No," he mouthed, shaking his head.

She pointed at Jonah and herself, made her sign for Mars, and then shut the door behind them. *Jesus would protect them.*

Not that Orient would have been any safer, but he is the only one who can communicate with them. She had not even known a hurricane was coming until he came for her. The image in his head of her house changes; the walls have collapsed. Bella is nowhere to be seen. His heart races. He should not have left them.

It had been eighteen years since he felt this level of panic—tied up in traffic on this same stretch of road. A call from André's cell phone, but André didn't speak when Paul answered. He remembers the frustration of yelling into the phone with nobody talking back, and then the meaning of the call flooding over him. Bella had managed to call with Andre's phone but could not talk. André was dead.

Since that day, Paul has traveled the five kilometers between Orient and Grand Case twice a day transporting Bella and her novelties to and from work and buying supplies for the restaurant at the warehouses along the way. The Land Rover has memorized each pothole and speed bump by the feel under its tires. He can judge the center of the road by his proximity to the buildings. Unless a light pole has blown across the road, he can make it.

"God loves me," he whispers as he inches forward.

Maria, hands on her hips, stands at the corner of *Boulevard de Grand Case* frowning back at the collapsed roof of her coffee shop's gazebo. Paul cranks down his window.

"Come stai, Maria?" His greeting in her native Italian usually brings a smile, but not today. "Are you okay?"

"Yes, yes. No worse than the last hurricane. Is everyone safe at Orient? Much destruction?"

"I don't know yet. I wanted to come here first."

She looks up the street at her neighbors milling about, pointing damage out to each other. "It's always the same, but this time without the flooding. I should be standing in knee-deep water. And look..." She points to a royal palm at the roadside stripped bare except for a single fluttering frond. "The wind has changed directions."

"Maybe it's not over."

Her head jerks to face him, eyes wide. Paul thinks this had been in her mind also.

"You are going to check on Bella? You should go now. Something is not right. Go!" She demands, waving him forward with her arms. "Bella and Jonah are safe, you'll see. But you need to get off the street before..."

Paul releases the clutch and eases away.

"God bless you," she yells.

Twice blessed, Paul thinks. Nothing bad can happen now.

Renewed gusts buffet the vehicle. A sheet of tin roofing, crumpled like foil, clatters across the road in front of the Land Rover's hood. Has the storm turned around for another swipe? No way of knowing, no time to think about it. He is committed now anyway.

When he pulls off *Ave du Cimetiere* in front of Bella's house, he is relieved to see it still standing, and then chides himself for being so worried. The house is basically a concrete pillbox. Even the roof is reinforced concrete. He had never appreciated its austere robustness until now. When he walks past the side of the house, he can see the bay. Rather than swollen waves battering Bella's foundation as he expected, the waterline is even farther away from the house than at low tide. *Did the storm suck the water out of the bay?*

Jonah, no shirt, barefoot, his usual canvas trousers, is wading in the surf. When he sees Paul, he laughs, wide-mouthed and toothless, waving both arms. He points to the deck, blown into a splintered pile of lumber below the rear door, laughs again as he bends down and slaps his knees.

The rear door that had opened onto the deck is now ten feet above the sand. Beside it the shutters of the kitchen window are open and Bella leans out beating a ladle against the outside wall to get their attention with one hand and pointing out into the bay with the other. He and Jonah both turn to follow her point. Somewhere beyond the scud of clouds is Anguilla, but he cannot see it. The layer of clouds just above the water is the blackest and it seems to be moving their way. He glances back to Bella, still jabbing her finger toward Anguilla. When he turns back, the black cloud has turned into a wave, a giant wave, a wall of water growing increasingly taller. Paul tries to throttle his panic, think rationally what can be done in the seconds before it hits. Nothing can be done.

Paul is found the following day lying between elevated crypts in the cemetery under debris washed out of the town when the wave receded. The boys who find him, taking him for dead, drag him by the arms to the side of the road for a rescue crew to pick up. This is where Bella discovers him. She too thinks Paul is dead and manhandles him into a wheelbarrow she had pirated from the rubble, wheels him inside her blown-out front doorway before continuing her search for Jonah.

When she returns at dusk, Paul's eyes are partially open. The pupils are not the same size. Just to double-check that he is dead, she finds a shard of glass in her yard, polishes the mud away on her dress and holds it under his nose. The faint fogging brings a smile to her mud-smeared face.

She wheels Paul through ankle-deep water from one room to the other searching for some dry place to lay him. The sofa and beds are mangled into soppy piles. In the kitchen, she rights the dining table and stretches his limp body on top. A half-way dry curtain jerked from the window over the sink is used to cover him; a potholder from the wall above the stove is his pillow.

In the night Paul wakes screaming, his only memory is of being swallowed. Unseen arms rock him back and forth against a warm bosom, the perfect succor for a frightened baby.

CHAPTER 44

The Prodigal Son

(Two weeks later)

The cocoon of morning fog is smothering. Bud slumps onto the scaly trunk of a royal palm washed onto the beach. Nicki trudges on, head tilted down, yellow sundress fluttering in front like a sail at luff, short strides like a prisoner toward a gallows. Ahead is the end of hope. He should catch up, be at her side when it comes into view. His body feels heavy, dead as the tree.

Nicki dissolves to a gold specter in the mist and then forms anew as she walks back. Delicate fingers sweep chestnut hair out of her face to behind her ears. The hint of a smile, or is it a grimace? Filmy rayon presses against her breasts and belly. She gathers her hem to keep it out of the surf and tucks the ball under her baby bump. As her fingernails lightly comb his hair, he looks up into her eyes, liquid turquoise like the ocean behind.

"Come on. Walking will make it better."

After she pulls him to his feet, he tastes the ocean in her hair. Her arms fold across her chest like angel wings as he gathers her in. There's movement against his stomach.

"He's awake," she says.

"It's a girl."

"Okay, if you want it to be a girl, then it's a girl—until it's born, and then it will be a boy."

"I'll beat you if it's a boy."

"It's not my doing. The sex is determined by the man."

Bud twirls her, lightly swatting her behind in mock anger. They walk on, her hand clasped in his, toward the waves breaking where the restaurant had been. Between the rotting sargassum piled two feet high at the water's edge and the jumble of creosote posts, broken concrete, and downed palms pushed against the undercut dunes, the beach is barely wide enough for them to walk side-by-side. Where they walk, the sand should be over their heads, the water a hundred yards farther out. That much beach had washed away during the hurricane.

A familiar palm, now on its side, naked roots exposed, conveys a memory. Rough hands bathing them together in a zinc tub in its shade, her whimpers at soap in her eyes, his squalls in protest and commiseration. They had grown up linked this way. If one got a pop on the butt for discipline, they both would slink off to pout.

He can feel her reflections in the twitch of her hand. "Is this where it was?" she asks. "Was the terrace here, or is it underwater now?"

He looks around for a landmark for orientation. "The floor is back there." He points to slabs of broken concrete. "The storm surge must have lifted the foundation and thrown it onto the cabins." Slanting beams jutting out of the sand mark where the cabins had been. "I think we're standing in the restaurant now."

Tears congeal on her cheeks like candle wax.

He walks her to where the center of the restaurant would have been, where tables would have been set during the day and then cleared for a dance floor at night. They sit back-to-back on a bronze colored flat rock exposed by beach erosion. Their backs press together holding each other erect.

He had to be here although there was nothing useful he could do. But he should have come alone, even after she insisted. He had hoped an afterglow of their childhood would temper the tragedy. Instead, a scab is washed away; a sore set ablaze by salt water.

He stands and walks around to kneel in front of her. He kisses the bulge in her dress and then lays his head in her lap. "You know they're dead, don't you?" He feels her stiffen and shudder. He had not accepted it as true himself until then.

While she sleeps, Bud sits on the little balcony of their room at the Mount Vernon Hotel overlooking the beach. Because it is on a bluff above the storm surge, the owners were able to reopen the rooms least damaged by the wind. Electric power is from a diesel generator humming in the background. He gazes down toward the jetty at the far end of the mile-long crescent beach where he had grown up.

On the beach below, yellow monsters growl as they push the wreckage of boutiques, beer parlors, and souvenir shops into piles to be hauled away. Anxious proprietors sit on the dunes behind. When the storm was imminent, they would have removed their merchandise and left their brightly painted shanties to fate. They could rebuild in days. Bud knows the beach itself is their worry. Erosion of the most popular beach in the Caribbean cannot be so easily fixed. No beach—no tourists.

After their walk in the morning, he and Nicki followed smoke to a roadside stand by the main road. Little Richard, a schoolmate, had stretched a canvas awning above a grill made from an oil drum cut in half lengthwise. He had salvaged tables, chairs, and enough unopened boxes of plastic plates and utensils from his demolished restaurant to get back into business. He even had beer, but it wasn't cold.

Over the years, Richard had worked his way up from a roadside lolo like this to a five-star restaurant in Grand Case. Bud did not doubt his enterprising friend would do it again. Richard joked the goats had all been blown away, but his barbecue dog was tasty—at least Bud hoped he was joking.

"The ocean will give back the sand," Little Richard assured him when they ordered ribs. "It might take a month, or maybe a year.

It will take that long to repair the harbors and airport anyway. We locals can survive anything for a year." When Bud suggested the beach might take ten years to return to what it had been, his friend crossed his index fingers in Bud's face. "This should not be repeated," he said sternly as if Bud had evoked a curse. When Richard returned with food, his customer smile covered the fear Bud had seen.

Bud steps from the balcony into the room and shuts the sliding glass door behind him, and then turns to open it again. The breaker for the AC unit had been removed. The generator couldn't support air-conditioning, only lights. The sliding glass door still has the X of duct tape from corner to corner intended to contain the glass shards if it shattered. He pulls off his stinky shirt and lies lightly beside Nicki sleeping, listening to the waves thrash against the boulders below.

He wants to leave the island now, but there is no way to call a cab. The cell towers are toppled and the landlines not yet repaired. The cab driver who brought them here from the airport agreed to pick them up out front in the morning. If he could just become unconscious until then...

Past the doorway, puffy gold-fringed clouds turn pink, then royal blue, and then disappear into the night. Nothing exists but the sound of the waves. At the border of sleep, snippets of himself and Nicki as children flicker like home movies. And then he dreams of waves, turning green when the sun shines through them as they rise, the crests shimmering white before they slump back into inky blue. Waves crouch and leap forward, an endless procession of gazelles stretching back to Africa.

CHAPTER 45

Broken Dreams

The cab picks them up three hours before departure time. Although the airport is normally twenty minutes away, today there will be delays for the demolition equipment and then the ambulances when bodies are found. The two-lane asphalt skirts the central hills to the coastal village of Grand Case. *Gendarmes* halt the cab at the roundabout where *Boulevard de Grand Case*, the primary street through the center of town, joins the main highway.

The cab driver talks over his shoulder. "From this point all the way to the airport is one-lane. Roadblocks at every intersection control the flow of traffic. It will be slow, but we will make it in time."

The driver points up *Boulevard de Grand Case* past a procession of dump trucks to a backhoe and a front-end loader clearing waist-high rubble from the street. "The town survived the front of the hurricane with only wind damage. When the eye of the storm passed over, the mayor, fortified with rum, ran down the street cheering that the storm was over. When the backside hit, the ocean rebounded with a monster wave that leveled the condos and restaurants fronting the bay. Only the cathedral withstood the pounding."

The church bell tower, its beige paint sandblasted into splotches, glares down on the shamble like an insulted matriarch.

After an hour, they drive through Marigot. The cab driver waves out his window at a dingy line three feet up the storefronts marking the height of the floodwaters. "Here, there is no beach in front of the town to lift the waves. The wharf undercut the surge. There was only flooding and wind damage."

Between the sidewalk restaurants and duty-free stores on their left and the limestone wharf on their right is a public park. When cruise ships are in, the park blossoms with the blue and orange tarps of an open-air market selling fresh coconut juice and island trinkets made in China.

The only permanent structure on the wharf is—was the ferry terminal. The Anguilla ferry sits upright atop the squashed ticket office. In the parking lot, a forty-foot schooner lies awkwardly tilted by its keel onto its gunwale.

"Did you lose much to the storm?" Nicki asks.

"No, my home is at the foot of those hills." The driver points out his open window at the red-tile-roofed shanties on the slope behind the town center. "The house was flooded, but not washed away like the houses below. I was smart enough to park the cab at an even higher elevation, so there was only slight damage from falling trees." He points this time to the car's roof that buckles down above his head. "My wife and daughter have been sleeping in the cab for the last two weeks, but we will move back into the house tomorrow."

"Can we help in any way?"

"No, no, ma'am. Thank you for the offer. You are the first American who has asked. There are many others more in need than me. I feel ashamed at being so lucky."

"I'm glad the cab survived and you still have an income."

"Yes, that is the best part."

They drive onto the man-made berm with a drawbridge in the middle that bisects Simpson Bay Lagoon. To their left, across several miles of water, hidden behind the mauve mountains at the center of the islands, is Orient Bay where they started. Both sides of the causeway are littered with half-submerged yachts, sometimes jammed into each other in piles of three or four.

Farther out, masts stick up like lollypop sticks marking where others sank while still at anchor.

At the roundabout on the Dutch end of the causeway, they enter Airport Road running atop a sliver of land between the lagoon and the ocean. "This stretch is called the Road of Broken Dreams now." The cab driver looks at Bud through the rearview mirror. "When it became probable that the hurricane would hit the Antilles, all the expensive boats from the other islands came here. This lagoon is considered the safest harbor to weather a storm. There must have been two thousand yachts at anchor when the storm came ashore. If they average a half million Euros each, that's...more money than I can count."

"Many can be salvaged."

"There will be much work for the boat yards, for sure."

Airport operations have been relocated to a World War II-era Quonset hut across the runway from the mangled terminal building. The east end of the runway was undermined and dips out of sight into Maho Bay. Much of the rest of the runway is buckled, but there's enough left for the turbo-prop commuter planes that hop between islands. Nicki finds the improvised latrine and then sits on their luggage in the rising humidity without complaint.

A van arrives selling snacks. Bud stuffs bags of peanuts and two plastic bottles of water into his canvas carry-on bag. They also have the local English-language newspaper, which he slips into his back pocket to read during the flight. After takeoff, the plane's wing dips in a sweeping turn to the northwest. Nicki seeks out his hand as they pass over despoiled memories of Orient Beach.

CHAPTER 46

Claudette

Island Gazette

Philipsburg, Sint Maarten ———— Thursday 21 September 2023

Editorial

We're back! At our *Island Gazette* office, we regularly patted ourselves on the back for being prepared for any emergency. Then Claudette did a little pirouette and we were out of business. Coming back to a submerged backup generator was embarrassing.

This morning we are still squeegeeing water from the pressroom. I won't bore you more with my whining. Most of you readers have suffered worse. I will advise, however, that we were only able to salvage a portion of our paper stock. We have managed to repair the generator and our press, but a newspaper must have paper.

Yesterday at 10 AM, our owner declared we could (**and would!**) put out an edition by noon today. The few reporters who could make it to work were dispatched to the major towns on both the Dutch and French sides of the island. All of the primary roads are open to one-way traffic now, although getting anywhere takes a long time. This morning, we combined what our reporters brought back with the latest government press releases into this one-page edition.

Most of you (or your neighbors) have battery-operated radios tuned to Miami, so I won't waste space repeating international news. I would like to print my snarky editorial about President Trump's declaration to the United Nations Security Council that global warming is a "third-world conspiracy." But blistering that pompous SOB, if done properly, would take too much space.

What you want most is news about our island: names of casualties, damage reports, forecasts for recovery. You want to know how your friends and relatives on the other side of the island are faring. I know our report will not cover everything, but I hope you appreciate our effort to keep you informed.

Claudette was named as a tropical storm shortly after departing Cape Verde on August 28. Her prowess increased steadily as she tracked west, then north. The National Hurricane Center upgraded her to Category 4 at 2:16 PM CST on September 8. Wind speed was measured to be 275 km/hr at 3:20 PM by the anemometer at the Juliana Airport before the weather station blew away. Satellite imagery tracked the eye of the storm directly over the Island at 3:46 PM. Maximum sustained winds were reported to 350 km/hr, toppling Irma's record of 293 km/hr set in 2017. The rainfall total in Philipsburg was 867mm, which surpasses the previous record of 700mm set by Lenny in 1999. By any measure, this is our worst hurricane yet.

After coming ashore at Bay Rouge, the eye of Claudette lingered over the French side of the island for an hour before crossing the straight to pummel Anguilla with the same force. The hurricane then hooked east into the Atlantic without directly hitting St. Bart or the other islands. Yesterday, Claudette was downgraded to a tropical storm doomed to screw herself out in the North Atlantic. Good riddance, Claudette, you #@&!

Sint Maarten News

The Sint Maarten Medical Center here in Philipsburg is operating with generator power. In addition to the many injuries, twelve deceased have been brought to the hospital so far. Some have been identified, but the *Gazette* has been asked to withhold names for now. Dozens of residents have been reported missing and, as of yet, there has not been an accounting of the tourists. Many bodies are likely trapped in the sunken yachts in Simpson Bay, so the final death toll may not be known for weeks. I know you don't want to hear this, but if a relative is still missing, you should check the morgue at the hospital.

Six inches of rain in three hours overflowed the salt pond behind Philipsburg—again. The storm drains immediately clogged—again, causing knee-deep flooding from Nisbeth Road to Front Street. For those of you old enough to remember the flooding with Lenny 24 years ago, it was six inches deeper this time.

The cruise ship Dodona Princess left Port Pointe Blanche last Thursday to outmaneuver Claudette in open water. Good thing, since the freighter Argosy III broke anchor and was thrown into the cruise ship pier. Several sunken yachts will have to be pulled from the channel before the port can reopen.

At the other end of Philipsburg, the new airport terminal doesn't look new anymore. It was designed to withstand a Category 5 hurricane—but guess what? The old terminal, (Quonset hut on the other side of the runway) was not damaged and reopened Saturday. The storm surge washed half of the runway into Maho Bay, but the other half has been approved for light commuter planes. Daily flights resumed Saturday to Guadeloupe and Cuba. Priority goes to officials with vouchers; and then remaining tickets are sold first-come, first-serve. Good luck with that.

Nothing official from the government about a recovery plan, other than there will be a study. As you know, all government studies take at least a year, so in the humble opinion of the editor, it will be two years before a major airline operates here again. Without cruise ships or airlines, the winter tourist season is already over.

Miami news reports a detachment of US Navy CB's will arrive aboard C-130 transport planes tomorrow afternoon. They are bringing pallets of bottled water to tide us over until the Southern Seas Desalination Plant can recover. They will also set up a mobile hospital at the airport. The Brits are sending an aircraft carrier with helicopters to aid Anguilla.

The high-rise condo complexes and casinos received only moderate wind damage and should be repairable. Considering how many foreign-owned establishments declared bankruptcy and left the island after Luis, this is a huge relief. Over half of our economy is dependent on tourism.

Opportunists beware: KPSM Chief Commissioner Petrus Flanders asked the *Gazette* to print this warning: "If a proprietor has made an attempt to secure the merchandise of a store, looting will be prosecuted as robbery." The metal roofs and walls of many stores are blown away. Canned goods from the Simple Market, for example, are strewn over acres and would be unsalable even if the owner could retrieve them. Our reporters observed people pilfering through the remains of grocery stores even as police looked on.

Our reporters estimated by driving through the countryside about thirty percent of residential homes remain uninhabitable. But hammers are pounding everywhere. If your home is still standing, please help your less-fortunate neighbors.

Saint Martin News

The French side of our island received the most punishment. Winds from the front of the storm pushed the ocean back against Anguilla, and then, after the eye passed over and the wind direction reversed, a ten-foot wave surged back. The concrete condos and restaurants facing the bay at Grand Case became battering rams to level the entire commercial district. Everything that would float, including people, washed into the salt flat behind the town. According to the Captain of Gendarmerie, sixty-two bodies have been recovered so far. Thirteen survivors have been dug out of the rubble. The search continues today, although the Captain expressed little hope for additional survivors.

Many of the residents who are still reported as missing are likely survivors who evacuated inland prior to the storm to stay with relatives. If you think your neighbors might be reporting you as missing, please update your status with the Gendarmerie. Most of the dead are likely tourists who either didn't know the danger or had no place to go. If you are religious, pray for our brethren. The heathen among you should reflect on where your soul might be if you lived in Grand Case.

Marigot only got a glancing blow from the storm surge and the commercial district survived. Vigorous recovery is underway. Our reporter estimated that ninety percent of the residences would be habitable again by this weekend.

Sandy Ground and all other low-lying coastal villages were flooded. Quartier d'Orléans and the inland neighborhoods at least six feet above normal high tide received only moderate wind damage. All of the condos on the hills surrounding Orient Bay survived. However, our reporter observed the wide white-sand beach that has attracted so many tourists in past years is gone, eroded back to the underlying bedrock. Bulldozers were at work yesterday clearing away the debris of the collapsed beach bars. The cabins and restaurant of the nudist resort at the end of the beach were completely swept away.

During the cleanup at Orient Beach, a curiosity was discovered. A bulldozer operator who thought he was pushing up a boulder, noted that his blade caused shiny streaks on the rock's surface. When he examined more closely what he had thought was a limestone slab, it turned out to be metal. Work temporarily stopped as the crew (plus our reporter) gathered around to speculate if such a large chunk of metal was part of a sunken ship. The foreman believes the artifact had been buried under the beach and uncovered by erosion during the storm. Our reporter notified the office of the President of the Collectivité who will investigate. In our weekend edition (if we have paper), we will report the solution to this puzzle.

Beware

Let me leave you with one final caution. The water, even if it is still flowing at your location, is suspect. The sewer systems have been compromised and the water pipes (sometimes buried in the same ditch with the sewer pipes) may be cracked. Drink bottled water if you can get it or add ten drops of Clorox per gallon to tap water and let it set for thirty minutes. The last thing we need right now is an epidemic.

Cuba

Nicki squirms in her seat so that her back is against the bulkhead and her sock feet in Bud's lap. He massages. She sighs with relief and her smile fades into sleep. Bud is jealous that she can sleep at will—anytime, anyplace. He reclines his seat and tries to blank his mind. As soon as he chases one memory away, another rushes in.

Nana Lily sets a coconut cake in front of him. Uncle Paul, on the far side of the table, strikes a match to light the candles. Nicki is in Paul's lap pouting that she is not the center of attention. Aunt Betty, Nicki's mother who had flown in the day before from the States, stands at Paul's shoulder singing. Betty's latest lover stands behind, looking over Betty's shoulder with a self-conscious grin.

By his side, Cousin William leans forward grinning eagerly at the cake. Behind William is Nursey, his grandmother, who had brought William from Anguilla in Webb's boat early that morning. Uncle Webb had been at his party the previous year but had died shortly after.

Bridget's arms squeeze him from behind as she kisses the top of his head. The surprise of her coming all the way from Paris with her husband and new baby made Momma cry with happiness. Later, the baby would nurse while Bridget ate cake. Momma would tell about Bridget and her two sisters playing with him like a doll when he was a baby. He would pretend to remember.

Paul lights the ten candles as the family sings. This still shot of their faces highlighted orange by the candle-glow is seared onto his brain by the electric shock of epiphany. These people he had grown up calling aunt or uncle or cousin were not actually related to him. Who were they? Who was he?

Across the table, Nicki, the only one not singing, knew what the sudden startle on his face meant, stared into his brain, read his thoughts. Although a year younger, she always figured things out first. With his eyes, he had asked if she was really his sister? She shrugged.

A shudder jolts Bud awake and he doesn't immediately know where he is. The dream remains vivid; a happy time, a haunting time—his tenth birthday. This moment is a stake driven into his childhood, where his subconscious returns in dreams seeking answers.

Nicki still sleeps soundly. Through the porthole behind her head, the flaps are lowered to half, the jolt that woke him. They are starting the descent to Cuba. A chime and the seatbelt sign flashes. Bud pinches a toe to wake his sister—his wife, the mother of his child.

All the flights back to the States are overbooked so there is no point waiting around the airport for a cancelation. The first available seats are on a puddle-jumper to Miami the following afternoon that connects to a red-eye flight back to Chicago. He pulls their one carry-on suitcase click-clacking across the tile into the stifling humidity outside the terminal. A faded '54 Chevy Bellaire pulls to the curb, luckily a four-door so Nicki does not have to scrunch past a folded front seat.

"Can we go back to the Isabel?" she asks.

"Sure…if they have a room."

"One night will cost a month's worth of baby food and diapers."

"We can walk Obispo until dark and get a good night's sleep."

On her cell phone, she finds the phone number and in her fluent Spanish negotiates a room with a balcony overlooking the *Plaza de Arms*, the best room in Havana.

"Hotel Santa Isabel, by the harbor," he says over the driver's shoulder.

She looks over at Bud with puppy-dog eyes.

"You deserve it. If we have only one night in Havana, it should be there."

She smiles and slouches back in the seat to ease the pressure on her stomach.

The streets through the city are clogged with a mixture of *nuevos ricos* European sports cars, fiftyish GM refurbs, and horse-drawn carts; two hundred years of vehicles competing equally for the right-of-way. Finally, the cab squeals to a stop in front of towering columns. The palace was originally built for an aristocrat in the Spanish colonial period, deflowered under communism into an apartment building, and then resurrected again in 1997 as the Hotel Santa Isabel to attract tourism to Cuba.

After unpacking and her first shower in three days, Nicki stands nude cooling in the breeze from the open window overlooking the plaza.

"Maybe you should stand back a little," Bud says walking out of the bathroom toweling his hair. "You'll wind up viral on the Internet."

She turns and reaches for a bra on the bed, "Here," she tosses it to him and backs up, "hook me up. Get some pants on. I can't wait to get out there, stretch my legs. Is that okay with you?"

They walk Obispo, jostled in thick humanity flowing between vegetable markets and trinket shops. The morning shade of the storefronts has receded, and Bud's polo clings to his back. Nicki, long hair bundled under a cloche hat, pulls him by one hand, eager to browse more shops and see the Marengo band they hear farther down the street. The tank top cascading from her breasts to her shorts hides her pooched stomach.

It happens again, a man, puzzle on his face, taking a second look as she passes. Bud jerks her back to face him. "You're overdoing it, don't you think? You and the baby need a nap." There's cleavage but her blouse is no more revealing than others he has seen. When he looks up, she is smiling at where his eyes had been. He feels a flutter inside—the effect, yet not the cause of why the man looked back.

"A little farther and we can take a break, get something to drink. Tomorrow we'll be cooped up in airplane terminals."

He frowns, still not convinced.

"Please…"

The magic word that always overrules. His face must reveal relent and she turns to lead him single-file through the throng of tourists. He stares at her butt squirming in the white shorts, swaying hips like a rocking boat. This is not it, not this alone. Her face? Full lips? Laughing eyes? The patina of her skin? No single feature warrants the attention.

He cautions himself against overreacting. Possessiveness—a byproduct of being in love. After all, the look on the man's face was more startle than lust, as if spotting a movie star. Or seeing the incarnation of the perfectly sculpted Venus every man carries in his head—mysterious, sensual, exotic, mesmerizing—the superlative against whom every flesh-and-blood woman is measured.

He thinks they are meandering aimlessly and then he catches a glimpse of the twin bell towers behind the two-story buildings. They walk out of the narrow street into the blaze of sun in the *Plaza de la Catedral*. On the far side of the blue cobblestone expanse, the baroque spires of the church flanked by the square bell towers blot out the sky. She grabs his hand, pulls him like a stubborn mule across the plaza onto the second step in front of the cathedral, and turns him to face the plaza.

"Say it again."

"I can't remember exactly." He does remember, the vows he had promised while holding her hands, lost in her eyes, how he had turned her to the crowd of strangers, squeezed her tight to his side, the lightheaded flood of adrenaline as he shouted that this woman was his.

"I remember what you said."

He grins at her and she grins back. "Ditto."

"I'm not good with words like you. I could never match such beautiful words. Gave me goose bumps then…and now, reliving it."

"Come on." He pulls her now. "You promised me a break."

"It was our wedding day. That's how I remember it."

They head to the Cuban side of the plaza and sit at a card table under a cloth awning. A wrinkled waiter, three-day-old stubble, takes their order and brings back two bottles of Cristal beer clenched by the necks in his fists, still dripping ice.

Across the plaza, a tuxedo-clad maître d seats Europeans and Asians in front of white tablecloths. Kushner Towers, the entirety of the far side, is a cleverly disguised New York hotel. The Havana government had insisted the facades of the original buildings be retained, but Bud imagines behind is a cliché glass-and-steel convention center with al fresco dining on the roof overlooking the harbor. The Kushner makes the rest of the plaza seem less quaint—more shabby.

In front of the Kushner, a larger-than-life gold-clad statue of Christopher Columbus atop a marble pedestal peers out to sea, a fitting tribute since his bones had once been kept in the cathedral's funerary. His travel-weary bones were returned to Spain after the Spanish American War—the Cuban War of Independence. Bud smiles remembering the bar fight he had started about the title of the war on his first trip to Cuba.

Chris is dressed correctly for a fifteenth-century sea captain, eyes squinched looking for India, lips pouting with determination. Donald Trump. How could the Historian of Havana not have figured that one out? On cloudy days, the church has the pink hue of the locally quarried coral used for construction. On sunny days, like today, everything facing the plaza is tinged yellow from glare off the statue.

Nicki taps his arm and points to the cathedral. The tall oak doors are swung open; a nun leads her class out onto the stoop, a surprising sight considering Castro had outlawed Catholicism after the revolution.

"Never thought I'd see a nun in Havana. Do they have a Catholic school inside?"

"Nana told me the new regime gave *Catedral de la Virgen María* back to the Jesuits with the condition they refurbish it and open it for tourism like the cathedrals in Europe—a partnership between church and state to improve the economy. Part of the deal was the Catholics could open a school and hold services as before."

Parents gather below the cathedral steps. The tourists, sensing a photo opportunity, rush to join them.

"Hurry," Nicki calls back over her shoulder as she runs. "I want to be in front."

Bud waves to the waiter, points to the table. He nods that he will save it.

The mothers smooth wrinkles from the pleated skirts of their daughters' school uniforms and then step backward into the audience. Little sandals shuffle as the nun arranges the girls shoulder-to-shoulder in a single line. The teacher walks down two steps, raises her hand. The girls' fidgeting stops. The nun smiles wide and with this cue, the girls smile as well.

The singing begins—Christmas carols in Spanish. Each girl stands demurely as the cameras click, singing to the cadence practiced at home rather than the waving hand of the nun. Some of the mothers kneeling behind the nun mouth the words. They finish with "Jesus Loves Me" in English to demonstrate the skills they are learning at school.

Nicki leans in close to be heard over the clapping. "Aren't they precious?"

They walk back to their table and Bud waves for fresh bottles of Cristal to replace the ones that had become warm. "The girls are about twelve, do you think? You were beautiful at that age."

"You didn't think I was beautiful after that?"

"You peaked at twelve and then again later. Between twelve and sixteen, you were awkward and disproportioned."

"I followed you around like a puppy and you ran off with the boys rather than play with me. You should have taken pity on what puberty did to me and been nicer. You didn't pay attention to me again until I grew these." Her thumbs point to her breasts.

"When you'd bare those things on the beach, my friends would run into the water to keep from embarrassing themselves."

Her smile widens and she covers it with her hand. "I'd tease them just to make that happen."

"It was mean."

"It worked on you sometimes."

"You don't know what it's like to feel possessed like that."

"I was getting even for earlier. I liked having power over you. Is that when you fell in love—when I was sixteen?"

"No. I'd already fallen for the twelve-year-old. Even now, when you give me that mischievous grin, I see the beguiling little witch who made my stomach hurt."

"So to you I'm a gap-toothed little girl with swollen boobs and a baby bump? Sounds perverted. Inside your head must be a really strange place."

"True. But you're my only perversion. That should give you some consolation. Now that the little girl is pregnant, she becomes more alluring every day. It gives me goose bumps to think I might touch her later."

"Are you seducing me? You don't have to seduce me you know."

"There it is then. Whatever I say will be construed as some teenager trying to get into your pants. Can't I say what I feel without having a purpose? For girls, love is more practical, don't you think? Girls just get pleased with themselves about a lover, like if they find a new pair of shoes that match their dress.

"It's not true that I don't love you. Do you think that?"

"I'm just saying the love thing is different for boys. A girl makes choices about whom to love. For a boy, love is something that happens to him and he's just along for the ride. Any choices are made by some reptile part of his brain."

"It's called gonads."

"Gonads then. My gonads want to touch you. Can I bathe you later?"

"You're sick. Sometimes I worry about you."

"Is that a yes?"

"Only because I can't see my legs. I suppose you'll want a favor in return."

"Whatever the little witch thinks is fair."

They walk to NAO Bar Paladar for *ropa vieja*, pulled beef over rice. As the sun sets, they move to a table on the sidewalk and he orders a *mojitos*, the rum version of a mint julep, and a Coke for Nicki. The sounds of the city—the clop of horses' hooves on cobblestone, a distant brass band—echo down the narrow street.

The cell phone in the back pocket of her shorts chimes. Their eyes share panic before she reaches for it.

"Email from the Embassy in Brazil. It will be another week before they can deliver a message to Mother. They don't even know exactly where she is—likely in the jungle with naked men hunting monkeys with a blowgun. News of the hurricane probably hasn't reached her."

"What will she do?"

"Nothing, of course. You know how my mother is. I might get a message back, or I might not."

"Her work is important."

"You don't have to defend her. My worse fear is becoming her. Please tell me I'm not like her."

"She's pretty—and smart."

Nicki kicks him under the table—hard. He reaches for his shin.

"I'm not like her. Why couldn't she be like your mother?"

He can't fight off the conjured image, his mother lying among the coral, her face wrinkled by the water, eyes half open. "My mother's dead."

Nicki's face goes from anger to shock and she reaches for his hand, "Oh, Bud, I'm sorry. It's just…"

She sits erect, staring at her glass as she spins it with one hand in a puddle of humidity. Without sobs, she cries. Her hand on his twitches almost imperceptibly as her mind races between memories. Tears drip from her cheeks into widening splotches on her blouse. He fights the urge to console, knowing she needs this release.

She takes her hand from his and wipes tears from her face, smearing eyeliner onto her cheeks. "As a girl, I fantasized Zuzu was my mother. Did you know that?"

"Mother loved you like her own. More than me, I think."

"Then it's settled. From now on, Zuzu was my mother as well."

"I like being your half-brother better; it doesn't sound as incestuous."

"Fine. You have your fantasy and I'll have mine. Besides, incest doesn't apply to cousins and half-siblings. Please don't use that word."

"It doesn't bother you what people will think?"

"Who? Our friends on the island assumed we were doing it even before we were. They're French; nobody cares. With our last names the same, we're just another married couple in Chicago. Zuzu and Nana would have been the only people shocked about the baby and…" The tears well in her eyes again.

During Spring Break, their previous trip to Saint Martin, was when Zuzu and Nana were to be told about the baby. That had been the plan. He and Nicki would sit them down together and just tell all—the baby, their ruse of being married, everything. They would face the wrath together, neither allowing the other to be singled out for blame. But Spring Break had been a zoo at the La Belle Creole and he and Nicki had been drafted to help. Every day they worked until midnight and then were back for the breakfast shift. Age kept Nana from darting in every direction at once like when they were kids, but she still had the drive and from behind the bar she kept everybody busy. He had never seen his mother so happy, the family working together again.

He and Nicki kept finding excuses to put off their bombshell. And then they were on the plane back to the States and it never happened. They had talked about telling them in a letter, but that never happened either. It seemed so chicken-shit after hiding it from them for a week.

"Maybe I'm a coward, but I'm glad I never had to tell mother," Bud says.

Nicki's face turns into a snarl, "My mother would look at us having a baby as some grand experiment for her to study. At least you had a mother, a caring mother. More than I ever had."

"I hope there is nothing to study. I mean six toes or anything like that."

A smile grows, a quiet chuckle, while her eyes are still bleary, "That would be neat."

"You're not worried?"

"Not about his toes." She lifts her glass in a toast. "To the first six-toed football star."

He clicks her glass with his. "To the first six-toed ballerina."

It is over, her skirmish with the past, as quickly as it had overcome her. He orders another round of drinks and, as they recount the remarkable changes happening to Cuba, let the dregs of their wearying trip drain away. Eventually, he will have to drag her back—discuss their situation, make decisions, plan—but it can wait until after the rawness of tragedy begins to heal.

A middle-aged Latino with thinning slicked-back hair and bolo tie walks into the island of light thrown through the café door. Bud thinks at first he is smiling at Nicki, but the man extends both hands to a chocolate-skinned girl who has been standing beside their table. The man kisses the girl lightly on the cheek and then stands back to admire her dress. The girl beams as she twirls to flourish the pleated skirt. "*Fantastica*," the man says as he circles her waist with his arm and guides her into the restaurant. The girl is pretty and Bud turns in his seat to watch her backside as they walk through the doorway.

"Quite a gentleman," Nicki declares, "unlike the Havana boys her age, I imagine. Bet he bought that dress."

"They're a couple, don't you think, meeting after work?"

The girl holds the man's arm as he talks with the headwaiter. Young men at the bar check her out and she returns their smiles.

"Married or not, she's still available. He may think he's the one, but for her, the game's not over."

"Why do you make it sound so adversarial?"

"The man is out with a girl half his age, a real looker. You don't think he feels like a winner?"

"The poor guy is probably madly in love and has deluded himself that she loves him too."

"He's just convenient. Another woman can tell in a second; males are born blind to such things."

The next morning, they breakfast on the roof overlooking the *Plaza de Arms*. Japanese tourists point cameras up at them, at the eighteenth-century façade of the palace. The exhaust stacks of their cruise ships in the harbor rise behind the red-tile roofs of the old city.

"I'll have papaya with eggs sunny-side up," he tells the waitress. She looks up at him instead of writing on her tab.

"No, no. Bring him *fruta bamba* with two eggs fried lightly. I'll have the oatmeal. Espresso for us both." Nicki repeats this in Spanish to be clear.

When the waitress leaves, Nicki covers her laugh with her napkin.

"What...?"

"Papaya is Spanish slang for vagina. You ordered pussy with eggs sunny-side up."

"How do you know these things? Is this what they teach in Spanish II?"

"No, actually my class knew all the sex words by the end of Spanish I."

"She's kinda cute. Maybe I do want papaya." He twists to watch the waitress walking away to demonstrate his manly lust. The girl is no more than twenty, long legs, darker than most Cubans, buttocks wobbling inside her knit pullover.

"I'll write her a note on the back of the bill. If you leave a generous tip, I'm sure she will come to the room. I'm not much fun as of late."

A joke. Most of their conversations are banter to avoid actually talking. Her offer is a smug jab, confident he would never make love to anyone but her. Even in school, he fought any boy who came onto her, not to defend the honor of his younger sister as the teachers assumed, but out of pure jealousy. The boys, even bigger boys in higher grades, learned to leave her alone or be prepared to fight past a bloody nose and gouged eyes.

But he also knows that if he were able to tell Nicki right now, with a straight face, and convince her he actually wanted the waitress, she would arrange it. She would do it as his sister and never feel bad about it later.

The girl stops to clear a table, and when she feels their eyes following her, glances at them with a shy smile. She becomes a young mother, with a husband who also makes eighteen dollars a month, who will save the scraps of the meals she serves in a paper bag to feed her family.

Bud turns to Nicki and reaches for her hand. "She'll get a generous tip, but don't bother with the note. I prefer to line up my women without help."

Nicki squeezes his hand and her lower lip turns out in a fake show of rejection, "I hate you. Do you know that?"

His face mimics hers. "I hate you, too."

Nicki returns to the room to pack, then a nap. Bud surfs the Internet in the lobby until time to wake her for the trip home.

CHAPTER 48

The Golden Maiden

Island Gazette

Philipsburg, Sint Maarten ——————— Friday 22 September 2023

Editorial

The Internet is back up. The *Gazette* will publish online until we are resupplied with paper. Thank you for your patience. We should be able to publish updates daily, even if Claudette's little brother Evander takes a turn and heads our way. The National Hurricane Center estimates atmospheric conditions are right for a Category 5 hurricane here on average once every twenty years. Well, guess what. Claudette proved conditions are perfect right now, so keep your guard up. Stockpile bottled water; have your plan ready.

As I read the final proof of today's edition, the casualty and damage statistics (page 2) sound dry and unfeeling. That's the editor's fault. Our reporters know that I will have them standing tall if they venture beyond the unvarnished facts or interject personal opinions and call it news.

But, as staff will attest, I exempt myself from these journalistic standards. Last night, as we compiled the latest list of casualties, sobs were heard throughout the newsroom. On behalf of our family at the *Island Gazette*, I want to extend heartfelt condolences for your losses. These were our neighbors and relatives as well.

Also, I want to publicly thank our guests from other nations who have left their safe and comfortable lives to assist with our recovery. Official messages of appreciation have been sent to your governments (see page 3), but this seems secondhand. On behalf of the residents of our island and our British cousins on Anguilla— THANK YOU!

The most intriguing news on the island is the "artifact" discovered at Orient Beach. Likely you have heard about it by now because the rumor mill abounds with theories as to its origin. This may turn into a more tantalizing mystery than the disappearance of the freighter Vasquez near the Bahamas in 2017. The Island needs a little diversion from the morose reality of the storm right now, so the *Island Gazette* will follow this developing story to conclusion. Philip Bergen of our staff is assigned to investigate and report

the latest in his column (see page 5). Please email any related facts (or just wild-eyed conjecture) to

p.bergen@ilangzt.com.

Philip Bergen Byline
(p.bergen@ilangzt.com)

The Mysterious Statue

Monday morning, the construction crew contracted to clear storm debris from Orient Beach discovered a lump of metal half-buried in the sand. There was no immediate explanation of how it came to be there. Helios Construction Foreman Jack Daniels (no relationship to the whiskey distillery) suspected it might be remains of a ship run aground during the storm. He left the object undisturbed until the St. Martin Parish Office of Homeland Security and Emergency Preparedness released it for disposal.

This morning, OHSEP representative Sébastien Perez arrived at Orient Beach to investigate. The artifact lies on the property of the nudist colony approximately where La Belle Creole café stood prior to the storm. From a distance, the object appears to be a flat granite slab, more brown than the typical sandstone. With a closer look, the yellow scrapes of the bulldozer blade are apparent. At Perez's direction, a trench was dug around the phenomenon to determine its overall size and shape—

roughly five feet long, two feet wide and one foot thick. A four-inch round pole, also metal, extends out of one end.

It wasn't until the metal lump was flipped over by a frontend loader and the sand swept away that it was revealed to be the statue of a woman. Daniels believes the statue is either solid metal or stone clad with bronze. If solid, he estimates its weight to be three metric tons.

According to Perez, there are no large ships reported sunk by the storm on this side of the island. He concluded that the artifact must have lain buried under the sand and was uncovered by beach erosion. Since this falls outside the responsibility of OHSEP, he left for Marigot to report his findings to the Saint Martin Territorial Council.

The statue of a bronze nude woman on Orient Beach seems appropriate. But how did it get there? I promise, I'll find out and it will be printed first in my column. So stay tuned.

CHAPTER 49

Chicago

(Two months later)

 ud stands at the sliding glass doors of Betty's fifteenth-floor condo watching snowflakes streak by the patio lights. He shivers. "I feel like a prisoner." He hears a snicker and turns to Nicki, sitting cross-legged on a sofa cushion she had pulled onto the floor in front of the faux fireplace. In the dimmed light, her face is aglow with the gas flame.

"If this is jail, I wouldn't mind a life sentence. You'll just have to endure winter for a few more months."

Bud looks about the posh room, the tribal masks on the wall, the memento wooden statues on the end tables flickering grotesque shadows onto the walls. Betty's home base, a place to recuperate between her excursions to study yet another lost tribe in a remote corner of the globe. It's probably worth a million, triple what she had paid twenty years ago; a gutsy investment for a young woman still working her way through graduate school. The abstract above the fireplace, a gaunt shaggy-headed man meditating on a beach, is their father, Nicki says. Betty painted it herself.

"Besides, Bud, Chicago was your idea."

Bud turns back to the window. Below, Lake Shore lights twinkle in the driving snowfall. Farther out, navigation beacons blink like fireflies floating in the Lake Superior blackness. How did a contented beachboy wind up in mid-winter Chicago?

Betty scheduled Christmas in Saint Martin before continuing on to join an expedition into the Brazilian rainforest. She ate Christmas day lunch at the La Belle Creole's bar while Zuzu filled drink orders. Nicki waited tables and Bud bussed. During the after-lunch lull, Nicki went behind the bar and washed glasses with Zuzu. Bud sat on a barstool beside Betty.

"I was telling Zuzu how much you love Chicago, Nicki."

Nicki didn't look up.

"You'd probably like to live in my condo, go to my alma mater Northwestern. I could put you on my checking account."

Nicki, unable to pass up a dig at her mother, snubbed the offer saying with a grin how happy she was being a waitress at La Belle Creole. Nicki knew this casual refusal, her lack of ambition, would drive her mother nuts—and it did.

Betty turned to Bud, "How about you then? You could start the spring semester in a couple of weeks."

Zuzu shook her head, opened her mouth to object when Betty cut her off.

"I owe you, Zuzu. This won't be full payment, but it will help me feel better about the debt."

Zuzu looked out at the ocean still shaking her head. "We've never been apart."

"You'll have to give him up sometime. Bud will get the itch to see what's beyond this island. Give him a chance at college."

"The cost—"

"I've been living on grant money for twenty years. My salary as a professor is direct deposited to an investment account. This won't even be interest on what I've got stashed away."

"Bud," Betty cupped his chin in her hand. "Want to start the spring semester? You graduated with honors, so there shouldn't be any problem getting in, but I'll send a note to the dean anyway. You're made of sterner stuff than your fickle sister. So go make something of yourself. The next four years are on me."

A week later, Bud pressed his face against the porthole of his window seat as his plane flew between a stratum of dingy overcast and the crinkled ice of Lake Superior. Ahead of the plane, tall obelisks emerged from the haze, some with red beacons flashing on top; others jutted up into slate-colored clouds. He turned his head to see if anyone else looked panicky, at the stewardess serving drinks, the stranger sleeping open-mouthed in the next seat, then back to the window to quell his claustrophobia.

He rehearsed what he should do after disembarking. Nicki had visited her mother in Chicago several times during school holidays and tried to prepare him.

"Follow the signs to luggage. A prompter on the wall will list your flight number and the conveyor your bag will be on. You'll need to spot your bag and pull it off as it comes around. Then look for an arrow that says taxi..."

She sounded so cosmopolitan as she went on and on, looking past him as she talked as if seeing the skyscrapers, rumbling trains, powdery snow she described. She made the condo elevator sound like a spaceship to Mars.

"I don't want to go," he told her.

"Nonsense, Bud. Don't be a dummy like me. This is your big chance."

"You won't miss me?"

"Of course. But you'll meet so many girls at college, you won't even think about me. I won't be able to beg you back here for a visit."

Somewhere after Miami, with every mile the plane carried him farther north, away from the island, away from Nicki, the giddiness of adventure morphed into dread. He pushed his hand into his pants pocket to assure himself he had not lost Nicki's notes—the address of the condo, code for the door.

Bud stepped out of a cab in a nylon blazer and the only pair of long pants he owned. He looked for the glistening snow Nicki had waxed on about, but all he saw was a mound of frozen sludge three feet high that he had to climb over to get to the condo entrance.

He called his mother as soon as he got inside Betty's condo. He took a deep breath, tried to quell his desperation before she answered.

"Everything's great," he told her. He told her how pretty the snow was, how friendly everybody was, how excited he was to start college. He said everything she wanted to hear, deserved to hear, while wiping tears from his eyes.

"Bud, are you alright. You sound sick."

"It's the weather change, the flying and stuff. Got my sinuses messed up. I'm great."

"Nana's right here. Says she's proud of you..." He hears his grandmother whispering in the background, "...and she's praying for you."

At that moment, Bud could see them clearly, behind the bar, bandanas over their hair, heads leaned together over the phone to hear his every word. If he could have reached through the phone line, touched them for only a moment, everything could have been made bearable. He had put his palm over the mouthpiece, screamed at the ceiling, bumped his head against the wall. He should admit defeat, tell the truth: *I shouldn't be here. I've never been cold before. I didn't even know what cold was. It hurts. This condo is turning me into a blubbering idiot. Please, Mom, send me a ticket—*

"Bud, are you still there?"

"Someone's at the door, Mom. I'll call you later. Love you. Tell Nana I love her."

Zuzu had agreed to let Nicki visit for a week after her graduation in May. Nicki found one excuse after another to extend the stay. *Bud wants me to show him...there's a concert coming up...*until the end of summer. It had been a fun time, a perfect time. When her pregnancy was confirmed, the stay became indefinite. Neither of them returned to the island until Spring Break weekend. Nicki had signed up for the fall semester at Northwestern. At least, that was to be her excuse for returning to Chicago.

"Bud, quit sulking and be a good coach. Let's practice." Bud sits behind her on the sofa and she scoots back between his knees. "I'll practice breathing and you can pretend to feed me ice chips."

Nicki has read everything online about natural childbirth, explained the whole birthing process to Bud a dozen times, always ending with a delicious grin as if already cradling the baby in her arms. At seven months, she enrolled them in a Lamaze class. Every Monday night for two hours they practiced—breathing, when to push, the words the coach should say and when.

"All the hype about excruciating pain is just women wanting sympathy," Shannon, their instructor, a fat mother of seven, assured them. "Babies are born every day without drugs. It will be an adventure for the two of you to share."

Bud massages Nicki's shoulders as she sucks in deep breaths and blows out through her teeth.

"I'm at seven centimeters, contractions five minutes apart. What do you say?"

"Squirt the damn thing out and let's go home?"

"You say that and I'll..." Nicki becomes walleyed, lips an O. Her whole body shudders. The first contraction slowly releases and she falls back against the sofa between Bud's knees, gasping for air, eyes darting as if looking for escape.

"False labor," Bud declares, and then forces a smile of reassurance when her face of terror looks up at him. "Relax. Remember, Shannon told us to expect this the last month. Just your body getting ready."

A weak smile creeps onto her face. The frightened, caged bird regains confidence. She sits up again and props forward onto her hands, "I can do this,'" she says. Then the smile stiffens to a glare, eyes flicking to him, and then away as if listening to a faraway voice. "It's coming back, Bud…" She jerks back between his knees, body stiff with anticipation. The contraction hits quick, and hard, forcing her breath into a moan. Her legs retract, arms hook around her knees, head arches forward. Taut tendons in her neck ripple; bulging eyes glare straight ahead. She uncoils finally, collapses back, and frantically gasps for air. Bud becomes light-headed, hyperventilating, vicariously feeling her panic.

Nicki goes limp, her breathing imperceptible, eyelids flaccid as if— Fear strikes Bud like a lightning bolt and he grabs her head and shakes until her eyes fly open.

"Bud, take me to the hospital. Something's wrong."

Bud jumps up and looks to the door. Shannon's words chastise him. *"Be kind but firm with her when she wants to give up. She will thank you later."* He turns back to Nicki, in charge again. "It's too soon. They will only send us home again."

"Bud, please hand me my cell phone," she says with controlled sternness.

He looks at her cell phone on the end table, then back to her.

"If you don't take me this instant, I'm calling 911 for an ambulance."

CHAPTER 50

The Arrival

S he has another contraction on the way to the hospital. Her water breaks. Bud blubbers like an idiot to a blue uniform at the emergency entrance. Luckily, Dr. Evans is on duty, the obstetrician Shannon described as *a liver-spotted curmudgeon from Tennessee with small supple hands.* Nicki looks relieved to see Shannon, a Certified Nurse Midwife, arrive to assist. These two handle all the natural childbirths for the hospital. Bud tries to shake his hand, but the doctor holds his gloved hands high, "Sterile," he says over his shoulder as he walks past into the labor room. Bud waits at the door for only a minute before the doctor comes out with Shannon. "She's yours for a while yet. Give her an IV with the usual cocktail. Get her prepped. When she gets to seven, bring her to delivery. Start an epidural and give me a page."

"But—" Shannon starts to object.

"But hell. She hasn't even started dilating and she's already begging. Let's skip all the drama this time. Start it at seven."

Bud tries to catch his arm, explain it's too soon, that they planned a natural childbirth.

"Sorry. No time to talk. Full moon you know. Busy night." And then he is gone around a corner.

"It's taking too long," Evans says to his nurse. "Is the sun up yet?"

"How would I know?" Shannon retorts.

Evans looks at the nurse, the black hollows above her mask, then bends back to look at Nicki, the part of her jacked up in stirrups, the crown of a head, then above the sheet at her sweat-drenched face, mouth a slit, eyelids clenched shut.

"She's done. We'll have to do some cut'n. Set me up for an episiotomy."

"Doctor Evans, if you don't improve your bedside manner, somebody's going to use one of these scalpels on you," the nurse says walking to the door.

Bud, sitting by the door resting his chin on his fists, enduring the groans, hears distant thunder in his ears and jumps to his feet. "No!"

The doctor looks over his shoulder as if he had forgotten Bud was in the room, then shuffles in place to face him. The edges of his mask are soaked with sweat, his eyes sunken, old, too old, too worn out. The mask moves atop the gray stubble—a smile maybe, a gesture of sympathy, or impatience.

"My call, Bud. You don't get a vote on this one. You can stay if you want, but I don't recommend it."

Bud goes to her side, looks down at the pink stripes across her forehead left by the elastic cap, the green squiggles of the heart monitor reflecting off her red-splotched cheeks, eyes still shut as if she no longer cares. When he drags the back of his fingers across her cold, clammy lips, her eyelids jerk but don't open. Gravity increases ten-fold pushing him toward the floor; he loses his balance.

"Bud—" The doctor catches his arm. "Let's me and you have a conference." Evans leads him into an adjacent room and pulls his mask down around his throat.

"We're fixin' to have us a baby, Bud. A healthy one, I can tell already."

"It's premature. This should be easier."

"Premature? Don't think so. A little over-baked if anything. Seven and a half, I'm betting. You should wait in here."

"But I promised—"

"Understand, and all that. I won't stop you, but you've got to stay in that chair, no matter what. You don't want to see up close anyway. Like sausage—don't need to know how it's made. Recovery will take a little longer, but she'll be back in working order in a couple or three months."

Bud wants to strangle him, get the smirk off his face. The doctor strips off his rubber gloves and pulls a fresh pair from a dispenser.

"If you choose to watch, it will take you longer to recover than her. You'll get a flashback every time you see her naked. You'll be limp as a dishrag."

Evans pushes open the swinging door with his elbow, stops and lets it swing back against his toe, looks at Bud over his shoulder. "How do you want it? Couple extra stitches and she'll be tight as a virgin." His grin slides away and he continues through the door. "Lighten up, Bud. Just delivery room humor."

Bud leans back against the exam table, trembling, weak after the jolt of adrenaline, the seething anger. He tests his wobbly legs, slips through the delivery room door, and plops into his chair. Evans' back is to him, bent between Nicki's legs. Then he stands to full height, stretches his elbows back like a hen fluttering her wings, a scalpel in his blood-smeared hand. The nurse holds the forceps as the doctor threads his blue-gloved fingers into the handles. Bud sees past him, the thick purple blood oozing onto the glare of stainless steel. He rushes back into the exam room and hangs over the deep sink, eyes watering as he gags. He hates these people hurting Nicki: this redneck doctor, the lying nurse—a baby wails from next door—the baby most of all.

CHAPTER 51

The Betrayal

Walking in without knocking startles her. Nicki hides her face behind the sheet, wipes at her eyes, and emerges with a fake smile. That she thinks she can get away with this makes Bud mad.

"Are you okay? Want me to call a nurse?"

"No, no. Just one of those postpartum things. We're fine."

The crown of the baby's head, a fluff of down above the sheet, is at one breast. The other breast is exposed, a spiderweb of blue and red veins under creamy skin, nipple gorged, a drip of white— transformed from its function of creating lust to its practical utility.

"He's fallen asleep. Would you put him in the bassinet?"

Bud pulls back the sheet, stands with his hands at the baby's back, afraid to touch it, not trusting himself.

"Roll him over, one hand under his head for support. You need to learn how to do it. Want a nurse to show you?"

Bud carries it to the little bed, lays it on its back, knees pumping, arms reaching for warmth, face a snarl, the beginning of a whine. Bud drapes a blanket atop, snugs its arms against its sides. The baby goes limp again with sleep, lips parted, the tip of his tongue flicking in-and-out through the gums as if still nursing, dreaming of the nipple.

Fat little feet stick out past the blanket. Already toenails. He imagines the baby in a ball inside her. He examines the toes again, fingering each one individually, so soft he can hardly feel them. He remembers the joke with Nicki about six toes, how she had laughed. Turned out to be four toes. Five toes actually, five toenails, but with a web of skin between the two toes adjacent to the big toe on both feet. He has seen this only once before—a friend, a playmate from childhood. He and Nicki had compared their feet to his, thinking nothing of it other than he was special.

He had done the research online. An errant gene, carried dormant in the DNA through generations, expressing itself randomly like a cleft palate, likely resulting from inbreeding in the heritage of one of the parents. The probability was rare that it would be passed from one generation to the next. He finds himself counting in his mind again, for the hundredth time, sometimes on his fingers, sometimes with a calendar—nine months back. He had been in Betty's fifteenth-floor condo overlooking Lake Superior. Alone, giddy as he cleaned preparing for Nicki's arrival, her college entrance paperwork spread on the dining table, already filled in except for her signatures.

"We have to name him," she says. "We can't wait any longer. They have to finish the birth certificate."

He feels her eyes eating into his back.

"We'll name him William," he says without turning. "William's a good name, don't you think?" The bed shuffles; bedsprings squeak. He doesn't need to see her face to know for sure. Silence is enough.

"I didn't know, Bud, not till he was born. I wasn't deceiving you. I thought…"

He thinks he hears a sob. He's never heard her cry, in all these years.

"Do you hate me?"

He doesn't answer, can't breathe.

"It didn't mean anything, Bud. I got lonely, with you off at school. It's always been you, Bud. Don't you believe me?"

"I've got to go back to the island."

"It was only that once, Bud, I swear. I was so lonely. We didn't intend for it to happen…neither of us."

He glances over his shoulder, the sheet balled into her face. He feels the urge to go to her then twists his head quickly back to the baby. It is already decided.

"He's beautiful, Bud. Our baby. Can't you forgive me?"

"Something's come up about the property. I have to leave as soon as you get home. Your mother called. Told her about the hurricane, all that—not about the baby. She left a number for you to call back. You can tell her then."

"Please—"

He knew the word was coming and cuts her off. "Sold the old Nissan today. Hired a private nurse to stay with you until you can take care of the baby yourself. Paid a month up front."

With the infirmity of doubt now solidified into certainty, he cannot stay for what will come next. He walks to the door slowly although he wants to run.

"Don't leave me, Bud."

He hesitates only a moment, flings the door wide, and walks through without looking back.

"Please…"

CHAPTER 52

Philipsburg

C ontent to be processed last, Bud steps out of the line snaking from the fold-down steps of the turboprop to the green canopy that now functions as Immigration and Customs. Behind the tent lies the jumbled remains of the destroyed terminal. He sets his canvas bag on the tarmac and walks away to get a better view. Black tarps cover gaping holes where plate glass had been. The American and Delta passenger ramps are crumpled at the loading doors. Four months and still no sign of repair or new construction.

Heat from the sunbaked tarmac seeps up through the soles of his loafers. He feels lighter without the oppressive winter coat—and all that goes with it. The air is hazy, tangibly thick with humidity. Already his shirt is clammy. He sucks a deep breath of ocean breeze. It smells good, like no other place—like home. The skin on his cheeks becomes tight, an odd sensation, his first smile in a week.

After Customs, Bud walks around the terminal to another tent, a holding area for arrivals awaiting buses or cabs. He expects to be attacked by grinning rental car agents, but with the airport parking lot at sea level, they would have lost their entire inventory. Bud requests a cab from the concierge, picks up a *Gazette* from a stack on his folding table, and sits in a plastic chair to wait.

Island Gazette

Philipsburg, Sint Maarten ———————— Thursday 5 December 2023

Claudette the Worst Ever

The National Hurricane Center yesterday confirmed Claudette was the strongest hurricane ever recorded in the Caribbean, exceeding Luis in 1995 by 30 percent and Irma in 2017 by 20 percent in size and wind speed. The NHC noted, "The trend toward more powerful hurricanes is alarming."

The French Collectivity merged its Missing-and-Presumed-Dead List with its Casualty List (see page 3). The Dutch side casualty numbers remain preliminary awaiting the raising of the last of the sunken yachts. Anguilla also has not issued a final casualty list.

Some of the missing may yet return safe and sound from trips abroad prior to the hurricane, but it is more probable the casualty lists will grow.

Recovery relief for Anguilla from the British seems ahead of what has been provided to Saint Martin by the Netherlands and France. Even before the storm came ashore, the British deployed the HMS Bulwark with two Chinook helicopters, beach landing craft, and a brigade of Royal Marines. The ship is currently anchored off Blowing Point.

President Trump demonstrated the USA support by buying the damaged Princess Casino before it went into foreclosure. On Twitter, Trump forecast reopening, "...probably never. It'll be used for tax write offs." He closed the Tweet with a promise to, "teach them how to fish rather than waste tax-payer dollars."

The island is preparing for the next tourist high season starting November 1st. The Sint Maarten Port Authority assured the cruise line industry the A. C. Wathey Pier will be reopened by November. Two cruise lines have added Philipsburg back to their ports of call. The first ship is scheduled for mid-November and another two for the first week in December. Even if the cruise ship pier is still under repair, the ships can anchor in the harbor and ferry tourists ashore.

On the French side, only the Mount Vernon on Orient Beach has reopened. Local entrepreneurs are providing concessions, (rental chairs, umbrellas, and drinks from portable coolers). All of the other resorts on the French side are shut down— either abandoned by the owners, awaiting insurance adjustments, or in various stages of repair.

Bud flips through the paper to the Saint Martin casualty list, two columns long, and looks for the names of his mother, grandmother, and stepbrother. Snippets of them flash from behind bleared eyes when he finds their names. They had been ever-present his entire life, but did he really know them? He had always felt too young to understand their adult world. Who were they really? What had been their private thoughts when they looked at him?

Page four is a collage of before-and-after pictures illustrating the progress in repairing island infrastructure. At the bottom of the page are pictures of the Golden Maiden—the statue being excavated from the sand and a second with it lying faceup at Fort Louis. He studies the pictures closely. Was this the boulder he and Nicki had sat on after the storm? How Nicki had looked that day flickers before him and he involuntarily pulls in a deep breath and concentrates on the paper. Nicki—now lost to him also.

Page 5

Philip Bergen Byline
(p.bergen@ilangzt.com)

Another Gold Statue Found!

Last Tuesday, Victor Dubois, President of the Saint Martin Territorial Council, informed the *Gazette* that a second gold statue has been discovered in the vicinity of Orient Beach.

Dr. Johan Dekker of the Leiden University School of Archeology requested that the Collectivity quarantine both Orient and Galion beaches as active archeological sites while his crew searches for additional artifacts.

Since the SMTC Gendarmerie is stretched thin already, the French Foreign Legion would have to be airlifted in to provide security. Another critical consideration is the effect of barricading two prime beaches just as the tourism industry is beginning to recover.

The compromise was for the two recovered statues to be removed to Fort Louis to facilitate security. The SMTC President arranged with the British HMS Bulwark supporting Anguilla to airlift them by helicopter to Fort Louis Wednesday. The two beaches will be quarantined for two weeks for Leiden's exclusive use. Both beaches will be reopened to the public on Valentine's Day.

Like with the Golden Maiden, international news agencies are announcing to the world this new discovery. Reportedly, incoming tourists are leaving their snorkeling equipment at home and bringing metal detectors instead. This is a welcome added attraction as long as everybody understands the rules.

President Duboise issued the following statement: "Leave any suspected antiquity where found and notify an authority. Failure to report discovered artifacts is a violation of the French Antiquity Laws. Leaving the island, all tourists and their baggage will be screened by security. Possessing contraband is considered smuggling and will definitely disrupt travel plans."

Leiden's Dr. Dekker speculates the statues were originally erected on the beach centuries ago and, due to wave action during subsequent storms, sank through the sand to bedrock. The Golden Maiden had remained hidden under the sand until beach erosion uncovered it during hurricane Claudette. His team is still investigating the origin of the statues.

Below is the timeline for the site:

Prior to 1960, the Saline Company utilized Orient Beach for loading salt for shipment to Europe. At the time, the beach was only accessible by footpath or by sea. In 1954, the schooner *Luisa B* ran aground at the midpoint of the beach while loading salt. This was the start of the reef that is there today.

After salt mining went kaput in 1960, the beach was deserted until the Le Galion Hotel was built at nearby Galion Beach in 1965. The French vacationers would hike a one-kilometer footpath to sunbathe *au naturel* on deserted Orient Beach.

In 1970, Alwin Smit, a Dutchman, bought the property behind the south end of the beach for a nudist resort he named Balneaire. Fences, cabins, and a restaurant were erected.

By 2000, the mega cruise ships had begun docking at Philipsburg and Juliana Airport had upgraded to airline industry standards. Overnight, the tourism industry sprang to life.

In preparation for extending roads and infrastructure to Orient Beach, the French required an impact study to assure compliance with French antiquity and environmental laws.

Tom Jensen, an archeology professor at Leiden University of the Netherlands, and a team of four of his students followed in the wake of road construction to ascertain if Arawak Indian culture was being disturbed. Pottery shards and a gold fishhook were all that was discovered.

With the roads complete, Saint Martin touted Orient in travel magazines as a pristine mile-long beach, the most beautiful in the Caribbean. Nudity was permitted on the south end of the beach past the reef. The rationale at the time was to retain income from the free-spirited French without offending the prudish Americans. The Americans as it turned out thought a nudist beach was the most fun since Disney World. The term "clothing optional" was coined and Orient Beach became a "must see" destination.

Restaurant La Belle Creole at Balneaire was built above the Golden Maiden statue. The restaurant was blown away by hurricanes Hugo in 1989, Luis in 1995, and Irma in 2017.

Each time it was rebuilt on the same concrete foundation. Claudette washed away the foundation as well.

Property records indicate the resort has changed ownership several times. The last purchase was by Delphinium SCA in 2001. Sterling Legion, a US citizen and sole owner of Delphinium, died in a boating accident in 2002. The most recent owners, the family of Sterling Legion, were killed by hurricane Claudette, so the current ownership may be in dispute.

Page 6

Contribute to Dear Roxy at
(d.roxy@ilangzt.com)

Dear Roxy:

My dear wife is deathly afraid of even run-of-the-mill thunderstorms, so when Claudette came ashore, she made me drag the mattress into the windowless bathroom and we slept underneath it for the rest of the night. With the thunder booming, lightning flashing, and rain beating on our tin roof, we made love like it was our last time. Roxy, it was the best we ever had.

Here's the rub. Since the hurricane, I can't get the wife interested unless we're underneath the mattress in the bathroom.

Even then, I have to get up in the middle of things to flash the light switch and flush the commode. The sex is still great, but I wish there were another way. Any suggestions?

– Worn-out in Cole Bay

Dear Worn-out:

Buy a second mattress to go underneath; turn the TV on with the sound off, and prop open the flush valve in the commode. If it's working, go with it.

The first listing under *Boats For Sale* is a 35-foot Beneteau moored at Dave's Marina behind Chesterfield's. *For sale by owner— as is.* Probably refloated after the hurricane.

The cab stops in front of Scotiabank on Back Street in Philipsburg.

"On second thought, take me on to Chesterfield's. I'll walk back to the bank from there," Bud says over the cab driver's shoulder. "Best breakfast in town. Can't remember when I ate last. Ever have their breakfast?"

"Oh, yes," the cab driver's accent sounds like he's talking around pebbles in his mouth, "Everyone eats there."

Bud stops inside the entrance to wait for Sonja to seat him. A waitress he's never seen, blonde ponytail, the only white person there, waves him to a table she is setting by the half-wall overlooking the dock. The top-hinged shutters propped to the outside let the breeze off the water flow through.

"Sonja off today?"

The girl glances at him as if he dropped in from Mars and then looks back to her order pad. "She didn't come back after the hurricane. That's all I know. She just didn't come back."

"Damn."

"They hired me temporary, but I think it will be permanent."

"Lord, I hope not." Bud catches himself, "I mean I hope she's all right."

"Name's Debbie. What would you like?"

The girl is all business, clearly not wanting to talk about Sonja anymore. "A ham omelet."

"We don't have fresh eggs yet. We have the egg substitute stuff. Will that do?"

"Sure. I may eat the tablecloth before I'm through." Bud is smiling but Debbie doesn't look up. "And maybe six slices of bacon and two orders of toast."

"No bacon. You can have more ham or sausage links."

"Sausage. Coffee with the meal, and give me a screwdriver for now—in a paper cup. I'll walk the pier until the meal is ready."

There are catamarans, runabouts, and a few offshore fishing boats, all dinged and scuffed, some still with sand on the deck after being refloated. Nobody is at any of them. In the last slip is the Beneteau single-mast cruiser with a For Sale sign showing through one porthole. Bud looks back at the restaurant to see if anyone is watching before stepping aboard. The rigging is intact, sails neatly sheathed in blue scabbards. He stoops to look through a porthole. No flood damage.

Back in the restaurant, he puts his cell phone beside his plate, hits send for the number he entered back at the sailboat, puts it on speakerphone, and takes a sip of coffee as he waits.

"Chesterfield's," the phone says, an echo in the background a half second out of sync.

Bud stares at his phone. "Calling about the Beneteau for sale."

"You a serious buyer?" An echo again. This time Bud traces the second voice to a white-aproned guy behind the bar looking at him.

Bud raises his voice and talks directly to the bartender, "I'm serious. Got the money in my pocket."

The bartender stares, makes a decision, "Hang up, and I'll call Geoff." He punches in a quick-dial, talks low while looking at Bud. When he lays the phone on the bar, he points at Bud, "He'll be right with you," then starts washing glasses.

"Geoff Ellander," he says with a Dutch accent as they shake. Geoff is overweight, receding brown hair, a rooster tail goatee dyed to match his dyed hair.

"Bud Legion."

Geoff slides into the chair across the table. "2010 Beneteau, owned by a friend of mine. I've sailed on it myself. Fast. Not regatta fast, but faster than most of what you see around here. Well maintained. Sails may be five years old, new jib roller, new GPS, new radar and radios, two spinnakers.

"Tell me about the seller."

"Luckiest guy alive. He and his wife do the island circuit every summer. They made it back to their home on Saint Bart just as his buddies were sailing their yachts here to Simpson Bay to weather the hurricane. They begged him to follow, but he stayed to board up his house. Now, he's the only one left with a boat."

"Glad to hear they sailed it. Not interested in some millionaire's vanity that's been tied to a dock for years. Why's he selling?"

"Hurricane spooked the wife—him too, I guess. They're too old to be sailing the open ocean anyway."

"How much?"

"Wants eighty K, US dollars."

"I'm on the way to the bank right now. Write down the data on the boat and I'll see what the book value is. If it's worth at least $80,000, then that's what I'll pay. Can you call the owner right now? See if he will meet me at Scotiabank tomorrow with all the paperwork? I want a quick sale, no negotiation."

"Sure, but don't you want to look inside, get a mechanic to look it over?"

"Nope. You're a good salesman, Geoff. I trust everything you say." Bud pushes back from the table and extends his hand. "Call me when you get things lined up. The bartender's got my number in his phone. It's been a pleasure."

CHAPTER 53

The Professor

Halfway up the concrete stairway to Fort Louis, Philip Bergin stops at the landing of a switchback. He holds to the pipe guardrail pretending to admire the view of the boat basin below, trying not to pant open-mouthed as the pretty young teacher leads her blue-and-white uniformed class past. The kids' heads keep getting in the way of looking up her skirt as they climb higher. The last time—the only time—he had been to Fort Louis had been on a class field trip like this, in grade school twenty years ago. It hadn't seemed so steep.

At the top of the steps, a narrow gateway chiseled through sandstone opens onto a level dirt path behind a chest-high parapet circling the dome of the hill like a crown. Sparkles dart across Philip's vision and he leans against the lichen-splotched wall until his heart, banging in his ears, recovers. Beside him, a rust-flaked cannon points through a crenel at luxury yachts moored in Marigot Harbor below.

Beyond the harbor, over the red terra-cotta tile roofs of the town, Simpson Bay shimmers like hammered silver plate. On the far side of the island, the Dutch side, high-rise resorts line the berm between Simpson Bay and the Atlantic—to the left, the white dash mark of a cruise ship docked at Philipsburg, to the right a gnat-sized airliner taking off from the airport. The hazy outlines of Saint Bart and neighboring islands sit atop the slate blue Atlantic. From this vantage, the Caribbean seems so small.

Philip turns around to the wide sandstone steps up the final grade to the top. This is where the statue will be—and Professor Jones. He checks his wristwatch; ten minutes until his appointment to interview her at the statue. The students sit on the steps fidgeting while their young teacher holds down her windblown skirt with one hand and points out landmarks with the other.

She explains this fort had thwarted a British invasion after Saint Martin was left on its own after the French Revolution. The brass plaque beside the cannon tells the story of the twenty-eight brave French soldiers fighting off a landing party of one hundred and sixty Brits from Anguilla. Even when the British landed ten miles away at unfortified Grand Case, they found the cannons could be turned to protect the land routes to the capital as well. The official language of the island would likely be English if not for these cannons.

Behind the kids on the top step, two *gendarmes*, handguns strapped to their sides, stand in front of a red-striped barricade. The French Tri-color flaps from the tip of a flagpole behind their heads. The stairway seems to lead straight into the puffy white clouds. Philip smiles. *The gateway to French Heaven.* He pulls his press pass from his jacket pocket. *And I've got the key to get in.*

After excusing himself and receiving a smile from the teacher, Philip navigates through the students to present his press pass to the *gendarme* on the left, a young Frenchman he had interviewed a few months back about a robbery. The summit is a boulder-strewn flat the size of a tennis court. Beside the flagpole base in the center, workers in canvas overalls nail together concrete forms around a skeleton of rebar. The gold statue lies prone on a wooden pallet behind them, a woman in a white lab coat crouched over it taking pictures. He tries to reconcile her with the Northwestern faculty photo he had found online, obviously taken a few decades earlier. If he replaced the shoulder-length bob with a salt-and-pepper dovetail, added maybe twenty pounds, and glasses...

"Dr. Jones?"

She continues taking her picture, moves to another vantage and takes another before looking up. "Philip Bergin, I presume."

"Thank you for granting me this interview. I am honored to meet you."

"Mr. Bergin—"

"Philip."

She smiles and he remembers the smile from the picture. Still beautiful, only a little past prime.

"Alright, if you're Philip, then I'm Betty. I've got a few more things planned before I leave for the day, but I'm a pretty good multi-tasker. Let me finish up while you ask me questions." She resumes walking around the statue taking pictures.

"Doctor…eh, Betty. Some of this will bore you to tears, but I've got to confirm this for the record." Philip pulls a hand-held recorder from his coat pocket. "Do you mind if I record a few notes as we go along?"

"As long as you're not recording my voice, I'm okay with it."

Philip pulls up the collar of his blazer and turns his back to the wind. "December 5th, 2023. Interview with Dr. Betty Jones, Professor emeritus of Northwestern University in Chicago. Professor Jones is a world-renowned anthropologist retained by the Leiden University School of Archeology to investigate the gold statues discovered at Orient Beach after the recent hurricane." He clicks the recorder off. "Betty, can you hear? Please correct me if I say something wrong."

"So far, so good," she says without looking up.

Philip continues, "At the time of this interview, Dr. Jones and I are at Fort Louis, the fortress overlooking Marigot Harbor, standing beside the life-size gold statue of a young woman. The President of the Territorial Council had the statue moved by helicopter to Fort Louis for security reasons. I will be interviewing Dr. Jones about the significance of this three-ton statue and the second statue, a turtle of about equal size, discovered last Tuesday.

"Dr. Jones arrived in Saint Martin two days ago from Brazil where she has been living with an indigenous tribe for the last three months. Dr. Jones has—had maintained a second home at Orient Beach for twenty years. Being knowledgeable of Saint Martin, combined with her intimate understanding of primitive cultures, makes her uniquely qualified to interpret these artifacts.

"The big question is: Where did they come from? In 1993, archeologists from Leiden performed the required digs at Orient Beach prior to new construction. Gold platters and tools discovered were attributed to the Arawak culture living there before Saint Martin was colonized by Europe. It is currently theorized these statues must be additional—"

Philip clicks the recorder off when Betty's head jerks around with a disapproving scowl. With a crooked finger, she beckons him to the statue. "Off the record?"

Philip nods.

"Have you looked at this thing? Look at her face—her cheekbones, the hair. What do you see?"

Philip studies the statue's features, coppery with surface corrosion, a few scuffmarks from the helicopter's sling.

"I'm here as a consultant to Leiden. Any findings will come from them. That's the chain of command." She stands up straight and gives him a hard look. "Anything official comes from them. Do you agree? If not, you can wait for Leiden's official report in about six years. That's how long it took them to publish the last time they were here."

"Then you're not going to tell me anything?"

"We can talk if you want, but if you quote me, we'll both be in trouble."

Philip looks away in disgust. A wasted trip.

"I've read your articles about the statue—pretty good journalism, I'd say. A little prone to speculate beyond the facts, maybe, but you've got a right to print your own candid opinions."

"Could be embarrassing if I guess wrong. That's why I need—"

"I want you to have your story. I don't want to wait six years either. Your press pass allows you to look at the statue. You seem like a bright boy." She points at the statue.

"I examined the statue the day it was dug up."

"I know. Look again. Tell me what you see?"

He glares back at Betty in the moment before she sets aside her camera and bends down with a whiskbroom to the face of the statue. *What kind of game is she playing?* As she brushes the eyes and cheeks, he remembers his first impression at the beach, an odd feeling that he had seen the face before. A girlfriend—from Amsterdam—"She's not Indian."

Betty doesn't look up but the sides of her face wrinkle with a smile. "Could be. An anthropologist might take pictures to compare the shape of the skull, cheekbones, width of the eyes with the norm of different races. Race could be determined easily enough."

"She's European, which means—"

"A conscientious reporter might also check the origin of the gold. Virgin gold includes trace elements that create a unique signature on a spectrograph. The country of origin, sometimes even a specific mine, is knowable. This doesn't work for most antiquities, even ones thousands of years old, because they are made from scrap gold collected from all over. But even knowing the statue is made from scrap gold is a clue to its origin.

"You're telling me—"

"I'm not telling you squat you couldn't learn off the Internet. But I bet if the right questions were asked to the right people, one might learn this analysis has already been done."

"Damn. What else are you not going to tell me?"

"The turtle statue I looked at yesterday. It's pretty battered and worn, but the pattern on the shell is still discernable. With a little investigation it might be determined that it's not a turtle at all, but a Galapagos tortoise."

When Philip doesn't respond, she looks up at him and he is suddenly aware of his open mouth.

"A reporter might even conclude these statues don't jibe with the current version of history. He might stumble right into a Pulitzer Prize."

"Betty, you're an interesting woman."

"What do you know about me?"

"I know you've been eating roots and roast monkey for the last three months and by the time we get back to the parking lot it will be almost dinner time."

Betty methodically returns her camera and tools to a canvas tote bag before walking close in front of his face and pulling off her glasses. "Are you coming on to a woman old enough to be your mother?"

"I...eh...could be."

"Think I might slip you some more tidbits over a second bottle of wine?"

"Could be. Or could be I'm after something else."

She steps back, cocks her head, studiously appraises him top to bottom, chuckles to herself, then steps close again to look into his eyes as if reading his brainwaves. A put-down was coming. Not his first. She was worth the try. He prepares his apology.

"I'm hungry for langouste and old wine served on a white tablecloth."

"What a coincidence. So am I."

"Nobody expecting you later?" she asks as they walk toward the barricade.

"Nope. How about you?"

"Langouste tail is not the only thing I'm hungry for, Mr. Bergin."

This freezes him mid-stride. She continues a few steps and turns. "Little Richards in Grand Case just reopened. About seven?"

"Professor Jones, I think this could be the start of a beautiful friendship."

CHAPTER 54

The Key

he bottom floor of the bank is an open lobby with teller windows against the rear wall. From the directory posted on a square pillar, he finds Florencia Josephs, Bank Manager. All offices, Bud notes, are on the second floor. Good planning considering the town floods during every hurricane. Bud finds the right door, which is open, and walks in.

"Afternoon. I'm Bud Legion here for a 2 PM appointment with Madame Josephs."

"Siddhartha?"

Bud catches himself glancing over his shoulder and chuckles. "Yeah, sorry. I go by Bud though Siddhartha is my legal name."

"Come on in, Bud," comes a smiling voice from an open door to his left. The secretary nods him that way.

A middle-aged ebony-skinned woman stands behind a metal desk with hand outstretched. Her hair pulled into a bun in the back says *professional*, the warm smile says *personable*.

"Friends call me Flora. Bud and Flora—is that alright with you?"

"Glad to meet you, Flora. You seem a little young for a bank manager."

"I'll take that as a compliment, but I assure you I'm old enough to be your mother. Let me offer my condolences for the loss of your mother, grandmother, and brother. Your mother's accounts are with a French bank in Marigot, I believe. You should go there also to see if there is any unfinished business. Your father banked here, but long before my time. I didn't know either of them personally.

"In 2002, just after you were born, I guess, your father opened a trust account at this bank in your name payable on your twenty-first birthday. A belated happy birthday, by the way. With the chaos after the hurricane, we had a hard time finding you, but we were able to get your email address from immigration. You live in the States now? I noticed the dot com on your email address."

"I go to school in Chicago. I'm trying to take care of the loose ends here in time to get back for spring term."

"Then pull up that chair. Let's get to it," she says sitting down, putting on reading glasses, and sweeping her hand over documents spread on her desk, "I've got everything we will need right here. First off, I'll need to check your passport to ensure you are indeed Siddhartha Legion." Flora thumbs through the stamped pages of the passport. "I'll need a copy for my files if you don't mind." She doesn't wait for a response. "Sophia," she calls out to the secretary. "Come get Mr. Legion's passport; make a copy and time-stamp it for his file.

"Let's look at your account history. Your father opened the account with one hundred thousand US dollars invested through the bank in mutual funds. In the twenty-one years since, the fund balance has grown to just under two hundred and fifty thousand US dollars. Now, you can leave the money in this account or, if you need money right away, move part of the money into a checking account."

"I bought a boat today. I would like to close the deal tomorrow here at the bank. And I'll need some money for college."

"Let's create a checking account then. You can start writing checks tomorrow. Since our home office is in Canada, there shouldn't be any problems with writing checks in the States.

"Sophia," she yells out the door again, "open a checking account for Mr. Legion using the information on the passport. When you get it, bring it in for signature."

"Done?" Bud asks.

"Hundred thousand get you by for a few months?" Bud smiles. "Done," she says back with a nod.

Flora leans back in her swivel chair, takes off her glasses, and sucks on a temple tip. "Your father rented a safe-deposit box here. It was transferred into your mother's name after he died. According to our records, your mother last opened it about ten years ago. Bud, I know you are aware your mother has been missing since the hurricane. About a week ago her name was added to the official casualty list and her legal status is now deceased. The contents of the safe-deposit box will go into probate."

"I didn't know about the box."

"So you don't know anything about the key? There would have been two keys."

"A key?" Bud slaps his pant leg, stands up and pulls out a key ring, throws it on the desk, and separates a brass key away from the others. "Could this be it?"

"It's one of our keys."

"Mom gave it to me a year ago before I went to Chicago. Wouldn't tell me what it was, only that I would need it one day."

"Well, today is the day. I can't let you take anything until after I get an order from probate court, but we can look inside if you want. Come on, just down the hall. We'll need my master key also."

Bud and Flora share a smile when his key turns. What could be in a safe-deposit box that hadn't been opened in ten years? Antique coins? Diamond encrusted jewelry? Knowing his mother, Bud didn't think so. Or, as it turned out when they opened the lid, musty smelling paper pouches of deeds and wills. Flora unfolds the deed at a standup desk, presses the creases flat with the palm of her hand, and stands back for Bud to read.

"I can't read legalese. You read it and give me the short version."

"This is a property plot for some place on the French side, someplace by the water."

"That would be La Belle Creole. That's the restaurant my mother and grandmother ran over on Orient Beach."

"This is for ten hectares, about twenty-five acres. They must have owned the whole resort."

"I don't think so. I would have known about that...wouldn't I?"

"Would you?"

Bud stares glassy-eyed at the floor.

"Well, let's look at the wills." Flora opens the documents one at a time and spreads the documents one on top of the other until she has scanned them all. "These are your father's and mother's wills and the will of somebody named Lily Ana Bartoli."

"That's my grandmother. She lived with us."

"Bud, do you have a lawyer?"

"Lawyer? Do I need a lawyer?"

"The bank has a *notaire* on retainer I'd recommend. I don't want to be guessing at what all this means. We need a good solid legal opinion. With your permission, I'll copy these documents and get a pro to work on it."

"Okay, I guess."

"Where are you staying?"

"Nowhere right now. I just got here."

"Uum...Bud, you've got a problem. With most of the hotels shut down due to storm damage, what's left on the island is rented short-term by relief workers."

"I could move into the boat...but not until tomorrow."

"The bank just foreclosed on a house in Guana Bay. The owners moved back to the States and left the bank holding the mortgage. No electricity or running water, but it's still furnished. You could stay there a few days."

"Could you do that? All I need is a bed. You can contact me by cellphone if you need me."

Flora steps out in the hallway and yells back toward her offices. "Sophia?" Sophia sticks her head past the doorway. "Would you please get me the key for the Burgess house?"

CHAPTER 55

Little Richard

Ruby's Place looks the same. It must have been rebuilt after the storm, but it had always looked cobbled together out of scrap lumber. Beside the kitchen on the flagstone plaza, Roy, Ruby's husband, stands between two split-in-half oil drums. Behind him, the smoky aroma of ribs billows up from a charcoal grill while in front he pings out impromptu calypso on his kettledrum. Roy stops playing long enough for a fist-bump before Bud ducks under the canvas awning slanting down over the bar in front of the kitchen.

Ruby, famous cherry-red hair spiked like flames atop her black face, slides off a barstool, wraps him in meaty arms, and pulls him tight to her jasmine-scented bosom. "Kiss me, you young stud." She air kisses at both cheeks, and then pushes him to arm's length. "Hear you're a college boy now. Thought you'd be too good for us niggers. Let me get you a beer." She slips through a lift-up door in the counter and comes back with two bottles of Corona with lime wedges sticking out the tops.

"Not many people on the streets."

"No tourists to speak of. No place on this side of the island for them to stay. I mostly opened up 'cause Roy needs something to do. The smell of them ribs and his music brings 'em out like flies to honey. But we mostly give away oxtail soup and johnny cakes these days. Locals ain't got no money."

"Things will turn around."

"Always do." Ruby's smile ends abruptly. "Sorry about your folks. Seems the storms take the best and leaves trash like me and Roy behind."

"You two are like the soul of this town. As soon as I heard that kettledrum, I knew everything would be okay."

"If you just got back, you've missed all the excitement. That statue they found at Orient turned out to be solid gold. Paper says it's worth a hundred million Euros. Can you imagine? You could buy this whole town for that much money."

She pulls him by the hand to a picnic table away from the grill for a better breeze. "Some beach bum chipped a finger off that statue before an army of *gendarmes* started guarding it day and night. One of those spidery-looking helicopters hauled it to Fort Louis a few days ago so it would be easier to guard until somebody figures out what to do with it." She waves toward the gap between the steep bluff at one end of the bay and the islet just offshore. "Helicopter came around that point, between Creole Rock and the beach with the statue dangling from its belly. Came right by the plaza, blades a-whopping. A sight to see, I'm telling you."

Roy drops his felt-tipped hammers in the kettledrum. "Heard some tourist with a metal detector found another one a couple of days ago." He turns to the grill, picks up tongs, and flips the rack of ribs. "Found it in a sinkhole on that exposed reef behind La Belle Creole—where the restaurant was anyway. Been lying out there in plain view looking like just another boulder. You've probably walked right by it yourself a hundred times."

"The guy gets to keep it?"

"Doubt that. The Governor posted a guard at the site like it belongs to him. He'll likely have it taken to Fort Louis like the other one. Wish they'd put them things where people could see 'em. They'd be tourists from all over the world flocking here to see the Golden Maiden—that's what they call her on the six o'clock news. I reckon she's famous all over the world now.

Roy picks up the rack of ribs with the tongs. "Ruby, fix Bud a plate of rice to go with these ribs."

Three more beers and a full stomach later, Bud walks toward the bus stop six blocks away at the intersection of *Boulevard de Grand Case* and the highway. The town dates to the oxcart era, so there is only room between storefronts for one-way car traffic. Parking has always been on the sidewalk, so he walks down the center of the street, stepping aside for the occasional taxi. Bud thinks of Chicago, the six lanes in front of Betty's condo, always choked with traffic. How could he have lived there?

Rubble has been cleared but still, Grand Case feels like a ghost town. The few buildings still standing, roofless concrete hulks, have sawhorses wrapped in barrier tape in front marking them as condemned, awaiting demolition.

Bud stops in front of steps leading up to a slab foundation covered in chipped tile. His memory sees what Little Richard's had once been—open double doors, candlelit tables covered with white linen, wine in tubs of ice, couples in evening dress. Bud tilts his head back and his mind projects on the blue sky the shuttered windows of Richard's second-floor loft. Nicki was too young to drink in the restaurant, so Richard kept a bottle for her upstairs. He and Nicki would lounge on a futon drinking rum colas, giggle at the conversations heard through the floor, and share other forbidden pleasures.

Electricity seems to surge through his body. Bud turns, clenches his eyes, pulls in a purging breath, and walks away. When he glances back there is only the dilapidated foundation. If only he could flush Nicki from his brain so easily.

Across from the bus stop, a hand-painted plywood sign hanging on the handrail in front of what had been Maria's Coffee Shop announces the "Grand opening of Little Richard's II". Richard is spreading tablecloths to cover mismatched tables on the terrace when Bud bear hugs him from behind.

"Bud, good buddy. Haven't seen you since the hurricane."

Bud stands back, looks around. "Totally new look. Got your flare. Where's Maria?"

"She made it through alright but decided not to reopen right away. Went back to Italy to visit relatives until things pick up here. She's renting this spot to me until I can get my place rebuilt."

"How's it working out?"

"Good. Better than operating out of a tent beside the road. If I can get the insurance company to settle up, I'll start rebuilding where I was before."

"Walked by the old place. Sad. What's left of the town is boarded up."

"For right now, it's better to be here beside the highway. It's one of those Catch-22 things. The tourists won't go downtown because nothing's open; nothing's open because there are no tourists. Somebody's got to get the old ball rolling again." Richard looks behind Bud. "Say, where's Nicki? She didn't come with you?"

"She's in Chicago—with the baby."

"Damn man. I'd forgot she was expecting. Congrat—"

"Richard…" Bud interrupts and then is at a loss for words. "How's your father?"

"The storm took the roof off our house but he's okay. He flew over to Guadalupe to stay with my uncle until I can scrounge up the materials to repair it. Charter fishing is dead anyway, so there was no point in him toughing it out here. "

"The boat made it?"

"Yep. Got lucky on that. Dad had it in dry dock for repairs when the hurricane hit. It's back in the water now. If you're going to be on the island a while, we should go fishing."

The boat, Richard's Dad at the helm, flashes into Bud's memory. He'd gone along as deckhand for charters on the weekends during high school. No pay, just half the tips.

"Can you get away?"

Richard looks at the waitress setting tables, into the little kitchen where he should be cooking. "Not really…but you could go. Boat's in the same slip over at Dave's Marina; key's in the bait box as usual. Dad wouldn't trust me to take her out, but he would you."

Richard's grin fades. "Look…we need to talk. We'll be open in thirty minutes and I won't have time later." Richard waves to the waitress setting tables, points to the one he was setting. She nods. "Bring us two Caribs." She nods again. Richard directs Bud toward a table by the street and they sit looking at each other until the waitress leaves.

"I was surprised to see you and Nicki together after the hurricane. Are you married yet?"

"No. We've split up."

"The ba—"

"The baby's not mine."

Richard stares back, the word baby frozen on his lips.

"Did you hear what I said?"

Richard lowers his head and stares blankly at the table. "I never thought it was."

"What…?"

"That's what I needed to tell you. You weren't the only one Nicki met upstairs."

"You knew?" The feeling of being zapped by a cattle prod returns.

"We were friends, Bud. She told me things. She loved you, but like a brother. Understand? She felt smothered."

Bud sneers viciously, "It wasn't like that."

"She kept saying she would tell you, but she didn't want you to be hurt. Also, I think she was afraid what you might do. When you left for college, she thought you would find somebody else. She started seeing this guy from Anguilla on weekends. Sometimes they met in the loft, but mostly she would go there. She was the happiest I'd ever seen her, until...until she became pregnant. He wouldn't have anything to do with her after she told him."

Bud's hands grip the sides of the table so tight it trembles. His chair tips onto the flagstone floor when he gets up to strangle Richard to shut him up.

Richard slowly rises from his chair, a haggard expression. "I'm sorry, Bud. Telling you this is the hardest thing I've ever done. I feel like shit."

Bud turns around and grabs the pipe rail separating the terrace from the highway, his body stiff, shaking at first, and then his shoulders slump. When he stoops to pick up the chair he feels weak, expended. Richard stands behind his chair, holding at the sides as if he might have to use it for defense, misery on his face.

"Richard, Nicki's a slut. If anybody else had said that, I'd—"

"She's just a girl."

"She's my sister, Richard. She let me think..." Bud found himself chuckling, and then sat down and cackled a maniacal, opened-mouth laugh without humor. "I was just handy when she needed a daddy. If anything, I'm getting out of this easy."

"You'll be alright then?"

"Let it go. This will be the last time we talk about it." Bud finishes the last half of his beer. "I feel a drunk coming on. I'd be safer here, if you don't mind? Just call me a cab if I pass out—or the *gendarmes* if I break anything."

Bud is slumped over his beer when a pleated blue skirt, shapely legs, and red shoes stand beside his table. He recognizes Betty without looking up. She pulls out a chair and sits without asking.

"Thought I'd find you here."

"Well, well. Aunt Betty." Bud slouches back, not even trying to hide his drunkenness. "Guess you've talked to your beautiful daughter then. How is she these days?"

"Do you care?"

"Of course. I love my little sister."

Betty stares hard at him until he can no longer hold his sneer. "I believe you do. If you can get past this, she wants you back."

"Does she now?"

"You're not her sister, by the way."

"Half-sister then."

"Not that either. Legion was not her father."

"That's not true."

"You're talking to her mother."

"I believe that, you lying bitch!"

"Look, maybe we should talk tomorrow when you're feeling better."

A sandy-haired man walks behind her chair, tweed jacket, Adam's apple working around the knot of a tie, "Who is this brat?"

"Philip. Give me a minute. Wait at the bar."

"I'll beat an apology out of him first."

A fight is exactly what Bud wants. "Go for it." He tries to get up, loses his balance, and falls awkwardly back in the chair.

Betty smiles sympathetically; sandy hair does not.

"Philip, this is Bud Legion, an old friend. Bud this is Philip Bremer, a new friend. Philip has invited me to dinner." Betty pulls a card and pen from her handbag, scribbles a number on the back of the card, and lays it on the table.

"You're Bud Legion?" sandy hair asks.

Betty takes Philip's arm and guides him away. "Bud, we'll talk tomorrow."

The waitress has their table ready, seats them, and lights the candle in the middle beside a gardenia floating in a silver dish. Philip moves the candle aside and leans toward Betty. "Bud Legion? Bud Legion of Orient Beach?"

Betty nods and reaches across to romantically take his hand in hers.

"I've got to set up an interview—" Philip starts to get up and Betty clamps his hand.

"Not tonight, Philip. As a matter of fact, not ever."

"You don't understand. Everybody's been looking for him. Best I can tell, he stands to inherit half of Orient Beach, and the statues as well. I've got to find out about him."

"I know more about him than he knows about himself."

Philip leans forward again, lays his hand atop hers. "And you'll tell me?"

"When we finish dining and you take me somewhere quiet, I'm going to tell you a story. Part of it, the part you can verify, will be true. If you print the rest and get sued for libel, I'll testify for the prosecution that you made up lies to sell papers."

"Don't do this to me."

"Philip, everything comes with conditions. Everything."

CHAPTER 56

The Inheritance

S ophia circles the conference room table pouring second cups of coffee for Monsieur Kritz, the boat seller, and Maître Sheridan, the bank's notaire. Both check their watches every thirty seconds—Kritz judging when he will have to leave to make the last flight back to Saint Bart and Sheridan calculating his fee in quarter-hour increments. Flora would not be able to keep them much longer.

"Maître, will you please review the terms of the contract once more?"

"Madame Josephs, this would be the third time. Monsieur Kritz's title to the yacht *Carpe Diem* is clean, without leans or attachments. Both parties have previously agreed to the sale price. Monsieur Legion will pay with a single check for the full amount. You have assured me his account has sufficient funds. All that is needed to complete the transaction are the check signed by your client and Monsieur Kritz's signature transferring the title."

"Madam Josephs, I've never met this—Siddhartha Legion." Kritz grins when he says the name. "He obviously has had second thoughts since you set up this meeting yesterday."

"At least, he could have called to cancel," Sheridan says scooting his chair back from the table.

Flora pushes an intercom button on a speakerphone in the center of the table, "Sophia, will you try Mr. Legion's cell phone again, please."

"No need," comes Sophia's reply, "he just walked into the outer office. Shall I show him in?"

Flora looks to Kritz who is checking his watch again. "If he's backed out, his apology will only take a minute. If the sale is still a go, we could finish up in fifteen," she advises.

Both men nod.

"Yes, bring him in, Sophia."

Bud, red ball cap over uncombed hair, three-day beard, shakes hands all around. Flora does the introductions and points him to a chair beside her. He looks sick.

"I didn't realize I was still on Central Time until Sophia called. Sorry to keep you waiting."

"You still want the yacht?" Kritz asks.

"Yes, of course."

Sheridan goes over the terms of sale again. "If this is agreeable to both parties, the only thing left is to fill in the date Mister Legion will take possession."

"Immediately," Bud says. "I want to move in today."

"Mr. Legion, it is customary to give the previous owner a few days to move his things out," Flora explains.

Bud turns to Kritz, "What sort of things."

"Not much. Galley stuff mostly—canned goods, pots and pans, wine, bedding, my tools, spare parts..."

"I'll need all that. What's it worth?"

"Three...four thousand."

"I'll increase my offer to eighty-four thousand if you leave everything."

"The wife has some knick-knacks, personal stuff—"

"And I'll need a shakedown cruise to learn the peculiarities of the boat. How about we sail it back to Saint Bart together. Your wife can take whatever she wants."

Kritz looks to Sheridan, "We need a new contract?"

"If you agree, I can do a pen-and-ink change on the existing contract."

"When do you want to sail?"

"It's a little late in the day. How about tomorrow?"

"Damn, son—I like your style, but I'm scheduled to fly back to Saint Bart in an hour."

"Cancel. Call your wife. Tell her you'll be sailing back with me tomorrow." Bud turns to Flora, "Would it be alright if Mister Kritz stays at the Burgess house with me tonight?"

"Sure."

Kritz stares solemnly at the table. "After today, I won't need any of that stuff anyway." He lifts his head with a smile. "The wife will want to say goodbye to *Carpe Diem*." Kritz extends his hand to Bud.

In another five minutes, everything is signed. Kritz exchanges the yacht keys for a check and leaves for the Burgess house.

"Hot damn!" Bud throws the keys on the table, a little-boy-at-Christmas grin. "I own a yacht."

Flora had suspected he was hung over, if not still drunk, when he first walked in and is glad to see him coming around. "Bud, do you even know how to sail?"

"I got my pilot's certification in the summers during high school. Don't worry, I'm not as dumb as I look."

"Do either of you need a break before we go into the estate documents?"

"Any coffee left?" Bud asks holding to the sides of his head.

Flora buzzes Sophia and asks for a decanter of coffee and another cup. "Also, bring a couple of ibuprofen from my desk drawer.

"Bud, I asked Maître Sheridan to look over the documents we found in the safe-deposit box yesterday and give us an opinion."

Sheridan scoots his chair closer, places a yellow legal pad and pen on the table. "First, I need to understand who I am representing. These documents refer to Siddhartha Legion. Madame Josephs calls you Bud. Is this a nickname?"

"Okay, here's the story. My father tagged me Buddha Siddhartha Legion on my birth certificate. My mother and grandmother thought it was sacrilegious or something and refused to use the name. Mom wanted to call me Sid, but Dad wouldn't go for that, so they agreed on Bud. Dad died when I was a baby, but the name stuck."

"So, Mr. Legion, are you requesting my services concerning your inheritance?"

Bud glances to Flora who nods then turns to Sheridan. "It's Bud. Mr. Legion was my father. Do you have a first name?"

Sheridan sits back, crosses his arms across the pooch of his stomach, and austerely locks eyes with Bud. "Yes, I do, but please refer to me as Maître Sheridan."

"I'd prefer not referring to you at all." Bud turns to Flora. "You know any lawyers who don't have a pencil stuck up their ass?"

Sheridan rises slowly and begins to repack his briefcase.

Flora jumps to her feet. "Gentlemen, let's start again." She looks Bud sternly in the eyes. "Maître Sheridan is the most qualified lawyer on the island in the realm of international law. I've known him for thirty years. He agreed to drop his other work and expedite the review of these documents as a favor to me. So Bud, to answer your first question: yes, Maître has a first name—Felix. He likes it about as well as you like Siddhartha. And, yes, I know other lawyers, but you're on your own if you insult him again. If we continue, you will call him by his title, Maître."

Bud opens his mouth to respond, but she has already turned to Sheridan.

"Maître, Bud lost his entire family in the hurricane. It is left to him to sort out his family's estate. Until yesterday he was unaware of the safety-deposit box or its contents. Bud just turned twenty-one. I'm asking you to look past his bluster and see an overwhelmed young man who needs the best legal advice he can get." Flora looks alternately back and forth between the men who are looking at the table. "Bud, the ball's in your court."

"Flora, nobody has spanked me so thoroughly since my mother. You're right. These wills and titles are over my head. I'll have to trust somebody—and I trust you. You trust…eh, Maître, so, yes, I would like to hire him to look after my interests."

Sheridan places his briefcase in the chair and props stiff-armed on the chair back as if making a point to a jury. "Flora, this bank is my client. As an officer of the bank, you have requested a legal opinion on a set of documents. At this point anyway, I am here to report my opinions to you. We can come back to the question of whether I represent Bud later."

She turns to Bud.

"You want me to leave?"

She turns back to Sheridan, "Maître?"

"Flora, Bud is your client. If you assure me what I say will not be a breach of confidentiality, he may stay."

"Gentlemen, you have turned me into a facilitator. Okay, here's how it's going to be. Bud, Maître's research and this meeting are on the bank's tab. He will be talking to me. This is going to happen whether you stay or leave. If you stay, you will keep your mouth shut."

"But—"

"If you have questions, you can ask me when Maître is finished. Do you agree?"

"Do I have a choice?"

"Find another bank; find another lawyer."

Bud sits back in his chair, tips the bill of his ball cap forward over his eyes and nods.

"I'll take that as a yes. Now, Maître, what have you found out?"

Sheridan sits again and painstakingly arranges the documents on the table in front of him. "Let's start with the deed. In October 2002, Sterling Legion formed Delphinium SCI, a French corporation, for the purpose of purchasing property in Saint Martin. Later that year, Delphinium purchased the property on this deed from Marcelo Leblanc, a French citizen. Everything looks in order. Delphinium owns the property.

"Next we'll go to the wills to trace the ownership of Delphinium. A legal firm in Nashville, Tennessee, USA drafted Sterling Legion's will in November 2002. They were also the administrator of his estate. I contacted that office yesterday. In Mr. Legion's file, they have a copy of this will, the marriage certificate to Zuzu, his second wife, and a birth certificate for Buddha Siddhartha Legion. I checked with the Parish Clerk of the Court in Marigot this morning. They have these exact documents on file. Mr. Legion meticulously left a broad trail to be found after his death. There is no question as to the validity of the documents you gave me.

"After Sterling Legion died in January 2003, his estate in its entirety passed by will to his wife Zuzu, a French citizen living in Saint Martin. So from 2003 until her recent death, Zuzu owned Delphinium, which owns the Orient property. In that time, the ownership of the property has not been contested in court and there are no leans against the property. Property taxes have been paid annually from a Delphinium account held by this bank.

"Now we go to the will of Zuzu Legion." Sheridan pulls a single legal-size page to the top of his pile. "In the event of her death, Zuzu bequeaths her estate in its entirety to her only son Buddha Siddhartha Legion. She further stipulates that if she dies before Bud reaches the age of majority, she appoints Lily Ana Bartoli as custodian. Because of Bud's age, this clause does not apply.

"Zuzu went missing after the recent hurricane and her body was never recovered. She was declared legally dead on October 8, 2023. Her estate is under the jurisdiction of the Parish Probate

Court. When probate is complete, probably in a couple of months, your client will own Delphinium and the Orient property.

"Nicki," Bud interrupts. "I have a half-sister—Nicole Legion."

Sheridan glances at Flora and then starts flipping through the documents on the table.

"She's my half-sister by a different mother—Betty Jones. I also have—had—a half-brother, Paul, by a third mother. He died in the hurricane also."

"Your siblings or their heirs might be entitled to inheritance from the estate of Sterling Legion if he had been a French citizen. French law specifies how an estate is distributed among the relatives. In the case of Sterling Legion, he was a US citizen who filed his will in a US court. Stipulations of the will take precedence over claims due to relationships. His will leaves his estate in its entirety to your mother. Your mother was a French citizen so her estate would go to you even if she hadn't left a will. The succession of ownership is clear."

Flora turns to Bud to check if he understands. His forehead is resting on the edge of the table, his shoulders jerking in sobs. She opens her mouth to ask what is wrong, and thinks how she would word it. *Is it all right to talk about your dead family like pieces on a chessboard?* She fights the motherly instinct to get up and hug him in a consoling embrace. It's better to just get this over with quickly.

"Go ahead, Maître."

"The current tax base for the Orient property is seven million Euros. This was with the improvements before the hurricane, so the property is worth about five million today."

"What does Bud need to do?"

"The named executor of Zuzu's will is Lily Ana Bartoli. This is Bud's grandmother?"

Flora nods, "She was also killed in the hurricane."

Bud gets up and walks to the window and fingers the slats of the Venetian blind apart to look down on the street below, his face hidden as Sheridan drones on in an unfeeling monotone. Flora imagines the words *killed* and *dead* as daggers embedded in Bud's back.

"The alternate executor is the French law firm in Marigot that drew up her will. The originals of these documents should be presented to them. They would take it from there. Then it's a matter of waiting for the wheels to turn in the Probate Court. Eventually, Bud would have a new title drawn up showing him owner of Delphinium and the property.

"Now comes the issue of the gold statues that were found on the property after the hurricane. Their combined value, even if just melted down into gold bars, is estimated at three hundred million Euros. The Saint Martin Executive Council has assigned temporary custody to the *Gendarmerie* to assure security of the statues until ownership can be determined. This could take years. A comrade of mine is already preparing a suit at the request of the President of Saint Martin that will claim the statues were discovered outside the property boundaries on Collectivity-controlled beachfront. This claim will be denied because the first statue was found buried underneath the rubble of the La Belle Creole restaurant owned by Delphinium. The second statue found was at an even higher elevation on the property. He will then file claim under the French Antiquates Law. Who knows where it will go from there. All claims will have to be litigated one at a time. It could be tied up in court for years. But, in my opinion, knowing what I do today, Delphinium will ultimately prevail in a claim of ownership."

"Bud…" Flora waits for Bud to sit back down and wipe his eyes with the back of his hands. "Do you understand? What do you want to do?"

"What do I want to do? Tomorrow I'm sailing to Saint Bart. I may stay a few days. After that, I want to sail...somewhere else, but not back here. I'm putting this island behind me. I'm sure as hell not spending the next few years in a courtroom."

"Bud," Flora tries to quell his rising anger, "you might not have a choice—"

"I don't want any of it—the property, the statues—none of it."

"Flora," Sheridan pushes back from the table. "I should leave—"

"No," Bud jumps to his feet, his face tortured. "Please...just tell me how to get out from under this."

"Bud, if you were my client, I'd advise you not to act your age."

Bud's face contorts into a snarl. He is about to respond when Flora cuts him off. "Maître, could you meet with me again tomorrow? I want to discuss this with Bud alone."

Sheridan puts out his palms as if fending off a blow from Flora, "I'm just saying—"

"I know, and you're right. There's too much on the table to just walk away. Say about three? I could come to your office if you like."

"I can move some things around. I'll come here."

Bud collapses in his chair, slouches back. "I won't."

"Bud, I bet you haven't eaten today. Give me a few minutes to close up my office and I'll let you show me your new yacht and treat me to an early dinner. Today, anyway, you can afford it."

The next day at three precisely, Sheridan walks into the outer office. Sophia is on the phone and waves him towards Flora's open door. Flora, in turn, waves to the chair in front of her desk. She lays a check in front of him.

"This is Bud's twenty thousand Euro retainer. He asked me to extend his apology for yesterday and requests you represent him and Delphinium."

Sheridan picks up the check, reads it, and then returns it to the desktop. "I don't think I can work with him."

"You won't have to. Get out your yellow pad. I need you to create some documents. First, of course, I need your standard contract to represent Bud and Delphinium. Next, I need a power of attorney naming me as Bud's agent. It should authorize me to write his name on checks or legal documents with my signature undersigned. Can you do that?"

"I suppose I could."

"Next I need a contract selling Bud's interests in Delphinium and the Orient property to his sister, Nichole Legion. The sale price is one Euro and other considerations. Here is her information." Flora pushes a paper across the desk.

"You two discussed this? Does he realize—"

"He does. This is the only plan I could talk him into. Otherwise, he's just going to sail off into the sunset. Also on this sheet are the other considerations. Nicole will donate the first statue, the one called the Golden Maiden, to the Collectivity of Saint Martin. You will have to wait until after probate and after Nicole reaches twenty-one this spring to execute the document, but we can compose the contract and get Bud's signature now. Nicole will sign. If she doesn't, she gets nothing. If she does, she's an instant millionaire. I think you can convince her."

"What about the other statue?"

"This is where you get to show your stuff. Show the Nicole contract to your buddy, the maître representing Saint Martin. Explain the Collectivity will receive the most valuable statue in exchange for dropping its claims. If the Collectivity claims are as weak as you say, they stand to lose both statues plus be out the cost of litigation."

"I think he will agree, but he won't like it. He was counting on buying a yacht with his fees."

"I told Bud I'd call him with your decision. Should I set another meeting with Bud to sign the documents in a week? After that, I'll only be able to reach him by cellphone when he's in a port somewhere."

"Flora, I think you and I should steal as much money as we can and run off together to Brazil."

Flora looks up, stunned until she sees the grin growing on Sheridan's face. "Twenty years ago, young law clerk Felix and bank teller Florencia could have done that. But now we're Maître Sheridan and Madame Josephs, respected pillars of the community. Our opportunity to become criminals has passed us by."

CHAPTER 57

William

ud idles a hundred yards back from the reef watching a giant wave, heaved twenty feet high, thunder through the spiny reef, feeling the spray from the collision caught by the wind sprinkle over him. When the wave reaches him, dissipated, still gurgling with foam, the boat bucks and turns the bow away like a skittish horse. In the trough of the wave, in the few seconds before the next wave, he looks for the narrow opening between two jagged outcrops.

It's been a long time, ten years at least, since he had accompanied Webb and William fishing on the other side. After pushing through the opening at full throttle, Webb had shown them the trench on sonar, starting shallow at the reef, extending ten miles as it widens and deepens into a valley leading to the six-thousand-foot deep underwater canyon.

"Tuna, dolphin, and sailfish herd the baitfish into my sweet spot," he had explained. "If there's any fish worth catchin' in this ocean, they'll be here." The place was not a secret, marked clearly on navigation maps, but none of the charter captains would risk scraping their boats and scaring the piss out of customers crossing the reef. A captain would go around, all the way to Shoal Bay, for a calm outlet to open water. After spending three hours getting to the sweet spot and allowing another three hours for the return, there was not enough time left in an eight-hour charter of actual fishing to suit tourists.

Webb would have gone straight to the reef, recognized the pattern of rocks, read the flow of water around them, and gunned his boat through. So would William. He's in his grandfather's boat, just on the other side of this thrashing machine.

Bud watches several waves come through, judging at what point in the formation of a wave he should be between the rocks to clear the reef cleanly, tries to steel his nerves, calm his pulse. The timing must be perfect. If he wrecks, there is no hope, not for the boat or himself. A quick death would not scare him, but first, he would be skinned alive on the coral then slowly ripped apart.

He closes his eyes, shudders, then looks above the calamity at the reef. *A calm sky. A perfect day. If it should happen, it will still be a good day. William will live and I will die. Let the ocean choose.* He aligns the boat in front of the gap between the towering black crags, waits, waits for the exact right instant and slams the throttles forward.

The ocean, swelled into high rollers near the reef, begins to level in deeper water. Bud can see ahead maybe twenty miles. The speck on the horizon resolves into a boat and he steers toward it. The other boat is floating free, bobbing in the waves. Either no one is aboard, or they are kneeling behind the gunwale adjusting tackle or baiting a hook. A stick-figure silhouette pops up, looks around for the motor sound, and then holds to the console as Bud approaches.

William waves, yells something Bud can't understand over the motors. Bud cuts the ignition, lowers his bumpers as he glides in, and throws a rope over to William.

"Bud, is it really you? What the living hell are you doing out here?"

"Tie me up, William. Brought you a beer. Thought you might be thirsty."

Bud opens his cooler takes out two cans of Budweiser, holds them over his head. William understands and readies to catch them. In the trough of a roller, with the boats relatively stable next to each other, Bud lofts the beers across one at a time.

"Come on over. Let me get a good look at you. Can you make it?"

Bud steps up to his foredeck, waits again for the boats to stabilize before jumping the gap. He lands in a crouch, holding to the rail with one hand, the other propped stiff-armed against William's foredeck, bracing for the boat's lurch over the next wave before standing.

William extends a hand to help Bud down into the cockpit, pulling him into a hug. "Man, it's good to see you. You're looking good."

"How are you fishing?"

"Longline today. Doing pretty good." William points to a twelve-pound grouper still bleeding on the deck, the line coming out of its mouth tied to a cleat atop the gunwale. Bud follows the other end of the line to the float, a twenty-gallon blue plastic drum bobbing fifty yards away. "Let me get this big boy on ice and we'll talk," William says. He turns, grabs pliers from a cup holder, crouches over the fish, and extracts the circle hook with the dexterity of a surgeon.

"How's Nicki?" William asks without looking up.

Bud doesn't answer. He reaches for one of the beers in a cup holder built into the cockpit shroud and pops the top. The knife is there, in the crease between the shroud and the windshield, as it should be, as it always is.

William opens the cooler with one hand, lifts the grouper onto the ice with the other, and lets the lid fall shut. Wiping his hands on a towel looped under his belt, he steps forward, smiling, hand outstretched for the beer. "How's Nicki?" William repeats. Bud steps forward also and puts the can in William's open hand. The beer slips from their fingers, clunks on the deck, spewing on their legs.

"That's what I wanted to talk to you about."

If there is pain, it doesn't register on William's face, only open-mouth startle, a question he can't bring to words. He looks down at Bud's hand, the handle of the fillet knife protruding below his ribcage, and tries to back away. Bud grips the handle with both hands and rips the blade upwards until it hooks behind William's sternum. William's face is frozen, taut neck muscles quivering. A drool of blood bubbles from his lips. Bud twists the blade and William's head falls forward, nestles against Bud's neck like a lover. Blood quits squirting on Bud's hands and he lets the body crumple at his feet.

William's blood drips from Bud's arms. He drops the knife and crawls onto the foredeck, pulling himself like a lizard to the rail before puking burning stomach acid. When he rolls to his back, he looks up at the lazy clouds, the same clouds as before. *Still a good day.* His numb mind registers only the drifting white puffs, the twirl of an albatross high above them, the sea sounds. Knotty muscles loosen. He closes his eyes and feels the tease of sleep. *If only I could sleep*; he hadn't slept the night before—or the night before that.

A hard thump of the boats against the bumper between them wakes him. Bud sits up and sweeps the horizon. To the south, a thin white line marks the reef. The wind and waves have drifted the boats toward it. Standing, he judges the reef to be less than a mile away. To the north is the dark silhouette of a fishing boat against the blue sky. Sea birds, like gnats, swirl behind marking a school of baitfish. The boat leaves the birds behind—probably not enough time before dark to circle around for another pass. Bud looks to the sun, low now, orange behind the haze, then down at William for the first time, surprised to see him there.

When he pinches William's arm, the flesh remains peaked. Bud pushes the hook William had disgorged from the grouper into the arm, pressing hard until the barb comes out the other side of the fold of skin. There's no bleeding. Bud pulls at the weight end of the longline, ten pounds at least, and looks aft at the blue barrel lazily tossing in the waves. He droops William on his stomach across the gunwale and unties the longline from the cleat before tipping him overboard. When Bud looks, the body is already out of sight.

Bud's clothes are sticky with coagulated blood. He strips, throwing everything over the side. The rubber hose used to flush the boat jerks like a snake when he turns on the pump. Brown streaked rivulets flow into the scupper.

He unties from William's boat and coils the rope in one hand before leaping across to his foredeck. The boats drift apart. He selects one engine before turning the ignition switch, listening to the outboard whir, cough, and then catch with a rumble. As he idles away, Bud looks back. William's boat is just as he first saw it. It will continue to drift into the reef and be pulverized. A few pieces may make it to shore, probably not enough to be recognized among the other flotsam.

William lives alone. He likely calls Nursey, his grandmother, every night to ease her mind that he is home safe. She might know where he was fishing. But even if she raises an alarm, nobody will come looking before noon tomorrow. The boat will be gone by then. If somebody thinks to pull in his longlines, they may find a shark. That much blood in the water will call sharks from miles around.

Bud bumps up the throttle, just to make the boat ride better in the waves, and heads to the west tip of Anguilla. There's no hurry. He should plan to arrive back at Dave's Marina between two and three in the morning, after the partygoers retire and before the charter captains ready their boats. He must walk from this boat down the pier under the glare of overhead dock lights to his sailboat. Hard to go unnoticed when you are naked.

CHAPTER 58

Man Adrift

Bud first sails *Carpe Diem* south to Antigua because the wind direction favors a broad reach and he can practice deploying the spinnaker single-handedly. At Martinique, he follows the trade winds west through the Windward Islands to Grenada and then in June north along the Venezuela coast to Curacao to spend the fall at anchor in the hurricane hole of Spanish Waters. In December, he beats against a headwind for two days and nights trying to return to Grenada and then reverses course to follow the trade winds again to Belize.

He pulls sails before reaching the reef and motors through the dark coral heads sprouting under the azure blue water. Ahead, a plank of driftwood bobs, and then he sees the fabric attached, and it becomes a body floating face down. He pulls alongside and the corpse drifts at the same speed as the boat. Shoulder length black hair wafts to and fro around the young man's head—in his twenties, Bud thinks. Judging from skin color, still pinkish, he has been dead only a few hours.

Climbing onto the foredeck, he scours the horizon for another boat, then the deserted beach a quarter mile away. He spits overboard and watches the current sweep the spittle toward open water. In another hour a cloud of small fish will form under the shadow of the man and by noon saltwater crocs will check out the commotion. By nightfall, the body will be gone.

If left on the beach, someone will find him and at least his family will know he is dead. Bud unlashes the two-man inflatable Zodiac from behind the helm chair, lowers it to the water, and ties it along the port side. With the gaff, he hooks the man's trouser pocket and pulls him into the dinghy.

Cranking the diesel again, he parallels the beach in water a few feet deeper than his five-foot draft, looking for a good anchorage. Ahead, a pier materializes and then the thatch roofs of a village rise above the palm thicket edging the shore. Arriving at a village with a dead man might be trouble. He should reverse course, dump the corpse, but by the time he decides, people are watching from shore.

Bud drops anchor off the end of the pier and lowers himself into the dinghy, stepping over the crumpled body to the aft seat to run the outboard. When he grounds on the beach, two boys who had been diving off the pier rush toward him, gawking first at his cargo and then suspiciously at him. The youngsters, their features a mixture of Indian, Spanish, and Negro, jabber among themselves then dash into the palmetto surrounding the village. They return following a barefoot, shirtless old man in ragged khaki pants massaging his gray-whiskered chin with one hand and gripping a machete beside his knee in the other. The old man kneels beside the dinghy and twists the head of the corpse. A gap opens in the neck where it had been hacked to the vertebra. He brushes the hair aside to see the face clearly.

"Aah...no." The old man says to the corpse before crossing himself and slumping onto his butt beside the dinghy. The boys remain quiet and still behind him out of respect.

"¿Hablas español?" the man asks.

"No. Francés o Holandés o Inglés."

"Inglés, un poco."

"I found him. I did not do this."

The man looks from Bud to the body, and then into Bud's eyes again.

"¿Comprende?" Bud asks.

"Te creo. I believe. I believe, or I kill you already."

A girl, thick-bodied, no taller than the boys but older, elbows past the boys. When she sees the dead man, her hands jerk to her face. Her shriek sends a chill through Bud.

"My son." The old man says and then points to the girl. "His wife."

"I'm sorry."

The old man turns to the boys. *"La tomas,"* he says pointing up the path.

The boys take the girl's elbows and try to turn her away. She jerks free but then acquiesces to being led back toward the village.

"Contrabandistas," the old man says. "Kill her also. Tonight, I think."

"No. Smugglers would not do that."

"My son steal from smugglers. They kill her…example…to others."

The old man seems sure of it. Bud does not know how to respond.

The man gets to his feet, glances once more at the body, and then leads Bud up the path the boys had used to a one-room, concrete-block house. Smoke seeps out the open doorway. The girl sits on a flat rock beside a fire pit in the center of the dirt floor weeping into her hands.

"Eat?" The old man points to a stack of tortillas in an enamel pan beside the fire.

"No. Gracias."

"Lolita, vierta el hombre café."

The girl wipes her eyes and nose on the hem of her skirt, snarls at Bud and then spits words at the old man fast and sharp as snakebites. The old man does not even look at her. She finally gets a cup and pours coffee from an aluminum pot.

"Thank you," Bud says, "I'm sorry about your husband."

"El ofrece simpatía," the old man tells her; she nods and sits on the rock again. "I tell her. She no talk *Inglés*." The old man points

to a wooden bench and they sit side by side. *"Te vas rapidamente."* He looks away searching for the English words. "You go now. The smugglers...*regreso*. Kill you." He walks to the doorway looks out toward the pier and the sailboat at the end. "Take my son." The old man looks back and Bud sees how hard this is for him to say. "Take him to the ocean."

"No. This is not my business. You should bury him."

"Mi hijo asesinado. My son murdered. You know. I know. *Pueblo*...the village know. They kill all who know. It better he never found. Nobody know."

Bud's face must show he does not believe the smugglers would kill a whole village. The old man nods his head to assure him it is true. "My son *estúpido*. The smugglers *estúpido*. If you as much *estúpido*, we die tonight."

Bud stands, looks down at the man's pleading face, then to the girl watching them. "No, I'll go now." He strides down to the beach, eager to dump the body and get back on his sailboat. The boys are still there and stand aside.

The old man follows, pulling the girl by her hand. "Save *la niña,* you take."

The girl, her face a rage, bends into the Zodiac to close her husband's eyes. Bud sits on the nose of the dinghy with his palms pressed to the sides of his head. All this is coming too fast. He can't think.

The old man grabs the two boys by their arms. *"No viste nada."* He looks each boy in the face. *"No viste nada." ¿Entiendes?"* He waits for each of them to nod. *"Escapada!"*

The boys scamper away without looking back.

The old man rushes to the girl, who is still leaning over the dinghy, and jerks her to her feet. He twists her toward the house and pushes her along while talking urgently in her ear in Spanish. Before they enter the palm thicket, the old man turns and calls back. *"Un momento por favor"* and vanishes before Bud can answer.

The old man returns with a black garbage bag over his shoulder, pulling the girl by the hand. She compliantly stumbles behind, looking at her feet as if in a daze.

"I pay you. All I have…in bag." He tosses the bag on top of his son's body then guides the girl onto the middle seat. "Go. Go," he urges Bud.

Bud wants to stop this, but he cannot think of the words to protest in Spanish or what else to do. He climbs in the back and lowers the outboard's foot into the water as the old man pushes them away.

When Bud cuts the motor at the yacht, he hears a wail from shore. The old man is on his knees at the water's edge, hands stretched to the sky, head tilted back in an anguished lament. The old man has finally given in to his pain. The memory of this horrendous day will dim over time, Bud thinks, but the cry of the broken man will return to wake him from sleep.

Past the reef, Bud pulls the throttle back and sets the autopilot on a heading away from shore. He goes aft and hand-over-hand pulls in the Zodiac. As he lifts the nose of the inflatable onto the transom, the corpse rolls out, sinking at first and then bobbing up in the wake.

Bud hesitates before pulling the dinghy on deck and looks to the sky. The wind has changed to blow from the north—both good and bad. Two days and nights with the wind at his back would get him back to Curacao. If he sets sail, the dinghy should be aboard. But a north wind also means a storm. Already the clouds are building and turning dark. Best to get back inside the reef and find a sheltered anchorage. After the tie line plays out through his hands, the dinghy jerks and then skips along as before.

Back at the helm, he sets *Carpe Diem* into a sweeping turn. Through the cabin doorway, Lolita lies facedown on the bench against the starboard bulkhead, only her filthy bare feet visible hanging off the end of the cushion. An undocumented passenger would be trouble in any port. The sooner he puts her ashore the better.

The girl comes up when she hears the anchor chain playing out. She ignores Bud and studies the shoreline.

"*No.*" She shouts to him and motions for him to move farther down the coast.

Bud reverses the transmission and backs *Carpe Diem* to set the anchor. When she rushes to grab his arm, he roughly pushes her onto the stern bench. Jumping back to her feet, she squalls a protest in rapid-fire Spanish. When Bud turns, hand raised to backhand her across the face, she sits down and draws a thumb across her throat as she points to the shore. Bud studies the coast. The beach is undisturbed; the jungle behind it like the rest he had passed. *What does she want?* Like him, he finally decides, she wants to live through the night.

As Bud winches up the anchor, she climbs onto the foredeck and holds onto the mast, her arm outstretched pointing the way. For another half hour, they motor inside the reef until the overcast sky begins to darken at sunset. In another fifteen minutes, it will be too dark to spot the coral heads. Just as Bud makes the decision to anchor and take his chances, Lolita points to a dip in the jungle canopy. A darker blue streak in the water indicates a channel leading to an opening in the lush green palmetto. Bud studies the girl, looking for doubt or fear. She adamantly urges him on.

Bud anchors in the middle of a lagoon the size of a soccer field as the shoreline fades into darkness. After the engine dies, he hops onto the foredeck. The moorage is ideal to wait out the coming storm—if he does not get boarded in the night. Already he cannot see the shore; there are only the undisturbed jungle sounds and no flicker of a campfire.

The faint form of Lolita gropes through the companionway into the cabin. Bud follows and flicks on the cabin lights just long enough to see her stretched on the bench behind the table again. His night vision is ruined, but he knows the cabin like an extension of his own body. Bud pulls the bed cover from the aft berth and tosses it at Lolita before going up to the cockpit.

From a side compartment, Bud retrieves a bottle of DEET and the Luger. If trouble comes, he won't be able to run. Even if he cut away the anchor, he would never find the lagoon opening in the dark. *Carpe Diem* would be a white plastic duck puttering around in a barrel, an easy target. He stretches onto the aft bench with the pistol on the deck beside him. No one can board without shaking the boat or making noise, he convinces himself. But if the bandits are as stupid as the old man said, they might try it.

At first light, Bud wakes to the roar of the dinghy motor. When he jumps to the rail, Lolita is speeding to shore—not looking back when he yells. She pulls the rubber dinghy beside a wooden skiff half-hidden under overhanging bushes and then vanishes into the jungle. This is why they are here, Bud thinks. She knows someone within walking distance and this is where she wants to be left. It is then, when he turns to put the Luger away, he sees the gun is missing.

The storm starts with a downpour. *Carpe Diem* lurches at the anchor line like a frightened animal. Bud watches out the porthole to see if the dinghy blows away. At dusk, the nose of the yacht rotates about the anchor to face the south and the rain slacks. Bud goes onto the foredeck and searches the shore. He could swim in to retrieve the dinghy, but without the Luger, he would be at the mercy of anyone waiting. The dinghy is a small price to pay to get rid of the girl and leave Belize alive.

Going back below, Bud's toe catches the black garbage bag Lolita had thrown under the table. Her clothes. Why would she leave without her clothes? He dumps the bag onto the table and stirs through Lolita's wadded dresses until he finds a zippered banker's pouch—inside, dozens of Ziploc sandwich bags of white powder. The old man's payment. Probably why his son had been killed.

"Damn," he whispers between his teeth when he realizes Lolita is going for the police. A murdered man, a kidnapped girl, and now drug smuggling. He scampers up on deck and looks where Lolita had disappeared. "Damn you," he yells and it echoes back from the far end of the lagoon.

If he can only make it through the night. A faint gibbous moon shines through the clouds. By morning the sea will be calm again and he will run as fast as *Carpe Diem* will carry him out into the Gulf, put all this behind. If he can just make it through the night…

With only a fillet knife as a weapon, there is no point standing guard; so Bud sleeps fitfully in the bunk below. In the gray half-light of morning, he is opening his last can of fruit cocktail when he hears an outboard motor. Through the rain-streaked cabin porthole, he watches Lolita, ochre hair matted around her face by the drizzle, cotton dress clinging to her stocky body, maneuver the dinghy toward the swimming platform at the stern. He goes topside to catch the tie line. She hands up a woven wicker basket mounded with food. On top is the Luger.

While Lolita showers in the head and changes into dry clothes from the garbage bag, Bud checks the contents of the basket—cans, cellophane pouches of beans, a moldy slab of bacon. When he sees the magazine of the Luger is empty, his eyes jerk to the head door, cracked open enough to see a sliver of her torso reflected in the vanity mirror. *What happened in the jungle?* Every scenario he thinks of ends in death—maybe deaths. The man found adrift has been avenged.

CHAPTER 59

Lolita

They sail in choppy water into a steady wind at close reach toward Grenada. Lolita, now wearing a faded blue one-piece bathing suit with a ruffled skirt, one an old woman might own, stands beside the helm chair watching his every adjustment intently. When he lets her sit in the helm chair and steer, she smiles for the first time. On the morning of the third day, Bud leaves her at the helm and goes below to plot their course. He intends to rest his eyes only a moment but doesn't wake until nightfall. His frantic rush to the cockpit frightens her. They are on the heading he last set. The sails are trimmed.

At Grenada, Bud anchors in Saint George's Bay and takes the Zodiac in immediately for provisions before the harbor patrol can get around to checking on the new arrival. The stores will not take his Euros and he returns empty-handed. Lolita watches as Bud stomps down the companionway into the galley, opening cupboard doors then slamming them shut. Only the food Lolita had brought remains and they are out of anything potable to drink. He slumps on the bench beside Lolita and lowers his head to the table, utterly defeated.

Lolita fetches the black garbage bag, gropes inside, and pulls out a canvas bag. Bud is topside readying *Carpe Diem* for departure when Lolita walks up the companionway with the wicker basket, a towel on top. As she walks past toward the dinghy, he catches her arm.

"What are you up to?"

Lolita lifts the towel from the basket to reveal a dozen sandwich bags of powder. She wrenches her arm from his grip and pulls in the dinghy rope. She is speeding to the wharf before Bud can think to stop her.

She will be caught. Bud imagines her in jail and then he sees himself there also with other drug dealers. When there is still no sign of her at dusk, Bud pulls anchor and motors a half-mile out to sea. Killing the engine and flicking the navigation lights off, he looks back at the lights from the wharf glinting off the water. In the dark, the shore patrol might not find him.

"Stupid bitch," he mutters.

Then he thinks of the efficiency she had divided up the stash into salable sizes and hidden them in the basket, her fearless face as she sped at full throttle to shore. She is not the simple wife waiting in a jungle shack for her husband to return. *This is not her first time.* Bud cranks *Carpe Diem* and motors to the same anchor spot as before. At dawn, Lolita returns with the basket full of provisions plus two cases of bottled water.

They anchor next for three nights inside the horseshoe reef of uninhabited Tobago Cays in the Grenadines. In the mornings, they swim ashore and nap on an islet beach. In the afternoons, Lolita snorkels the reef, walking ashore with langouste, tails flapping as she grips their backs, to roast on the coals of a driftwood fire. Bud watches Lolita do it all—catch their food, build the fire, cook—not asking permission or trying to explain what she is doing. She could survive anywhere.

As they leisurely work their way east through the Windward Islands, they take shifts at the helm. Bud has taught Lolita how to use the propane stove, and during his shift, she cooks and brings him food before sleeping. On the first night of a two-day sail from Guadeloupe to Saint Bart, they both remain on deck. With their bodies only apparitions to each other in the starlight, Lolita begins to talk for the first time. In her rapid Spanish, Bud can only guess what she is saying and tries to slow her down. She continues at her own speed and Bud realizes she does not intend for him to understand.

All through the night, she talks, stopping only when she chokes with tears. When the sun creeps out of the sea, Lolita is different—evolved somehow during the night. His stare makes her uncomfortable and she goes below to make a breakfast of bacon and bread fried in the bacon grease.

The next night, Bud remains at the helm alone. He hears Lolita bumping around in the aft bunk beneath his feet.

"¿Estás bien?" he calls down to her.

"Sí," she replies and then she is quiet. Bud imagines her stretched on the bunk asleep.

The sea is flat, the wind steady. He flicks off the cockpit lights and looks up to verify he can see the sails in the glint of starlight. A familiar constellation behind the mast becomes his heading. As he fights away sleep, he wishes Lolita would come up and talk again. Remembering her face when she had brought up his breakfast, the hint of a smile that had replaced the hardness, Bud thinks she had disgorged all that haunted her.

Bud begins talking aloud, his voice projected out to the ghosts at the edge of darkness, rambling on about the cabin behind the beach where he grew up, the hundreds of little details about the restaurant his family ran, recalling events about their life together, the five of them—him, his mother, Nana, Uncle Paul, Nicki. His rising euphoria tanks when Nicki slips into his monolog and he pounds the steering wheel trying to expunge her.

"Durar."

The voice seemed to come out of the black sea and hang in his ears. Had he imagined it?

"Continuer la historia!" Lolita yells from below, not giving permission but demanding he continue.

"Nicki…" he repeats. A crack in a dam, memories percolating through, spurting, gushing. He tells Lolita how they shared one life growing up, how her happiness had been the only measure of his own. Nicki, his sister; Nicki, his lover—the shame amidst the ecstasy. The baby, the symbol of her treachery, undeniable proof. How he hates her with the same intensity he had loved her—love and hate, two edges of the same sword impaling him.

He gives Lolita every reason to despise Nicki, but the arguments sound weak when said out loud. Was it Nicki's fault she could not fall in love with her brother? Was he not the deviant one? Looking back, had she not tried to dissuade him dozens of times—subtle hints so as not to hurt him, with enough compassion that he could dismiss her words as one of her passing moods.

As the horizon lightens before dawn, he tells Lolita about William, his friend since childhood, his rival. How he was viciously murdered—not as punishment for betraying Nicki, his justification at the time, but in jealous revenge. How the murder had rendered him trash blowing across the ocean at the will of the wind. That the Luger is not for protection but rather assurance his torment has a limit.

CHAPTER 60

Return of the Native

Bud radios ten miles out from Saint Bart and is directed to tie up dockside in the inner harbor before reporting to the Gustavia Port Authority. Lolita, an adept sailor now, helps him pull sails and they motor past the bows of mega yachts, their sterns moored to the harbor wharf.

The boardwalk surrounding the tiny harbor is crowded with café tables set up *al fresco*. Yacht owners in their obligatory white caps with black visors drink their morning coffee while their mates bustle from one duty-free shop to the next, designer sundresses fluttering.

This is *Carpe Diem*'s home port. When Bud presents the boat registration and his passport, he expects the process to be perfunctory and it is. This registration will get him into ports of the sister island of Saint Martin as well. At the Scotiabank next to the Port Captain's Office, he withdraws ten thousand Euros, all they will let him have on short notice. He sets up to come back in three days for the rest.

When he returns to *Carpe Diem*, Lolita's face is pressed against a porthole watching with big eyes the parade on the boardwalk. Bud has to coax her topside and after a score of headshakes finally gets her ashore. Their clothes are dirty rags, so first they shop. As they pass the window displays, Bud points out outfits. They will not look as sexy on her as the willowy mannequins, but he feels her shame walking among the exquisitely dressed European women. At one window she does not shake her head, so they go in. He explains to the clerk in French that she will be talking to him but pleasing the lady.

Lolita tries on leather pumps but cannot get the hang of walking in heels and they settle on chic leather deck shoes. They buy two dresses, shorts, blouses, undergarments, and a new bathing suit. There are no one-piece suits, so she picks out the bikini with the most material, blue like the other one. She won't come out of the dressing room to model it for him, so he doubts she will wear it in public.

Bud parks Lolita in front of a café and orders fruit punch for her to drink while he buys a new wardrobe for himself at a men's shop next door. The hotels are perched on the slopes of the hills one street back from the harbor. Bud enters the lobby of the first one they come to. He takes a three-room suite with a balcony overlooking the harbor—nine hundred and fifty euros a night with a three-night minimum. Bud pays up front from his dwindling role of bills. There are still docking fees to pay, plus fuel and provisions to buy. Surely he can make ten thousand euros last three days.

The following morning, Bud arranges with the concierge for a manicurist and hairdresser before spending the morning drinking coffee on the boardwalk. At noon, as he watches the boats moving in and out of the harbor, a girl walks into his line of sight—Lolita, a caterpillar morphed into a butterfly. The shaggy hair is now a short flapper cut with waves at the sides, her fingernails painted bright red to match her lipstick. She reads something into Bud's open-mouthed gawk and she slips self-consciously into the chair across from him and frowns at the table.

"Maravilloso," he says and reaches across to touch her. Her hands fly up to cover her face. *"Perfecto,"* he croons. Between the fingers of the hands covering her face, a smile grows.

As they eat breakfast platters, Lolita glances furtively at the women at the other tables, adjusting how she holds her fork, her pinky finger flicking out delicately when she sips coffee. *She is a quick study*, Bud thinks, *who could blend with this scene in a week*. The yacht captains would take notice, not of island trash as yesterday, but the exotic beauty that must belong to someone in their circle.

Sitting across from her, Bud feels scruffy. He has not had a shave or haircut in a year. He waves over the waiter and orders a plate of pastries. The waiter speaks Spanish, so he relays for Lolita to stay while he finds a barbershop. In the barber's mirror, he examines his leathery face creased with crow's-feet from the constant scrunch against the sun's glare. He can barely recognize the boy that left Saint Martin a year ago. He decides against the shave and has the beard trimmed to match his new persona.

Their last morning in Gustavia is spent restocking provisions and readying *Carpe Diem* to sail. At noon, Bud anchors in *Anse de Colombier* on the tip of Saint Bart, a good jumping off point for the short sail to Saint Martin the following day. The cove is part of a nature reserve forty-five minutes by footpath from the nearest road, so they have the pristine beach to themselves. Bud starts a driftwood fire while Lolita, snorkel and mask in hand, walks toward the rocky end of the beach.

As Bud watches the fire die down, a chartered catamaran sails into the cove and drops anchor just offshore so the clients, four young women on holiday, can swim and sunbathe. The catamaran blocks his view of Lolita bobbing in the water as she searches for supper. After an hour of not seeing her, he strolls past the bare-breasted women to find Lolita stretched out on the sand behind a car-size boulder with her bikini top off like the catamaran women. When Bud stands in front of her with a grin, deliberately staring at her sunny-side up bosom, she gives him a withering *if-you-laugh-I'll-scratch-your-eyes-out* glare.

The next afternoon, they tie the Zodiac to the wharf in front of Marigot, stretching their legs with a walk through the flea market set up in the adjacent park. Bud is glad to see the flea market bustling with tourists bargaining for souvenir T-shirts and local crafts. In the center of the park, where a fountain had been prior to the hurricane, there is a docking station for a new attraction, a cable driven gondola, like one might see at a ski resort. The cables slump over the red tile roofs to Fort Louis on the bluff overlooking the harbor.

"What's this all about?" Bud asks a sunburnt American standing in line. The man gives Bud a sideways glare like he thinks Bud is an idiot.

"The Golden Maiden, man. We're going up to get pictures with the Golden Maiden in the background...prove to the folks back home we've been here." Bud puts a euro in one of the tourist binoculars on the wharf. The statue, back arched, face tilted to Heaven like a returning angel, gleams atop a pole mounted on a granite pedestal. The French Tri-color flutters from the pole underneath. Bud boosts Lolita up to look also before the binoculars time out. She is not impressed.

While they are eating at one of the outdoor restaurants across the street from the park, Lolita catches his left hand when he reaches for his beer. She taps the wedding ring and asks with her expression. How can he explain? Half of a simple wedding set he and Nicki had bought at a pawnshop in Havana and had resized. He takes it off and tries it on Lolita's dwarf-sized fingers. It only fits on her thumb.

"Nicki," he says. She must remember the name from his rants that night on the boat and nods in sympathy.

"*Mañana*. Tomorrow you will meet Nicki."

CHAPTER 61

Orient Beach

*I*n front of Orient Beach, Bud hooks to the mooring ball next to the catamaran *TikiTaki*. The nudies are wading out, drinks held high, for the sunset nude cruise around the island. Most are blood-red from their first day in the sun and already drunk. Lolita goes below in disgust, but he knows she is watching through a porthole.

With binoculars, Bud inspects the new La Belle Creole—shaped just like the previous one, only elevated on concrete piers, probably anchored to bedrock. The restaurant might survive the next hurricane, but everything built on the beach is just another taunt to Mother Nature. Even as blue metal panels are nailed to the restaurant's roof joists, a wood deck underneath the floor among the round piers is crowded with customers. There is a walkup bar in the back, but it is too shadowy inside to see who is running it. He thinks he recognizes Betty walk out on the beach and look back at the construction crew. She turns and looks directly at *Carpe Diem*. Knowing Betty, she would know the name of his boat, but the wind has the transom facing out to sea.

As *TikiTaki* raises sails on the far side of the reef, Lolita comes back up and sits beside Bud on the aft bench. He jumps up and acts like he is pulling off his swim trunks. Lolita pulls him back down and wags her finger. She smiles easily now, swatting his arm when he teases her.

Bud takes her hand and points to the ring on her thumb. "Nicki." Then he points to La Belle Creole. "Nicki—take this to her." Lolita acts confused, but Bud thinks she understands. *"Regresara, por favor."* Her eyes become wet, not from what he is saying, but the pain she reads in his face. Bud shuts his eyes. *It is the only way.* She touches his arm before going aft to pull in the dinghy. Bud thinks of his grandmother, her story of arriving at Saint Martin with nothing more than her bathing suit and a dinghy. Lolita has that kind of grit.

He will miss her.

~~~

The Creole girl pulls the rubber dinghy out of the surf. When she looks back at the yacht, the bearded man points to the restaurant. He has sent her in for booze, Betty thinks. The girl leaves her deck shoes in the dinghy to more easily walk in the powdery sand, then picks a path through the congestion of umbrellas and beach chairs, averting her eyes when she passes a nudist. She walks to the steps of the deck underneath the restaurant and stops, seemingly unsure what to do next.

Betty calls out to her, "Do you want liquor?"

"Nicki?"

Betty reflexively glances to the bar at the back of the deck. The girl points to where Betty looked.

"*¿Está Nicki?*"

The girl reads the answer in Betty's face, mounts the steps and strides purposely between tables. Betty follows, expecting trouble.

The girl pulls the ring from her thumb and plops it on the bar. Nicki gives her a questioning look before picking it up and examining it, comparing it to the ring on her own finger. The girl discerns what she wants to know from Nicki's gasp.

"Bud." The girl turns and points. "No!" she shouts when she sees the yacht she arrived in leaving. She bolts back out to the beach, running along the water's edge to the dinghy. The yacht is already past the reef, the jib sail raised. The girl frantically tries to push the dinghy back in the water and then, when she realizes it is too late, sits on the nose of it crying into her hands.

"Is that Bud?" Nicki asks Betty.

"Is that his ring?"

Nicki slips the ring on her pointer finger, Bud's ring size. "Yes." She looks out at the yacht, the mainsail at the midpoint of being hoisted. "We've got to stop him. He murdered William. I just know it."

"Call the shore patrol. They'll pick him up, but I don't think you could prove anything. Even if he admitted it, what would that get you?"

"We can't just let him get away."

"Nicki, you're the reason William is dead. Bud let you get away."

Nicki looks out at the girl. "Why dump his girlfriend here?"

"My guess is they're not lovers, if that's what you're thinking. She's in trouble and Bud wants you to take care of her. That ring is her letter of introduction."

Betty walks to the edge of the deck, watches the girl walk knee-deep into the surf, chin jutted out defiantly even as her shoulders heave with sobs. The girl has been here before. Had Lily Ana not stood destitute at that very spot—and Zuzu while deciding to take her own life? Had she herself, pregnant and alone, not looked to the ocean that way? She thinks of the enigmatic Golden Maiden stuck in the sand facing the bay.

Nicki walks up behind Betty. "What should I do?"

Betty leans back against the wooden rail and looks Nicki in the eyes. "You'll do the right thing. This place has a tradition of being a safe harbor for wayward women—you included." Betty turns and looks out at the girl again. "I'll take over the bar. You both speak Spanish. Why not take her to the cabin to meet the baby? You two have things to discuss."

CHAPTER 62

Santiago de Cuba

A fter registering with the Santiago Port Authority and stretching his legs with a walk through town, Bud stops at a grill set up on the wharf. A girl with a quadroon shade of skin and her hair tucked under a red bandana only smiles when he tries to order first in Dutch and then in French. Finally, he points to a simmering pot of fish stew thick with vegetables. She waves him toward a picnic table set up under a canvas sunshade and follows him with a crock bowl. Bud sits across from a man in a khaki uniform bent over a plate of black beans and rice.

"Dutch?" the man asks as he wipes his mouth with his sleeve.

"American."

He points to *Carpe Diem* at anchor in the harbor. "You fly a Dutch flag. You are a smuggler then?"

Bud puts a finger to his lips. "Not so loud, there may be police around."

The man sits back and laughs.

"You speak good English."

"It is my chief qualification for being a *Guarda Frontera*. I was born in Havana but I lived in Key West for twenty years. I never became a citizen, you see, and they finally got around to kicking me out."

"So, what did you do in Key West?"

"Yes, well that is my other qualification. I was a smuggler—drugs, contraband, people—anything that needed to go back and forth."

The girl returns with change for his ten-euro note in pesos, two bills and various coins. Bud has no idea what they are worth.

"Did she cheat me?" Bud talks to the man but smiles shyly up at the girl who is pretty.

"She is a notorious swindler. She's already given herself a generous tip."

The girl walks around the table to behind the man and playfully cuffs him on the ear. The man throws up his arm as if to ward off a second blow.

"Poppa is a liar," the girl says in perfect English.

The man rocks back in open-mouth laughter at Bud's surprise.

"Siddhartha—that is your name, I believe. This is my daughter, Emma."

"How do you know my name?"

"I am a border patrolman. Did I not tell you? And you are a smuggler, so of course, I know your name."

"I'm not a smuggler."

"The smuggler talk is only a joke. But why are you here?"

"No reason other than there was a favorable wind."

"Just passing through then. So where to next?"

"East, I suppose, or maybe I will sell the boat and stay here."

"Two weeks. An American can only stay in Cuba for two weeks without a special permit."

"Then I'll be French. I've got dual citizenship. How long can a Frenchman stay?

"The American part of you will have to leave in two weeks."

Bud finds himself staring at Emma standing behind her father as he talks. She is short like Lolita, of indeterminate origin, but something about her, the impish grin maybe, reminds him of Nicki. Bud looks past them at *Carpe Diem* gently bucking in the harbor, impatiently calling to him. She had meant freedom to him only a year ago, but now she is a prison.

"Do you suppose I can find a room in town? I could use a real bath and a real bed."

The girl grabs her father's shoulders from behind and smiles brightly at Bud. "Poppa, Dora would put him up. It would be perfect."

The excited tone of his daughter's voice causes the man to crane his head back to study her face and then he faces Bud solemnly. "Young man, you should get back on that boat and sail away before this one sets a hook in you."

Emma rolls her eyes and pops the back of the man's neck. Again, he throws up his elbows in mock defense before she stalks back to the grill.

"Are you serious about selling the boat? I know a man who's looking for one about that size."

"Guess I'll need it to get out of here. If I could stay, I'd sell it."

"Stay? My friend this is the most backwater place in the world."

"That's why I like it. The rest of the Caribbean is one big tourist trap."

"Can't say I don't like it here myself after twenty years doing the hustle in Key West." The man reaches a hairy paw across the table as he is getting up. "People around here call me Diego. I'll talk with my friend about the boat. If he likes it, maybe something can be worked out."

"But—"

"Sometimes things work out is all I'm saying," Diego says as he carries his plate and Bud's bowl back and dumps them in a galvanized tub beside the grill. Diego talks to him but stares at his daughter. "If you'll come back to the wharf an hour before dark, Emma here will take you to see Dora." A smile creeps onto the corners of Emma's lips as she washes the dishes but she does not look up. "If she is not in my house by nine PM, you will become a smuggler again. Do you understand?" Bud does not answer because Diego is still looking at his daughter.

On the first anniversary of hurricane Claudette, Bud sells *Carpe Diem* to a corrupt Cuban government official. As part of the deal, Bud assumes the identity of a Havana dissident the official thinks is either dead or hiding in Miami. Bud names Emma's first child Siddhartha, Sid for short.

On the island of Saint Martin, the name Siddhartha Legion enters into the realm of legend. Over time, it is variously rumored he died at sea, he never really existed at all, or he became a hermit in the USA writing novels under a pen name.

Epilogue

'He's dreaming now,' said Tweedledee:
'And if he left off dreaming about you,
where do you suppose you'd be?'
'Where I am now, of course,' said Alice.
'You'd go out—bang!—just like a candle!'
– Lewis Carroll

(2 years later)

Lolita sips lemonade at a cocktail table on the elevated veranda of La Belle Creole. Below, the resort's yellow umbrellas blossom in neat rows like sunflowers with their blooms turned to the sun. Far up the beach, mixed among the gawkers walking the waterline, she spots a plump black woman in a flower-print muumuu leading a stooped, stringy-haired white man in surfer pants.

Bella, her gray-streaked hair stuffed under a stack of wide-brim beach hats, dozens of shell necklaces draped onto the slope of her bulging bosom, trudges barefoot to Paul's usual spot in front of La Belle Creole. From one of the cloth bags hanging from her shoulder, she pulls out a yellow beach towel and spreads it a few feet back from the surf. She twists Paul to face her and flashes quick motions with her hands. Paul holds to her as he struggles out of his bathing suit and then stands statue-still as she slathers him with lotion.

After giving Paul a quick hug, Bella looks up at Lolita watching from the veranda. Bella points to Paul and then to Lolita. Lolita nods that she will keep an eye on him. The cocktail table is strategically located to simultaneously observe Nicki's son Junior in the sandbox at the foot of the stairs and the demented old man on the beach. This is just another of the responsibilities shared by Nicki, Betty, and Lolita. One of them is always sitting here taking a break from the restaurant, a diversion they all look forward to.

Paul watches Bella walking away until she turns and waves and he waves back. He then pivots in tiny steps to center himself on the towel facing the ocean before lowering himself to his rump.

With his tangled hair and scruffy whiskers, Paul reminds her of her father-in-law in Belize. Other times, when she catches the profile of his gaunt chiseled face, she thinks of the *gringo* that brought her here.

Long-term guests who understand Paul's handicaps, make a point to walk over and greet him as soon as he is settled. His response is wildly flapping arms and an exuberant grin. If they say, "Good morning," he tries to politely repeat it back. It sounds like a gull squawking, but judging from his visitors' faces, he shares his joy perfectly.

Even after his friends walk down the beach or back to their umbrellas, Lolita knows that Paul is not alone. His face and arms are continually animated as if in conversation. He might spontaneously laugh or cover his face with his hands as if someone has said something disturbing. Her brother had been like this, an imbecile from birth, but also a *hechicero*. His body was present in this world but his soul was already in another realm.

A short bald man with bird legs sticking out beneath a threadbare towel wrapped around his beer gut stops in front of Paul. Paul smiles and pats the sand beside him inviting the man to sit.

"What is your name in this illusion?" the man asks as he lowers himself cross-legged on the sand.

Paul's reply sounds like nonsense, even to his own ears, but he knows this man understands.

"I'm glad to be in unison with you, Paul. My illusion name is Siddhartha. Just call me Sid." Sid looks up and down the beach. To them, it is deserted. Sid points to the end of the beach. "See that mountain, how it slopes down to the cliff, and that little islet sloughed off at the end? I think I've been here before—maybe more than once. Sure is a beautiful spot."

Paul smiles that he agrees.

"You know, once there was a shaman who lived here—called himself OldOne. Maybe you've met him—kind'a wild-looking guy, only four toes on each foot. We strolled on the beach and talked while his family huddled around his illusion waiting for him to wake up and tell them of his adventure. I wonder if he told them about me?"

Paul squeals gibberish and points to a tattooed man walking out of the surf pulling a brick at the end of a rope.

"Did one of you combine with me?" OldOne asks, shaking the water out of his hair like a dog.

"That would be me, I guess. Sit a spell and dry out. I was telling Paul here about the last time I was here—you know, about your family and all, how happy and content everybody was. Not too hot or too cold so you didn't need clothes. And Ocean always provided plenty to eat. Paul, they gave birth in Ocean and buried in Ocean. They knew after their illusions were over they would become pinpoints of light in the sky. A very progressive people.

"I told this to a fellow named Jesus who enlightened me, that it must be some time in the future when earth becomes perfect. He said he didn't think perfect was in that direction. To him, it sounded more like what his father called Eden, a place that existed way back. He said his father knows everything and he would ask. But I never ran into Jesus again, so I still don't know.

OldOne squeegees water from his face with his hand. "Well, perfect didn't last. We had a visitor."

Friar Simón walks up in his robe, an ax sticking out of his back. He does not seem to be aware of the ax until Paul points and squawks.

Simón looks over his shoulder. "Oh that. I got that fighting for a woman."

"To be killed fighting for a woman is noble," Sid says.

OldOne throws up his hands, "We never had such a death. It's not, as you suggest, noble. If one of my women caused this, I hope she was put to death."

"No," Simón says sitting across from OldOne. They sit in a horseshoe with the opening toward Ocean, all looking out at the water.

"I've had a few centuries to think about this," Simón continues. "She was young and desirable and I fell in love. These things were not her fault."

OldOne slaps the sand causing Paul to cringe. "So it was this Love, whatever it is, that killed you? Is this another evil you brought with your god? I hope this Love didn't infect my descendants."

OldOne has not quite reached Nirvana, Paul thinks.

Sid stands up and looks at the islet at the end of the beach, concentrating as if recalling something.

"Hello again, Siddhartha. Were you calling me?" Legion is about to greet the rest of the unison, when a little blond-haired boy, no more than three, crawls into Paul's lap and twists around to look at the group.

"Hello. My name is Junior." Everyone understands his jabber. "This is my Uncle Paul. Welcome to our beach." And then excitedly he points at OldOne's feet. "Look, Uncle Paul, he only has four toes like me!"

Nicki charges down the steps onto the beach. She grabs Junior by an arm and yanks him out of Paul's lap, swatting his bare bottom, making him dance and squall as she marches him away from the water.

"You little brat. You'll get worse if you ever go to the water again without someone with you. You know better than that. Now hush that blubbering."

His mother sits with Junior on a pallet in the shade of a palm behind the beach.

"Now lay down. It's time for your nap."

Between sniffles, Junior tries to tell her about the man with four toes, but his mother never listens.

They both turn to squeaks coming from the undergrowth behind them. Mother pushes aside a palmetto palm and there is a yellow dog in a wallowed-out crater in the sand with a litter of pups nuzzling her swollen tits.

"Look, Junior."

Junior instantly forgets about the spanking and crawls toward the puppies.

"Hold up there." Nicki lifts Junior into her lap. "They're not old enough to play with yet."

"I want to hold one," Junior squeals with his arms outstretched.

His mother seems to understand this time. She shakes her head at first and then a smile grows on her face. "Yes," she says emphatically. "You'll have to leave them alone until the mother weans them; then you can pick out one of the males. We'll call him Beau."

Nicki turns her head and looks up at Meme Betty leaning on the rail of the deck above watching.

"Now lay down and I'll tell you a story about a dog named Beau and your Uncle Paul and Meme Betty. It's a story Uncle Paul told me when I was about your age. Now there's a lot you won't understand, but when you get older it'll make sense. When it does—and it may be years from now—you should write it all down and keep it in a safe place so you can tell your children. If you don't pass it on, it will be like it never happened. Don't worry about remembering everything I say exactly. It's all a fable anyway. Do you know what a fable is?"

"A fairy tale somebody makes up," Junior babbles. Again, she seems to understand.

"It's like a fairy tale, but fables are about real people and they are always true. They start by one person telling a story, like when Uncle Paul told me, and it gets told again like I'm telling you. Even if a person is part of the fable, they can't understand everything that's going on, so the storyteller has to imagine parts of the story. That's why it's already a fable the first time it's told. Understand?"

Junior nods his head so she will keep talking. Most of what his mother says does not make sense, but he loves the sound of her voice.

"So later, when you think back on this, don't worry about remembering what I say perfectly. What you don't remember, you can fill in for yourself and it will still be true."

END